SCARS
OF
REDEMPTION

D.S. QUINTON

ISBN: 978-7366590-0-7

Development Editor: Andrew Lowe

Copy Editor: James Osborne

Cover design: Jeff Brown Graphics

Interior formatting: Mark Thomas / Coverness.com

PROLOGUE

In 1963, a most unfortunate thing happened. A book was found.

The book had been wrapped in cloth, bound by twine, covered in burlap, tied with rope and hidden in an alcove behind a false wall in a den.

The city was New Orleans.

The book was a grimoire.

The day the Grimoire Dark was found, everything changed. Old superstitions, arcane and forgotten, suddenly returned. Archaic fears, once dismissed as childhood nightmares, resurfaced with cold certainty. Ancient horrors, long buried, awoke. And the spirits moaned that the dead would be many.

The greatest of the horrors, the Gris-gris man, terrorized the Crescent City that year. Binding the souls of those who crossed his path, he searched for a soul more coveted than any other, that held the key to great power. He found the soul and nearly restored himself but for the actions of a few brave people.

The night Del and an unlikely band of heroes fought the Gris-

gris man, her illusion of living a normal life shattered. Her unnatural abilities—considered a gift by some—felt like a curse to her and the people that died, *That Night* would haunt her forever.

Her wounds were grave, and recovering from the ordeal took time. Eventually, after many months, her dreams of a normal life returned, and she wondered on her future.

But dreams are never what they seem, and monsters are never where you look.

She thought her journey of nightmares had come to an end. Little did she know, it had just begun.

CHAPTER 1

D elphine Larouche often dreamt of the dead, but it was not often she went looking for them. Tonight would be different.

She knew that some individuals looked for dead *people (corpses)*: policemen, firemen, or grave robbers, for instance. Even newspaper reporters looked for dead people—when they were trying to scoop a big story. But rarely did they look for the dead *in their other state*. They simply didn't *know* the dead existed in another state.

How nice for them.

The remnants of last night's dream vanished as she grabbed the morning paper from the front porch. A fading smell of magnolia blossoms hung on the air. By the end of June, the scent would be gone.

She closed the large front door behind her and tiptoed down the hall. The floorboards were kind to her this morning; they barely squeaked. She hoped for twenty minutes alone with the paper before one of the others came down and asked for their favorite section.

She entered the kitchen, poured her coffee, and scanned the headlines.

"Equal pay *and* civil rights?" Del said to no one. She snapped the newspaper open and laid it on the kitchen table.

The morning sun cast a warm, airy glow into the room, but the effect was as if magic floated right out of the paper. In a way it did. The *Times-Picayune* was a treasure trove to her, bringing news of the larger world and making it all seem a little less scary.

She carefully flattened the crease where the paper had been folded. She did this from left to right, in order to push any wrinkles off the page. She leaned forward and sniffed (but not before verifying she was still alone). There was something about the smell of a newspaper that she loved. The woody, dusty smell of the paper, combined with the chemical ink aroma, triggered a special feeling, a promise of mystery, knowledge and freedom.

In the orphanage the newspaper had been her only link to the outside world, making it seem smaller and less scary. To Jimmy—the mentally handicapped boy she'd protected there—the paper was a constant source of fun. Besides the funny papers, it was good material for hats and other craft items—but never boats. He was afraid of those.

She read the headline again.

The Times-Picayune

June 10th, 1963

President John F. Kennedy Signs Equal Pay Act into Law.

To anyone reading the same story, the idea of equal pay for equal work should be obvious. Who would think otherwise? Although… the fact that it had to be made into a law in the first place…

As optimistic as Del was, she wasn't completely naïve of the world she lived in. How could she be? She was reminded of her place in it every time she tried to do her job as a newspaper reporter.

But you're not really a reporter if they don't even let you in the door.

Yes, there was that.

She couldn't claim anything about unequal pay when she didn't even get a chance to do the job. Over the last few months, as her wounds healed and the weather warmed, she'd diligently attended the satellite office of *The Times-Picayune* newspaper, waiting for an assignment. She remembered how excited she was when she'd learned she had the position. That was the day she nearly ran Frank over on the sidewalk. That day felt like it was far in her past now.

Granted, the editor had called the job an *internship*, which Del thought would include training, but was more like a trial. A test run, really. The only problem was that the guys in that particular office had no need of an intern, didn't want an intern, and especially didn't want one that looked like her. As the days became weeks, then stretched into months, the three men in the satellite office made a game of how they could get rid of Del. Often, it included running bogus errands all over town.

"Run across town to the print supply and see how many packages of Super White paper they have left. This batch is gettin' dingy," one of them would say. They'd all lean back in their chairs and laugh.

They'd ask for typewriter ribbons, several bottles of the new product called Liquid Paper—which they quickly nick-named White-Out, *"to fix all these dark splotches"*—and a hundred other useless items.

Finally, tiring of the game, they resorted to simply locking the outside door and pretending they couldn't hear her knocking, even though she could see them through the window.

Because she wasn't being given assignments, she had nothing to turn in. And because she was considered an *intern reporter*, with no assignments, that meant she didn't have a paycheck. When she spoke to the editor about her dilemma, he simply said to *make herself more useful*, and that was how she'd start climbing the corporate ladder.

Del had never heard the term 'corporate ladder' before, but began to wonder if it even had a rung for her to start with.

She pondered this, then turned her attention back to the paper and another article. She sipped her coffee and read. This one stated that the Civil Rights movement—which Del felt officially began with Rosa Parks on the bus—was gaining steam and would soon see significant gains under the current president. He, President Kennedy—almost too handsome for the office, she thought—had already had several meetings on the subject.

"Good morning, Del," Armand Baptiste said as he entered the kitchen. "What does the world have in store for us today?"

Armand, her kind benefactor, had reached the status of *eccentric surrogate uncle* in her mind. The kind who usually knows best, but may let you get away with more than he should.

"Equal pay! Right here in black and white. Can you believe it? And a lot more after that." She smiled and thought of the possibilities.

"Good for him," Armand said as he scanned the headline. "Mark my words, he'll do wonderful things for the country. All he needs is a little time."

Little did anyone know JFK's time was almost up. It would end less than six months later in Dallas, in the cold sunshine of a November day. But no one was looking for monsters then.

"I have to talk to my editor at the *Picayune* again," Del exclaimed.

"I need a real assignment. I'm missing out on the most important events of our time!"

Having poured his coffee, Armand turned towards her. The mouth-end of his unlit pipe became a conductor's baton. "Yes, how is the newspaper business? Are you getting—"

"No! I'm not getting anything." Del folded the paper and slapped it onto the table. She crossed her arms tightly over her chest. A rapid drumming emanated from beneath the table where her foot tapped out her annoyance.

"I see." Armand clutched his pipe between his teeth. "Well, perhaps a different office would—"

"I already asked. I have to report to the one I'm at."

"The one with the men that…"

"Yeah." Del nodded. "With the men that can't stand the sight of me." Her foot drumming became slow and deliberate. "I just need to land my first story. It doesn't have to be a major scoop, just a chance to show I can do it."

Armand stroked his beard. How hard it must be for her, he thought. Life wasn't fair, and she'd been dealt a hard hand to play. He saw greatness in her, but how it would manifest was yet to be determined. He hoped he could play some small part in that discovery.

"And my old typewriter," he said. "It's working out?"

"Oh yeah, it's great. I've been practicing. I'm up to thirty words a minute now."

"Thirty words per minute you say? Very respectable."

"I guess. I'd probably be faster by now, but Jimmy always wants to practice, right when I start. Says he's going to get a job at the newspaper with me."

"The young man idolizes you."

"I told him he has to learn his letters first. I'm teaching him." Then Del's face darkened. "It's not like they taught him anything in that orphanage anyway. All Sister Eulalie wanted to do was send him away because of his *condition*." Her foot tapping sped up.

"Please, the morning is much too pleasant to bring up those old horrors," Armand said.

Del sighed. "I know. But I'll teach him to write, just wait and see. And I'll teach him to type, too." Then she added, "You don't mind, do you?"

Snapping out of a deep thought, Armand was surprised at the question. "What? Why, of course not. It's your typewriter now. Do with it as you wish."

"Thanks. I'm sure it will help, if I can just get a story to work on."

"Well," Armand began, "you could always," and here he chose his words carefully, "*look* for your big story." He held up his hand and waggled his fingers just like Frank did when he would talk about her *trancing*. The wrinkle of Del's mouth told Armand that wasn't the best suggestion.

She knew that she could use her *gift* to go looking for something bad that was about to happen; she did have the sight after all. But the thought didn't sit well with her. It was like she'd be wishing for someone to get hurt or robbed, just so she could write a story. And she certainly didn't want to do that.

"I know, but... it just seems like snooping. You know what I mean?"

"I believe I do," Armand said. He began organizing the things needed to make breakfast. "And good for you for having the courage to stick to your convictions."

Del sighed again. "Yeah, if only everyone else did the same."

Armand smiled. Del was wise beyond her years, he thought. She just didn't know it yet.

"I guess it's a good thing Mama Dedé set me up with another one of her clients, huh?" Del traced a lazy shape across the newspaper. "Otherwise, I wouldn't have any money at all."

"That's right," said Armand. "Another client. Tonight. Yes?"

"Yeah."

"What do you think it will be? A haunting? A voice from the past?"

"Psshh… as protective as Mama Dedé is? It's probably someone who lost their keys."

CHAPTER 2

A grizzled hand lashed out of the swirling mist and caught Del on the back of the neck. Three jagged cuts opened her skin and ran across her left shoulder. In an instant, they burned with unnatural fire. She cried out in pain.

Del stood amidst a whirlwind of madness and faced her attacker. Dust and debris swirled around her, choking her breath and clouding her sight. This wasn't what she'd expected at all.

Her leather boots anchored her youthful legs to the rocking floor— she would not fall. The ends of her headband fluttered wildly—a rattler warning the attacker to be ware. Her light-brown face and sculpted jaw were locked in granite determination—she would not falter. Her eyes—sparkling and fierce—penetrated the dark gloom and saw beyond the veil. They were piercing flames of life in a storm of death.

The outline of the Spirit Hunter stood beautiful and deadly.

The shape of the spirit shifted, grotesque and wanting.

Debris hit Del's temple and rocked her head. A cut opened there. Her eyes closed on instinct and the phantom vanished.

She was alone in the room, so she couldn't fully trance out, leaving her body defenseless, but she couldn't fight the thing like this. In fact, she hadn't expected a fight at all. Mama D said this would be an easy one.

She spun around and leapt backwards, moving toward the center of the room. She knew the floor would warp when she did this—the entity was tricky—but also knew it was an illusion of movement. The floor was solid. But in her mind, and in the minds of people who'd recently stayed here, the feeling of falling forever was too much to bear. This malevolent thing before her was claiming the room for itself.

As she fought to maintain her balance, she remembered something Mama D had told her about *projecting*. It may be a way she could trick the specter, but she'd never tried it like this.

Her trancing had become stronger over the last few months. Projecting was similar, her mentor had said, you just had to imagine what you wanted to look like, otherwise you were just mirroring yourself in another place.

Just as the apparition reappeared—this time attached to the wall above the door—Del slipped out of the current moment and into her trance, projecting. She was instantly hovering above the scene and could see her own body still standing in the middle of the nightmare.

While trancing, Del could see everything. She was still surprised by this ability—only realizing she had it a few months ago. It was a feeling like nothing she'd ever experienced; it gave her the feeling of simultaneously floating and mindreading, but it was more than that. When trancing, she felt connected to something beyond her everyday life. There was energy, so much energy, beyond what people could see or feel, and she was tapped into it. She could observe people in a scene and even see a split second *in front of them*. She could sense the hands on the clocks waiting to move. She could feel the wood in the room age by tiny degrees. Now, on top of that, she was projecting an image of herself and feeling these things all at once.

From her trance she saw the specter hovering against the wall and became overwhelmed with pity. It wasn't a monstrous demon or hellish abomination at all—those she *had* seen—but was an old woman, barely visible, her essence nearly washed out. The spirit wore the rags of someone from a different time. She was very old, Del thought. New Orleans had been around a long time. The entity emanated profound sadness. She could feel it. Its outer shape—the one that Del's physical body and eyes were dealing with—was that of a monstrous swirl of dark smoke. It had enough power to fling objects around, which were possibly what Del felt cut her neck. It also had the ability to cast visions into the minds of the living; her mind thought the floor was falling even now. But Del didn't sense horror from the thing. She sensed fear. The old spirit was scared.

Del called out from her trancing mind. *Woman. I am here. Don't fear me.*

The phantasm twisted its head around and stared up at the image Del had projected above it—a shimmering silver orb that pulsed with energy.

The face of the old woman stretched into a grotesque mask of shock. The eyes bulged and popped. The mouth distorted with a long grimace, then disappeared into smoke, only to instantly reform as a face. The wretched thing twisted in fear as it clung above the door.

Then Del felt her body tilt.

The few seconds it took to trance out and observe the spirit were precious moments *not* spent maintaining her body's balance. She couldn't be in both places at once. She only hoped she could move between the two fast enough to *appear* that she did.

The spirit felt the shift in the air that announced Del's balance was leaving. Its attention turned to the body, preparing to seize upon it as it fell.

Del saw the spirit's intention to send an old vase crashing to the floor just where her head would hit. She slipped out of her trance and righted her body—her eyes sparking with fearsome light—and caught the vase before it broke. Righting her balance and locking her legs against a final descent of the floor, she slipped back into her trance and sent a fiery burst of silver light throughout the room. The spirit of the old woman looked from Del's body to her projected, silver-orb entity and back again. Del appeared to be in two places at once. And one version of Del was a monstrous cloud of energy.

The phantasm shrieked and flew from the room. Across the city, several sleeping people dreamed of a tattered spirit that night. It flew south into the swamp.

Del slipped out of her trance and collapsed onto the floor, exhausted. The session was finished.

CHAPTER 3

In the early hours of morning, Del floated to the surface of
a strange dream. Her covers hung partially off the bed but
remained twisted around her feet. She was having another rough
night of sleep, and the old air-conditioner wasn't helping. Some days
it struggled to regulate the large house, especially as June heated up,
but now it was too cold. She'd been tired when she stumbled into bed
last night and forgotten to check the thermostat.

Now she groped for the covers, pulled a corner over her shoulder
and shivered. The room was still dark, but freezing, and she pleaded
with the sandman to let her fall back asleep. It was too early—or late,
depending on how you thought of it. Figments of last night's session
floated in her mind.

(That poor woman.)

Go to sleep.

(That poor spirit.)

Go to sleep. Stop thinking. Sleep…

A car door shut somewhere outside the large house.

Turning on her side, she pulled a second pillow onto her exposed ear, leaving just enough room to breathe.

Sleep... sleeeep... sle...

A light, airy sound came from between the pillows as Del sighed and slipped back into a dreamless slumber.

Then the ceiling looked at her.

From all perspectives, the richly decorated room only had one occupant. Observing it as someone passing through the door, one would see well-constructed mahogany furniture from the late 1800s; tall walls adorned with paintings of the New Orleans harbor, a four-poster bed with a languid, sleeping Del, and a small crystal jar on the nightstand that held a single strand of hair wrapped around a thimble. This perspective gave the impression of someone with wealth—or at least someone who may inherit it, in time.

But looking beyond the furniture and paintings, which oftentimes transferred with the house, one would see a different tale: a closet stuffed with old clothing—perhaps as old as the furniture—that did not fit the current occupant; dust beneath the bed, where rows of shoes did not exist; dresser drawers empty and hollow, not hiding childhood treasures. The only items in the room that hinted at a real, live occupant were either folded neatly in a small, smoke-stained suitcase, or strewn about the floor as a teenager would do: a bandeau headband, a white bra and t-shirt with ripped collar, worn jeans and battered leather boots. It was too warm for the motorcycle jacket, so it hung over the back of a desk chair.

These items would tell an observer that the occupant was merely passing through, or unsure of their tenancy, and liked to remain *prepared*.

The ceiling stain—from an old, repaired leak—was barely visible and had been forgotten long ago. Before Del's arrival it was a simple stain, content in its plainness. After the girl's arrival, it became something else.

Through slow forces, the brown water lines moved, twisted and reshaped. It was crude, the shape it took, but it was functional. Within the stain, a faint eye had formed. Unnatural energy fed it when Del was in the room. And tonight, it was awake.

It looked down upon the occupant. It did not see the strewn clothes or empty drawers. It had long forgotten these material things. The eye—now clearly defined and getting larger—saw many other things. Lying there on the bed, making the slightest of sounds—almost cat-like—was a human body. The white panties, partially hidden by covers, stood bright against the light brown skin of the body. The eye was drawn to the contrast. It looked beyond the skin and saw a strange mix of colors flowing, just beneath the surface. The eye could peer deeply. The colors within the girl ebbed and flowed. They were wild: silver and black lightning. The thing attached to the eye sensed it like a feeling of static electricity in the air.

The eye grew bulbous and watery. The surface stretched and strained off the ceiling, attached to the plaster with long threads of membrane. It hung, bulging, to within a few feet of the skin. Two other orbs formed from the stain as well and began their descent. They were of different size and shape, but they were drawn to the contrasting colors as well, for they were once human—and they remembered.

The eyes captured a kaleidoscope of images, for they all turned in different directions and peered at different parts. One, fascinated by the thigh, followed its line beneath the cover. One observed the small of the back and the unbroken color up to the neck. The other eye focused on one thing only: the three long scratches that ran from the neck to the shoulder blade.

It wanted to touch them.

Del twitched her foot, kicked off the covers and rolled onto her back. Only the pillow covered her head. Two of the eyes faded back into the ceiling. The first hovered closely, gazing.

Del rested in thin sleep until she felt the first rays of sun stream beneath the window shade. She stuck her legs in the air to stretch and one leg passed through the hovering eye with a shimmering disturbance. She felt a cold breeze brush over her leg and pulled her knees to her chest, throwing off the pillow.

The eye was gone.

She lay there for several seconds, forcing her eyes open. She shivered again and wondered if Armand had not only fixed the air conditioning, but left it on high. Letting the pillow drop to the floor, she sat up, rubbed her eyes and decided on a shower.

She felt another cold draft and quickly grabbed her robe.

CHAPTER 4

Spider hated these early morning jobs. But that was the business he was in. Hell, he couldn't really call this an *early* job. He didn't have to wake up for it. The bars were still open—at least some of them. It was a late *thing* he had to do. That's how he described it anyway, and the people he spoke with understood. "I got a *thing* I gotta do later," Spider would say, thumbing over his shoulder, as if the task was always right behind him.

He would also flick his lighter three times—even if it flamed right away—before lighting his cigarettes. Some things were simply tradition, and a man in his business needed some stability.

Flick. Flick. Flick. Burn. Inhale.

"I got this *thing.*"

Spider would thumb and people would nod.

In his business, people either nodded or said, "Spider, go to the other side of town and meet this guy." And Spider went.

Or people would say, "Wait for this dude and bring the package back." And Spider waited and brought back the package.

It was easier for Spider to do it this way. Any other way required him to think ahead and figure things out. This made him squirmy. And he didn't like it when he felt squirmy.

Many of the bad things in his life happened around these times. '*Episodes*,' one of the doctors had called them. His head would hurt during *episodes*. Then the medicine would be given, then months would go by where he did little more than sleep, then he had to make money somehow so he would scutter out into the night and people would tell him what to do. Short, skinny guys with twitchy fingers never got to be the boss, they just did what they were told. So, he just waited for someone to tell him something, then he went and did it.

He pulled into the alley and gave himself a vigorous thumbs-up due to the absence of streetlamps.

They were all out.

Somehow Spider associated this event with himself and his ability to do his job, as if the streetlights knew he was coming and had turned off in reverence.

This was one small victory in a whole line of tasks he had to do tonight. He almost had to take notes, but decided he could remember everything if he tried.

He remembered to turn his headlights off well before he turned towards the alley. He remembered to fix the hole in his muffler, so it wasn't so loud. He remembered the flashlight and the blanket. He parked and opened the trunk. Then he walked down the alley.

*

A tangle of brown hair moved in the dark as the little girl woke in the St. Augustine Orphanage. Her sleepy brown eyes opened, first one, then the other, and peered at the gloom from behind her covers. She started to cry out, but remembered there was a rule against that. She didn't like this place; Mommy wasn't here.

She liked that she had a bed and didn't have to sleep on the stinky couch. It had bugs in it. And they had lots of food here. Sometimes her belly hurt from eating so much. Despite the food and warm bed, she didn't know anyone here and wanted to return home.

Listening to the other kids sleep, she wondered where all the other mommies and daddies had gone. There were a lot of kids here.

A shadow moved in the far corner of the room. It was a large, open room with rows of beds, and it had a lot of shadows. But this shadow looked different. It was toward the back by an old coat closet. She didn't like that closet. In the dark, the coats made ghost shapes, and it was always hotter or colder back there than in the big room.

The girl clenched shut her eyes, hoping the shadow wouldn't see her. That's what her mommy had told her to do at her old house.

There she'd been told the thing moving in the corner was just a mouse anyway, and why couldn't she be quiet for a while?

She had tried to be quiet *and* to close her eyes, but when the mouse dragged away the puppy, she'd gotten scared and made some noise. She didn't like that mouse. It had found the little puppy, Pickle, that got left under their porch, and pulled it into a hole by its head. She'd seen it.

In the orphanage, outside the dark closet room, she lay still until she thought the mouse had gone away. Maybe it was just one of the coats after all, she thought. Her eyelids drooped shut.

Then something whispered her name.

"Claaraaaa...," the voice said softly.

She peaked out of the covers and looked around. "Mommy?" she whispered.

The shadows in the corner moved again.

The little girl peered closely, and thought she saw the outline of a woman; it was thin and slight.

"Mommy?"

The thing in the corner grew bolder at the girl's words. "Come, darliiinnnnggg," it whispered. "Come to mommaaaaa."

The girl felt a wind blow her hair, as if a door had opened, and the shadow seemed to slide further back. Maybe Mommy was leaving already.

She sat up in bed and pulled the covers tight around her. She wanted to scream for help, but also didn't want to get in trouble. She sat frozen with wide eyes. She slowly shook her head no.

For an instant a low growl reverberated off the floor. She felt it vibrate up through her bed. It settled in her body, near her heart and made her feel sick. It felt the same as when her mom yelled at her about wanting to keep a deformed puppy that its own mother didn't even want. Besides, Pickle was a stupid name for a dog.

Clara had never had a puppy before, and wished she could have been able to pet it just once before it went away. She couldn't reach it, so she never got to pet it. She'd heard it whining under the porch. When she looked through a hole in the board where a piece had fallen out, she saw it and thought it could see her. Until the mouse came.

As soon as the thought of Pickle entered her mind, the growl faded and a faint, warm glow appeared in the corner.

Maybe someone had woken up and turned on a light, she thought. But deep down she knew it wasn't that. She hoped the light would wake up the other kids and they would scream out, but that didn't happen either. As the light grew brighter, she saw a little shape lying on the floor. Then it moved.

The thing in the corner whispered, "I found hiiiimmmmm."

"Who?"

"Piiiiiiicckkllllllle."

"Pickle?"

"Yeeessssssss. He neeeedddsssss yoooouuuuuuu."

Clara looked around once more at the sleeping children. She doubted she would ever see these kids again, but didn't know why she thought that. It was just a feeling.

Her little toes touched the cold floor and left warm tracks toward the glowing light. It was fading quickly.

"Pickle," she whispered and hurried. "Com'ere Pickle, Pickle, Pi—"

A sharp little scream pierced the night air, but was engulfed by a black mist. The scream fell, dead and silent, like a shadow on the floor.

Clara and Pickle were gone.

CHAPTER 5

Del sat on the toilet wrapped in her robe waiting for the water to heat up. Armand's boiler, like his air conditioner, was finicky.

She rubbed her shoulders. The bad night of sleep seemed to be settling there, that and the trancing session. She'd learned over the last few months what the aftereffect of trancing felt like. It was not just a mental fatigue; it settled into her muscles as well. Granted, now that she was out of the orphanage and living in Armand's house with Mama Dedé, she had been active: exploring the city when she had time, taking Jimmy to movies when she had money, and trying to find her first real story, but she didn't think she'd been so active to account for the soreness.

She'd left the bathroom lights off; her eyes told her they wanted to stay shut. When the steam began to roll over the curtain, she stood up, dropped her robe and stepped in.

As the water heated her skin, she wondered about last night's session and what she could have done differently. It was nothing like she'd expected. Her newly found power—closer to a curse really—was unwieldy. One moment she thought it was under control, the next moment she was dealing with some new ability or danger.

Was it too much to ask for a normal problem?

She was a modern girl after all—or at least wanted to be one—and wanted normal problems to deal with, like having a little money for clothes, or going out, or perhaps even having a boy *(girl?)* friend. But with her donated clothes that lay on the floor of her temporary bedroom, the concepts of *modern* and *normal* seemed miles away. Then on top of all that, when the knowledge that she descended from a long line of Voodoo practitioners—Marie Laveau of all people—came to her, she couldn't believe it. But many others could. And did.

After that terrible night in the cemetery, and despite their best efforts to stay quiet about the whole thing, people began approaching Mama Dedé about Del. Maybe she could perform a reading or enchantment for them? Maybe a quick blessing? As if Del actually knew how to do those things.

It was as if Mama D had suddenly become Del's agent. Most of the requests Mama D could handle very well on her own, Del knew this. But on occasion, the senior woman—who *had* taught Del how to trance—had asked her to help during a particular session.

She didn't think Mama D was pushing her into the occult life, but she knew the woman believed in her ability. And Del had to admit, the things she had performed *That Night* in the cemetery were extraordinary. But she hadn't been able to save everyone. Things had gone wrong then just like they had last night. And she could never be sure when they would go wrong again.

Del adjusted the temperature and lathered her hair. Her hands ran down the back of her neck and she flinched at the sting the cuts sent out.

"Oww. What is that?" she said in the thickening steam. She'd forgotten about the scratches until now.

As if answering her call for assistance, a slight disturbance formed in the steam just above Del's head. It quivered with excitement, hovering in front of the showerhead and soon becoming part of it. If the water were not flowing through it, the shape would sometimes resemble an eye, then a mouth—alternating between the senses of sight and taste. But the water streams pulled the essence apart, stretching it and sending it reaching, with long liquid fingers, towards Del.

It hung there, suspended, and watched.

Del remembered the first time Mama D had asked her to help with one of her trancing sessions. Del was both flattered and scared. She wasn't concerned about her ability to do the job, just what it meant for her future. Did she really want to establish a reputation in this business? A business that she had so adamantly refused to believe in until the evidence was literally staring her in the face.

The spirit crept along the tendrils of water towards Del's skin, hovering, stretching, quivering, just out of reach. It inspected her closely as the streamlets moved out ahead, hitting her body and running down.

Mama D meant well by introducing her to clients. It gave Del something to do while she looked for real work—though she was starting to believe she'd never get a chance at the newspaper. It also put some money in her pocket, more than she had imagined she could make. It seemed that people in need of that kind of help were very generous. So, Del began taking on her own clients. Last night's job had been the toughest so far.

The lustful entity, morphing between gaze and hunger, reached for the fresh cuts first. The skin was soft and tender there. Weeping and salivating at the same time, the steam-shape dissolved into the water streams and let its essence wash over the young woman, running down her skin, into the cuts, over her shoulder blades, down, down.

Lost in her thoughts, Del felt her temperature rise. The water was hot now. Her breath was quick and shallow. The steam lightened her head. The hot streams massaged her body. She suddenly felt wonderful. The water was heavy, encompassing. She wanted to fall into it. Wrap herself in the heavy wetness and dissolve. She wondered if a lover's touch felt like this: constant, gentle pressure that sunk to her core. She felt like crying.

The thing with a thousand gazing eyes sheeting over Del had its own needs. It twisted in agony and want, transforming over and over, and became all mouth. Now a thousand slathering tongues, dripping hot saliva, protruded from the showerhead. The invisible tongues sheening the surface of every water droplet lashed and lathered everything in their path, splashing against the ceiling, running down the walls, cascading onto the floor.

The orgy of heavy steam and slathering tongues was suddenly accented by a dark mist. A single black stream slithered out of the showerhead and moved on its own accord. It did not flow with the other tongues; it wavered, sampling the air. Then, like a snake at its prey, it struck its target. The black tongue lashed out at Del, hitting below her left armpit and snaking across her breasts. Its touch was vile and cold, like death groping.

Del screamed and slapped at the invisible thing in the shower. Pulled violently out of her daydream, she spun around, looking everywhere. The room was still dark. Water sprayed in competing directions from the calcium buildup in the showerhead.

She threw back the shower curtain and stared into the steam cloud.

She pulled the curtain to the other side as if someone could be hiding behind the four inches blocked from her view. She checked the shower knobs and they seemed to be working correctly, although she thought the hot water may be running low now. Maybe a jet of cold water had suddenly come up from the tank and not mixed properly, giving her the sudden jolt of cold. Although, she would swear she felt like it had reached around her. She turned off the water, stepped out and flipped on an overhead light that blinked awake. She quickly toweled dry and donned her robe.

Something wasn't right.

CHAPTER 6

Mama Dedé walked through the backdoor of Armand's house into the kitchen. She drank in the homey sight of Del sitting at the table with her coffee and paper. The warm smells of breakfast and pipe tobacco accented the air.

She still wasn't used to calling this place home, but it was becoming easier each day to imagine it. She'd loved the old Prudhomme house. It did have more scars than normal, but that was simply due to the number of girls that had lived under its roof.

After Mama D's house—The Transitional Home for Girls—burnt down, Armand had been kind enough to offer them rooms for as long as they wanted to stay. The old woman was quite comfortable already, her and Armand interacting like an old married couple who had long ago taken to separate rooms. They went about their business with a mutual respect, and lived comfortably separate lives that overlapped mostly during breakfast and dinner.

"Woo, wee!" Mama Dedé huffed. "That boy gonna run me ragged." She fanned herself with a plump, ringed hand. "Ever since I told

Jimmy he could catch a bird if he sprinkled salt on its tail, he's got me out there every hour trying to help him." Del smiled up at her. "Maybe I should tell him my heavy feet been scarin' 'em away, and I'd be better to watch from the porch."

She sat down at the table and dabbed a white handkerchief at her neck and large bosoms. "Gonna be a hot one today."

Del nodded. "Yeah, I think the air conditioner is on the fritz. My room was freezing last night."

Mama Dedé watched Del carefully. "How'd your session go, honey?"

"It was OK."

She thought about the scratches on her shoulder, but didn't want to give up that bit at the moment.

"Just OK? Were you able to set the spirit to sleep?"

Waiting for an answer, she noticed a small bead of sweat break across Del's temple. Next, the observant woman noticed a flush rise in her cheeks.

Del sat uncomfortably in her chair. "I'm not sure that one was ready to go back to sleep just yet."

Mama D. watched as more beads of sweat sprouted on Del's upper lip and leaned back in her protesting chair. She sighed deeply and locked her hands over her large stomach.

Del looked up from her plate of eggs and glanced at the woman. A stern, knowing stare gazed back at her.

"What?" Del said.

"Hhmmpphh! What 'what'?" the woman responded. "You gonna sit there and sweat with your robe pulled up to your ears, or you gonna tell me what happened?" She heaved herself from the table and went for coffee. "You know I'll find out if I want."

Del watched her walk to the counter, pour a steaming cup of coffee, then turn and look back, leaning against the old cabinet.

With one hand on her wide hip, she sipped her coffee with a stern *sssssiipp* and narrowed her eyes at Del.

Del sighed and looked out the back window for Jimmy. She saw he was safely occupied with some fascinating oddity, then swiveled in her chair toward the old woman. She flapped the lapels of her robe open, letting in a cooling draft of air, and exposed her left shoulder.

"What in the name of..." Mama Dedé went to inspect her wounds. "What is that?"

Del started to cover up. "It'll be fine. It's just a—"

Mama D. pulled the robe further down her shoulder. "Oh, lawd! Girl, you tell me right now what happened."

Pulling the robe tight around her shoulders, Del nodded and checked again that Jimmy was out of earshot. "I got scratched somehow—"

"I'd say!"

"It was kind of a bad one this time. Not like the other two I've done."

Mama D sat down. "I was afraid we started you too soon." She shook her head in disgust. "I should have never let you—"

"But it was my decision," Del interrupted. "I'm a grown woman and..."

The old woman leaned back and looked down her nose at Del.

"...and well... I have to make money somehow, so I just did it." She looked back at her eggs.

Mama D softened. "Del, honey, why you so hellbent on making money? You—"

"You know why!" Del pulled her robe tight and looked to the

30

interior of the house, hoping Armand hadn't heard her. "You know why," she said quietly. "I can't stay here forever. I'm glad that Jimmy and I have a place to stay. And Armand is so kind to us, but…" She shrunk in her chair.

Mama Dedé nodded. "OK, enough of that. I know you got the itch to make your own way. It's in you and nothin's gonna change it, but you got to slow down. You're learning fast, but you got to give your own mind time to adjust to the things you're learning." She leaned forward, resting her chin on her hands. "The spirits, they don't usually reach out and touch."

"They don't?"

"No." She shook her head slowly. "Almost never. They can knock a lot of things off the shelves, slam doors and play havoc with the lights. But they rarely touch."

"I didn't know that."

"Mmm-hmmm. Did you at least put the spirit down?"

Del's mouth twisted to the side.

"No, I don't think so. It was just an old woman. She got scared and—"

"Got scared? Of what?"

"I don't know. Me, I guess."

"You? How in the worl—? What did you do that *scared* a spirit away?"

"Maybe when I was projecting…"

"Projecting? Honey, you just supposed to guide those spirits back to sleep. There's a verse for that. It's too dangerous to be *trancing* by yourself, much less projecting with a spirit in the room."

"There was no other way," Del said. "She wasn't about to go on her own. She'd already done this," pointing to her neck, "before I thought about trancing on her. That's when I saw it was a woman. Or what was left of her. The spirit was... almost gone, somehow."

Mama Dedé was silent for a long time. Her heavy chin resting on her clasped hands.

Finally, she said, "You know, it's not the big ones I'm worried about. After watching you that night in the cemetery, seeing the way you handled that tricky old bastard, I'm not worried about those at all."

"Then what are you worried about?" Del asked.

"All these little things that happen. They add up, you know. They take a toll over time. You ever heard of death by a thousand cuts?"

CHAPTER 7

Frank Morgan left the St. Augustine orphanage at 8:43 Wednesday morning. His morning cigar, a pleasant Nicaraguan blend with a light Connecticut wrapper, jutted from the side of his mouth. He opened the door to his 1953 Chevrolet Bel Air and sat in a perfectly molded shape of his round bottom. The convertible top was already down.

He sat his small notebook on the passenger seat and waved at Sister Francine as she closed the front door. She had taken over after the mysterious disappearance of Sister Eulalie, a few months ago. He had a good feeling that the horrible things that had been allowed to transpire here were finally at an end, now that Eulalie was gone. He knew that she would never come back, although there were only a few people that knew that. During the fire that destroyed Mama Dedé's house in spectacular fashion, Frank and Armand had whisked Del and the woman away. Sister Eulalie—beyond saving—was still burning in the back courtyard when they left. But when they returned the next day to speak with the fire department—many of them known by Frank for years—no body was found. Not even the remnants of one. Quite literally, the terrible Sister Eulalie had disappeared in a cloud of smoke.

Pushing that horror from his mind, he turned back to the current one. He rubbed his eyes, opened his notebook and reread his notes. They were scant:

Clara Boynell, 6 yrs. old, approx. 3' tall.

Brown hair. Brown eyes.

Missing.

They couldn't even say what she might have been wearing. Pajamas of course, but no color or pattern could be remembered. What a shame.

She was the second child to go missing from an orphanage this week, the third in two weeks. And he didn't like these types of cases. They rarely turned out well.

Early this spring, after the (also mysterious) disappearance of Henri Guillaume, his former police captain, Sergeant Allen Conroy had been appointed interim department chief. He was a good man, and Frank thought he would do well in his new position. It was Captain Conroy who had called Frank as soon as the first kid went missing. Frank Morgan was still a legend to most of the younger officers on the force, and to have him helping the NOPD in any capacity was considered a great asset. Frank was happy to work a case or two when he could, just to keep his retirement interesting.

The last thing his city needed was a damn serial kidnapper wreaking havoc. But three missing orphans in two weeks pointed to just that. They were all young too, which meant they were unlikely to be runaways.

No sign of forced entry. No ransom notes. No trace of where they'd gone. Like so many people in the Crescent City, they just up and vanished.

He sat the notepad down again, checked his mirror and backed out. He turned right on Governor Nichols Street and drove toward the Mississippi River. He'd meander a bit. He had to think this one out.

*

Spider woke up in a panic. He was sweating badly. Had he forgotten something?

He hadn't drunk much the night before—he'd had a *thing* to do—so he was surprised at how much he was sweating. His heart pounded in his chest. He thought he may be having a heart attack.

Grabbing his cigarettes from a wooden orange crate that sat next to the bed, he shook one out from a prone position. He didn't want to risk sitting up yet until his heart slowed down.

He held the cigarette in his mouth, but didn't light it. It wasn't safe to smoke in bed.

He closed his eyes and let the coffin nail hang from the side of his mouth. *What did you forget?*

(You'd forget your head if it wasn't attached.)

I didn't forget anything.

(Then why are you so nervous, spider dick?)

Stop calling me that! My name is Spider.

(Spider dick, spider dick, here's a big one, have a lick.)

He opened his eyes and his youthful tormentors faded away.

Fucking retards and bullies, that's all they were. Neanderthals. He couldn't help it if he hadn't grown very fast as a kid. Pops must have shot the good load into some hooker before he came home and dribbled him out.

He thought the nickname of 'Spider' was pretty cool, until he realized the kids thought of him as a bug that scurried around in the shadows. But that's what he did. It was easier to get through life that way. Just wait in the shadows until someone told you what to do.

(The trunk! Did you unlock it?)

His heart, which had been slowing down, ratcheted up a notch.

Yeah, I unlocked it.

(It's got to be hot in there. Are you sure?)

Last night's events replayed in his head: he parked in the alley, he got out—no, first he turned off his lights, *then* he parked in the alley; then he walked down the alley... then... What did he do then?

What *did* he do?

He rubbed his head and sat up. He needed a smoke to remember.

Flick. Flick. Flick. Burn. Inhale.

Spider smoked and thought. One was easier than the other.

After a long period of thinking, a long gray ash fell onto a nervous, shaky hand. It was cast out onto the floor, away from the bed.

He remembered driving away.

Then he ran over something in the road.

(No! The thing made a noise, shithead.)

Oh yeah, the package he was delivering made a noise. All the way from the trunk. So, he'd turned the radio up louder like he'd been told.

Then what?

Then he'd parked somewhere.

(In another alley?)

Yeah, in an alley. A different one.

(And then?)

And then he'd unlocked the trunk!

See there, he had remembered everything.

Spider crushed out the cigarette. Into the fat bottom of a smiling porcelain Geisha girl it went. He couldn't remember where that came from, but had no time to wonder about it.

He had a *thing*.

CHAPTER 8

L   ater that morning, Del, dressed in her standard jeans and t-shirt
    (burnt orange which matched the colors in her headband)
    stood in the wood-paneled parlor of Armand's house, facing a
mirror. After the odd sensation in the shower, she wanted to put some
happy thoughts in her head. And this was her favorite room.

The entire house was grand beyond scale: dark mahogany accented
every wall; creepy old paintings of people she didn't know hung from
wires (but this was a good creepy); rich fabric framed ornate windows,
and intricate wallpaper stretched to the ceilings. The first time she'd
walked into the parlor she'd fallen in love.

The spacious but cozy room had quaint couches and chairs spaced
around the walls. They sat snugly between a large fireplace, an upright
piano and two large windows that looked out the front of the house.
Interspersed between all this was a standup bass and guitar on stands
and three old violins that held a place of honor on the floor-to-ceiling
bookshelves.

Del imagined the former owners having grand parties here. After a decadent meal, in front of a roaring fire, the guests would sit in the parlor and listen to wonderful music late into the night. Handsome men and beautiful women would take turns playing the instruments; the little table and chairs would be moved out of the center to make way for an impromptu dance; courting couples would flirt and steal away into other rooms.

Armand had given her permission to play any instrument she wanted, saying it was good for mental development and that everyone needed a hobby. Del agreed, but really just wanted to hear the romantic music of that lost time. So, after a brief explanation of how to read music and some new strings, Del decided she would learn to play the violin. This was her practice time.

An old music stand sat near the center of the room, directly in front of the fireplace, which had a large mirror over the mantel. She could watch her form this way. She opened her book to "Twinkle, Twinkle, Little Star" and began.

After several misstarts and a bit more rosin on her bow, she started in full strength. A high-pitched semblance of screaming banshees reverberated through the house.

Del fiddled away, watching her reflection in the mirror, seemingly oblivious to the ancient dust particles that the high frequency sounds shook loose from the ceiling. Just as she thought she was hitting her stride, her concentration was broken by a plea of surrender.

"BBAAAHHHH! WHAT DAT SOUND??" Jimmy yelled, running through the parlor door. His hands were clamped tightly over his ears and his flat face was scrunched into a grimace of pain.

"DEH, YOU CACK'N MY EAHS!"

Del stopped and looked at the boy she had grown up with in the orphanage. They were nearly like brother and sister now.

"What's the matter?" she asked. "I'm practicing."

The boy tentatively lowered his hands, just in case Del started up again quickly.

"Pact-a-sing?"

"Yeah, I have to—"

"Deh, dat soun' 'ike poop."

"Jimmy!" Del cocked her head. "That's not nice. I have to practice if I'm going to get better. Maybe I can get a job in a band one day and—"

The left side of Jimmy's face wrinkled, flaring his nostril. He considered this idea, briefly shaking his head. After a moment his eyes brightened and he said, "Maybe you get a job an schop wood."

"Chop wood?"

"Yeah, dat be puwty good I guess."

Satisfied with his suggestion, he turned on his heels and headed out of the parlor. Passing Armand on the way, he said, "Hi, Aman!" Then whispered, "I fought Deh kiwen a cat." He marched toward the back door. "But she not. She yust pact-a-sing."

"Indeed?" said Armand. "That would be a trick, considering we don't have a feline friend."

Del plopped into the chair next to a small table. She watched Armand's nimble fingers sprinkle invisible dust in the air. She knew he was working out an odd word association in his mind. He inspected the shelves, muttering to himself.

"No. No feline friends..." He touched one violin, then the other. "Feline, cat, string." His fingers danced, collecting bits of the story that was hiding in those objects. "Yarn. No, not yarn. String... dust... Yes, of course!" He looked at Del, finger pointing triumphantly in the air. "Did you ever hear the strange story of the Weeping Violin?"

Del chuckled as her shoulders drooped. "No, but I think that's what mine was doing earlier. Jimmy's right, that did sound like I was killing a cat."

"Oh, not to worry," Armand said, gently patting other objects in the room. "It even took the great composers years to master their craft. You've barely begun your ten-thousand-hour journey."

"Ten thousand hours?"

Armand took the chair across from Del.

"Well, some manage it a bit quicker, but in general, yes."

Del seemed to deflate even more.

He continued, "Why, depending on how much you practice, it could be done in... five years or so."

"Five. Years?"

"Don't look so glum. You'd only be twenty-three, with your whole life ahead of you."

Del looked at the beautiful throw rug beneath her feet and bit the side of her lip. She couldn't save up enough money for that rug in five years, let alone for a house to put it in.

Armand had seen this look before on Del. Although he went about his research quietly, allowing his guests—now his extended family—to get acquainted with their new home, he was a keen observer. He'd often seen Del wandering the large rooms, gazing at the old items, feeling the rich wood. She was an old soul, he'd thought many times. In more ways than one.

Handing her a small stack of letters, he said, "You know, there are other ways."

She tentatively took the stack.

"There are some who believe that one should not... focus broadly, just to reinforce their weaknesses. But should put all their energy into their... natural strengths."

She looked at him and caught a twinkle in his eye.

He raised his hands in slight surrender. "Simply put, energy spent on natural talents, is more efficiently used than…"

"Killing cats?"

His bushy moustache smiled.

"I would say, '…tasks with a poor possibility of return.'"

She shuffled through the letters. It was as she had feared. They were all addressed to her and decorated roughly the same way: custom drawn filigree and veves covered the envelopes. The handwriting varied, and the formality of the letters were different, but she knew they all carried the same message, the same request.

The letters were addressed to Delphine the Spirit Hunter, and inside they would all request her help.

CHAPTER 9

F rank parked at the wharf and turned off the engine. He had done several slow loops through the city, letting his mind wander. He wasn't surprised that he'd ended up here.

He watched as a long, low barge crawled its way up the Mississippi. The rippling waves flowed against it, giving him the false sensation that it wasn't moving, or that it was moving backward. Two competing forces in an odd dance of willpower. And wasn't that how life worked after all? Everything and everyone struggling for their own space in a sea of competing tides. Some people sailed upriver

(Like Del)   .

as if they had a magic wind at their back. The waters of strife parting before them. Others had a constant flow pushing against them and no matter how hard they tried, they never moved forward, expending all their energy just to stay afloat.

(Like Del?)

He ashed his cigar, almost opened his door, but saw some kids wandering down by the river's edge. He sat back and watched.

There were all types of people that wandered this area, and he thought about the last time he was down here. That was on official business. That kid—young man really—had met a terrible end, right down the wharf from here. Being torn apart by a beast was bad enough, but having your head eaten…

A dark thought pricked the depths of his mind, causing his skin to crawl. It was just a shadow, a fragment of an idea, but Frank knew it would grow if he gave it time.

The macabre events of *That Night* had never left him. He knew they would stay with him for the rest of his life. He just hoped he'd be able to forget them when he was dead. Lying there for eternity knowing that something like the Gris-gris man was possible was more than he could stand to imagine. But now, thinking about his current case, and watching the kids on the wharf, the old nightmare bubbled back to the surface. Why? He didn't quite know.

He knew the clues were in him. He was a good detective, and naturally recorded details without thinking about it. He just needed to get them to line up—to associate with one another—and form a plausible theory. He thought he'd try a little Armand trick to get his mind unstuck.

He closed his eyes and imagined he was touching objects in Armand's study.

Da dead boy, da beast, da eaten head… just da brains really, but… Then there'd been da binding spell. Don't forget dat. Dat's what Henri— dat sum'bitch—was trying to use to bind up da Gris-gris man, but when he got sucked into da void—

"Aw hell," Frank said, frustrated at his digression. Startled, he opened his eyes and looked around to see if anyone had seen him talking to himself.

Dis ain't workin'. Where's Armand when you need him to pull some strange notion outta da air?

He looked back where the kids had been, but they were gone. He looked up and down the wharf, but they were nowhere in sight. He didn't think he'd been daydreaming that long. But wasn't that the problem with these things? You think you're on top of things, so you glance away for just a second, then...

Suddenly the words of Loo'siana Slim popped into his head. He was the first man Frank had met when he began investigating a reported *gator attack* earlier this spring. Slim warned them of the swamp and not to follow any fifolets—the spirits that lived there.

Slim had said, "Da fifolet... it'll just lead you on and on, just 'round another tree, then," throwing up his hands, "you just be gone."

A breeze chilled Frank's neck as a cloud floated overhead. As if by invitation, the thought previously stuck in Frank's mind surfaced. This chilled him even further.

He started his car, backed out and quickly left. There was someone he needed to speak with. A terrible feeling had settled over him. It wasn't a hunch—something he could contribute to good policework— no, this was more like a gut-punch from something he didn't want to consider. Something he'd wanted to forget. And if he was right, he was afraid that other kids would soon...

just be gone.

CHAPTER 10

Frank knocked on the backdoor of Armand's house as he opened it. Over the last few months, knocking had become optional, considering how close they had all become, but his manners were deeply engrained.

"Hallo?" he said, peering into the kitchen. He walked in, shut the door and made his way to the table where a lone sausage lay waiting. Just as the sausage approached Frank's mouth a high-pitched screech bellowed from the parlor. Nearly dropping the morsel, he stuck the snack in his mouth, wiped his hand on a discarded napkin and held his hands over his ears as he tiptoed through the foyer and up the steps to the second floor.

As expected, Armand was looking for something within his large volume of books.

Frank was always amazed at this second-floor study. The curving staircase that ran up the right side—straight off the foyer—brought him to a large, balcony-type room that looked down upon the main entryway into the grand house. A large concave bookshelf stood floor to ceiling, directly in the middle of the room; dark halls on both sides disappeared behind it. A large wooden table sat in front of the shelves, covered with books and papers. Above all of this, a unique bit of architecture opened through the second-floor ceiling, ending with a domed skylight that jutted out of the roof. The natural light was amazing here.

He spied his friend, impeccably dressed in a shabby-professor sort of way, pipe hanging from the side of his mouth, sprinkling invisible dust with his fingers in an effort to find a lost thought. And he was wearing earmuffs.

"Let's see," Armand said to the books. He touched them gently. "*European Myths, Native American Beliefs*, yes, native... *Birds of Myth*, Oh yes! The Thunderbird... no, not the Thunderbird. *Birds of Myth*... Ooo... *moroi*. Yes of course!" His finger poked the air as he turned. "Why, hello mon ami! Have you ever heard the strange story of Polyphonte?"

Frank sat in his usual chair in front of the fireplace and lit his cigar. Armand sat across from him and puffed his pipe.

"What brings you out today, my friend?"

Frank eyed Armand quizzically and pointed to his ear.

"Oh!" Armand said, gently pulling one earmuff aside. "Is it over yet?"

A wry smile painted Frank's face. "I think she just finished," he said quietly.

Setting the earmuffs on the table, Armand patted them. "Quite handy, you know."

"Yep."

"So, what brings you out?"

Frank leaned back and brushed air from his stretching shirt. He was settling into a deep thought.

"Oh, no. Don't tell me you found another..." then he whispered, "grimoire."

"Hell, no! If I had, I'da burnt da damn thing before I brought it here."

Armand looked slightly hurt.

"Oh, you know what I mean."

"Yes, yes. No worries. But what is it? You look troubled."

Frank adjusted in his seat.

"Well, I think I got a... hell, I don't know what I got besides some missin' kids. But da way dey went missin' is da problem."

"Fascinating," Armand said. "Do tell."

Frank blew a smoke ring that drifted out in an ever-expanding circle. When it disintegrated, he said, "Almost two weeks ago, a kid went missin' from Poydras Orphan Asylum, Alvie something. Little kid, seven or eight, I think. It's in my notes. Then last week, Willy Jenkins goes missin' from St. Vincent's. He's a little older, hadn't been there long, so... could be a runaway, but I doubt it.

"Den, just last night, a little girl named Clara, younger, six years old, goes missin' from da same place Del and Jimmy was at—good ole' St. Augustine's.

"Anyway, no witnesses, no suspects. Da damn kids just up and vanished."

He drew deeply on his cigar and tried not to imagine what was happening to them at that very moment.

"I want to help!" Del said from the parlor below. She bounded up the stairs with rapid-fire steps and jumped to an exclamation point besides Frank. She kissed his temple.

"Hi, Frank. Can I help?"

"Del-bell! How you doin' honey?—Hey, wait a minute. You weren't spyin' on us, were you? You know, with da..." And here he wiggled his fingers and whistled.

"No, Frank. I wouldn't do that. It's just..." She bounded over to the small couch by the railing and fell into it. "Well, it's just that sometimes... I hear things without trying."

She looked at Frank, then at something on the floor.

"I can't help it, honest. I was just working on reading my music, then suddenly I was—" She pulled her legs beneath her and leaned into the couch. "I don't know, I just kinda had a daydream and could suddenly hear you guys talking."

She glanced back.

"I didn't mean to."

"Dat's OK, honey," Frank said. "No harm done." He cast a quick glance at Armand, who was already watching Frank. "How much did you hear?"

The side of Del's mouth twisted as she looked around the room.

"Umm... All of it?"

Frank's cigar drooped briefly. "Damn," he mumbled, which sent ashes cascading down his shirt.

"Come on, Frank," she said. "I could really help. You know, with research, or note taking. I might even be able to get those old farts to—uh, I mean... this might win me some favor at the office."

She looked hopefully at Frank.

"You know, after I was... out for so long, after... you know... the whole cemetery thing, then..."

She jumped up to plead her case better, but her hands were on her hips.

"You know, I could understand if I was actually working, then got *sick*," (*air quotes*) "but I never got an assignment, not a real one anyway, and I caught their stupid jokes, ha ha, they didn't think I did, but they weren't that funny anyway, and actually kind of stupid, but they don't know that, because they're not that smart and what do they expect anyway, for the country to never change?!"

Her wind exhausted, she sat on the couch with a thump and crossed her arms tight.

Frank squirmed in his chair and looked at Armand.

Armand's face replied, *You're asking me?*

"Well, honey..." Frank sighed. "I'm not sure what Mama Dedé would say about me gettin' you involved in another..." He trailed off.

"Another what, Frank?" Mama Dedé said from downstairs. She had just returned from her errands.

"Damn," Frank said under his breath. "Dese women and der spooky hearin."

"I heard that too, Frank."

Heavy steps moved toward the staircase. Mama Dedé was coming up.

CHAPTER 11

The large woman huffed up the stairs to the second floor. Frank and Armand sat silent, listening to each stair as it squeaked a warning. Del watched, always amused at the two men's discomfort at a potential scolding from Mama Dedé. Her stress was suddenly gone.

"Woo!" Mama Dedé made the last step. She wiped her brow, walked around Frank and sat in her designated chair at the fireplace table. At these second-floor-fireplace meetings, where serious group talks occurred, Del's spot was still on the small couch by the railing.

Eying Frank and Armand, she called over her shoulder to Del, "Honey, do I need to hex one or both of these knuckleheads?"

The men started to plead their innocence when Del spoke. "No, I guess not. Not yet anyway." She smiled slightly but felt the embarrassing realization that she was once again *outside* the adult conversation. She pulled at a loose thread on the afghan that hung over the couch.

"OK, Frank. Out with it," the woman said. "What are you into now?"

Turning toward the old woman, Frank saw Del's expectant face behind Mama D, looking back from the small sofa. She was trying to send him a signal.

"Well…" He adjusted his girth and sat his cigar in the ashtray. "I was just tellin' Armand about dis case I got. Kinda spooky, but… hell, I don't know. It's some missin' kids I'm followin' up on and—"

"And Frank was thinking I could help," Del said quickly.

Frank nearly let his surprise overtake his face, but played it off as a bit of indigestion. Mama D eyed him closely. Del's eyes silently pleaded with Frank from behind her. Armand, sitting in the chair to the woman's left, gave a slight nod of encouragement to Del as the woman's attention was on Frank. He started to mouth something when he heard, "Frenchy, I can hear your moustache moving in the air. You got something to say, say it."

Armand went on the defensive. "Mon chéri, I just—"

"Don't 'mon sherry' me. If you and Frank are puttin' ideas in that girl's head, I want to know what they are."

"I wasn't—" Frank started.

Armand cut in. "I think she should explore her natural strengths, that's all. What a fascinating life she could have."

"And you would know the dangers of doing that, would ya? She nearly got herself killed the last time she tried to help Frank."

"I didn't—" Frank tried.

"But that was not his fault," said Armand. "He didn't read from the book. He may have shot her on accident, but—"

"No, I didn't—"

"Yeah, and on top of all that—"

"Stop it!" Del said. "Just stop it."

The group fell silent and turned towards the girl.

"I'm sitting right here, you know. You act like I'm not even here."

The group looked at their hands or cigar or pipe, and cleared their throats.

"Del, honey," Mama D said, "we didn't mean to be talkin' about you with you sittin' right here. It's just—"

"I know," Del said. "It's just that everyone has their opinion about what I should and shouldn't do. But you've even had me do some hunting. Just last night."

Now it was the old woman's turn to squirm in her chair.

"Well now… when that job came in… I've just been so busy lately and… well, you know. But I didn't think it was gonna be like it turned out. And certainly not any type of *hunting*. Just a case of—"

"But I did fine," Del said. She felt the scratches on her neck flare. "…mostly. Besides, what Frank's talking about is newspaper business. Reporting. Isn't that right, Frank?"

Frank breathed deeply and held his breath. After a slow release he said, "I think…" He searched his thoughts. "I *think* der's a bad person on da loose. But I *know* we got three orphans missin'. And I know I ain't got any leads, so…"

"And I want to help if I can," Del said.

*

Del sat on the back porch in a creaky rocking chair and watched the birds fight for position in a birdbath; she and Jimmy had cleaned it this spring. To help Armand with the large house and yard, they'd volunteered to clear the overgrown courtyard, and had weeded several stone planters.

She thought the yard must have been grand in its day, and tried to imagine what it looked like in its heyday. The flowers were standard for the South: iris and diamond flowers, azaleas and lilacs, but they had been planted with a larger vision; bordered by arrowwood bushes and magnolia trees, the courtyard created a magical feel of mystery. Here, she thought, even the stones had secrets.

But out of all the features in the garden, Del's favorite was the massive stone maiden that stood watch, in a pool, from its center.

Remembering when she'd first visited the house, she thought that an eight-foot-tall statue rising out of a black pool of water was a bad omen. Later she'd learned that it was only six feet tall and stood on a two-foot-high stone base, but the effect was the same—it was a beautiful and ominous sight.

The maiden was ringed by a low stone wall that made a surrounding pool. Streaming water from a stone jug held in her arms cascaded into the pool and cast faerie-like voices onto the wind. Sometimes she imagined the maiden had its own voice.

After the conversation in the library, Mama D had made a house call, Jimmy was upstairs and Del was left alone. She was thinking about everything that had happened since yesterday.

Sunbeams bounced off the maiden and through the splashing water, sending a bright radiance dancing across the courtyard. Del's face was highlighted with light brown freckles and sharp splinters of light that cut her silhouette into many pieces. The day was growing hot.

No wind blew. Even the shade of the porch was stifling—like an old attic left to bake for a hundred years. Del squinted her eyes against the flickering light and they grew heavy. Small beads of sweat broke out on her skin. Her mind slipped towards a daydream as she wondered about her future.

In the shade of the porch, along the high ceiling above her head, a small spider worked its magic repairing a web. Behind the web, the trim boards met in a nearly perfect forty-five-degree angle where the ceiling and walls came together. Over the years, as age took its toll, a small gap had formed in the corner. The gap appeared as a tiny black void that sunk deep into the house.

As Del dozed, a dark shadow formed in the gap of the wood. Darker than any shadow that had ever touched the house, the wood seemed to shrink away from it, giving it room to grow. Like a stain, the dark thing corrupted the wood and crawled across it, reaching in all directions. The heat pushing her down, Del breathed slowly and dozed.

The shadow spread out from the center void, an unnatural force driving its growth. It touched the silvery anchor strands of the web and the beautiful creation froze. A second later, gravity pulled the web into a million weightless shards. The tiny, frozen fragments, along with the dead spider, fell silently to the porch as the black thing moved down the wall.

It slid silently toward the floorboards. A fly, buzzing in the summer heat, flew too close to the dark thing and was snatched from the air by a black filament that shot out from the mass; sticky tendrils wrapping it tight and sucking it into oblivion. The dark shape had substance now. An oily sheen colored its cold black surface. It reached the bottom of the wall, then moved on.

The stone maiden, long ago placed to greet visitors entering the gate against the road, turned her head slowly. Faint vibrations of deep cracking rippled across the water's surface. The head, now twisted violently over her right shoulder, stared across the courtyard at the black shadow creeping toward Del. Whatever inhabited the stone form watched on in silence.

The thing ebbed slowly across the old porch as if smelling its way to food. It stopped near the line of sunlight that cut across Del's feet on an angle. It vibrated slightly, testing, then slid back. It moved away from the light. But there was darkness beneath the rocker.

A black pool formed on the surface of the dusty planks beneath Del. Where the old boards had separated and left gaps, the blackness flowed. Down, beneath the porch it sank, where it was cold and dark. The spiders, crickets and ants beneath the porch died instantly. They were consumed into the mass and it filled the whole space beneath the porch. It was getting larger.

The stone maiden watched as the black tumor corrupted the earth just inches below Del. The earth shuddered in revulsion as the vile thing settled in; a freezing death-horror with an insatiable appetite.

Several tendrils emerged from between the planks and slithered up the legs of the rocker. A small bead of sweat dripped from the back of Del's leg and fell into the black pool. It shivered with the taste.

The squeak of the screen door called to Del's mind. She realized her feet were hot from the harsh sunlight and folded her right foot beneath the chair instinctively. Just as she did, a black tendril lashed out and stung her between her second and third toe.

"Deh!" Jimmy said, as the screen door stretched its old spring.

"Ow!" Del yelled. Her eyes flew open as she pulled her foot forward to see what had bit her.

"Dere you are!" Jimmy crashed into the chairback to hug Del—stepping on the front of the rocker—just as Del leaned forward. The combined momentum sent her sprawling toward the two steps that led to the courtyard.

The black tendril held fast to the soft skin between her toes as it was stretched into the sunlight. The filament evaporated into the air with a tiny wisp of smoke. Only the maiden saw.

Del flailed her arms and partially recovered her balance as she fell into the sunlight of the courtyard. Landing on her hands and feet, she rolled to the side and sat down hard on the stone path.

"Damn it," she said grabbing her foot. "Jimmy, you need to be more—"

She looked up just as the beaming smile of Jimmy faded at the harsh words.

Jimmy stood processing the scene.

"I yust wanted to hug you."

He stepped down.

"Did you huwt you foot?"

Del inspected the space between her toes and grimaced. "That's OK, Jimmy. I didn't mean to yell at you. It's just that something bit me, and it really hurts."

"Bit you 'ike dis?" Jimmy scrunched his face and gnashed his teeth. His fingers became claws. "Cunch, cunch, cunch."

Del normally would have laughed, but the pain in her foot was too great. She couldn't decide if the bite felt hot or cold. Like a fire-ant, she thought, only with frozen fangs.

The stone maiden watched as the black horror slunk beneath the porch and into the depths under the house. It hadn't left completely, but it had retreated. The spirit in the maiden felt the boy must be powerful to accomplish such a thing.

CHAPTER 12

Clara woke from a nap and looked around. She didn't like the look of this place. She didn't think a new mommy or daddy would find her in this orphanage. If that's what it was.

A heavy, dirty smell hung in the air. The room was cold and dark. A small sliver of light shone beneath the door. A faint red glow was cast into the room from a high, covered window. She whimpered and pulled a smelly cover up to her chin.

She listened to the walls and thought she heard footsteps. Her stomach growled.

"Mommy?" she said weakly.

Mommy hadn't been around for a while.

"Pickle?"

She listened for a response. There was no one else to ask for.

A sob broke the silence and startled her. Two more echoed off the walls before she realized it was her.

"Quiet, you dummy!" a voice whispered from under the door. "Don't let 'em know you awake."

Clara looked at the sliver of light where the voice came from. A shadow flicker that looked like a bug made her pull the covers tighter.

"Who's there?" she whispered.

A long time went by and the voice said nothing. She tried again, a little louder. "Who are you?"

"Shhhh... My name's Willy," the voice said. "Now hush up."

"But I'm sca—"

Heavy footsteps echoed overhead. A fine dust cloud wafted down from the old floor joists where the steps had just passed. Clara watched the ceiling where the footsteps sounded. They seemed to walk away from her position.

"AH-CHOO!" The sneeze, caused by the floating dust particles, burst out of her before she knew it was there. She pulled the cover around her ears, hoping it would keep the sound in the room.

"Oh no," Willy whispered, somewhere outside her room.

The footsteps on the ceiling walked slowly back, creaking each board with special care. They stopped somewhere just above—and outside—of Clara's room. She held her breath.

A commotion could be heard above, then the footsteps walked quickly away. A moment later she heard two sets of footsteps, shuffling against each other. One big, one small, she thought.

A door opened in the room above her. The way her bed was positioned, the sound came from the wall at the end of her tiny room. The sound grew louder, closer. They weren't in the ceiling any longer, they were in the wall. Muffled and coming down.

A nail groaned as the big feet touched down on the last step. The small feet no longer tried to keep up. They dropped lazily from one step to the next as the shoes were dragged along. The dead thud of the little shoes made Clara sick to her stomach, but she didn't know why.

An old door groaned open right next to Clara's room and she threw the covers over her head. She squeezed her eyes tight, trying to keep every last sound inside her.

The squeak of bed springs floated through the knit of her covers. The door closed and locked. The big feet shuffled outside the door. She thought they were coming to her room.

Her breath burned in her chest as she clamped her mouth tight. She willed the feet to run away so she could breathe and not be heard. She felt dizzy. Her breath was about to come out.

Just as the big feet squeaked the bottom step, a small puff of used air escaped her mouth. She gasped in fresh air and listened.

The feet were going up.

*

Flick. Flick. Flick.

Spider listened closely, letting the flame burn. He thought he'd heard something. He knew that his packages sometimes made noise in the trunk, which is why he always turned the radio up.

He was a man who could follow instructions.

But there was nothing in his trunk besides some blankets, a jack and a tire iron. Oh, and a pillow. But now that he thought about it, the jack and tire iron didn't do him much good because he'd taken the spare tire out to make room for the packages.

Also, he wasn't in his car anyway. The sounds were coming from somewhere in the house.

Was someone talking? He was sure he'd heard something.

Quickly looking left, then right over his shoulders, he thought he was sure to catch whoever was behind him. He was smart like that.

There was no one.

Was someone trying to give him instructions on his next task?

No. He didn't think so. Usually those instructions were more direct.

Spider, get the hell out of here and go do that thing.

Spider, meet this guy and give him this envelope.

Spider, turn up the radio if the packages start making noise.

He lit his cigarette, inhaled deeply and shot two streams of smoke out his nostrils. The smoke always made him think of a dragon.

Spider the Dragon King. That's how he imagined himself. Twenty feet—no, fuck that—fifty feet tall and made of iron. A dick ten feet long that shot molten lava.

A rare smile turned the side of his mouth. His eyes gleamed.

Who's squirming now, baby? Not Spider.

If he was a dragon, he'd grow black wings that would sail him through the night. The *Silent Hunter*. He could be the boss then. Nobody would fuck with Spider the Dragon King. And he'd get all the pussy. Until then, the little things would have to do.

A movement outside the window brought him back. He slid to one side and peered out through the slit in the drapes. Then he looked the other way, being just as careful. After a few minutes he decided it was All Clear. That was an important step to achieve.

Making ready to leave, he went through his laundry list of prep tasks. These were things he had to do before he did the real tasks. These things helped keep him out of jail.

He was driving the '55 Plymouth tonight, having just used the Ford Vic the night before. The Vic was a '51 two-door, midnight black. He liked that one the best because it felt and looked the most like a gangster car, he thought. It wasn't a Caddy—which he would drive if he was the boss—but the Vic had style.

The '55 Plymouth Belvedere was too modern for him. Even though it was several years old, the lines were sharper, and it had too much chrome.

He'd changed the plates on both cars last week, but was now changing them daily. He'd been getting more requests for his services lately.

He'd also made sure both trunks had blankets, but only had one extra pillow. Oh, well.

The air had been checked in all four tires—very important when you didn't carry a spare. And the taillights and brake lights all worked. Which wasn't easy to check by yourself, but he was resourceful.

Extra pack of smokes. He was ready.

He had a *thing* tonight.

CHAPTER 13

"You sure you want to do this?" Frank asked as he checked the rearview mirror.

Del gave a look like a parent telling a child 'no' for the tenth time.

"Yes, I'm sure." Looking at Frank, she emphasized this with large eyes. "Positive!"

"Ok, Ok. No need to…" His cigar moved from one side of his mouth to the other. "I'm concerned about what we might find. When kids go missin'… well… it usually ain't good. Not to mention da last time you…"

"I know. I'll be careful," Del said. "I need to do something… you know, some kind of real job. And get out of that house—"

She fidgeted in her seat and chewed at a nail.

Frank puffed silently as he turned the car onto Octavia St.

"Somethin' wrong at da house?"

Del looked surprised, then realized she shouldn't have been. "No."

Frank waited. After an uncomfortable silence, he switched on the radio and scanned for a ballgame.

"Wait! Go back!" Del said. She pointed at the dial as if Frank could see the frequency.

He scanned back slowly.

"Right there!"

"Twist and Shout" by the Isley Brothers poured from the speakers. Del loved this song, and began to dance in her seat. She would love it even more twelve months later when a mop-haired band of boys from Liverpool rereleased it, taking the nation by storm.

Frank waited for the song to end. He didn't hate it, and it did have a beat, but it was certainly no Sinatra.

When the radio announcer began talking, Frank turned the volume down and asked, "So… Jimmy OK?"

Del settled back into her contemplative mood and attacked another nail.

"Yeah, he's fine." She sighed. "Good, actually. He's doing good. I'm teaching him his letters."

"Dat's good. And I thought Mama D had some work lined up for you."

"Yeah, some. But that's just it. She's given me a few extra jobs that she couldn't get to. And I'm starting to get my own requests. They're coming straight to the house."

Frank whistled his surprise. "Really? Right to da house?"

"They're letters mostly. But sometimes I see people walking around in front of the house, on the street. Like they're thinking about coming up and asking, but they don't. I also—"

She stopped and considered what she was about to say.

"Also, what?"

What was she wanting to say? Something had been bothering her the last few days, but she couldn't put her finger on it. Actually, something had been building up for a while; several weeks in fact.

"OK, we're here," Frank said, putting the car in park.

"Where are we?"

"We at da Poydras Orphan Asylum. This is where da first kid went missin' from." He turned toward her with a serious face and said, "Now listen up."

He described the three missing children:

Alvin *'Alvie'* Foreshaw, White, seven years old, blond hair, blue eyes. Skinny. Went missing almost two weeks ago.

Willy Jenkins, African-American, nine years old, black hair, brown eyes. Plump. Went missing five days ago.

Clara Boynell, Creole, six years old, brown hair, brown eyes. Thin. Went missing last night.

"I doubt we'll find 'em all alive. If we find 'em at all."

Del started to protest, but Frank shook his head. She was to listen now.

"Damn case didn't come to me 'til da second kid." He checked his notes. "Willy. So, we're gonna start at da beginning. We're gonna walk through each orphanage. I'm gonna ask questions. You can take whatever notes you want. When I'm finished, you can ask more questions if you want. If you... feel anything while we in there, keep it to yourself 'til we get outside. We can talk about," he wiggled his fingers, "in da car."

*

At seven-thirty that evening, Frank and Del arrived back at Armand's house. They had visited all three orphanages, ending with St. Augustine's. That was the hardest for Del to visit, considering she'd spent so much time there. It also felt eerily empty without Jo, and in some strange way, Sister Eulalie. It was like walking into a bad dream from long ago, but this dream still had the ability to turn her stomach sour.

They sat around the kitchen table as Armand dished out gumbo. He was very proud of his recipe.

"Well?" Armand asked. "What was it like? Did you get any leads? Any good vibes?" His eyes twinkled.

Del saw Mama D standing in the foyer outside the kitchen door. Her hands on her wide hips. She obviously wasn't happy with Del's decision to get involved, nor Armand's insatiable curiosity. She turned and headed up the stairs.

"Yeah, I got some good notes," Del said. "I think." She mixed the ball of rice into the spicy liquid of her meal. "I mean, I'm not sure what a newspaper would want to print, so… I'm writing down whatever I can think of."

"That's good," Armand coaxed. "Every journey begins with the first step."

Frank spoke between spoonfuls. "Der wasn't a print or broken lock to be found. Be a bad endin' I'm afraid, unless Del can…"

Wiping his mouth, he reconsidered his words. "Dis ain't on you honey, so forget what I just said. You just do what you feel is right."

Armand coughed lightly and stared at Frank to try again.

"I mean… what you're comfortable with doin'. You know, not that you need to… ah, hell! I knew dis was a bad idea."

He sat his spoon down and puffed at his cigar. It had gone out. He dropped it in the ashtray with disgust.

"I know what you're saying," Del said. "It'll be fine. I won't go too far."

She looked through the kitchen door to where Mama D had been.

"And I'll explain to her that this is my choice. Maybe... maybe I can use this ability in a real job somehow. You know, investigating with... real clues and just a little of," here she wiggled her fingers at Frank and whistled.

Embarrassment colored Frank's face. Grumbling, he said, "Well, now... I didn't mean anything by—"

Armand slapped Frank on the back, laughing. "That was a good one, mon ami! Just go with it."

Frank sat silent for a long moment. He hated when his competitive friend got the upper hand. Dipping his spoon in the dark liquid, Frank eyed Armand, pointed the spoon at him and said, "Da roux. Is burnt."

"Pfff!" Armand twisted his moustache. "But you are mistaken, my friend. The roux is perfectly seasoned and—"

Del let the banter fade into the background as she took her bowl and walked toward the parlor.

Moving from the kitchen into the foyer, she felt a cold draft brush her neck. She shivered and looked quickly at the front door, which was closed tight. She'd meant to ask Armand about the air conditioner, but would do it later.

She entered the parlor where Jimmy was playing at something on the floor. Her favorite couch was waiting for her. Actually, she had several favorite couches and chairs in this house. Plopping down, a bit of juice from her bowl splashed over the edge and onto the old material. She grimaced slightly and looked up to see if her mishap had been discovered. She quickly rubbed the spot with her finger and licked it clean. She'd have to remember to clean that tomorrow as well.

"Bah! Boof. Geh away!" Jimmy waved his hands in front of his face.

Del took a bite and grimaced. Her delicious gumbo was suddenly cold. A small film of fat already forming on the top. She wrinkled her nose and reached to set the bowl on a table.

"Blah! Plltt! Bleck! I said geh away." Jimmy fought more invisible foes.

"Jimmy, what are you playing? Is that a new game?"

The boy slapped at his face and frantically waved his hands over his head.

"Aahhh, dese 'tupid bugs! Geh. Away." He turned and looked at Del. "Deh, da 'tupid bugs keep fwyin' in my nose!"

"Bugs? I don't see any—"

A sense of dread hit her as she realized that something was wrong. Jimmy wasn't playing a game. Almost without thinking, she slipped into a trance and was suddenly hovering above the parlor. What she saw was terrifying.

The soup bowl began a slow escape from her fingers.

Jimmy was covered with hundreds of tiny spirit lights.

They were crawling all over him.

CHAPTER 14

On the corner of Dauphine and Mandeville Streets, in the old Faubourg Marigny section of the Crescent City, sat a two-story building. No one was sure how long the building had been there, or who the owner was, but the taxes were paid regularly. So, no one asked.

The front of the building was ornamented with carved wooden balusters in need of paint and windows covered on the inside with decaying newspapers. From the street view, the building appeared to have been used as a warehouse, but now sat abandoned.

Half-way down the block a dark opening led to a small alley that crept behind the front-building. The unnamed alley dead-ended in the center of the block at a singularly odd building.

It hadn't had a visitor in a long time, so no one paid it any attention.

It was an odd building in every way imaginable. It had windows, trimmed with paint so faded the colors nearly washed together, barely hinting that a window even existed. It had a door, so weathered and decrepit that it seemed to have *grown* as a scab over a large wound in the wall; it could easily pass as a shadow. And it had walls of such strange geometry that if someone were to peer directly at them, they would warp in such a way that the person may never see an actual edge. It simply slid from one's vision.

Among these oddities, it had something else. An old faded sign.

And, this sign, like on all odd buildings, hung *above* the scab-shadow-door, as opposed to the side of it. The sign had always been there—but no one remembered it. Legend said that it would creak on certain occasions with a high-pitched cry, but only the old-timers believed that. No one could ever remember hearing it. So, the building that couldn't be seen, with the faded sign that no one heard, remained hidden. And since no one remembered where to look, the legend of this place remained forgotten.

It wasn't unusual for shudders and signs to creak during storms, but this sign only moved on special occasions, despite what the wind wanted. It was moved by a different force.

Above the sign, a rusted tin shade blended with the shadows and shielded a single, dirty light bulb.

In the dark of the alley on this particular day, another strange thing occurred: the light flickered on for no one to see. When it did, it cast a sickly green light over the sign. Faint lettering that hadn't been read in years suddenly appeared in the feeble light. Finely painted filigree, outlining bold lettering glowed in the early evening twilight. The sign read:

Madame Broussard's Curio Shoppe

The building was having a guest tonight.

*

Deep inside the odd building, preparations were being made. The two people who understood the building worked quietly and diligently putting things into place. A heavy red curtain, detailed with gold embroidered tassels was taken out of a chest, strung along a verdigris rod which was hung on heavy metal hooks that jutted from a brick wall. An ancient wooden chair with thick arms was uncovered and positioned two feet in front of the curtain. Three smaller chairs sat to one side of the room.

"How is the inventory?" Madame Broussard called from a side room.

"Der fine," an old woman's voice called back. "Aldoh, da one's 'bout to spoil."

She was afraid of that. Children were hardier in her day.

A plain wooden table sat four feet in front of the chair. It would soon be covered with an array of the madam's finest curiosities. She had a very particular customer coming tonight and had been saving her best.

Entering from the side, Madame Broussard wiped her perfectly clean hands and inspected the main room.

Her black, graying hair was done up in a knot. Wisps hung around her face, framing a finely sculpted jaw line. Gray eyes saw everything.

She pushed the strands behind her ears with elegant hands that hid their age. When she did this, two oblong rings with different colored stones glinted from her ring fingers: lizard green on her left, cat-eye yellow on her right. Her fingers adjusted a strand of Tahitian South Sea black pearls that shone out against her long pale neck. Matching single pearls hung from each earlobe. Her skin was nearly without blemish, and hadn't seen the sun in a long time. The only other color that accented her face was a respectable medium red that outlined her lips. Her hands smoothed the sides of a long black-velvet dress that hung gracefully off her shoulders and whispered across the floor.

She nodded her satisfaction; it was nearly ready. Choosing which curio items to make available was still pending, but there was one pressing matter to attend first. Approaching the ancient chair that sat before the heavy drapes, she opened a small velvet bag attached to her belt. She withdrew a charred finger bone and kneeled at the edge of the red drapes.

On the floor, starting at the wall near the outer edge of the drapes, she drew a heavy black line. It continued in a wide semi-circle that went out past the chair and ended back at the brick wall, at the other side of the drapery. The line was *not* made of chalk, like most practitioners used. Chalk lines were effective for most of her clientele, but not the one coming tonight.

The black line made from the charred finger bone appeared something like grease on the floor, but beyond that, no other comparison could be made.

Outside the half-circle, she marked symbols on the floor, all of which were beyond description. They were so old, the writing no longer existed to explain them and the only thing that remembered how to make them was the old bone itself.

Finishing, she stood up and stepped back, ensuring there was no gap in the protective spell. She was looking at a black semi-circle, seven feet in diameter, that encircled the chair and drapes. During her transaction, she and her goods would be on the outside of the half circle; her guest—if everything held—would remain securely on the inside of the half circle.

CHAPTER 15

Willy crept to the door of his room and listened. He hadn't heard the footsteps for hours. In fact, he hadn't heard Alvie either. When he first came here, he used to hear a constant singing from the other room: *I got no strings, to hold me down, to make me fret, or make me frown...* That Alvie kid was some kind of Pinocchio fan.

This morning he'd heard the song, but it was closer to a moan. Willy sang the words back to him—the few that he knew—in hopes the kid would perk up. But Alvie's voice had slowly faded away. He was quiet now.

Maybe he was just sleeping. Hopefully. Willy couldn't remember when he'd last slept. The days ran together in the darkness.

He felt like he was in a root cellar for some reason. He had an old memory of one—or something like it. When he laid in the orphanage at nights, sometimes old people visited him in his dreams; sometimes in his daydreams as well. He thought it was his grandfather.

Everyone has a grandfather, don't they?

He had a faint memory of playing somewhere that always smelled wet. In New Orleans, that could be anywhere, but his memory told him it was a building. It had potatoes in it, he was pretty sure. The unused ones always grew eyes. After a while, they sprouted long feelers in the dark and he would pretend he was in a faraway jungle in search of gold. The potato feelers were deadly, stinging plants.

Also, in this memory, it seemed that the foundation of the building went down a few steps, but always turned to mud. That wasn't the case here. There were no basements. There was too much water.

He pulled a thin sliver of metal from behind a piece of wood trim. He'd hidden it there. He wasn't sure what it was—an old rusted piece of wire or broken spring, maybe—but it had worked once before.

If he only had a skeleton key, this would be easier, but he didn't expect to find one laying around. He quietly slid the piece of metal into the keyhole and began to twist. Lock picking wasn't something he'd ever considered before now. But he had to find a way out.

Several more twists and the tumblers fell into place. He felt the vibration in his fingers. He turned the wire and helped the old flip-lock unlatch. Now for the others.

He pulled the door back just enough to squeeze his stomach through, then he was standing in a junk-filled room.

The only light source was from under the door at the top of the stairs, which was probably locked as well. He didn't risk looking for a light switch down here, so he felt his way around.

He knew the new kid—a girl—was in the last room, but he wanted to check on Alvie first. He had made a lot of noise when they brought him down the last time, but he wasn't making noise now.

Willy felt his way along the wall. A small squeak scampered away in the darkness and he held his breath. He didn't like rats. His home—before he was taken to the orphanage—was full of them. He'd heard that some kid on the next block only had nine toes because a rat ate one off when he was little. He never got a chance to find out if the story was true, before he was sent away.

A loud rumble from his stomach reminded him that it was close to dinner. If he could get both the other kids ready, maybe they could break out tonight after they ate. But he didn't know how much time he had left.

His hand bumped across an old doorknob. Small impressions around the edge of the knob pressed into his hand. It felt like it had been worn nearly smooth. He felt for a thumb-turn, but there was none. He'd have to pick this one as well.

He inserted the piece of metal and jiggled it.

"Hello?" the girl said, from the other side of the door. "Who's there? Billy?"

"Hush up," he said. "And it's Willy. Now just wait."

"But I'm scared." The voice was on the edge of tears.

"Shhh. I'm gonna get us out. Now be quiet for a minute."

Click-click. The lock turned.

Willy slid inside the dark room where Alvie slept, and pulled the door shut.

He thought Alvie was dead.

"Phew, it stinks in here," he mumbled.

He shuffled around the room in complete darkness. His arms stuck out like feelers and his eyes were wide saucers. The gloom settled to different shades and he thought he could tell where the bed was.

Two steps in the new direction and he banged his shin on an iron bedrail. He stifled a yelp behind clenched teeth as he fell forward.

Instinctively, his hands shot out, right hand hitting the wall, left hand landing on a thin mattress.

Alvie was gone.

Willy felt around for his friend. In a place like this, you made friends quickly. All he felt were damp blankets.

A floorboard creaked above. Someone was moving.

He jumped up and walked quickly back to the door. Reaching for the knob, he stopped and spun around. Panic crashed over him.

"Oh, shiii-ooot… My wire!"

When falling against the bed he'd opened his hands, not realizing he'd dropped his trusty lock pick.

Not wanting to bang his leg again, he crawled on all fours back to the bed. He groped the thin sheet that once covered Alvie. He grimaced in the dark. He hoped the kid wasn't dead. He didn't sound too good the last time he'd heard him. And he was skinny. Willy knew this because he had been in here once before, planning their escape. That was before the girl came along.

His hands flew over the bed, feeling everywhere. Somewhere above him dishes clanked. It was dinner time.

Panic clouded his mind as he slapped at the bed. The seconds flew by. He heard another click and recognized it immediately. The door to the stairs had just been unlocked. His heart jumped into his throat.

His fingers scraped along the stone wall by the bed and something pricked his finger. He gently felt around, and it poked him again. The wire! It had fallen between the wall and the bed, snagging on the cover.

He pulled it out of the crevasse as he heard the old door squeak open. He had to decide quick: try to relock both doors, or just his.

Whether it was survival mode or not, he couldn't say, but an image of Alvie dying flashed in his mind. He stood up and took two long steps in the direction of the door with his arms extended. He found the handle by memory and slid outside.

Closing the door gently, he had just enough time to slip into his room and position the pick. He recognized the squeaks of the individual stairs now, and knew that the loudest squeak was on the last step right after the two short, high-pitched squeaks.

He jiggled the pick until he felt it catch. At the same time, he heard a faint *squeak-squeak* from the stairs and turned the lock. The tumblers seemed to echo in a concert hall. He imagined seeing each piece of metal grinding and clanking against one another as the sound bounced off the walls, announcing his attempted escape. Just as the tumblers clicked, a loud squeak let out from the bottom stair and the two sounds cancelled themselves out somewhere in the dank air.

The footsteps stopped. They never stopped on the bottom step before. They must have heard.

Long seconds passed where Willy prayed the pick to come out of the lock without a scrape. He listened at the door with barely a breath.

The footsteps paused as if considering the dark echoes. Finally, the last step squeaked its relief and the footsteps moved on. They were unconcerned.

Another *click* and light skimmed beneath the door. The footsteps came in his direction.

He tiptoed backwards and sat on the edge of his bed. He didn't want to risk squeaking the bedsprings.

He waited for the inevitable.

CHAPTER 16

"Get away from him!" Del screamed from her trance.

The spirit-wisps were crawling all over Jimmy. Shapeless things without faces, they floated above his head, then dove at his eyes and ears. They blinked in and out of existence like stars; a ghostly universe with Jimmy at its center.

She was still clumsy with her new power, and wasn't sure how to fight the dead things. Trancing was for watching scenes, and watching had its dangers—Mama D had told her that—but this was completely different.

She'd *guided* people during a trance once. *That Night* in the cemetery she'd controlled Frank, Armand and Jimmy. Something closer to *suggestion* really, but it had kept them alive.

But now, seeing the dead things crawling over her friend, all she felt was white-hot rage. It coursed through her body.

She saw herself sitting on the couch, frozen in time, staring at Jimmy. She saw him frozen in mid-swat, shooing away what he thought were gnats. She saw the rest of the parlor room. But it had a strange red and blue shimmer about it. This meant the scene was both moving away from her (getting older) and moving towards her (getting ready to happen) at the same time. She'd never seen this before, and it was terrifying. Like watching a car wreck in slow motion and you knew where it would fall, she saw everything at once. She couldn't stop her actions now any more than she could stop the car wreck. She was *outside* of her mind.

The result emerged as a scream. Not knowing how to protect him, she simply screamed. But it was more than that. Much more.

The energy of it had built up, not in her physical lungs, but from somewhere behind her *essence*. In her trance she felt it come from *inside*.

The scream flowed through her trancing self, then out into the room. She saw it as waves of energy rippling out in all directions.

The spirit-things held tight to Jimmy's face for a second; they were feeding on him. Then they were cast off, gradually at first in ones and twos, then faster. The cosmic wind of Del's rage had reached gale force.

As energy pulsed from her core, she felt the heavy weight of gravity take hold. It wanted some of Del too. Feeling the pull too late, her mind began to fall, and there was no stopping it either.

The waves of rage that pulsed out of her were elemental. They distorted her, pulling her mind forward—in all directions—and slammed her through the floor. The last of the spirit-gnats were cast from Jimmy on a searing heat wave that crashed through the walls of the house and into oblivion.

Trancing-Del, however, continued to fall.

She raced away through a dank and crumbling substance; an ancient substrate far underground. The house and parlor room were far behind her now.

Then she was in a dark abyss, floating free. It loomed and shifted: down, over, outside and backwards, the space moved away in all directions. She fell through the blackness and her mind stretched. Invisible threads of energy pulled at her sanity; pinhole voids that warped reality sucked at her being, threatening to pull her apart. In her mind, her arms and legs flailed, trying to right herself. She felt another scream rise in her throat but pushed it down, afraid it would only send her flying away faster.

What she feared most was tumbling out of control—it had happened before, and she'd barely survived—so she concentrated on her core. Her core—the Del-orb—was heavy. It was how she stayed anchored to reality. She didn't know what it was or how it worked, but she imagined a large spinning mass, a huge silver orb of power and essence. She was one and the same with it.

As she imagined the Del-orb spinning, she felt her own weight increase. Her physical body—somewhere far away in the parlor—didn't change, but her essence (her soul?) did.

Suddenly the scales tipped, and she felt herself flying backwards, the gravity of the Del-orb had overcome and begun to pull her strands back together. The deadly pinholes that sucked at her mind fell away into the darkness. The abyss dissolved. The dank substrate slid beneath her just as the parlor room closed over her head.

She reentered herself just as her sitting body tipped sideways. The soup bowl, having just left her fingers, bounced off the floor sending cold liquid and shrimp flying everywhere. Del slid off the couch to one knee and watched as the dark liquid spilled across the floor.

"What was that?" Mama Dedé yelled from the second floor. "Lawd God, what happened?" Heavy footsteps headed down the stairs.

Tears of surprise and fear sprung out of Del's eyes as she clasped her hands over her mouth. She had no idea what had just happened. She wasn't even sure if all of it *had* happened.

"Deh…" Jimmy said, rolling on the floor. "Deh, what'd you do?"

"Del, I'm coming!" More heavy steps.

She quickly wiped her eyes, but the tears wouldn't stop. The surprise fall *out of this world* was behind her now, but the stress of the journey was just emerging.

"Jimmy," she whispered, wiping her face. "You're OK. Just sit up. You'll be fine."

"Deh, wha—?"

"What happened?" Mama Dedé hustled through the door panting. Del burst out laughing. And crying.

She picked up pieces of shrimp and dangled them in the air.

"See Jimmy, they're not real monsters, just little shrimpy monsters." She let out a howl and rocked back on her legs. The tears flowed under the cover of a bad joke.

Mama D surveyed the room and the mess on the floor. She let Del expend her energy, but didn't join in on the fun. Something was wrong here.

Frank and Armand appeared behind her. Their discussion about burnt roux had led them to debate cigar over pipe, and neither had heard the initial disturbance.

Armand peeked over the woman's wide shoulders and said, "No injuries? Well, nothing that a bowl of water and towel can't fix. Come mon ami, the porch awaits us!"

The woman stood silent as the two men departed. Her eyes never left Del, who was now scooping up bits of rice. Del felt the probing eyes and wondered how long she could keep up the charade.

She found one last shrimp beneath the sofa, picked it up and wiggled it at Jimmy with a weak smile.

Jimmy watched her with confusion. He didn't remember a joke about a shrimp. Besides, they weren't funny or scary. He decided right then there were two jobs not suited for Del: playing the violin and telling jokes.

"Well?" Mama D waited.

Del set the bowl down and crossed her legs Indian style. She didn't want to lie to the woman, it was just that she didn't know what to tell her. It was bad enough that her body seemed to have a mind of its own the last few months, but how could she explain this? Slipping in and out of trances without trying. Dark voids. Ghost bugs. Feeling like someone was watching her. Feeling frustrated and angry. If this was all due to hormones, maybe she didn't want them.

"It was nothing," she said. "We were just playing a little game and—"

"I felt it." Her hands clamped to her hips. "From all the way up the steps, I felt it. Whatever you're doin'... Don't."

Del nodded silently, picked up the bowl and pulled Jimmy to his feet.

"Come on Jimmy, let's get this mess cleaned up."

Del smiled weakly as she squeezed past the woman.

CHAPTER 17

Later that night Del sat at a small table in her room, prepared for another trance. Frank was coming by in the morning, and she hoped she could tell him something about the missing kids. If she couldn't, what good was this *gift* of hers anyway?

The tea that Mama Dedé used for trancing sat in front of her. She wanted to do this right. She wasn't sure what had happened earlier in the parlor, but was concerned about the *slips* she'd been having. It was as if her trancing-self had a will of its own.

She drank the strong tea and closed her eyes. Instantly her mind was hovering above the room and the feeling of flying overtook her. It was one of her favorite parts of trancing, and she'd do it more often, but Mama D had warned her not to get in the habit. It was too easy to let yourself get lost in the worlds of others, she'd said. Some people never came back from extended trancing. Others, they didn't come back the same.

The vision-mist swirled as her mind expanded. She thought of the Poydras Orphan Asylum. The first one she and Frank had visited.

Alvie Foreshaw had been there less than a year. A skinny little blonde-haired boy with glasses.

A view of the orphanage formed in front of her. The scene was tinged red, as it grew older, but the vision was in faded shades of gray, like an old black and white photo. Shadow people, the past images of those who made the scene, came and went. Moons rose and clouds cast shadows scampering over the world. Day after day sped by.

She spied a little boy she thought was Alvie, but couldn't be sure. The vision had a pulsating film of graininess to it. She tried to focus it but couldn't—something was preventing her.

As she worked the scene, she was conscious of an odd movement in her mind. It felt as if a wind was blowing against her, pushing her off course just as she was about to bring the image into focus.

This is new.

Since when did old scenes try not to be viewed?

Next, she tried to spin the scene, view it from a different angle, but it spun back to its original position, like it was on a spring hinge. Frustrated, she floated closer, hovering as near as she could to the boy.

That has to be Alvie.

The vision skipped and she was thrown back. The grainy, shadow people moved on in their dead world. She felt like a kite in a growing storm. Alvie was no longer there.

She didn't know if this scene was where he went missing or if he just wasn't in it, but felt it was important. She reversed the movie reel in her head and spied the boy again. This time it was dark, and he was going to bed. She let the scene run in the background of her thoughts as she quickly checked on her physical body, wondering where the sensation of movement was coming from.

Everything was fine in her room. She was still sitting calmly at the table.

She turned back to the trancing scene and the traffic on the dark street was gone. The city was nearly asleep. The lights in the orphanage clicked off. The streetlamps came on.

A car arrived. Its lights were off.

That's odd, she thought. *Who would be—?*

The dark car drove slowly past the orphanage, then turned on a side street. Next, it went down the back alley and stopped.

Del watched intently as something began to move inside. The scene flickered again, this time nearly fading out completely. An old T.V. set with a bad reception.

What's happening? Why is it doing this?

She was looking at the inside of the orphanage when a strange light flashed, then disappeared. The scene jumped forward and her mind rocked with another blast of cosmic wind.

Damn it!

Alvie and the car were gone.

Del watched the images a while longer, sure the moment of his capture had just slipped by. Something was still interfering with her trance, but she was so close to seeing the person in the car, she had to stick with it. She was determined to get as close as possible, despite the brewing storm.

The thought of experiencing a storm during a trance had never occurred to her. Mama Dedé had never mentioned such a thing—or the static—so she wasn't sure if this was normal or not. She suddenly wished she had the old woman trancing with her. Mentally, she bit a nail.

With all her concentration she pulled at the scene. One minute she was close to bringing it into focus, the next she was floating above a grainy image. She wrestled the images in her mind. They didn't want to be tamed. It was its own thing, and was intent to play out and age as all other cosmic mysteries. The girl didn't even belong here. In this world she was an outsider. In this world, she was the ghost.

Del focused on the sidewalk that ran in front of the orphanage. She was frustrated and tired. The cosmic wind was sapping her strength. With each tug of her mind the sidewalk came closer, like reeling in a giant fish. The scene was clearer, but the tension on her mind was incredible. A strange pressure built up around her. It felt like her ears were about to pop.

She pulled the scene close. The sidewalk was inches away. The picture was the clearest ever. She imagined the colors getting sharper, more vibrant.

Suddenly, a great ripping sound filled her head as a flash of light split the scene in half. A sharp pain shot through her left eye. Del slipped sideways in her mind as her foot touched the sidewalk. In an instant, everything changed.

As the light settled to a normal hue, Del looked around at an unbelievable sight. The trancing scene was gone. She saw people. Real people walking up and down the sidewalk where she stood. The focus was so clear it almost hurt her eyes. But they were real—they had to be. The telltale signs of a trance, the red and blue shift, were gone. Where it went, she had no idea.

The day was warm and sunny. The streets were filled with carriages and horses. Top hats and parasols bobbed to lively chatter. A steam whistle sounded from a boat far away.

Where am I? Am I dead?

She didn't think she was dead.

Isn't this how people describe dying? Not that they'd really know, but that's what they say: one minute you're alive, the next... you're just gone.

But this wasn't like that exactly. She *was* somewhere, just not where she expected to be.

This was no longer the scene she'd been watching. It wasn't the right time of day. It wasn't connected to anything she'd been thinking about. And as far as she knew, one couldn't just trance about *anything*. There had to be at least some small connection.

But there was no connection to this place. This was no time she'd ever read about. The street felt familiar, but the buildings were small. She sensed that some of them were homes, but she didn't know why she felt that. The dress of the people was strange and their speech even stranger. She heard French and broken English. Snippets of Spanish also. Looking around for a landmark, she saw a steeple towering above the low rooflines. Another steam whistle oriented her to a different part of the river.

That looks like the Saint Louis Cathedral. Only smaller.

She knew the iconic cathedral well. It bordered Jackson Square and faced the Mississippi River. But the three tall steeples where different.

And where are all the other buildings? Where are the cars?

Her heart thudded as the answer came to her.

Del had slipped into an old version of New Orleans.

CHAPTER 18

S he stood still for a moment, fearful of breaking the spell.

The people walked right by her, so she was surely still invisible to them. But they looked so real, so... *present*, she had to fight the instinct to reach out and touch them.

Del recognized the old-style dresses worn by the women. The white fabric jutted out, widening at the hips. Covered with colored aprons, they looked to be lost in folds and folds of fabric. Most sleeves puffed out from the upper arm down to the wrist. Some shoulders were exposed.

The men wore a variety of light-colored pants, with dark coats and cravats. She always thought the fluffy neckwear made the men look feminine, but maybe it was just the way they posed in the old photos. Now she thought they were rather dashing.

She turned and walked slowly down the sidewalk. Her mouth hung open in surprise. People passed right through her without even so much as a shimmer. It was disorienting at first, to have a leg or hand suddenly sticking out of her stomach, but soon she didn't notice it.

A horse-drawn carriage came towards her and she stuck her hand out and watched it pass right through the horse, driver's leg and carriage. That time she felt something.

It seemed as if she could feel a slight presence of an object when she initiated the contact, but nothing else interacted with her.

She walked on for a while, meandering toward the spires of the cathedral, gawking in all directions. People sold everything she could imagine on the streets: fruits, chickens, fish, large spools of rope, nets, lamp oil and fabric.

She smiled at the charming city and its romance. The formality of the people and their mannerisms captivated her.

Then she turned a corner.

At first, she didn't realize what she was seeing. A throng of people filled the dead-end street. Large stone buildings stood in a horse-shoe shape and walled the crowd on three sides. A man stood on a wooden stage and called the crowd to attention. The sale was about to begin.

It was a slave market.

When the first person was marched on stage her stomach dropped. It was a girl about her age, and she was pregnant. Del stood in shock as the sale progressed. Person after person was sold like so many spools of rope and fish nets. The disgust coated her like a cloud of smoke, and she thought would vomit.

She wanted to help these people. She wanted to scream and blast away the wanton desire of one man to control another. But she knew these people were beyond her help. She turned away, intent on retracing her steps. There *were* people she could help, if she could just find her way back.

She walked back to the main street she had appeared on and turned west. The day was progressing quickly, and the sun was low in her eyes. Another disturbing sight stopped her.

Sitting amongst the bustle of street goers was a small girl. She sat on the edge of the sidewalk with her feet in the street. A dingy cotton dress, nearly falling to rags, hung about her. She threw rocks at anyone who walked over her. The rocks went right through the people with no affect. But a bad toss sent one skipping into Del's leg. She felt a slight tinge as the pebble passed through her with a tiny ripple.

So much for her theory of initiating first contact.

Del moved closer to the girl, who seemed not to notice her. Long dirty hair hung around her face. Her bare feet and hands were nearly the same color as the street, and her arms looked like sticks. A fat woman walked over the girl and stopped right above her; her very wide dress completely enveloped the girl and Del wrinkled her nose at the thought of those large thighs squishing the girl's head.

Del expected to see the girl float out of the smothering confinement, for surely she was a ghost and could do so. But she saw nothing. A moment later a carriage pulled up and two men helped the women in. The car tilted precariously.

The ghost girl threw a handful of sand and gravel at the women, penetrating her face and thick neck. With sad eyes, she looked at Del—*through her*, perhaps—then cast her gaze back to the street.

As Del edged closer, a troubled feeling came over her. Shading her eyes from the low sun streaming down the street, she saw a large dark circle beneath the girl. She hadn't noticed it before, but it spread out from the sidewalk and slid off the curb, into the street. The girl sat nearly in the center of it.

Do ghosts cast shadows?

She didn't think so, but no longer knew what was real. Maybe her mind had finally cracked.

"Hello?" Del said gently to the girl. "Can you see me?"

The girl shrugged her shoulders, perhaps at random.

"You can, can't you? Are you trancing? Are you lost?"

The girl shrugged again.

Del squatted a few feet away from the girl, just outside the dark circle. She wasn't sure why, but she didn't want to step inside it.

"My name is Del. What's yours?"

The ghost-girl sat and picked at rocks, occasionally throwing one at a passerby. She seemed to be talking to herself, when suddenly she whispered, "I am pretty, I am Mist." The ghost words seeped into Del's mind.

She blinked in confusion as her skin prickled. Somewhere in a room of Armand's house, goosebumps crawled across her neck.

"How did you—?"

"I lost the boy who stole the kiss." Now the words sang in a low whisper. "The day is long since I've been bound, forever-ever in the ground."

Del stood up and stepped back. The dark circle seemed to have inched toward her feet.

She looked around. The throngs of people still flowed, but the sun was low. Dark shadows stretched down the street and crept out of the alleys. She suddenly felt she'd stayed here too long.

"Can I help you... somehow?" Del asked. "I don't know what I can do, but—"

The ghost-girl spoke as an oracle:

"Never dead, the boy of string,

"Puppet dance, he'll dangle and sing.

"Fear for the girl yet to be bound,

"Forever-ever in the ground."

She scratched a dirty nail between the cobblestones. The slow, silent scrape grated on Del's mind like nails on a chalkboard.

"What are you saying?" Del asked. Her heart pounded in her ears. "Do you know who I'm looking for? Are you speaking to me? Do you know about the—?"

Someone stepped on the girl. She glared after them and threw another pebble. "Goodbye," Mist said.

"Del..." Mama Dedé's voice trickled into her mind. "I'm here... Where are you...?"

Del felt her mind slip again. She was violently jolted back into her trance. The city street faded as night overtook the scene. She watched the little girl fade away in a blink of static.

She opened her eyes and saw the old woman sitting across from her. She was back in her room.

"Where'd you go?" the woman asked.

Del wiped a small trickle of blood from her nose. She wasn't sure.

CHAPTER 19

The house was quiet.

Jimmy was tucked away tightly, his new Bugs Bunny slippers sat neatly by his bed side. The last thing he thought about before sleep overtook him was the strange thing Del had done in the parlor. He still didn't remember the joke about the shrimp. But he did remember that Del had seemed to fly up in the air, then knocked him down.

But that was silly. Del couldn't fly.

He was sorry that he always had silly thoughts, but couldn't help it. He told himself he would concentrate really hard tonight and try to dream of Del's shrimp joke. He'd surprise her in the morning by cracking the joke on her. Del filled his mind and he sank into a deep sleep.

Del, after taking two aspirins, laid in bed and thought of the ghost-bugs that had been on Jimmy earlier, and the ghost-girl she'd found. She knew that something was happening with her, but didn't know what. Mist had tried to tell her something, but the meaning escaped her. She was frustrated and exhausted.

Almost too tired to sleep, she tossed in the hot room as the air conditioner stumbled along. She slipped into a fitful sleep and kicked at the sheets around her legs.

Armand snored lightly, the soft night breeze blowing the curtains through an open window.

Mama Dedé sat in the parlor, trancing.

The spirits in Armand's house were currently quiet, but overall, they had become more restless.

The old woman had felt a dark presence growing over the last several weeks. She had told no one, for she feared it would only make the spirits bolder. They could sense fear, and many fed on it. Others were simply bored, or jealous of the living, sometimes conducting their minor haunts. But this was different.

She feared that what had happened the night in the cemetery had let more things into this world than had been taken out. The void that had opened was unnatural. Jo being sucked into the void was terrible. But the things already deep inside it, they were madness. And she feared they'd seen Del.

She couldn't understand why the spirits felt quiet tonight. Ever since the parlor incident with Del and Jimmy earlier in the evening, all activity had ceased. It was if the creeping spirits had gone into hiding. They hadn't left completely; she was sure of that. But they were lurking somewhere just out of sight.

Lurking. And growing, she feared.

But she was determined to find out what Del and Jimmy had been up to. So, she was now visiting the parlor scene of just a few hours ago.

As she floated above the scene in her mind—she was just above the door looking into the room—she saw Del walk in with her bowl of gumbo. Mama Dedé knew right away that something was wrong;

Jimmy was being swarmed by spirits.

She watched as Jimmy swatted at the *invisible bugs* he thought bothered him. The *bugs* were something like fifolets as far as she could tell, small spirit orbs of varying color that floated in the swamps. Many people had been led to their deaths trying to catch fifolets.

But these were different. Fifolets weren't this aggressive. She'd never dealt with this type of spirit before, and knew little about them. She'd research them in the morning.

As she watched Del sitting on the couch, with Jimmy on the floor, the scene of the trance suddenly blurred. It faded with a crackle of static. The objects seeming to melt together.

This had never happened before either. Something was wrong indeed.

Mama Dedé moved to a different angle and the scene refocused. She was now over one corner of the room; Jimmy was on the floor to her right; Del was on the couch to her left. The scene moved slowly, as if it were controlling its own speed. That, or she was hyper-aware that something else was happening.

Jimmy swatted slowly at the bugs.

Del spoke in slow, frozen words.

The trancing scene began to ice over.

Mama Dedé felt a shiver run up her back.

Around the edges of the scene—like a window on a winter morning—a light filament of ice crystals formed. In slow, creeping tendrils, the ice began to cloud her vision. She looked around the Parlor, but everything looked the same. She ran the movie reel backwards, then forward again. Same thing.

She tried to move closer into the scene, but the distortion was there also. Then she saw it.

A black shadow had formed on the wall behind Del. It came out from behind the heavy crown molding where a small section of wall jutted out. The shadow was under its own power. It formed against the pattern of light in the room and headed to the floor.

Del spoke in slow motion, and Jimmy barely moved as the thing slid down the wall. In real-time it would be moving quite fast. It was aggressive.

It touched the floor behind the couch and disappeared. Mama D watched in horror, wondering where the thing would show itself.

Something spooked Del and she went into her own trance. And without any preparation at all! The woman didn't know she could do that.

Del's power had grown quickly over the last few months. She was already playing at things the woman didn't understand. The physical Del was sitting on the couch, but the spirit-Del had just appeared above Jimmy. The silver drops swirled on a whirlwind and formed the Del-orb. The last time the woman had seen this, Del was lost in her own trance, and had nearly come undone. Spinning out of control, Del had nearly flown apart in her own mind, but had saved herself eventually. Later, Del told her that she had focused on her core and created an inner gravity stronger than the bellowing voice of the Gris-gris man who had trapped her. The Del-orb was beautiful and terrible to behold. And it had reformed.

But she's still holding her soup bowl. How is that possible?

The old woman's core power was trancing. She was better than most everyone she knew, except Marie Laveau of course. But a trance took great concentration, so much so that she had to sit at a table doing nothing else. This way, her mind had to spend little time tending to her physical body, and could focus on exploring the scenes. But Del had slipped into her trance right in the middle of doing something else. *How powerful is this girl?* she wondered.

Her stomach clenched as the scene progressed. The black shadow had just emerged from behind the couch. In the milliseconds it'd taken Del to slip into her trance (to understand what was happening to Jimmy) the black entity had raced across the floor, up the legs of the couch, and hovered behind Del's head.

The woman wanted to scream a warning. She'd never felt anything so cold.

Black tendrils snaked off the shadow as it surrounded Del. The couch was moving. Thousands of tiny shadow-threads had come through the cushions to explore the essence of Del. They wavered gently like black seaweed in a current. They tingled with static.

Then she heard it: tiny, minute tearing sounds, like thorns of a blackberry bush pricking at small fingers. The black shadow-threads had grown barbed hooks that tore the fabric to get at Del.

Just then, a brilliant flash of light blinded the scene. The Del-orb exploded outward in a white-hot flash. Seconds later the echoing words of '*Get away from him!*' passed her ears and she understood that this was what she'd felt from the second-floor room earlier in the day.

A cosmic blast of energy flew out at the biting spirits, obliterating them on a great and terrible wave. The shock wave blasted through the walls and into the night. Mama Dedé feared that every dead thing in the city felt that disturbance.

When the flash of light subsided, the Del-orb was gone.

The physical Del was still sitting on the couch in the woman's trance, but the bowl was falling to the floor. The spirits were gone. Jimmy had just begun to topple over.

The boy felt the blast, she realized. *How is THAT possible?*

As the scene settled, the black tendrils and shadow-threads paused. They hadn't been destroyed. They hadn't been scared off. They hovered as if inspecting the scene. Then, slowly, they retreated. An instant later the shadow was gone, having retreated somewhere into the house.

Mama Dedé stared at the unbelievable scene. The Del-spirit had flown through the floor and beyond her sight. Del's essence was far beyond where the old woman could go. Del was truly on her own.

CHAPTER 20

At 11:29 at night, Madame Broussard sat in a richly carved Elizabethan chair, awaiting her guest. Her hands were gathered in her lap, but her fingers were loosely intertwined. The eye-shaped rings—lizard-green and cat-yellow—needed their own view.

A few select items had been placed on the table that sat in front of the Chair of Honor. The chair would remain inside the black semi-circle she'd drawn on the floor. She thought of this as the Circle of Protection.

Candlelight flickered at the edges of the room, occasionally lashing out sideways at other candles' encroachment upon its covey of shadows. The battle between light and dark was as old as the cosmos, and infected all things.

At 11:30 a rumble from deep in the earth vibrated the odd building. The heavy red drapes shivered in anticipation. Her guest was arriving.

The elegant woman with the neatly tucked graying hair and matching eyes stood up and walked behind the podium. It sat safely behind the long table. She would not move any closer to the chair in the circle this evening.

The rumble became a violent shaking and the old plank-board floor twisted and groaned. Dust particles fled from the high ceiling and candle flames danced—an attempt at escape—but were held tight by their wicks. They would witness the visitor.

A gush of stinking air blew the heavy drapes apart and a silhouette appeared against the brick wall. First shadow, then shade discolored it; a moldering of the brick began, and an old thing came forth.

The silhouette—just a hint really—grew to the size of a man. It shimmered for a moment, as if testing the air, then belched itself into existence in grotesque distortions, feeling for the correct size. It expanded and contracted, coating the porous brick with an oily black grease.

Once settled, the shape took physical form and peeled itself from the wall. The peeling sound was that of an animal being butchered. Its skin, pulled downward, being separated from the meat by the tearing of millions of tendrils, each one breaking at the last moment of agony.

Viscous dark shadow was its first layer of *skin*, first an arm and leg, then a head and body. The shadow-man slowly pulled himself from some unseen depths and emerged into the showroom of Madame Broussard's Curio Shoppe.

The woman tucked an errant piece of hair behind her ear and smiled.

"Mr. Scarmish, how nice to see you again."

The shadow-man twisted its head in contortions beyond that of a normal spine. Its skin was now a menagerie of color, dark grays and blacks that fell backward into oblivion. It was an optical illusion, one moment appearing three-dimensional *in the room*, the next moment, a three-dimensional depression sinking backwards out of the wall.

Its voice echoed from all directions at once. "Thank you for receiving me. It's been… a long time. I believe."

"Yes," the woman said, wondering about the final two words. Then added, "Too long."

Shadow-hands stretched off the wall, feeling the empty space, and reached over the back of the chair, touching the warm wood. Things like fingers felt the crevasses and tried to remember. The old wood cracked and shrank under the deadly touch. A dark form—now free of the wall—stepped around the chair and the rest of the man joined it in due time; stretching, distorted shadow-tendrils keeping the pieces loosely connected.

The place in the head where eyes should be shimmered with a color less dark than the rest. The head tilted slightly and inspected the black line and symbols on the floor. The body walked to the line. A shimmer of heat appeared as the protective spell interacted with the shadow-presence. The heat waves radiated in great ripples, from floor to ceiling, and further distorted the image of the man-shape.

The dark voice echoed, "Is this necessary?" The wavering shape of hands spread out in appeal. "We've been… associates for so long, after all."

Madame Broussard smiled slightly and said, "It's best for us both. Good fences, and all that."

Mr. Scarmish tilted his head toward the ceiling as if contemplating the mysteries of the universe. A stinking sigh emanated from his chest and vibrated the fine hairs of her arms. "Very well," he said and sat down. "If we must, we must."

Long, wispy fingers grasped the arms of the chair, and beneath the unnatural touch the heavy oak crumbled into dust.

"What do you have for me?" he asked.

Madame Broussard described each item on the table.

A length of old chain with a blood-stained shackle at one end had come from the attic of the infamous LaLaurie house. Madame LaLaurie had kept her slaves chained there, and regularly tortured them. She was discovered after a fire burnt part of the house and the town's people had come to help. Madame Broussard felt that a spirit was still attached to the chain and could be salvaged.

Mr. Scarmish nodded absently.

Next on the table was a nondescript voodoo doll about four inches tall. No hair or clothes adorned it, just bumpy brown leather for skin. It had two red beads for eyes and a long rusty hat pin that stuck down through its shoulder and came out its rectum. "This," the woman said, "has a heavy presence, but I've yet to unlock its secret."

Shadow-eyes flickered as if some bit of recognition passed through them. Mr. Scarmish cocked his head and tried to sense the object from where he sat. There was something familiar about the piece.

Next was the partial skeleton of a strange creature. A true abomination, she described. On the table lay the partially burned bones and skin of a weasel-like animal. A cat-sized head was grotesquely deformed, with a large beak that had grown where its mouth should have been. The head had been separated from the spine—the top three vertebrates being crushed—but the bottom half of the monster was intact. Five of the six legs hung from the spine, all ending with three sharp claws. The foot-long spine curved, ending with the stump of a tail that was split into two pieces at its base.

The man nodded in appreciation at the artistry it had taken to create such a monstrosity, but he did not smile. A dark mood fell over his shadow-face as the drapes rustled nervously.

He stood up and walked behind the chair, letting his fingers drag across the shimmering spell-wall; light sparks fell to the floor where he touched it. A faint smell of burnt hair floated into the room. He squeezed the back of the chair and twisted his head slowly as if his shirt collar were too tight, although he wore no clothes. A low drumming could be felt through the floor as if an anxious heart beat restlessly.

"Trinkets," his voice echoed. "I did not rise for trinkets." He levelled a gaze at his hostess. "Now stop wasting my time. I despise this semi-solid form. What of the young roots? I have used much of my own on my deep journey, but am very close to discovering the secret. I need a dozen more to sustain me."

A dozen more?

"And," he continued, "I need a special one. A female. For the twins."

Over the last several minutes his skin had formed an opaque sheen. Madame Broussard had watched for it carefully, judging his temperament. The sheen came from an electricity that leaked out of him. She imagined millions of microscopic lightning bolts flashing over the surface of his skin. He seemed to be heating up. He was sweating power.

The glow across his skin made him look as if he were covered with the same dark coating as her pearls, and she touched her necklace absently. His eyes now glowed a low ebb of light, metal gray against shiny, pearl black skin. She imagined just for a second what it might feel like to touch that skin. To have all its power flow deep inside her, filling her beyond capacity and laying her to waste.

A knowing tilt of his head brought her back to his question. She felt him smirking at her.

She motioned to the old woman who had been hiding in the shadows. She sent out the first child with a push.

A skinny blonde-haired boy stumbled forward. He staggered as if he'd been drugged, or was nearly dead. But he was beautiful in his frailty.

The man was glistening now. He was fire and black lightning. He was hunger and lust. He paced the confines of his small circle and burnt his fingers along the shimmering walls of the spell.

The boys glasses slipped down his nose as he stumbled forward. He was singing quietly: *I got no strings, to hold me down...* He looked in all directions, blinking at the strange room. Dried tear lines stained his cheeks.

The shimmering man stopped in front of his chair and looked at the wretched thing the woman had presented him.

His voice was soft now, cooing. "Why, he's nearly skin and bones."

The boy's eyes looked at the table and fell upon the weasel skeleton. They grew large with fear. He walked wide to avoid the hellish thing.

The woman yelled, "Boy, stay here!"

"He's nothing but sinew and string," Scarmish said. Rivulets of saliva slipped down his chin.

The boy didn't see the shimmering man. Everything was shimmering beneath his teary eyes, and his glasses were smudged with fingerprints. The monster skeleton with the beak was all he could see.

"Boy! Come back!"

The boy circled in front of the table.

"But he smells... wonderful!"

The sign outside the odd building began to sway.

A flash of light exploded as the man reached through the spell wall. Waves of burnt flesh reeked through the room, although he had none. In an instant, he'd grabbed the boy by the neck and pulled him to his shimmering face. The boy, still staring at the beaked skull, only had time to register a slight surprise before a searing bolt of heat sent spasms through his body. A long, spiked tongue shot into the back of his skull and an orgy of slurping sounds filled the air. The spell wall sizzled and popped against the man's shiny skin, but he felt nothing; his own hunger had overtaken him.

"Mr. Scarmish!"

The boy's glasses flew off and tumbled under the table. The man's metal-grey eyes turned brilliant white as they rolled back in his head. He convulsed as he slurped the sweet essence from the boy's body.

"Stop that—"

The boy bucked and jerked. His arms moved on their own.

"—right now!"

The man gnawed and grunted. He was nearly at the core. His eyes rolled over and over, flashing gray then white.

The sign outside squealed an agonizing pitch.

"He's not—"

The boy's shoe flew off as his legs thrashed the air. He was dancing.

Her rings flared with life. One lizard-green eye and one cat-yellow eye formed in the oblong stones. They saw the betrayal and looked into the man's core, searching for a way to stop him.

"—your—"

The top of the man's head burst into flames as he leaned into the back of the boys neck, crossing well over the spell boundary.

"—property!"

At that moment, an odd picture entered the woman's mind. The boy reminded her of Pinocchio. His spindly arms and legs dancing on the air. Invisible strings running deep into his core, pulling tendons and wire. His eyes, frozen in terror forever, searched her face for answers, but found none.

The sign swung in a frenzy.

The boy began to shrivel. The core of his being was nearly exhausted. The violent shaking flailed his arms and legs in all directions. His head smashed from side to side as the man dug for morsels and shook his prey like a beast. His tongue came loose from the back of his throat and flopped wildly in his mouth, hanging by shreds of muscle. It made a lolling, gaggling sound, as if trying to speak on its own. A loud snap echoed as the boy's left arm came apart at the elbow. Now the lower half spun like a windmill, stretching the skin to the point of ripping.

"MISTER!"

The vertebrae in his neck snapped.

"SCARMISH!"

The shining, dripping man pulled his spiked tongue from the back of the skull and skin ripped away when he did. He threw his head back. A shuddering, glottal sound bubbled from his throat as translucent grease ran down his chin and neck. In his moment of ecstasy, the hand holding the boy clenched and severed the remaining muscles. The boys head fell to the floor with the crack of a large egg. Blood and ooze spilled out and was quickly absorbed by the waiting planks. Nothing would be wasted.

As the man collapsed back into his chair, his hand released the remains of the dancing boy and a pile of bones wrapped in skin dropped to the floor. Brittle echoes bounced around the room before fading to pleasant memories.

The sign outside stopped swinging.

Madame Broussard looked on in disgust as a long, black tongue searched the man's face for traces of sweet liquid.

Slumped to one side, the man pointed a trembling finger at the remains of Alvie Foreshaw. With a shaky voice he said, "Put him on my bill."

CHAPTER 21

Del ate her toast standing up and slurped loudly at her coffee. Despite having trouble falling asleep the night before, she was raring to go this morning. She walked quickly to the front window again, then came back and took another bite.

"Don't get in such a twist," Mama Dedé said. "You know he's liable to be late."

Jimmy looked up from his pancakes. "Who's 'ate? Deh?"

"I'm not in a twist," Del said. "I'm just… I want to get going. I might have a lead."

Mama Dedé eyed her and sat her cup down loudly. "Yeah, about that. I want to ask you—"

"Here he comes," she said. She took another loud slurp, grabbed an uneaten sausage from Jimmy's plate and wrapped it with her toast. "She you latah," she said with her mouth full.

"What time you comin' back?"

"Don't know," Del said, closing the back door. "Maybe late."

The door slammed shut.

"Hey!" Jimmy said, looking at his plate. "Whey'd it go? Da' snausage got away!"

The Mama D watched as Del jumped into Frank's car and he backed out of the drive.

*

"OK, Frank, what are we doing today?" Del asked. "Do you have any leads yet? I might have one, but I'm not sure. Do we have anyone to stake out? I wrote down everything I could think—oh shoot, I left it in my room."

"Whoa, honey," said Frank. "I hardly got my head woke up."

The sweet smell of cigar tobacco and flowers surrounded her, despite the convertible top being down. Del had learned that Frank—like Armand with his pipe tobacco—smoked different types of cigars in the morning, versus the afternoon or evening. The *breakfast cigars* as he called them were mild and (now that she was used to them) not altogether unpleasant, especially when mixed with the sweet smell of flowering gardens. In her mind, she wove these aromas together with that of pipe tobacco, oiled wood and old books, and a pleasant picture of home formed in her mind.

"I gotta drop by da station first, den we hit da road. OK?"

Del seemed lost in her thoughts, so Frank didn't press the question. They arrived at the police station fifteen minutes later. Frank had been assigned there when he was a beat cop, and then later on when he became detective. Since he was officially not on the force any longer, he shouldn't have parked in one of the reserved spots, but he did anyway.

"You just stay here; I'll be back in—"

"I want to go in. I need to see how things work behind the scenes. How else am I ever going to get a job?"

Frank's shoulders drooped slightly, telegraphing his concern. "Ok, I figured that would be da response. We'll only be in dere for a minute, so… just ignore… well…"

"What?"

He grunted. "Never mind. Come on."

They entered the station and a sea of eyes turned toward them. At eight-thirty in the morning, the night and day shifts were still mingling around the water cooler, despite the shift-change meeting having just ended. In the South, everyone moved on to the next part of their day with relative ease.

The whistles and catcalls started immediately.

Frank had meant to mention this to Mama Dedé, but never having had a daughter of his own, wasn't sure if the topic was something he was even supposed to notice, so he'd never found the words. But, Del's shirts were simply getting too tight.

He told himself that it must be something wrong with Armand's washer. He didn't want to think of the alternative. Whatever it was, it'd caused her jeans to start shrinking as well.

Also, to his chagrin, Del didn't seem to notice. Her colorful headbands—today with vibrant oranges and blues—always drew attention to her freckled brown face. From there, some colored tee-shirt accented a youthful body. Then there were the jeans, seeming to hide runner's legs. And it always ended with the knee-high leather boots. Frank hated those boots, but couldn't quite say why. Her old sneakers had been just fine with him.

Frank said, "Just come back to my desk," and pushed through the swinging rail gate. The sea of blue uniforms parted before him.

"Hey, look what Frank caught!" said one voice.

"Woo wee!"

"A wild cat!" said another.

"Who dat?"

"Watch out, dat cat got claws!"

The men howled and leered as Del walked silently towards Frank's desk. His wake through the sea of blue closing quickly.

Frank stood at his desk shuffling papers. His temporary landmark sat near the far wall, which gave him a view onto the room.

A lanky officer who always wore sunglasses inside motioned to the group, then let his hand swing and smacked Del hard on the butt, sounding a dull *Slap!* He squeezed as much cheek as he could before she twisted away and turned on him.

A shock of embarrassment colored her cheeks as her eyes flashed a warning. Her mouth was a thin, tight line.

The men howled.

"Hey! Watch dat!" Frank yelled, pointing a cigar finger at the culprit.

"Watch it, Ronnie," someone warned. "You 'bout to get bit!"

More laughter.

Mr. Ronnie-indoor-sunglasses looked at Del and watched the trail of goosebumps slide down her neck and collect beneath her shirt in two tight bumps. His lip curled in satisfaction.

When Del realized what he was staring at she clasped her arms tight over her chest and pushed her way to Frank's desk. She stood against its front and glared at her aggressor.

"Don't mind him," Frank said quietly from behind her.

The only thing Del heard was the fading sound of laughter. Despite the contorted faces of the men telling her the party was still going strong, the sound was quickly fading from her ears. She was slipping.

It happened before she knew it was coming.

Ronnie, having just poured himself a celebratory cup of coffee, was leering at Del as the cup came towards his mouth. The curl of his upper lip had just slipped behind the Styrofoam cup.

One instant she was leaning against the desk, the next, she was in a trance, staring at Ronnie from inside his cup; one silver-demon eye leering out at him. Several seconds later (Ronnie was rather slow, she found out) he was flailing at the vision, covered in hot coffee.

The room erupted again. This time, Ronnie was the object of interest.

Ronnie sputtered and howled in pain. He grabbed a handful of napkins and dabbed gently at his face. Removing his sunglasses, he looked around to see if anyone had seen the eye, then looked back at Del. The slightest smirk curled the left side of her mouth, and her eyes gleamed.

"Ok, let's go," Frank said as he tucked his files under his arm and moved around the desk.

Del leaned up from the desk and took the lead. The blue sea parted. Ronnie dabbed his shirt and glared. The young woman walked out with a strong jaw leading the way. Although she was shorter than all of them, her stature was large.

In the car, Frank relit his cigar, puffed and glanced in the mirror. He then turned to Del and said, "Did you, uh… have anything to do with…?" He nodded his head towards the station.

Del turned and said, "Seems you hired a clumsy cop, Frank."

"Ppfff! I didn't hire da damn fool!" He could see in her face that she was sticking to her story, so he dropped the line of questioning.

"Ok, dat's fine. He got what he deserved. Let's go catch us a bad guy."

CHAPTER 22

Three hours later, after multiple trips past orphanages, halfway houses and shelters, and an agonizingly long time sitting in the car *watching*—Del was still trying to determine *what* they were looking for—she let out a groan and twisted in her seat.

"Can we take a walk or something?" she asked. "What are we looking for anyway?"

Frank snorted as his eyes flew open. He slapped away dead ashes and grumbled.

"I was just goin' over da notes in my head. And we looking for a spark of inspiration right now, honey. Dis is what da job is, I'm afraid."

"Yeah, but—"

"Tell me about your vision again. Let's see if we missed something."

She sighed at the thought of repeating the story—it hadn't been very successful—but did anyway.

"I only went back and looked at the Poydras orphanage, but I looked outside, also. Eventually, I saw a car come down the back alley, late at night. I saw who I thought was the first boy, but the whole scene was kind of jumbled up."

"Jumbled?"

Del shrugged. "I don't know what it was. I have to ask Mama D what went wrong."

"So, you couldn't see his face?" Frank asked.

"Whose?"

"Da guy driving da car."

"No. But I didn't say it was a guy. I—"

"It's a guy. I'd put money on it. Dere may be others helpin' him, but this is dicey work. Anyway, you say you don't know what kind of car it was?"

"No. Just old, like yours." A frown turned her mouth. "Sorry, you know what I mean."

"Eh, don't worry. How old like mine?"

"What do you mean?"

"Think about da body style. Long? Short? Rounded?"

"Yes! It was rounder than yours. Sort of. Roundish, anyway."

"Hmmm…" Frank began to flip through the catalog of car knowledge he kept in his head. "Del-bell, let me think on dis a while." He dug for his wallet. "There's an ice cream shop around da corner." He pointed up and to the right. "Why don't you run over there and—"

"Ok!" Del pulled the door handle open.

"Now, hold on, I—"

"Don't worry," she said. "It's on me." Her face beamed.

"On you?" He whistled. "You sure?"

"Yeah, I have my own money. Well… some. Those side-jobs that I got from Mama Dedé… they pay pretty good actually."

"They do? Well, that's good to know."

"What flavor?"

"Huh? Oh, chocolate for me," he said. Then he held an invisible cone and measured its height with his other hand. "A big one."

She smiled and closed the door. In an instant she was running down the sidewalk.

*

The air in the ice cream shop was heavenly. Besides being much cooler than outside, the sweet smells of waffle cones, ice cream and fudge made her mouth water. She stood gaping at the brightly colored posters of giant sundaes and triple-scoop cones.

A group of high-school kids stood around the counter shuffling for position. At least, Del thought they looked her age, but suddenly realized she wasn't sure. Two of the girls turned and stared at her and she realized she'd been holding the door open the entire time. She stepped in, letting the door swing shut with a jingle. The girls turned away and giggled.

Del stood behind the throng of kids—young adults really, she reminded herself—and spied at the flavors between elbows and shoulders. The boys in the group couldn't decide which butt they wanted to pinch; the girls couldn't decide how long they'd let them before mocking surprise. It was hard to tell who was paired with who, or if everyone was open game.

A tall black boy leaning against the counter turned around and spotted Del. A smile snuck off his face just as she looked his way. The girl next to him—having not stopped talking since Del entered—noticed the break in his attention, turned and glared at Del, shoving her hips toward the boy.

Del rocked on her boots and looked back at the posters. She went on like she hadn't noticed.

Finally, after the group exhausted their frivolous demands (*No. More caramel. Just a little. Too much! I'm watching my figure. Three cherries please. You're out of sprinkles?*) they filled all the small tables and spilled out on the sidewalk. Del stepped up to order.

The boy behind the counter was working hard. The girls had been tyrants.

Brown waves of hair spilled out from beneath his white paper hat, which was crumpled to one side. His apron was covered with every color of the rainbow. He was frantically trying to wipe his work area clean, still looking down when he said, "Welcome to the Ice Cream Emporium. I'll be right with you."

"Oh, no hurry," Del said. "You look pretty busy."

"Yeah, it's a hot one. My name is John—" He looked up and his mouth fell open like it had a bad hinge. Slow-motion surprise, crossed with wonder, swept over his face.

Del, surprised by his surprise, thought maybe she had a crumb of toast stuck to her lip. The slightest look of fear caused her mouth to draw back in a grimace as she covered it with her hand.

The boy, surprised by her surprise and look of disgust, feared he had ice cream on his face again, and quickly wiped his cheeks, leaving a dark smudge of fudge in the process.

He started again. "John..."

Del cocked her head. "Your name is Jon-jon?"

"WHAT?" the boy said too loudly due to a poorly timed lull in the conversation.

Del's eyes grew wide with surprise.

Half the room turned and gawked.

As an awkward silence smothered them both, he fidgeted on his black rubber mat, looking for stable ground.

"Oh. Sorry," he said, finally closing his mouth. His tan cheeks burned red. He bit absently at an already chewed nail, then, as if suddenly remembering something about health code violations, wiped his hands on the bottom of his apron, crumbling it into a sticky ball.

She eyed him with curiosity. Then, noticing that most of the onlookers had lost interest, pointed to her own cheek, mirroring his, and wiped gently.

His shoulders sank as his pride completely evaporated. He grabbed a towel, gave two hard swipes at his cheek, and threw it into the sink.

A despondent voice said, "I'm Johnathan. Can I help you?" He glanced from the ice cream tubs to Del and back.

When he looked up again, she caught a glimpse of nervous brown eyes and the longest eyelashes she'd ever seen on a boy. His gaze headed for the tubs again, but she hooked it before it could flee. Her eyes, pulling hard, invited it to stay and linger. His chin raised in hope and he blinked a new look onto his face.

She noticed that messy brown hair spilled out on all sides of his paper hat and a line of sweat had broken across the front of it. A deep tan covered his arms and extended all the way to his long, straight fingers.

She smiled and said, "Hi, my name's Del."

A bright smile lit his face as his eyes sparkled.

"Hi, Del. I'm Johnathan."

His faced clenched as soon as the words left his mouth. He quickly tried to count how many times he'd just said his name to this *very* interesting girl.

A low chuckle opened his eyes. Del was still smiling.

"Yeah, I got that."

CHAPTER 23

Ten minutes later, the order still hadn't been placed, but neither Del nor Johnathan noticed.

"Now, this one over here," he said, "is Pecan Cream. Kinda reminds me of my grandmother." He scooped another tiny spoon full of ice cream and handed it to Del.

"I still have these to taste," Del said, holding up a miniature spoonful of Double Chocolate in one hand and Summer Mint in the other.

"That's OK, here." And he held the spoon over the counter as close as he dared to Del's mouth. He swallowed a lump in his throat. He couldn't decide if looking into her eyes or at her lips was better, and decided on both. "It uhh…" His voice became quiet and breathy. A freckle by the edge of her lip caught his attention. "It uhhh… the flavors…" She had several nice freckles, he realized. "…they'll be better in this… uhhh…" Del's mouth opened slightly. His eyes widened in response. Square, white teeth shone bright behind her lips. "…the…" The tip of her tongue peeked out to accept the sweet offering. "…order of … the tongue…" The soft dimple of her upper lip closed around the tiny spoon. "…affects the taste." He slowly pulled the spoon back and stared at a tiny trail of cream that had curled up the front of her lip, leaving a slight sheen there. A second later her tongue peeked out again to wipe it away.

A wavering breath leaked out of his swollen chest.

The order of the what affects the taste? passed through Del's mind and evaporated.

The mirror on the wall behind Del reflected the spellbound, ogling face of a boy in a crumpled paper hat. He would remember this encounter for the rest of his life.

He gave me ice cream that reminds him of his grandmother. Del sighed. Satisfied.

A loud crash from the backroom broke the spell. Mumbled curses floated through the open doorway behind the counter. Boxes scraped across the floor. Shadows betrayed movement. A tattooed arm came into view, then disappeared. A stab of pain like brain-freeze shot through Del's head, but she knew it wasn't the ice cream.

She gasped and stepped back from the counter.

"Who's back there?" she said with wide eyes.

"What?" Johnathan said. He watched in dismay as Del backed away from him. "What's wro—?"

"In the back. Who is that?"

Johnathan glanced over his shoulder, but turned quickly back, not wanting to lose sight of this amazing girl.

"I don't know, delivery guy, I guess. They're always making—"

He stopped talking as Del backed out the door.

"Hey wait!"

She turned and ran.

The door closed with a happy jingle.

*

Frank was searching the radio for a ballgame when he saw Del pounding down the sidewalk. She ran to his side of the car, breathless.

"Frank! Hurry! We got to—"

He looked at what she was carrying and grimaced.

"They uhh... kinda small, don'tcha think?"

Her face creased in confusion as she looked down at her hands. Two tiny sampling spoons were still clutched tightly between her fingers.

She threw them down and grasped the top of his door, shaking the car. "Come on! We gotta go! Quick!"

He eyed her and turned the ignition at the same time. "Get in. What is it?"

She ran around to the other side and climbed in.

"There's someone in the ice cream shop! I was talking and Johnathan gave me samples and there was a noise in the back and then my head hurt and I saw the tattoo and—"

"Whoa! Slow down, honey. I'm not followin' ya."

She huffed once and sank back into the seat.

"Where's the alley?"

"Which alley?"

"To the ice cream shop! How do they get deliveries into the back?"

"Hell..." Frank twisted his girth in the creaking seat. "Back dat way, should be. Let me see, we at..."

"Spin around!"

"Spin around?"

"Turn, I mean! Hurry!" Del looked in all directions, trying to see who may have just walked out onto the sidewalk. But the Ice Cream

Emporium door was up and around the corner to her right. People could be going anywhere.

Frank threw the car in gear, looked over his left shoulder and stuck his arm out the window. Pulling into the street, he pointed his intention to the other drivers and simply made an opening for himself. His U-turn faced them the other direction and he stopped, double-parked in front of the Georgette Grocer and Deli. They were having a sale on pickle-loaf.

"What are we lookin' for?"

"A man with a tattoo. He should be coming out the back any minute!"

Frank drew an invisible map over the steering wheel with his finger. The ice cream shop was now to his eight o'clock, across the street. There was no alley opening on this side. It must be one of the funny L-shaped alleys that cut the city block into unequal parts—one-quarter to three-quarters instead of fifty-fifty—he thought. The car lurched forward as he pulled back into traffic. He turned left the first chance he got. He was now on the back side of the block, behind a building that was behind the ice cream parlor.

"What kinda tattoo?"

"I don't know."

"Well, what's he look like?"

"I don't know that either."

Here, the buildings were different. It wasn't a perfect city block with tall buildings on all four corners and neatly defined alleys. He passed a single-story building on his left which gave way to an open gravel parking lot which bled off the lot where an automotive repair shop sat. An alley system didn't really exist here. The trash dumpsters, which was pretty much all the alleys were used for, just sat randomly around the edges of the lot.

"Ppfff!" Del let out a disgusted breath of air.

Frank pulled to the side again and put the car in park.

He looked at Del and put his arm on the back of the seat.

"Who do you think we're looking for?"

"I told you—"

"No." He held his hand up. "You didn't tell me anything, but to go chase my tail."

She rolled her eyes and crossed her arms.

"So, I got my tail. And now I'm looking at my backside. Dis what I'm supposed to see?"

She blew another little puff of air out of her nose. "No."

"Ok. Den here's what we're gonna do. We're gonna drive around da block and park across from da ice cream shop. In da front so we can see. Then you're gonna tell me what you think we're lookin' for. Ok?"

Del nodded in silence.

CHAPTER 24

*F**lick. Flick. Flick.* Burn. Inhale.

Spider was on the move.

He pulled the '51 Ford Victoria away from the stoplight and glided down the street. The day was hot, but he felt good. He felt like the boss today, now that his deliveries were done.

Spider: Man of the Hour. Peopled called Spider when things needed to get done. He had people asking him for things day and night, because he made things happen.

He also knew how to keep a low profile.

It'd taken him a while, but he'd finally learned the lesson by the time he'd dropped out of high school. In grade school, you act up and you get your fingers wacked. He liked trying to anticipate the timing of the ruler cutting towards his hands and pull them away at the last second. It was like *Bloody Knuckles,* a game he would learn later, where you and an opponent squared off against each other with fists touching in midair, trying to rap the other's knuckles before they could pull their hand away. He always won because he was quick like a spider.

Then in junior high he learned to keep a low profile, or you got your head wacked. And it was always from behind where you couldn't see it coming. Teachers wacked his head with books. Bigger kids wacked his head with big thumping fingers if he smarted off—even if he didn't. He'd learned to sense those things coming, like a spider with a thousand eyes in his head.

Then in the real world, he knew instinctively to keep a low profile, or you got your whole body wacked. That was usually from behind as well. But only once.

Yep, keeping a low profile and swapping cars (which really go hand in hand) had kept him out of jail. Combined with having a sticky web—he caught a lot of things with his web—he was in high demand.

He was nearly his own enterprise.

The part-time work making side deliveries during the day was a great cover. The appearance of a *normal* job—one that sent him to many different places, but rarely the same one consistently—was great for his nighttime work. He loved the night work best. Just wait for the call, then go do the *thing*.

He didn't have any jobs scheduled for the evening, so was thinking about going to the new titty bar, The Golden Globes, across town tonight. Maybe he could catch a juicy morsel.

He made several turns on his way home, always watching his mirror. It took longer this way, but it was better than having someone find out where he lived. After several more minutes, he turned into an alley that didn't look like much and stopped between some old buildings. He got out, opened a garage door that didn't look like it would open and drove his car into blackness. He knew exactly where to stop before bumping into something. Spiders worked well in the dark.

He shut the garage door and walked up a short flight of steps and into a small kitchen. He grabbed a beer from the fridge, walked into a sparse front room that overlooked a crumbling street and plopped down in an old chair. After several large gulps and a healthy burp, he leaned his head back and closed his eyes. He began to think about the titty joint and what wonders he would find there.

Then his phone rang.

At first, he thought it was someone calling to speak to Spider the Dragon King in his private room at The Golden Globes, but the image faded quickly, and he groped for the phone.

He was in high demand. This phone hadn't rung so much since... we'll, it had never rung this much. *It's going to be a good summer,* he thought.

He picked up the phone and listened. After nearly a minute the person on the other end was still talking. They were giving slow, methodical details. He began to wonder if he'd remember them all. This made him squirmy.

He made as many mental notes as he could. Nodding his head along the way as if the voice on the phone could see he was paying attention. The voice disappeared with a click.

No titty bar for him tonight. Packages had to be moved again for safe keeping. He had a *thing.*

*

Willy stifled a yawn and whispered beneath his door. "Are you awake?" He'd been in and out of sleep for a while, and couldn't tell what day it was. He only knew he was in the same room because of the smell.

There was no sound from the other room.

Ah, man. Am I the only one left?

He groaned as his stomach hurt. Sharp pains shot through his gut and a wave of heat flushed him. He had to use the bucket again. And fast.

"Ohhh... wait. Wait."

He pulled his pants off as fast as he could and hobbled to the corner. Taking too long of steps might make it all come out before he got there, but he wasn't sure that would matter; it already stunk.

Whoever lived above them—the person keeping them—hadn't been in the room for a while. He was beginning to wonder if they'd forgotten he was here.

Something crunched beneath his sneakers as he straddled the bucket. Whatever it was, at least it couldn't crawl up his leg now. Who knew where it'd go if it did?

A loud rumble vibrated through his gut as he let loose. The force was so great his knees almost gave way, causing him to fall backward. A low moan slipped out of him as he shuddered and struggled for balance. After several more spasms he thought he was finished. Whatever they'd fed him was causing his stomach trouble. Maybe it was poison.

He cleaned himself up the best he could and hobbled back to the bed, pulling his pants up but leaving them unhooked. He rubbed his tender stomach and pulled the blanket over his shoulders. He shivered and fell into a fitful sleep.

CHAPTER 25

Del was quiet on the ride home. She and Frank had sat in front of the ice cream shop another twenty minutes before he decided to leave. No one of suspicion had come out. She'd explained that it was more of a feeling than anything, but the glimpse of the man's arm had put her on high alert.

"But you didn't see da tattoo?" Frank asked again.

"No. I'm not even sure it was a tattoo," she said. "It could have been a burn I guess, but... no, I'm pretty sure it was a tattoo. An old one. You know... faded."

"So, he was a white guy?"

She looked surprised. "I don't know. I didn't say—"

"Tattoo on a black guy is kinda hard to see."

"Oh, yeah, you're right. You know, I'd say the color of his arm was sort of like... dirt. I think he was a white guy that'd had too much sun."

Frank grunted. "Yeah, laborer, dock worker arms."

Del twisted her mouth and bounced her knees as the car rolled along. She wanted to be out of the car.

"Sorry that I... I wish I'd been more alert. Maybe we would've caught the guy by now."

"Not your fault, Del-bell. And, I doubt it. Police work is slow business most da time. I'd say we're lucky to even have somethin'. If you'da come out any sooner, we might still have nothin'. What took so long anyway?"

Del tapped a nervous little dance with her feet and remembered Pecan Cream ice cream on her tongue. She saw Johnathan's soft brown eyes watching the spoon move toward her own lips, his eyes widening in surprise and anticipation. He was asking her if there was anything else he could get for her.

She sighed. "Not a thing."

Frank turned at the odd response. "What?"

"Huh?" Del looked around, realizing she'd spoken out loud. She wondered what secret she'd just let slip.

She saw the confused look on Frank's face and used it to exit the awkward conversation. "The large crowd in front of me ate all the sprinkles AND the cherries. Can you believe it? Not a thing left I wanted." She turned her head as if to watch a passing thing of interest and hid her smile.

Frank's cigar drooped in confusion.

Teenagers.

As they pulled into Armand's, Jimmy stood up and waved. He was planting something in one of the stone containers in the yard.

"Deh!" Jimmy cracked a wide smile. "You not 'ate!" He checked his watch to make sure. "You yust in time for pway—"

Del rushed past him. "Sorry, Jimmy Wawoo. Gotta do some work. We'll play later."

And she was gone.

Jimmy grunted and sat down on the ground. He wondered what was wrong with Del lately. Ever since they came to Armand's house, she'd been different. She must have grown up a lot when she left the orphanage. In there, she was his best friend. After she left, she'd still come by, but not as often. She must have made a lot of new friends. Then, when they moved in here, he thought they'd have all sorts of fun together, but when she knocked him down the other night, he got scared. He couldn't remember how she did it, or why. It might have been because of the bugs that got after him, or because he didn't remember the shrimp joke. But either way, she didn't have to yell at him. He couldn't help that he didn't remember what she'd said, but she was scary and ugly when she yelled like that—sort of like a monster. And now she had work to do and couldn't play.

He dropped his hand-shovel in the dirt and walked up the back steps. He sat on the top board and looked at his shoes.

"Pfoo. Geh away," he said quietly, waving his hands.

The invisible bugs were coming back.

*

In her room, Del tranced.

She was looking for the man who'd brought a delivery into the back of the Ice Cream Emporium.

She hovered above the scene in her mind and watched her younger self—younger by sixty minutes perhaps—walk into the shop. She sped past the catty girls and their ridiculous demands and stopped as she stepped up to the counter for the first time.

She watched carefully as Johnathan wiped his face and bit his nail. She lingered on the tasting scene and relived it in her present-mind and her trancing-mind, simultaneously. It was a wonderful stereo moment, until static suddenly interrupted the picture.

She huffed silently and tackled the scene again. It had jumped forward a bit, but this was a good part as well, Johnathan looking shy and smiling at her.

How tall is he, I wonder? I bet he has strong legs. I wonder if—

A crashing noise made her jump. It came from the back of the store, and she remembered why she was here. She pushed the Johnathan scene away with a sigh and changed the angle of viewing.

A shadow moved in the back of the store. The delivery guy was there! She was sure of it. She'd catch sight of him in a minute or so.

She stole a look back at Johnathan for just a second and wondered what his hair looked like without the hat. His hair looked really soft.

Checking back on the delivery man, she realized that in the last few seconds, she had floated away in her trancing scene and was now outside the building. She was well above the roof now, and saw nothing.

She grumbled under her breath.

The cars on the streets moved in slow motion and she thought of the alley. She turned the building in her mind and looked at the parked cars. There were several.

Long brown eyelashes fluttered in front of her and she tasted something cold and sweet on her lips.

A box dropped in the back of the shop.

She looked through the open door behind the counter. He was almost in sight.

Johnathan licked his own lips in response to her.

The arm came and went.

Aarrgghhh! Concentrate!

The scene rolled away from her with a crack of static.

Damn it! What's wrong??

She saw herself licking the ice cream from her lips. Her heart fluttered. Whether it was a trance flutter or real-life, she couldn't tell.

She saw an arm and concentrated.

Wet lips.

A shadow.

Brown eyes. So cute.

Please!!!

A tattoo.

Hold still!

Brown hair. Wavy.

An insect.

Concentrate! WHAT IS THAT?!

She felt it this time.

Her whole trancing body slipped violently sideways, and the scene was obliterated. She plunged through freezing darkness and slammed into the night air of a different time.

She was back in old New Orleans.

CHAPTER 26

Del wobbled and grabbed a brick wall. She'd never felt a jolt that strong before. She didn't think trances should be this physical. Surely Mama Dedé would have warned her of it.

She looked around the dimly lit street. Gas lamps flickered, lending a soft glow to the dreamy world. This *vivid trance*—which was how she'd come to think of these events—felt different than the first. It had been jarring, but the scene had been clear—like she had stood there, in that world at that time, but no one could see her. This trance was different.

Perhaps because it was night, but she felt like she'd been painted onto the front of a canvas and the picture had come to life. The people walking by still moved normally, but the far edges of the scene were blurry. The old world ceased to exist were the light from the streetlamps faded. Even the outer edge of her vision was blurry, like the world didn't exist until she looked in that direction.

She observed the couples as they strolled the streets. It was after dinnertime, and people were either going home or onto their nightly entertainment.

A handsome couple came toward her. The man in his coat and tails. The woman in her wide dress and petite hat. She was striking. A long, graceful arm swung by her side as the other held gently beneath the man's elbow.

They passed right through her, but when they did the woman shivered and stopped.

"Oh! How strange," she said.

"What is it, darling?" he said, still extending his arm to her.

The pretty blonde woman turned and stared right through Del. They were only inches apart.

"I don't know," she said. "I just had the strangest feeling."

Del smelled her perfume. Or thought she did.

"A sensation, really."

The scent of lilac filled the air. Del leaned forward, tilting her head to the right. She stopped as close as she could to the woman and breathed deeply. The smell was heady.

The woman sensed something. She felt a presence very near her, and it made her heart flutter. It was a dangerous feeling, exciting. It was a secret.

Feeling the slightest breeze brush her cheek, the woman turned to her left. Her lips brushed Del's invisible ones, but they both felt it. The slightest spark of electricity had reached across an eon and touched them. Both sets of eyes flew open.

Del looked at the woman. Saw her skin. Watched her inhale a quick, shallow breath. Small goosebumps rose on the woman's neck as her pupils dilated.

The woman looked deep through Del's eyes, scanning the night, searching for the mystery that had touched her skin. Something was there, she knew it, and the woman wanted the mystery to see her. She swallowed hard, but her eyes went on searching.

"Come, darling," the man prompted. "It was just the wind. The doctor's dinner conversation was exhausting. I'm tired and want to go to sleep."

The woman turned reluctantly and joined her husband. He was walking briskly now, and she had trouble keeping up.

Del did not.

Like a moth to a flame, Del followed the woman without thinking. It didn't register where they turned, but she knew she could close her eyes and the woman's lilac scent would pull her forward. And so, she followed.

The couple came to a large stone house. A night doorman tipped his hat and held open the door. Del followed them inside.

They exchanged small talk as they walked up the stairs and to the back of the grand house. They entered a small parlor and kissed goodnight. The man turned and went through the door to the right. The woman went through the door to the left.

Del went left also.

Behind the heavy oak door was a soft, plush room. And it smelled of the lilac woman.

A four-poster bed stood in the center. Low-burning candles sat on small tables to each side.

A dark mahogany room divider stood off to one side. A movement of shadow from behind it caught Del's attention. The woman was undressing. Del stood, hypnotized. And waited.

Seconds turned into minutes as she imagined the scene behind the wood panels. The thought of changing her viewing angle never occurred to her. The tiny flickers of candlelight that escaped between the panel folds brought snippets of images to her. Just enough.

A pale shoulder blade slipped out of the last fold of material.

The small of the back glistened. The material must have been heavy.

The warm line of a full hip as it turned.

Long arms that extended above the panels, guiding on the sheerest of night gowns.

Then she was standing in front of Del.

For a brief, terrifying second Del thought the woman saw her, but instead, she lifted a heavy train of golden hair high in the air and let it spill across her shoulders.

She sat down at a small table and began to brush the golden waves.

Before she realized, Del was standing behind the woman, watching her in the mirror. She wasn't sure how long she'd been there when the woman let the brush go with a frustrated sigh and stood up. Del saw her sheer image in the mirror as her hair passed across Del's face. She smelled lilac again. And something else.

The woman slipped beneath the sheets, but was not still. Her legs moved beneath the covers slowly and her hands could not find rest. Her head rolled slowly from side to side.

Del came as close as she dared to the woman and bent over her, gazing into her lovely face. The woman's eyes were closed but active. Del drew closer. Like on the street, their lips reached across eons to touch. And each one felt the other's presence in the night. The woman gasped but did not open her eyes. Her lips were barely parted. Soft, sweet breath escaped as she pushed the covers down to her hips. Her nightgown began to slide up.

Del stared into her face. Slowly moving her head from side to side, she brushed the woman's lips with her own. She felt every ridge. The woman squirmed and pulled the covers down with her feet. Her hands roamed as her lips parted. She spoke in a soft, lilting voice:

"Oh, gentle spirit of the night, whose wanton touch evades my sight,

"Flee me not for fear of fright. I give myself to thee."

Del hovered, mesmerized by the woman.

The woman felt Del hesitate and spoke again.

"Come close and feel this heart of mine, night whispers now will make it thine,

"These lips are soft and sweet like wine. I give myself to thee.

"This magic night was made for us, waste it not and seize it thus.

"So, take me now *sweet succubus*, and let my spirit free."

Del felt an overwhelming pull from the woman, as if she'd been called forth by an incantation.

Sweet succubus? What did she mean?

As easily as a bee finds the flower, Del found herself straddling the woman. She felt only the bed and its inviting softness, afraid to touch her directly or for too long, and break the spell.

As if feeling a shift in the pressure of the room, the woman smiled slightly and pulled a candle from its stand. With slow deliberate moves, she traced the curves of her nightgown with one finger from the hand that held the candle. Del watched the woman's skin respond to the proximity of the flame.

The woman's desire manifested itself in the flaming tip of the candle and Del felt it reach for her across the ages. The desire was fundamental, and had always been in her. It needed but the faintest touch to ignite. And ignite it had. The woman moved the candle with firm intention, exploring the space above her as if Del were physically there. Somehow, she knew the shape of Del, as if she'd molded her with her own hands; a creator that spent a lifetime sculpting the most beautiful thing she could imagine.

With each movement of the candle, with each lick of the flame, Del imagined she felt the woman's intention. The candle flame, like a lover's tongue, confirmed the young woman's thoughts and opened other mysteries yet to be dreamt of. For in many ways, she was as new as a blossoming spring.

With each shudder of Del's body, the lilac woman imagined she felt a response: a surprised flinch, an intake of breath, a constricting of nerve ends, a static tingle, a wave of heat; she felt all these things travel the ages and settle over her like a layer of silk fire. She searched the darkness for her lover and for brief seconds—that she would remember the rest of her life—imagined the night air shimmering into supple contours and whispered requests. The woman obliged.

Del dreamed a thousand desires and spoke to the night in murmurs and soft whimpers. She lost herself in the eyes of the lilac woman. They were deep pools consuming her, and she was lost. Her arms and legs trembled as she supported herself just above the woman, still fearing to reach for the nonexistent body and break the spell. Her fingers clutched unconsciously, digging into the soft dough of the bed and woman, as they had become one in her mind. The candle flame scorched the air and Del leaned into it, coaxing it down, down. The woman, knowing her desire well, responded. In an instant, Del was overcome with a fire like none she'd ever imagined. "Oh…" she breathed as her eyes sprung wide. "Oh…" Her breath pleaded. "OH." Her eyes squeezed tight as she fell forward, forgetting her imagined boundary. Del meant to surrender and let the woman absorb her in the undulating waves that caressed them. She buried her face into the pillow and abandoned herself.

As Del fell forward, the lilac woman felt the static tingle of Del's lips pass through her own, then her own eyes sprung wide. The essence of Del had penetrated her completely, and she experienced something never before imagined: tongue passed into tongue, navel sunk beneath navel, then their minds became one. For a shuddering second, the electricity that Del generated flowed into the woman's mind, down her spine and through every nerve ending, locking her head, toes and hands in one great spasm. Her mouth froze with a grimace of ecstasy. The candle snapped in the woman's grip and snuffed out against her trembling leg. Her head rocked in sharp stabs as she tried to process the sensation. She breathed in short, ragged bursts. Her outstretched toes cramped to the point of locking. Her eyes slowly rolled back.

Connected to the beautiful, struggling woman, Del saw into her core. She floated freely in the woman's desire and took her fill of it. The intoxication of total control was like nothing she'd ever felt before, and she was drunk with it. Del nearly lost herself, then suddenly—from another source of willpower—pulled away, breaking the spell. She flung herself from the bed and staggered to her feet.

The woman cried out softly, "Oh! Don't go…" Her eyes roamed the dark. Her fingers trembled. "Who— whoever you are. Please stay."

Del stumbled backward. Her mind twisted with fire and confusion.

What am I doing?

She was already outside the large oak door, but still heard a whispered plea.

"Please stay…"

What am I doing?!

She ran down the steps and through the front door. Out in the dark night it had begun to rain. The impact of the lilac woman boiled through Del's body and she screamed at the night.

Clasping her hands behind her head, she walked in a tight circle around the street and cried. It was several minutes before she realized the rain was cooling her.

What was happening to her? She felt like she was losing control of her mind. And her body. She couldn't tell who had more control, the woman with her strange poem, or herself. She continued to walk the tight path, around and around, circling whatever abnormality was at her core, trying to identify it. She was oblivious to all others.

A beggar in an alley stared out from beneath his tattered blanket and said a silent prayer. The next morning, he would swear that he'd seen an apparition floating around in a circle late that night. He knew it was a circle because it appeared to be steaming from the rain.

CHAPTER 27

Eventually Del broke free of her circle and followed whichever street lay in front of her. The surreal vision of the painted canvas stayed with her. But now she felt like she was walking into a nightmare painting, an old street scene that had to suck the living into so it could exist.

A bell struck somewhere in the distance. It was eleven o'clock in the evening on a cold night that may or may not have ever existed. She couldn't tell what was real any longer, and feared she was hallucinating.

This wasn't real, she decided.

She was soaking wet and shouldn't be. All the other times she'd tranced, she'd never felt anything physical—at least not from the scene. It wasn't supposed to happen this way. These were simply snippets of life that had occurred already.

And as far as the future scenes were concerned, sometimes it was a picture of something that was close to happening, she knew that. But they still weren't physical things. And those were so blurred—because of the uncertainly surrounding them—that they were hard to look at anyway. But still nothing physical.

But what she was seeing now had apparently happened a long time ago.

Was this the 1700s or the 1800s, she wondered? She didn't know.

A low building on the corner became her new destination. Only because it looked warm. Whether it was her imagination making her cold or not, she had to get off the street. She didn't feel safe.

She entered the building and felt a crash of déjà vu. The sign outside had simply advertised a blacksmith shop, but there was clearly a pub being operated here. She'd only seen the large front room, but was sure she knew the place. Smoky, sweaty air assaulted her, along with a din of nearly unintelligible speech. The place seemed to be jammed full of sailors—or men of less repute trying to *appear* to be sailors. A fire burned brightly in a stone fireplace and oil lanterns hung from metal hooks on the walls. Other paraphernalia dotted the rafters: loops of rope, large metal hooks, a medieval looking metal spear that might be a harpoon. And the smell of fish was overwhelming.

Del moved effortlessly through the crowded room and experienced none of the electric static she'd felt with the woman on the street.

Maybe the lilac woman was *a hallucination. Maybe I* am *losing my mind.* The thought of both disturbed her.

She moved past the fire, then behind the bar. She still wasn't used to the feeling of passing through people and tried to avoid them as much as possible.

Barmaids and prostitutes squeezed past each other, sometimes sneering and sometimes winking. The voices didn't let up. Behind the bar, Del saw two rooms: one appeared to be a rudimentary kitchen were an unpleasant smelling fish stew bubbled; the other a more private meeting place, away from prying ears.

Del moved into the shadows of the meeting room and listened.

Five men were huddled close together, speaking barely above whispers. A strange ship had docked earlier in the evening, although no one recalled seeing it hail into port. Rumors about it were spreading quickly. It was as if it had materialized straight out of a thick fog that rolled in unexpectedly.

It was badly weathered, almost completely black with rot, and was missing half its bow railing. Remnants of it hung over the side as if some great and terrible creature had reached out of the ocean depths, trying to pull it under, and only managed to claw one side.

No signal cannon had been fired when it entered port, and the flag was so tattered that its country of origin could not be determined.

It docked with its sails stowed, yet no one pulled an oar. Stranger even, only one person had disembarked from the ship; the sailors had neither been seen nor heard, and only a single lantern burned in the captain's quarters this very hour. The singularly emaciated man that did disembark hailed the very man sitting with his back to the wall now and bade him to find four other strong men that could keep their tongues quiet. There was a good wage to be paid for heavy work tonight, but it could only be done between the hours of midnight and three a.m., which was quickly approaching.

The men all made signs to ward off evil and drank to seal it. The oldest man in the group spoke up.

"Dat be black doins ye be hailed fer, an' I'll have no part!"

Some men grumbled their agreeance.

The old man continued. "What ship ken stay afloat black wit' rot? No crew ta heel 'er in? Stink ah death yawnin' about?" He gulped another drink which partially ran down his wiry whiskers. "I hear dat fish be dying very now," his finger stabbing the table, "what swims too close to it. Dat be da devil's own, I say!" A wide eye stole across each man and they looked away, fearing a hex may be somewhere inside it.

The man who called the meeting countered, "Yer ale's mushed yer head an' da fish died cause ya dipped yer dirty arse in da harbor. I don't care what da cargo be. And tain't da firs' or las' time sumpin's been moved in da dark!"

"Fools, ye be," the old man said. He pointed at each one. "Ye know not what lurks in da wee hours. Der's a strange mist what came in wit' da black ship. Mark my words, der's spirits about and der lookin' for souls."

Del thought the man looked at her just then, and she faded further back into the shadows.

"Bah! We be wastin' time. Now who's wit' me? Speak up."

"Whar we haulin' too?" another man asked.

"O'er Dauphine Street. Broussard's Imports."

Most of the men grunted acquiescence. Madame Broussard was known to have a thriving import/export business. Her husband had established it right after arriving in the Crescent City. No one remembered when that was or where they hailed from. It was said that he later traveled north up the Mississippi to establish another location at the confluence of several rivers. He'd never returned, but was reported to have found 'a rich source of material.' However, no one could imagine what would be so valued to import or export from a remote part of wilderness in the middle of the country. And this was just fine with the Broussards.

Four of the five men in the back room of the blacksmith shop went on to complete their work later that evening. At three a.m. their names were lost to history. But their souls remained.

Del had to get out of this place. She suddenly felt she'd stayed too long again, and had to find a way home. She left the men to their planning and entered the front room, where she stopped. Not believing what she saw. There, sitting before a dying fire was a little girl.

The room bustled, but no one saw the girl. They stepped right through her.

The ghost girl, Del thought and hurried to the front. She stopped in shock as she stared at the wretched thing. It wasn't the same one.

The poor girl that sat before her now must have been born horribly deformed. Her legs were folded beneath her. She wore similarly dirty clothes like the other one. Even the long stringy hair was the same. But instead of spindly arms, hers had grown long and thick. They reached the floor and curved away from her body in great flaps of flesh. They looked like flippers.

The girl sat right in front of the fire and stared at the worn boards of the shop. She made no notice of Del and occasionally scratched at the dirty floor as if drawing a picture. She waved in annoyance at the dirty boots that trampled it, making a fleshy, wet sound as her long arms slapped the floor.

Del stepped carefully to the right of the girl and positioned herself by the front window. There was a small vacancy at the side of the fireplace that no one occupied.

"Hello," she said softly. "Can you hear me?"

The girl drew at her picture and shrugged her thick shoulders.

A narrow, dark shadow stretched out from the girl, but not in the direction of the flickering flames. The shadow stretched towards Del, sideways from the firelight.

Del crept backwards until her back was against the front wall. This was another shadow she didn't want to touch.

"Why are you here? Do you know about the missing kids? Do you know where they are?"

"I am pretty, I am Scar," the girl said to the floor.

A wave of nausea swept Del. The voice was similar to the first girl's. Only this one was a hollow echo. And the greeting was the same—*I am pretty.* "You do hear me. Why am I here? How do I find—?"

"Never dead but deep we are.

"Come journey forth, you won't be found.

"Forever-ever, in the ground."

The narrow shadow shot out between Del's feet and she saw tiny shadow-fingers scratching the floor towards her. She leapt straight in the air to avoid them and stumbled backwards out the front of the building. She didn't have time to consider if she'd trip over the wall—which wasn't supposed to happen—or if it was her own clumsiness, before she sprawled out into the street. She landed on the wet cobblestones and looked around wildly for other errant shadows.

Just then, the old man from the back room—who would survive the night—exited the front door of the blacksmith shop pub and turned left. He was muttering to himself.

"...got ta' watch da tangled spirit. Black root goes deep."

At least she thought he was talking to himself.

He looked back over his shoulder at where Del sat in the street. One eye seemed to glint a warning. Or a hex.

"Wait. What does that mean?" Del yelled.

The scene began dissolving quickly.

Suddenly she was falling backward through the cobblestone street; the surreal painting of another time flying away from her.

"What does that mean?" she called through the void.

Before she even landed in the chair in her room, she could taste the coppery bite of blood running down the back of her throat.

She choked on it as she called out...

CHAPTER 28

"What does that mean?"

"What?" Mama Dedé said from the other side of her door. "I said, 'Come on down and get some supper.' You been in there all day."

Del looked out her bedroom window and saw that the sun was low. She felt like she'd spent a full day or more in old New Orleans, but based on Mama Dedé's request, assumed it was still the same day.

She couldn't remember what time she and Frank had returned home, but her stomach rumbled that it'd been hours earlier. The thought of food turned her stomach as she gagged again on the rich fluid stuck in the back of her throat. She coughed and spit a wad of blood into her hand and nearly vomited.

"You alright, honey?" the woman called as the doorknob turned.

Del jumped up and leaned into the door with her hand. "I'm changing. I'm fine." She hung her head and shivered. "I'll be down in a minute."

She stood quietly listening to Mama D traverse the stairs, muttering under her breath.

Del cleaned up in the bathroom down the hall. She looked terrible. Her face had gone ashen and she rubbed at shadows under her eyes. She needed sleep, but wanted to get the thoughts out of her head before she did.

She joined the others at the table and looked weakly at the mound of fried fish sitting on it. The smell of the bubbling fish stew from her trance wafted over her and she felt her temperature rise. She opted for a handful of fries and started dipping them in tartar sauce.

After several minutes, Del grabbed another handful of fries. She needed more tartar sauce as well.

"Good lawd, honey," Mama D exclaimed.

"What?" Del said with half a fry sticking out of her mouth.

The woman smacked her lips apart. "You givin' my arteries a fit."

Del didn't follow.

Mama D rolled her eyes and nodded at her plate. "That!"

"What?"

"The fries are already dead. You don't have to drown 'em."

Incredulous, Del said, "But I like tartar sauce."

"You don't got to *drink* it is all I'm sayin'." The woman looked around the table for support. "Besides, poor Frank hardly got any."

Simultaneous surprise hit Frank and Del. A fry drooped from her mouth as his simply hung open. Frank receiving pity from Mama D was rare indeed.

Mama Dedé straightened slightly in her chair and delicately wiped her thick fingers. "Close up your mouths." She shot a nasty look at them and grabbed another piece of fish.

"So Frank," Armand broke in. "What of the case? How is our young investigative reporter doing?" His moustache smiled at Del. "Has she solved all your cold cases already? Hmm?"

Armand enjoyed poking the Frank-bear.

"Well, uh…" Frank stole a glance at Del and saw her staring a hole through her plate, wondering if he would tell them about the wild goose chase she sent them on.

"…she's comin' along just fine. I might be slowin' her down a bit." Frank leaned back in his chair, now fully in control of the narrative. "You know how dese kids are. Damn world don't move fast enough for 'em. And police work is slow business. But other'n that, we know she's got da mind for it. So…"

Del shot a thankful smile at Frank.

"Of course, she does!" Armand crowed. "Our young Del is terribly gifted."

Armand continued, but his voice faded away from Del.

Terribly gifted… Depends on how you look at it, she thought. *Gifted with something terrible? Terrible with my gift?*

Her confidence returning, Del said, "You know, Frank, after we got home, a few more things came to me. I wanted to run them by you to see if they had meat."

Frank whistled at her recovery and nodded. "Ok, let me hear 'em."

"On the ride back—then again in my room—I tranced and got a better look at the delivery guy."

"You see his face?"

"No, the trance was… interrupted by something," Del said hesitantly.

"Interrupted?" Mama D questioned.

"It was just… I don't know, I was having trouble focusing, is all."

The woman watched her closely. Interruptions weren't a normal part of trancing as far as she knew.

"Anyway, I got a better look at the tattoo."

Frank perked up.

"It was on his left arm. Right here." She pointed to her own forearm. "I think it was a spider. Actually, I'm pretty sure of it."

"A spider?" Frank puffed his cigar in contemplation. "Hey, dat's a good clue." He nodded slowly as he flipped perp pictures in his mind.

"Also," Del looked at Armand, "has anyone ever heard of… the *tangled spirit* before?" She glanced sideways at Mama Dedé. As feared, there was a mixture of hurt and suspicion on her face at not being consulted directly on the subject. The old woman nodded slightly as if she understood Del's reasoning, but her face was no less harsh.

"The tangled spirit," Armand said, drawing the words out slowly. He stood up, stroking his beard. "Where have I heard that before?"

He walked away absently. His fingers kneaded the air, searching for his own clue.

Del and Jimmy cleared the plates, but left the dwindling bowls of fish and French fries on the table. They were a family of grazers. Someone was sure to snatch the last few pieces before the night was over. Besides, Armand wasn't overly concerned about the table being straightened. They still ate with it partially covered with old boxes and stacks of research folders.

Upstairs, Armand was busy touching everything in his study. Random words floated over the railing and fell like the soft snow of a fairy tale.

Frank had grabbed the brandy on the way up and had already poured himself one as he slid the other to Armand.

"Oh, thank you, mon ami," Armand said, turning back to his

books. "Please, help yourself to…whatever…is this doing on the wrong shelf?"

Frank shrugged his shoulders, nodding at his glass, and topped it a bit higher. He sat in his usual spot, on his side of the fireplace table.

Several minutes later, Del and Jimmy arrived with cups of hot cocoa topped with heavy whipping cream. Mama Dedé was nowhere to be found.

CHAPTER 29

Armand climbed the librarian's ladder that stood against his curved bookshelf. A tarnished metal track ran from left to right in a concave fashion. He was near the top of a twelve-foot ceiling. He was talking to the books.

"Where are you?" He dug to the back of the top shelf. With his left leg, he pushed himself along the track while holding the ladder with one hand and fishing with the other. Frank grimaced at the precarious scene.

Armand read the titles of several old volumes: "Let's see... *Shipwrecks of the 1780s, ...1790s, Spirits and Their Abnormalities.*" He grabbed this one with his right hand, hopped from his right foot to his left on a rung and swung toward his guests. His body hung partially off the ladder, causing it to slowly slide back to the left.

"Spirit abnormalities," he said, holding the thin book. "Can you believe such a thing?" He read the back. "Dr. Archibald Bertrand Normal. A. B. Normal. Sounds like a quack to me." He shoved the book back in.

Like an acrobat, he switched leg positions again. With a hard push from his left, he sent himself sliding to the right. Rickety wheels clattering beneath him.

"Holy hell," Frank muttered and sipped his brandy.

"Of course!" Armand announced from his perch. Sliding down the ladder, somehow with an armful of books, he turned and said, "Have you ever heard the story of the Tormented Lady?"

Frank interrupted. "Uh, actually, before we get to dat, I was hopin' dat Del... well, we got missin' kids. And I'm afraid our time is 'bout up."

"Oh, of course," Armand said. "How terrible of me." He set his books down and took his spot by the fireplace. "You are right, mon ami. We should be... well, you... It's just that Del's question was so fascinating. I got carried away. What did you have in mind?"

"You're right, Frank," said Del. "We shouldn't be wasting time. I can trance again and—"

"Well," Frank said timidly, "what I was thinkin' was..."

Mama Dedé ascended the steps just then with a pot of tea and two cups.

"Oh." Del understood immediately.

Frank stood up to give his seat to the elder woman. "Maybe dere's somethin' you missed," Frank said.

Del looked at the floor and toed the edge of the floor rug.

"Maybe Mama D can help spot it."

Del absently pressed her hip into the front of Armand's worktable and straightened the rug tassels with her foot. She thought of what the woman would see at the ice cream counter. That was bad enough. Embarrassing. She hoped to God she couldn't see her in old New Orleans.

"Yeah, sure. I might have missed something."

Armand motioned for Del to take his seat. He tipped the brandy decanter toward Frank, who came like a moth to a flame. The men watched in silence.

Mama Dedé poured tea into two cups.

"I don't need it," Del said quickly. She sat down. A matter-of-fact look on her face.

The woman set the pot down and returned Del's long stare. "I know you don't. But it's how I taught you."

Frank thought there was a hint of emphasis on the word 'I' and exchanged an uncomfortable glance with Armand.

A heavy breath huffed out of Del as she grabbed the teacup. She raised it in a 'bottom's up' salute to the old woman and drank it in one gulp.

The sides of Mama Dedé's mouth drew down, somewhere between embarrassment and disappointment. She swallowed her tea, set the cup down and closed her eyes.

The men waited.

*

Mama Dedé saw Del's essence immediately. The cloud of silver droplets never ceased to amaze her. Before she could orient on the room they were in—this was how she'd taught Del to trance together after all—the girl was gone. She'd sped away to whatever scene had occurred earlier in the day.

The woman followed the essence of Del in the dream world, floating through an infinite sea of color and sensations. She had an idea of where Del would go. She knew about the ice cream shop, because Frank had mentioned it to her earlier when he'd asked for help. She just didn't know why Del wouldn't wait.

Then it occurred to her.

Del didn't know that she and Frank had spoken earlier. Del thought the woman was wholly reliant upon being able to follow her presence through the trance-mist. Del meant to lose her.

Mama Dedé settled into deep concentration. Deeper than she'd been in several months. Her search this spring for Marie Laveau and the Unbinding Spell was the last time she'd been this deep. It took a lot out of her. Her mentor, Abigail Clemmons, a hard woman and strict practitioner of the arts had warned her not to go too deep, too often.

Da spirits catch da scent a'yer root and it drives 'em mad. Stronger den yer bleed an musk combined. Yer root is da very essence of da ting you are. Core a'yer soul. Dark and rich, like marrow. You go too deep an' yer root goes too. Leaves a trail. Now da tings beyond death ken find ya. And dey never lose yer scent.

Settled now, the woman flashed forward then back. She reoriented, saw the quickly fading trail of Del-silver, and followed. The trail, like the time Del was truly lost, spread out in a thin mist through the ether. Usually, she only saw a faint presence that someone had been trancing around a scene, but with Del, she could somehow see *where* she'd gone, as well as *what* she'd been looking at. It was fascinating and unnerving at the same time. Mama D knew that Del had greatness in her, but also knew that it came with a terrible price. She wondered how much Del had already paid.

She followed the silver trail as it twisted and turned. Scenes started and stopped. One minute it was daylight in the garden behind Armand's house, the next it was night and Frank was helping Armand cook them dinner. She thought she heard a debate about ingredients, but didn't wait long enough to hear who prevailed. Del was leading her on a wild goose chase.

Around and around Del tranced, and the woman followed. A new scene floated into view. Frank and Armand stood around a bottle of brandy, staring at two women sitting in front of a fireplace. She'd gone in a circle again. Mama D was watching the scene where she was trancing, trying to follow Del.

That damn girl…

The trail led on, but was now mixed with the fading remnants of the other trails. The silver droplets of Del floated away in a random scattering; red and blue shifts of light bounced in all directions. The woman had nearly lost the trail, and was tiring. There was one more thing she thought to do.

She focused all her attention on a scene she knew Del had been at. It was in her trail of memories, and would ring in Del's consciousness if the woman had enough power. She concentrated.

A flash went off in Del's mind. Something new had happened. Like gravity, the scene in question came to her. She didn't move *to* it like before. She *pulled* it into view. It was the scene of her standing in the ice cream shop. Johnathan was feeding her.

"Enough playin' around!" Mama Dedé's voice echoed in her head. Only it was a replay.

It was as if the woman had already been at this scene, somehow knowing Del would end up here, or at least that it would be stuck in her mind, and anticipating her juvenile trick, had laid the reprimand over the memory track of the original scene. Then somehow, she'd made the scene flash in Del's mind.

Apparently, the woman hadn't taught Del everything yet.

The essence of Del and of Mama Dedé, two abnormal forces, floated just off the ice cream shop scene. Each was aware of the other.

Del felt the other woman pull at the scene. She was in control of it.

Mama D inspected the frozen image of the ice cream parlor, but didn't play it forward or backward. She turned it over in her mind, then, like a magic trick, the scene split in two.

Del suddenly realized that the woman had detected the original scene, where Del had first met Johnathan, and the secondary version when Del was trancing on the first. The second version was blurred with static.

The woman watched the original scene unravel; two teenagers flirting over an ice cream counter.

Well, isn't that cute. He's so nervous.

Del closed her trancing-eyes as if this would shield her from the embarrassment that was sure to come.

Why you rollin' your ankles out like that? What're you doin, butt-crunches?

I am not!

Oooo... Now he's feedin' you ice cream? Yumm-mmmyy!

Mama D, please.

He's just so nervous he—whoa, peek behind the counter, from this angle he don't look nervous no more.

Mama D!

The woman chuckled to herself. Del saw it as a slight shimmer across her yellow essence.

Now the second version of the scene began to play.

The gist of the scene was there, but the images jumped around like a bad movie reel.

Del swallowed hard in her physical body. Her trancing-self felt the lump go down her throat. What would be revealed next?

The tattooed arm came into view and froze. The woman proceeded slowly. A frame-by-frame view of Del's failed trancing session unfolded. Lips and eyelashes flashed into focus, then faded away. The tattoo-insect came close, then went black.

The original scene started up again. The angle was changed to focus on the storeroom, but it was blurry. The image fell away, then was pulled back. The building spun again, then snapped back like a hidden spring held its original orientation.

I see something! Del said in her mind. *Can I drive?*

A soft feeling of air through her mind told her the scene had been given over to her. She ignored the images with Johnathan in them. She concentrated, but not as hard as before; she was afraid of slipping right in front of her mentor.

She saw three quick flashes of light.

Flick. Flick. Flick.

Then she smelled smoke.

Del wasn't sure why the scene was blurry. It was as if someone had rubbed paint thinner on just one part of a painting, obscuring this one character. No matter where the man walked—she was sure it was a man with a spider tattoo—his face was never visible. In fact, he sometimes faded into the shadows of the room, which made him hard to track. But his cigarette smoke didn't fade.

She followed the smoke out the side door.

Wait. Side door? Didn't he park in an alley at the back of the building?

The side door of the ice cream shop opened upon a covered area—which at some point in the past had been open to the sky—that now looked like a small indoor courtyard. It was simply a covered area that people used to get between buildings. It didn't look like an alley, so never registered with Del.

The trail of smoke wound through a labyrinth of stone halls and exited out the side of another building. An area that Frank had driven past, after Del took him the wrong way.

No wonder they didn't see him!

The smoking man with the tattoo was still blurred, but his car wasn't. It was an old Ford, she could see the emblem. She looked closely at the headlights

(like bug eyes)

and fenders

(round, not pointy).

It was a neat car she thought

(like a gangsters).

She knew this was it. She knew this person had something to do with the missing kids. She just needed more details.

What else? What else about the car, so Frank could figure out what it was?

Torpedoes. It has torpedo tips on the bumper. And the windshield is in two pieces. A split windshield!

She felt the older woman pull on the scene. She was trying to get Del's attention, and spoke.

License! What's the license say? Del, release it. You're too deep.

Just a minute! I almost got it.

Del!

The girl focused tightly on the car as it drove away. She could feel the pull of the scene; it wanted to fade into the past, but she was trying to follow, and Mama D was pulling her the other direction.

The purple license plate. Just focus.

A dirty rectangle came into view. It had a yellow line that ran around the outside with blurry letters and numbers.

Wait! I'm almost there!

786 came into view just as the scene faded out. The pull of opposite directions was too much to overcome.

She floated in a black ether and felt Mama Dede's presence moving toward her.

CHAPTER 30

I almost had it! Del screamed in her mind.

You almost went too deep! Mama D responded.

But I was so close!

Yeah, you don't know how close you were to getting your butt in trouble. You got to get yourself under control.

What do you mean? I did fine this time, I didn't— Del almost gave it away.

Mama Dedé pulled Del toward her body in Armand's house.

Del let herself be led.

You damn near obliterated that first scene, the woman replied. *You know why there was so much static? Your hormones just about burnt it up!*

My hormones?

Yeah, your hormones. They're messin' with the internal works. Literally. That's why I told you to drink—

"—that tea before each session."

Frank and Armand jumped as the two women came out of their trances in mid-sentence.

"You think this tea is only to help you get *into* a trance? You think it only helps with *expanding* your mind? Fool girl, you got to listen!"

The men made their way quietly to the couch by the balcony rail.

"It helps just as much with keeping your mind intact! It keeps your mind from expanding *too* much. It keeps you from slippin'."

Del's eyes told that she was caught.

"Yeah, I know you been slippin'. You know how I know? When your essence just *disappears* out of the scene, I know you done slipped! I told you before, everyone, and I mean everyone, leaves a trail, or a faint image around the scenes they've been trancin' on. But there's only one way for that trail to disappear completely. You tore through the fabric."

She waved for one of the men to help her up. Her legs were stiff. Armand jumped to the rescue.

"And when you do, you don't know where you'll end up. And because of that, there's no guarantee you'll get back. Ever."

Armand stole glances from Del to the elder woman. He knew which side of this conversation he would stay on.

"Damn, I need a drink," the woman said. "Can someone pour me a—?"

"I'll get it." Frank was faster than Armand this time.

Hoping to distill the tension, Armand cleared his throat. "So, ladies... any success? How did the session go?" His bushy eyebrows raised in anticipation.

"Well," Mama Dedé said, remembering the wild goose chase, "we got off to... kind of a slow start. Wouldn't you say?" She looked at Del.

Del pulled her feet beneath her and sat uncomfortably. "Yeah, I guess so." Her voice was small.

After an awkward silence, Mama D released the tension. "But Del came through. I think she got something you can use."

"Really?" Frank said. "Do tell."

Del exhaled and sent a smile of thanks to the woman. Mama Dedé winked in return and took her seat. A glass of brandy swished in her hand.

Del described the car in detail to Frank. He was certain it was a Ford Victoria, early '50s model.

The girl described the tattoo in better detail. It was definitely a spider on the man's left arm. He was white but his arm was deeply colored, like too much sun for too long.

"Truck driver's tan," Frank said. "Left arm is always dark from hangin' out da window. Tattoos on that arm are always a splotchy mess."

Del knew he smoked and that he had a habit of flicking his lighter several times.

Best of all, she knew the first three letters of his license plate were "786."

Armand beamed at Frank and nudged his shoulder as if to say, *I told you so.* He walked around the room swelling with great pride.

"Frenchy," Mama D said, "you about to peacock right outta that vest. Were you trancin' behind us and I didn't know it?"

Armand felt the sting. "Oh, well no, it's just…" He beamed at Del. "I *knew* you could do it!" He raised his glass to her.

Del, having just shed the embarrassment of Mama Dedé's cover, felt it again at Armand's over-confidence in her. In this situation, Frank was the pillar to which she turned.

"What now? Does this help?" Del was humble.

"Del-bell, dis helps a lot." He set his glass down. "So much so, that

I'm goin' to da station. I'll call for ya in da mornin'. Let's see where we're at then."

"Mon ami, you're going? Tonight?"

Frank headed for the stairs. "Dese kids got one day left, if any. If we don't find 'em tomorrow. Don't think we ever will."

The group fell silent as Frank descended the stairs.

CHAPTER 31

N ear the corner of Dauphine and Mandeville Streets, in the center of a block that no one thought of, the odd building that no one could find—save by special invitation—stood in shadow and waited.

The lamp did not cast its sickly green light crawling down the wall, nor did the sign cry out horrendous agony. But it was not dead.

In fact, this odd building was very much alive. Having felt the life force of so many unfortunate souls pass through its walls—for the years had been so long—it had absorbed the discarded shards of life and held them fast. Remnants of breath, cries and screams; droplets of blood, urine and tears; fragments of bone, skin and teeth; essence of mind, spirit and souls; many things had been shed within the walls of this building. And it had absorbed them all.

It was a living thing now, this building. Its dry mortar and hard brick, its ancient wood and antique furniture, its plaster and wallpaper, had digested the life fragments, and there they had become one. The building breathed the dying breath of ten-thousand screams. It drank a thousand gallons of spilled bladders and split veins, one drop at a time. It grew a skin of dust from an uncountable number of shattered bones and grinding teeth.

And yet its hunger was never slaked—like others.

Madame Broussard looked at the faded, black semi-circle on the floor of her showroom and shook her head, remembering the lurid behavior of last night's visitor. Mr. Scarmish had always been a difficult customer—she'd known him a long time—but for him to be so out of control was unexpected.

Granted, he'd been gone a long time—how long she couldn't begin to guess. There had been rumor amongst a very inner circle that he had been consumed completely, root and all. But she knew it unwise to believe idle gossip.

The people she dealt with on a yearly basis changed little. They kept their essence intact and thus could still behave in a reasonable manner if they chose to. Those that stayed away from the living world longer, that traveled deeper—like Mr. Scarmish—did not remain intact. They became fragmented and disturbed. And the few—*he may be one of them*, she thought—that went so far as to search for the Ultra Tempus *(those beyond time)* were never heard from again, as far as she knew.

Because of all this, she had to be cautious; hers was a dangerous business.

She wasn't concerned with the typical dangers that a normal woman—or man for that matter—worried over. In the old days, muggers and rapists came to a quick and violent end if they accosted her in an alley—and oh how she loved to stalk those alleys. No, her concern was of the darker things. For as old and learned as she was, there were many things far beyond her ability and understanding. One of which was what Mr. Scarmish may have become.

Last night's spell had held, but not as well as she'd expected.

She looked at the place on the wall where the entry curtain had hung. A black stain lay upon it that wasn't there before her visitor came. The building would absorb it eventually, but all trace of Mr. Scarmish should have vanished by now. It was as if the wall couldn't stomach the residue of her dark visitor.

The spell should have held completely. Why didn't it? He reached right through it like it was merely an unpleasant experience.

She had thought about this all day, and had no explanation. In fact, there were several things she had no explanation for, and they all concerned her.

A few months ago, she'd felt a *rip behind the skin*. That's how she thought of the mortal world anyway; a thin layer of skin that was maintained with makeup and rouge. A pleasant face to look at, but one that hid unimaginable horrors writhing just beneath the surface. That world beneath was *much* larger, she knew. But mortals had no capacity to grasp it, except for the mentalists, psychics and psychotics. How ironic, she thought, that the ones who had seen into the other side were so often locked up as insane or ignored as lunatics. The only ones that had been of real concern were the old Spirit Hunters, because they had a reasonable grip on both worlds. But they were all gone.

The cause of the rip hadn't been discovered. There were rumors on this, but that's all they were. Regardless, since that time, she'd had a surprising uptick in business—which was welcomed—but it felt like too much was happening, too quickly. The spirits that had sought her out, should not be. The whispered stories that had passed her ears, should never have been uttered. Those were dangerous rumors indeed.

The rip had turned into a gate and what flowed through it was dark insanity. Whoever had caused the rip must be powerful, she thought. That person would surely be the target of every malevolent spirit out there, trying to feed from the energy source. That person was someone she would like to meet.

She inventoried her goods, marked her ledger and sighed. She was running low on rootstock. She was also disappointed that Mr. Scarmish had dismissed the curios she'd presented him—she thought they were lovely items—but he was particular. Apparently, he'd become even more so over the years. But a dozen more roots? And in only a few days' time. How could she manage that? She could offer him *some* of what she had—if they were still viable; the young didn't fare well in this building—but locating new ones took time. They didn't exactly grow on trees.

She would ensure her supply chain stayed functional, but she couldn't overtax it. It did no one any good to become so brash as to get caught. But she didn't understand the sudden need for so much rootstock. He'd never needed that much before.

She was very curious what Mr. Scarmish was up to.

CHAPTER 32

J immy laid in his bed and stared out the window. He was reciting a list of things he had to do, so he wouldn't forget them. He was going to surprise Del this weekend.

First, he was going to help Armand make breakfast in the morning. He wanted to draw a picture of himself in Del's pancakes so she would remember him when she went to work. Then, he'd decorate his face with strawberries for the eyes and bacon for his mouth. He would get her glass of orange juice and… there was something else she liked.

What ese? 'Tupid head, doan fohget!

Toast and jelly.

Oh, and peanut butter for his nose.

Next, he would ask Mama Dedé if she'd take them to the movies on Saturday. He'd see if there were chores he could do around the house to earn some money. He was going to buy the popcorn.

Then after the movie, they could watch the trains come in. If he had enough money left over, maybe he'd buy her an ice cream.

Jimmy smiled and pulled the soft blanket up to his chin. He liked his new room.

*

Clara shivered under her thin blanket. Her lower jaw shook so hard her teeth clattered together. It wasn't cold that shook her little body though, it was shock.

All day long, an angel had been whispering beneath her door. She thought she might be dead and that he was trying to tell her how to get to heaven—or at least how to get out of this place—but she couldn't understand him. She was tired and fell asleep a lot.

She knew it was a boy angel by his voice, but couldn't understand why it came from under the door instead of out of the ceiling. She didn't think too long on this because she'd also dreamed of her little dog Pickle. Well, it had almost been her dog, but then the mouse came.

She wondered if Pickle was in heaven already. Maybe it was his voice she heard coming from under the door. That made more sense somehow. He wasn't very big, after all.

A large tear had collected at the corner of her eye. Her head lay sideways on the dirty pillow as she stared at the wall. Something crawled up it in the shadows. She squeezed her eyes shut and the tear ran across the bridge of her nose.

*

Willy snuck back to his room. He was afraid the little girl might be gone already. He'd tried talking to her as long as he could, but didn't want to get caught. He'd yet to make it up the stairs—they were too creaky—so he still didn't have a way out. Besides, his stomach was cramping, and he didn't think he could get out if he did know the way. He'd decided he wouldn't eat any more food, because he thought someone was trying to poison him.

Or maybe it was drugs. People drugged kids and did all sorts of bad things to them. If someone came in his room and tried to do something to him, he'd fight them however he could. He decided that he'd keep his lock pick in his pocket at all times. Maybe he could poke an eye out.

He didn't know where he was, but knew he had to get out soon. He wouldn't purposefully leave the girl, but If she really *was* gone, it *would* be easier, he thought. Sometimes she made a lot of noise. And she'd been quiet for a while.

He wished he knew her name, at least. He felt bad that he'd yelled at her that first day.

Maybe it was better that she *was* gone already. Hopefully, she was in a better place with her mom or dad.

That thought helped him sleep a little.

*

Del twisted in her bed. She was tired and wanted to fall asleep, but her mind was restless. She wondered if Frank had found anything from the clues she'd given him today.

She thought the entire thing would make a great newspaper story, but wasn't sure how to write it. Nor was she sure how she could explain her part in the capture. Trancing detectives weren't a thing.

She thought about Johnathan and wondered what he was doing at this moment.

Is he sleeping?

What does he sleep in?

Is he thinking about me and what I sleep in?

A tingle rippled through her and she adjusted the covers. The temperature was never right in her room.

Maybe she'd drop by the Ice Cream Emporium this weekend. She didn't have anything else to do.

Maybe he's not working this weekend.

She rolled onto her side and watched a slice of light cut across her wall. Weird, she didn't remember the lights from passing cars making it up this far, but—

Maybe he has a girlfriend!

Del rolled onto her back and angrily fluffed her pillow. She shoved it back beneath her head and glared at the ceiling. Slowly moving tree branches from outside cast odd shapes above her, and she imagined floating clouds.

She supposed she could find out if he had a girlfriend.

You can't spy!

But what if his girlfriend was way prettier than she was?

Stop it!

What if she has a job?

You have a job. Sort of.

What if she has a family and a home?

Del sighed and stared at the ceiling.

She imagined his face somewhere in the shifting colors. With enough concentration, she thought she could see him in the shadows, as if he were hovering above, watching her.

She closed her eyes, willing herself to fall asleep, but soon thought of the lilac woman. Her heartbeat picked up and she felt another funny feeling inside.

The scene ran quickly through her head: the static tingle when the woman passed through her; their lips brushing across time and space; her room; the smell.

Now she imagined the woman's face in the ceiling shadows, and they shifted from one to the other: first Johnathan, then the woman, then both in rapid succession. In Del's mind they were both watching her.

Above her, the shadows formed of their own accord. They were not created by passing cars or waving tree limbs outside the window. They were in motion from another source, and that source was growing stronger.

The shape of an eye *was* there also, but it wasn't imagined, and it didn't belong to the woman or Johnathan. It had emerged from a dark place, waiting until it felt safe. Its position was above the bed. It had a full view from here.

It knew that the young woman lying there was powerful. She had shown it not long ago when she had pushed all the spirits from the house. All but one, anyway.

Most of the spirits had left for good. It was one of the few that had returned. It didn't know why. It was simply drawn back to this spot. Not because the ceiling held anything of interest. It was because of the young woman in the bed. She had drawn it to her. For what purpose, it didn't know. But it would stay there, watching and waiting, until something happened. It would watch her for as long as it took.

It would be hours before Del fell asleep.

CHAPTER 33

Early the next morning Frank burst through the backdoor of Armand's house. His unshaven face and eyebags announced he'd been up all night.

"Where's Del?" he asked Armand. "We got a good lead and I need her help."

"Mon ami," Armand said, "you look terrible. Sit down and have some coffee." He poured a large cup and handed it to Frank.

"Have you been up all night?"

"Yep," Frank said. He sipped at the hot liquid and nodded his thanks. "But it was worth it. I got a suspect. Gonna pull him in today for questioning. I just need a little help trackin' him down."

"Ah, dang it!" Jimmy said from the stove. "'Tupid head got sqwonshed."

He set the spatula down on the counter. Remnants of a torn pancake-face hung from the working end. He wiped his fingers on his shirt.

Armand glanced over the boy's shoulder. "I don't know that it's quite *sqwonshed* really, perhaps just a bit *sqwinshed.*" He patted Jimmy's shoulder. "I'm sure it will be fine."

"Frank, I'm coming," Del said faintly from upstairs.

"Sleeping beauty awakes," Armand said, pouring another cup.

Slow heavy steps announced Del's descent. Her boots thudded, but not the bass drum version that usually echoed throughout the house.

"Alas, the horses are tame this morning," Armand said, winking at Frank.

Jimmy carefully placed the pancake face on Del's plate and dropped two strawberries on the eyes—they looked in different directions. A flimsy piece of bacon made a lopsided grin. Frank thought it resembled a melted Playdoh man from a B-horror movie, but said nothing.

Del's burnt orange T-shirt announced her presence, but the dark circles under her eyes told of a bad night's sleep.

She sat in her chair and grabbed her cup. "Thanks, Armand," she said. Her words were mostly lost in her cup, and came out as coffee-mumbles.

Jimmy said something. She could feel him fidgeting in his chair.

Her half-opened eyes stared at her plate over the top of the cup. The image reminded her of the strange dreams she'd had the night before. The many swirling faces of her nighttime fantasies.

Frank was saying something.

All she could focus on was the distorted face on her plate. She debated if it really looked like that, or if her imagination was working overtime. She didn't want to ask. Jimmy, sitting on her left, said something again and snorted. Her sluggish mind rejected making the translation and let the words slip by.

She yawned wide and her watery eyes made the table setting look like a Picasso. Images twisted and untwisted.

She thought about going back to bed, but what kind of reporter would that make her? Didn't she have to burn the midnight oil—or the candle at both ends—to get the story? She wanted to help Frank if she could, but couldn't seem to concentrate. The face on her plate changed. Its lopsided grin became a wet, glistening tongue and the eyes were staring at her. The strawberries looked like bulging red eyes straining off the plate. They were creeping her out.

The bacon-tongue grew. The tip of it reared off the plate.

Creepy eyes.

She'd seen creepy eyes last night.

The tongue made crude *licking* motions.

The eyes bulged out at her.

In one of her dreams—

Jimmy was still talking.

—creepy eyes dripped from the ceiling and—

Del looked at Jimmy and her heart leapt into her throat.

"Get off!" she screamed and slapped at Jimmy's face. Her coffee sloshed onto the table.

"Owww!" Jimmy yelled, grabbing his cheek.

"Del-bell!" Frank spit out his bacon.

Del pulled at Jimmy's shirt, slapping, looking, then grabbed his head roughly and twisted it from side to side.

"'Top hitting me!" Jimmy flailed his arms.

"What was that?" Del said. Her bloodshot eyes, wide and watery, searched Jimmy.

His arms covered his head.

Del blinked her eyes and stared at the boy. His terrified eyes peeked out from behind his elbows.

She looked at her plate. The pancake face was soaked with coffee, but beyond that, it looked normal. Her heart raced as she searched the breakfast items for answers. They had none.

"Jimmy, I'm sorry. I didn't mean to—

"There was something on your face." She turned to Frank. "Did you see it?"

Frank grimaced. "Well…" He pointed at his bacon.

She rubbed her eyes again, trying to refocus. "Jimmy, something was on your face and—"

Jimmy growled under his breath. "Hhhrrggg! 'Tupid Deh! Dat was my face on dere!"

He gave her an ugly look and left the table.

"Jimmy, wait! I'm sor—"

The screen door slammed behind him as he stomped onto the back porch and down into the courtyard.

She pleaded her case with Frank. "Really? You didn't see that? I didn't mean to hit him that hard. It just… it just looked like something was… crawling on him."

"Crawlin'? Like a bug? Or…" he lowered his voice, "something else?"

Del heard the implication and knew what he was asking.

"Something else," she said, staring at the ruined breakfast.

She began sopping up the liquid with her napkin.

"I don't know, maybe it was my imagination. I didn't sleep very well last night."

CHAPTER 34

"You alright, Del-bell?" Frank asked as he drove out of Armand's gate.

"Yeah, I'm fine," she said. Her booted foot tapped rapidly on the floor of the car. She leaned against the door and chewed a nail. "Just sleepy eyes, I guess."

"Yeah, OK. So, you ready to work?"

Her thoughts drifted. She felt a strange mix of want and guilt when she recalled the dream fragments from last night. She'd wanted Johnathan to come to her in her dreams. He did for a while—she thought. But so did the lilac woman. Or maybe it was reversed. Maybe she went looking for them. Either way, it was a frustrating dream and she felt angry that both had eluded her.

How stupid, she thought. Who gets mad at dream-people and—

"Del-bell?"

"What?" She jerked her hand from her mouth and looked at Frank.

He eyed her with concern.

"I'm ready. I'm ready." She squirmed in her seat. "Who are we looking for?"

Frank described his suspect. "Willis Lewis Morris—"

"What? Are those his aliases?"

Frank chuckled. "Nope. I guess da poor bastard's momma couldn't decide between a couple of first names, so she just stuck 'em together." He puffed his cigar and looked at his red eyes in the mirror. "Anyway, Mr. Willis Lewis Morris, aka, *The Man with Two First Names*, aka, *Spider*, has a couple of cars registered to him. One to a Willis Morris and da other to a Lewis Morris. And as you might guess, one car is a '51 Vic and da other is a '55 Plymouth."

Del listened intently.

"Also, da 786-license number doesn't belong to either one, so it must be stolen. Anyway, he's had some run-ins with da law, but has stayed outta da spotlight for a long time. Licenses are registered to a fake address—or maybe an old one dat got rezoned—but dat's where you come in. I need you to sniff him out."

Del smiled. Her boots danced on the floor. Finally. Something she could really help with.

"Where do we start?"

"I'm gonna drive past da fake address again. It's close enough to being real, but ain't there. I did it earlier this mornin' but my mind ain't thinkin' well. I doubt I missed it, but you might be able to see somethin' I can't. We'll go from there."

"OK. Where is it?"

"Dauphine and Mandeville."

Ten minutes later, Frank drove east on Dauphine approaching Mandeville.

"Far as I can tell, 2331 Dauphine just ain't here," he said with certainty. "And especially no suite #8."

"Suite eight? Like a hotel?"

Frank pulled to the side and parked. The stop sign for Mandeville was ten feet in front of the car.

"Da only thing close is this old building on da corner: 2340. But it's been shuttered for years."

Del looked at the charming, two-story building on her right. The old brick walls were covered with years of grime, but the curving, second-story balcony—round at the corners—still held an air of elegance. Many balconies had wrought-iron railings, but she liked the old wooden balusters. It gave the building a quaint *Old West* feel.

She thought she could see remnants of the red and blue paint that had colored the posts, supporting the balcony, when they were new.

She felt sorry for the building. It had been beautiful once, but years of neglect seemed to have sucked the life from it. The profile of the building lay across the street in distorted slants, and Del realized it had a third floor—they had parked too close to see it. The dormered windows jutted from the roofline cutting sharp shadow-angles in the morning light. Maybe it *had* been a hotel once.

She wondered what it had looked like when it was new.

She wondered if she could sneak a quick look at its past.

"Frank, I think I'm getting a vibe," she lied.

"You are?"

"Let me sit here a minute and see if I pick up anything."

"OK, great. I think I'll stretch my legs a bit and walk around da block. I'll be back in ten minutes or so."

"I'll be here," she said. And she slipped into her trance.

*

Madame Broussard, laying in the depths of sleep, opened her gray eyes. Her black hair, spread about her head like dark wings, contrasted with her pale skin, but faded into the black silk sheets. Something had just disturbed her sleep. This was unusual, for her normal rest was that of the dead.

Sitting up, the luxurious hair slid down her back in long, flat sheets. She listened to the building. It was sending her a warning.

The dark room came to life when her feet touched the floor. The deep blackness crept back into the walls as faint lines of a living fresco seeped out.

This was her vision onto the world.

A silhouette of the Crescent City etched its way across the walls of her bedroom—it would cover every wall on this floor, and follow her wherever she walked. A living spider web of humanity was drawn there: lines—like veins—snaked out in all directions from one central point—the curio shoppe; the cardinal points of the compass oriented across the walls; the horizon—spread all around her—sloped and rolled with the moving of the seasons and tilt of the earth; the moon—fading into its daytime slumber—showed pale, like her eyes; the sun a black disc with a thin fire-red circle around it, its path of destruction already burning across the plaster sky.

She had relied on this fresco for many years—more than she could remember. She had been confined to this building for a long time. But today—for the first time ever—something was wrong with the picture. Whole sections of it were out of focus.

Why hasn't it oriented? she wondered. It had never done this before. Not once.

She watched it with growing concern. Madame Broussard stood in the middle of her own room, protected by inner walls that would never betray her to light, hidden by outer walls that couldn't be found, and felt real concern. She hadn't felt this for many, *many* years.

She walked the perimeter of the room—her bed being in the center—watching the fresco struggle into existence. She recognized the larger landmarks: the river never really changed; the swamps were always there; the red spots on the map that marked safe feeding grounds came and went with the years, but she was used to that; the horrendous black perimeter just outside her walls was there of course, but whole sections of the map—the parts that mankind could influence—ebbed between the present day and sometime in the past.

It was as if the layers of history were being peeled back, and the fresco was trying to reflect it.

She went to a dark chifforobe that stood against a wall. Within it was a large wooden picture frame with no picture or back. She rarely used this item, as it did carry some risk, but needed a better view today. She took it to one wall and hung it from an iron hook sunk deep into the brick. There were many such hooks on the walls of the building. They all had a special purpose.

The fresco behind the frame stopped its ebb and flow and became something very close to a window. It reflected the actual scene outside the wall, appearing as a finely drawn landscape.

She stood to the side, not looking. Her eyes searched the ceiling for how long it had been since she'd used the frame window. She couldn't remember, and all she saw on the ceiling were black and white sketches of floating clouds.

After the black perimeter had been set around her, inside her building, she'd worked hard to forget what that world looked like. She learned to be satisfied with her living fresco, which until this morning, she could control to watch any time from present to past.

She didn't visit past scenes often, only when she was feeling particularly melancholy in the late hours of an October evening. She still remembered the smells of the night air when she arrived on these shores; it was a cold evening in late October and the air was rich. In many ways she considered it as her birthday in the new world. Youth and power flowing through her veins; the possibilities of the world laid bare before her.

She could never have another day like that one.

She sighed and straightened her shoulders. No use dwelling on the past. She turned and looked onto the world.

The finely drawn image of the outside world came into view. It was nearly lifelike. She was looking west, and through a combined effect of her picture frame and the fresco, she could see the well of humanity as it rushed away to the far reaches. How she longed to be free of her building and flee into the deserted lands where it was wild. At least, she thought it was still wild there.

After several minutes she moved the frame to the south wall. This counterclockwise motion always felt right to her—as if she were rolling back time. The view south was romantic. The ports were there. She could smell the briny gulf breeze as it blew through the fetid swamps. Freshly salted rotten corpses—that was the smell. At least, that was the base. There was another element beneath it all, but very few could detect it. A dark, ancient concentrate.

She'd never tasted that forbidden concentrate, but had smelled it once. It was rich and dark like nothing else, but it wasn't for humans, or for her. Tasting it would be akin to sucking the marrow from all your ancestors—no one could survive it. Nothing from *this world* could survive it. The concentrate was only for the dark thing rumored to live beyond the swamps, somewhere in the depths.

She turned from this dangerous thought and looked east.

East was bittersweet for her. An ancestry, long and heralded lay far away to the east. She had family there once—many years ago. She wondered if any of them remembered her.

Looking this direction, the image in the fresco-window was badly distorted. The source of the disturbance was close. The sketched buildings sagged and twisted; the horizon tilted wildly; the black sun disc slid backwards and to one side as if it were being pulled off its trajectory by a great force.

Why is this happening? What is causing it?

Her hand went quickly to her black pearl necklace. She stroked it lovingly; nervously.

Who is causing this?

Had Mr. Scarmish returned? Was he trying to penetrate her protective prison cell? Had he seen past the hiding spell?

She cautiously removed the frame and walked to the north wall. She knew the disturbance had centered here before she hung it. By the time she'd made her counterclockwise rotation, the fresco had nearly disappeared from this wall. Pulled into the depths of plaster, the faint lines of the human world struggled to be seen. Something— or someone—was twisting the fabric. And whoever it was, they were close, powerful, or both.

She hung the frame on the north wall.

She stepped back in shock and stared at the image.

No. It wasn't an image. It was a nightmare. Through her frame she saw the current face of the world as it was being peeled back. But she wasn't manipulating it. She had some ability to sift through the layers of time in a vision, but it was a methodical thing—like turning the pages of a book. This was more of a molestation.

Present time—the ever-lurching forever-monster—did not give up its momentum. It was not interested in what just happened even a second ago. It only knew forward. But something—or someone—was wanting to look back. Someone was forcing the layers of time apart, peering into them, then moving on. This person could not stop the forever-monster, but they appeared to be trying to tug its tail.

The effect on the image in the frame was hellish.

Madame Broussard looked at the world outside her north wall and watched it twist and sink below the surface of the wall. What should be a gray day-scape had been wrenched away, pulled under, leaving a blank space where part of her past had once existed. A spot of sinking sand had formed on the wall behind the picture frame and disappeared everything around it. Even the stars were pulled down.

Then, her view of north was gone. Whatever magic her window frame could muster was overthrown. She watched as the sheets of time were pulled down, one by one, and what images she could make out got older and older. Suddenly they were older than the span of a normal human life. And the person kept searching.

They manipulated the scenes of time with ease—almost flagrantly. Like discarded playing cards in a drawer, the layers of time were tossed aside with abandon. They were looking for something specific, but they were being hasty. It was too fast, too dangerous, to search in such a manner. It created too much disturbance. It was sure to draw attention. It was like when she felt the rip beneath the skin just a few months—

A loud boom split the air and she screamed. The building tilted sideways, casting her backward. The shock wave caused her to lose her balance and the frame to fly from the iron peg. For a brief second the sand-trap image that had formed behind the frame traveled with it and she could see it fall toward her. Only it was no longer just a place where things disappeared. As Madame Broussard and the picture frame hit the floor, the image changed from a disappearing place, to the hint of something else. An outline was there beneath the sands of time. As the frame splintered into pieces, the thing out in space looked in and saw a woman screaming.

CHAPTER 35

"What da hell was that?" Frank yelled as he ran back to the car. "Del-bell, you alright?"

Del came out of her trance and grabbed her head. Her skull was squeezing her brain and her ears were ringing. She thought she was about to vomit.

The car rocked as Frank got in. Her face turned toward the sidewalk. She worked at convincing herself she was back in the present. She'd tranced through so many versions of this place, she wasn't sure.

Frank was speaking somewhere to her left. Her ringing ears where now pulsing to the beat of her heart. Words seeped in.

"—gotta say someth— —da hospital. —felt like— —nose—bleeding."

A handkerchief was pressed against her nose. One hand came down to hold it in place. The car began to move.

"Wait," she finally whispered. "Just give me a minute."

Frank said something again. She smelled a cigar. The ringing in her ears faded.

Whatever had just happened to her was a blur. Her mind felt scrambled. Images swirled. She'd been onto something she'd never seen before, but as fast as she'd found it, it was flying away.

"Go left." She nodded at the intersection in front of them.

Frank followed without question.

With eyes closed and hands clamped to her nose and head, Del led Frank through a series of turns which ended only a few blocks from their starting place.

"Pull over. He's right around here."

"Do you... see him?" Frank asked cautiously.

Del finally opened her eyes and laid her head back against the seat. Her nose had stopped bleeding, but she was pale.

"I saw him. He's been around that last place a lot, but..."

"But what?"

She looked at Frank. "There's something wrong with that place back there. I could see traces of him all around. He drives around the block."

"Around it? But never stops?"

She sighed. "I can't tell. He comes in from the same two directions and—"

"Well, Dauphine and Mandeville are both one-way streets."

"But then he drives around and around the block and then... well, I just lose him. He disappears into a cloud. But I think he goes somewhere inside."

Frank groaned. "Inside? Inside where?"

"Exactly. Inside where?"

The tip of Frank's cigar went around in a circle as he chewed the mouth-end. The look on her face told him she was as perplexed as he was.

"But you think he comes over here?" he coaxed.

A glimmer of light colored her face. "Yes. He almost always comes this way. I think this is where he lives."

Frank switched on the CB radio mounted beneath the dashboard. Del had never noticed it as something separate before. She thought it was just more knobs and dials.

"Are you calling for backup?"

"Just checkin' to see who's around. May need to call someone, but let's see what we—"

"Frank! There he is!"

She pointed across the street to a shambling figure walking down the backstairs of a tenement house.

Frank threw the car in gear and zipped across the street. He sat at the entrance to the alley, blocking one direction out. Spider hadn't seemed to notice their arrival.

Like a street magician, while Del was watching Spider, Frank had reached across, pulled his revolver from the glovebox and slid it into place under his arm. It was a well-practiced move.

"Are you sure dat's him?"

The car crept forward.

"Yes, I'm sure. Trust me, I—"

Frank held up his hand and nodded, but his eyes were focused forward. The signal was: *I trust you, but be quiet for now.*

Spider had just disappeared into a garage.

"We're going to lose him! I know—"

His big hand became the finger of silence.

An old garage door swung up.

Frank crept the car down the alley.

A long moment seemed to pass where Del thought nothing was

happening. She slipped into a quick trance and saw several possibilities.

"He has a gun," she said quietly.

A puff of car exhaust came out the open garage door.

"It's under his seat."

Frank crept forward.

"He's leaving!"

The black Plymouth backed out into the alley.

Frank hit the gas.

Del saw the outcome.

With perfect timing and a quick adjustment to align the bumpers, Frank braked the candy apple red convertible just as the bumpers of the two cars met. The bump was subtle, but caused Spider to jump in his seat.

Frank was out the door before Del could say anything.

"Whoa there, buddy! You just backed into me!"

He pulled the door to the Plymouth open. Spider was still looking around to see what had happened.

Del smiled watching Frank work.

The large man, normally bumbling and complacent, was all business now. He was speaking quickly and flashed a badge, which seemed to disorient Spider even further. He had a clear line of sight into the car and was deftly helping the smaller man out.

Spider tried to respond to the volley of questions Frank threw at him, but was suddenly turned and pushed against the car. With his arms locked behind him, he had no leverage against Frank's weight. A glint of metal flashed in the sun just as the handcuffs slipped around Spider's skinny wrists. Another magician's trick.

"There now," Frank said, turning the man around. "Now we can have us a chat."

Spider stammered.

Frank reached in and turned off the engine.

"You stand right there," he said. "I got to see what kind of damage you did to my car."

"What? I… I didn't even… Are you a cop?" Spider's twitchy eyes looked from Frank to Del. He wanted badly to have a cigarette. His fingers flicked an invisible lighter behind his back. He began to feel squirmy.

"Well, I showed you a badge, didn't I?" Frank asked as he sat in his own seat. Del thought she saw a quick wink.

He picked up the mic of the CB, holding it high in front of his face. Spider saw it through the windshield. Frank whispered. "Honey, just stay in da car for now. But let me know if you get any vibes." He definitely winked that time.

He backed the car up and spoke loudly. "OK, Cappin'. Here's the plate number." And he read the license plate number in a booming voice.

Spider turned a shade paler and looked up and down the alley. His foot tapped rapidly in the gravel.

"OK, let's see what kinda damage got done." Frank exited his car and walked between the two. Spider stammered a feeble protest, but the old detective was ready.

"My cappin' is gonna run down that seven, eight, six plate while we wait. Seems like it's on da wrong car. Just hang tight."

Spider stopped his protest and tried to think. *Which plate is on? 786… where is it?* He wished he could see the front or back. He was afraid he'd forgotten a step.

"Well, would you look at this." Frank was bent over looking at the back of the Plymouth. The keys he'd palmed when turning off the engine slid out from his thick fingers. One of them slipped easily into the trunk lock. Frank turned it as he said, "You got some damage here."

The trunk popped open.

"Seems your trunk lock is broke."

Spider's eyes were wide saucers.

"What do we have here?"

"Blankets?" Del asked as she joined him. "Why are there—?"

Frank already had Spider by the arm and was dragging him to the rear of the car. "What da hell you been transportin' back here?"

Red splotches crept up his face as his chest heaved. Spider stammered. "I... it's just deliveries. I—"

Frank pulled Spider close. The skinny man flopped like a rag doll. "What kind of delivery needs to be wrapped in a blanket with a pilla?"

"Oh my god. Frank, look." Del held a long brown hair between her fingers.

Spider seemed surprised to see it.

"Can you use it?" Frank asked Del.

"I'll try."

"OK, *Spider*. Where are those kids?" Frank did his best to control his anger as he pushed the stammering man toward the house.

CHAPTER 36

Jimmy sat on the short wall that surrounded the fountain and watched his reflection in the water. His pancake surprise hadn't turned out like he'd wanted. He didn't know what was wrong with Del lately, but was glad he had someone to talk to about it.

"And den she hit my face and said sumptin' was on it. But it was yust my face on dere!"

The voice spoke to Jimmy, and he considered it.

"I doan know why."

He traced his finger along a crack in the cement between the old stones.

"Maybe…"

Shadows rippled across the surface of the water. Jimmy didn't notice that they corresponded with the voice.

"Bad? I doan know."

He sat Indian style on the narrow ledge and pulled at his shoelaces. He wanted to see how long he could keep his balance.

"Maybe she a wittle bad. I fink dere bad fings in her room."

The stone maiden that stood watch over the courtyard had much to say about this. Jimmy listened.

The rippling voice was soothing.

The water looked inviting.

Jimmy saw an image beneath the surface of the water.

"Yeah."

"I doan know."

"Maybe."

He felt chill air settle around him and shivered. The water in the fountain pool looked cold. And deep. He felt sleepy looking at it.

"Yeah, and guess what? She talk to people at night."

He watched the reflection of angry clouds float in front of the sun. They reminded him of Del's dark face this morning. She had a dark face a lot of mornings. Not exactly like a monster face, more like someone in a monster movie. Maybe she *was* turning bad.

"Yeah, and den guess what? She knock me down and said I toad a joke and spiwed da soup, but I didn't tell da joke."

A cold wind blew and soothed the boy. The stone eyes of the maiden, cast in deep shadows, watched.

The water rippled.

"Wha?"

Jimmy saw something in the bottom of the pool. It glittered from an errant ray of light. He leaned forward.

The water rippled again. It tried to show him.

"What?"

He leaned further and saw Del's face in the deep pool.

The stone maiden closed her eyes.

Jimmy tumbled into the water and began to flail. He felt arms pull him down.

*

Upstairs in her bedroom, Mama D thought about the strange events of late. She'd heard about the outburst at the breakfast table this morning. After Frank and Del left, she'd spoken with Armand. They were both concerned.

"I know that girl has got herself into somethin'," she told Armand. "Problem is, I haven't been able to figure out what."

Armand stroked his moustache in thought. "Yes, I must say, I've felt an uneasy presence about young Del of late, somewhat distant."

"Mmm-hmm."

"And I don't believe she is sleeping well. The circles under her eyes. It's a bad sign you know."

She nodded.

"By the way," Armand proceeded gently. "I've been meaning to ask you, last night... the two of you were discussing something."

"Yeah, I was wonderin' when you'd ask."

He pulled at his moustache. "If it's a delicate subject..."

"I never had to worry about slippin'—although Marie's warned me about it. The power ain't in me."

"What? Why, I would think—"

She waved him off. "Frenchy, I know my limits. And to tell you the truth, I don't know if I'd want the ability to go deep. I mean, *really* deep."

"Go deep? How do you mean?"

"You heard us talkin'. At least part of it, I guess. I taught her to use the tea, like I'd been taught. It helps get started at trancin'. But Del didn't need much help. She took to it pretty quick. But it helps to keep your mind intact; not allow you to trance too deep. The more you expand your mind, the more vulnerable you become."

"Vulnerable? To what?"

She looked at him over cupped hands and considered her words.

"The Gris-gris man, he was bad business. Like I've said before, 'black business.' But as far as I know, he never went deep. John, I mean. Either he didn't know how, or couldn't do it.

"Oh, he called up that hellish spirit alright, but he had help from the spells. Now, Marie could do it, so she's said. Warned me about it. She said if you go deep, a couple of things can happen."

Armand was all ears.

"First, you start slippin'. It's already happening to Del."

"But what is it?" Armand asked. "I have no frame of reference."

"Instead of just seein' the scenes, somehow you slip *into* the scenes. You're more physically there than just by trancing. It's like going through the door instead of just lookin' in the window. You do that and you might not get back out."

"But if you do?" Armand drew slowly on his pipe.

"What? Get back out?"

Armand nodded attentively.

"If you do, you don't know what you'll bring with you. There's things beyond imagination in the deep. Who knows if man has even seen 'em before? But, there's a bigger problem."

"Bigger?"

"You create too much disturbance when you slip and go deep. You start to leave a... trail."

"Fascinating."

She sighed heavily. "Yeah, until things follow you home."

Armand considered this for a long time.

"Do you think that has happened? Has something followed our Del home?"

The woman leaned back in her chair and locked eyes with Armand. She wanted her next statement to land beyond the *fascination* part of his brain.

"I think somethin' followed her home that night from the cemetery. I think more have gathered since she's been here. Hell, I know the word is out—so to speak—because I have people asking about her abilities. If she hadn't already slipped, I'd have more customers lined up for her than she'd know what to do with.

"It can be a good livin'. She could eventually get herself a little house. But she's stubborn and thinks she knows how to handle things. I shouldn'ta given her that first customer. It was too soon. But I wanted her to see the possibilities. Wanted her to have some hope at a normal life. Whatever that might be."

Armand nodded. "Yes. I agree. Hope is a good thing. It springs eternal."

"But since then, once she started slippin', I'm more afraid that… well, she's powerful. Deep things like power. They eat it up."

Armand continue nodding as he looked out the side window. The day had suddenly grown dark.

*

Beneath the dark clouds, an eerie silence had spread across the courtyard. A cold wind rippled across the water.

Jimmy floated on the surface of the murky pool.

He had stopped flailing.

CHAPTER 37

Spider sat in his small kitchen pleading his case. "I told you, I don't know nothin' about no kids! I make deliveries. That's it."

Frank stood in the short hall that ran from the backdoor into the house. He leaned over a half-wall that gave some visibility from the kitchen. He'd been through the entire place already, and there was nothing to be found. It was a fairly clean, sparsely furnished rental.

"Deliveries for who?" Frank asked again. "You never told me a company."

"You know how it is." Spider was sweating now. "You make it where you can. A little here, a little there. I make things happen. But I'm no kiddy freak!"

"You gotta go somewhere to make your pickups and deliveries. Where's that?"

"Like I said, they're all over. People just say, 'Hey, Spider, go do this thing,' and I do the thing. Sometimes they say, 'Be here at a certain time,' and I'm there."

Spider squirmed. He flicked the invisible lighter behind his back. He needed a smoke.

"I could really use a smoke. You think you could...?" He nodded to the kitchen table.

Frank puffed his cigar, leaned forward, and blew the cloud toward the sweaty, squirmy man. "Maybe."

Spider's head rocked on a loose spring. This was torture. There was no one to tell him his next step. There was too much thinking involved. Too many possibilities for Spider to consider. The pain of resignation spread across his face.

His voice became low and conspiratorial. He glanced over his shoulder at the cabinets, leaned forward and looked down the hall, then back at Frank. "Sometimes there's special deliveries."

Frank puffed his cigar and savored the flavor. "Go on."

Spider squirmed as his legs began to scissor back and forth, back and forth.

Frank thought he was going to pee on himself.

Spider's face became a red grimace. Now the top half of his body rocked forward and back, half the speed of his legs. Veins stood out on his temples and a low groan escaped his throat.

On second thought, I think he's gonna shit himself.

Spider's legs scissored rapidly. If he didn't speak soon his head would explode. Tears welled behind his eyes. He growled low, between clenched teeth, then a change came over him. His legs slowed. His face relaxed a bit. He breathed deeply and spoke slow and calm.

"Sometimes there're special deliveries. But for those, they just call Spider directly and tell him where to be. He shows up, someone loads the car, he drives to the drop off, someone unloads the car. See ya later, alligator. Spider goes on his way."

A chill ran across Frank's neck as he listened to this new voice. He looked up and down the hall as if someone had just snuck by him.

"Who calls?"

"No names. Just a voice."

"Man or woman?"

Spider's eyes considered this briefly, but the answer came quickly. "Can't tell."

"Where do they call?"

Spider looked around with surprise. "Here, man. They call Spider here. Then he does his thing."

Frank looked around for a phone. Nothing on the hallway wall. He walked into the living room. A black phone sat on a small table next to a sofa. He picked it up, dialed a number, then dropped it in the cradle.

He stormed down the short hall toward Spider, but was interrupted by a voice at the backdoor.

"Police! Frank, are you there?" Sergeant Shelby Fontenot walked through the door.

Frank eyed Spider as if the man had just escaped a terrible punishment.

"Sergeant," Frank said, "glad to see ya." He was still staring at Spider. "Only, I wish it was under better circumstances."

Sergeant Fontenot had been on duty when Frank made the real call from his radio. The department was used to hearing him from time to time, and made him a priority to assist.

"What we got?"

Frank motioned him out onto the small back porch landing. He closed the door behind him. "A real scumbag is what we got. Officially, dat little fender-bender out there." The sergeant looked back at the two cars and scratched his head. "Unofficially, suspicion of kidnapping."

"Kidnapping?"

"Yeah, when his trunk popped open, I got a good look. Blanket and pilla in the back."

"In the trunk?"

"Uh-huh. Might find a strand of hair or two."

"The orphan kids?"

"Maybe. I've been lookin' for him for a while."

"What about inside? You look around?" the sergeant asked.

"Nothin'." Frank looked disappointed.

The sergeant considered the situation. He walked down the steps and inspected the cars. "Fender bender?"

Frank was relighting. "Musta' felt harder than what it was. But da trunk popped right open."

"You don't say? Well, that was fortunate."

Frank shrugged.

Shelby Fontenot inspected the trunk. "No spare. Just a damn pilla and blanket. Pretty suspicious to me, Frank. I can sweat him for a day, and get a couple guys to canvas the block, but if nothing turns up…"

"I know da routine. Do what you can, and I'll keep lookin'."

The sergeant called for another squad car, then went to retrieve Spider. Del joined Frank at his car.

"What's gonna hap—?"

"You got da hair still?" Frank interrupted.

"What? Yeah, it's—"

"Leave part of it."

"What?"

He walked to the open door of the Plymouth and discretely tossed the keys onto the driver seat.

"That may be da only piece of evidence they find. So, they need to find it. But keep some for…" Frank whistled and wiggled his fingers.

"OK, got it." Del approached the trunk, then hesitated. She looked back at Frank, who was already opening his door.

He cleared his throat with a puff of cigar smoke. "Hrrr-onda-pilla!"

Del nodded and dropped half of the strand of hair on the pillow and tucked the other half in her pocket. The sergeant and Spider exited the back door just then. Del began a leisurely stroll toward Frank's car, whistling off key.

Under his breath, Frank said, "OK, Sherlock, let's go," and started the engine.

He waved a salute at the sergeant as they drove off. "I'll consider charges once I assess the damage!" he called out over his shoulder.

Spider looked confused.

Frank drove slowly down the street, blowing puffs of smoke above his head. His thick arm hung out the window as he considered the day's events. Del leaned her head back and allowed herself a brief smile as the sun emerged from behind a cloud. She thought maybe she'd like to be a detective now, more than a reporter.

"So, what'dya think?" she said. The pressure of questions being too great to hold in. "He's our guy, right? What now? I thought the kids would be there. I—"

The pointer finger of Frank's driving hand stopped her. Deep bags had settled beneath his eyes. He yawned and rubbed his stubbled chin.

"You did good, Del-bell." He nodded at her. "Real good. I wouldn't have found him by myself. And I know it wasn't easy on you." Here he considered his words. "You know, with whatever happened dis morning while you were…" He wiggled his fingers again.

"Why do you always do that?" she asked. "You can say the word you know? It's just trancing."

"Yeah, OK. Just trancin'. Anyway, whatever happened, well… I can't help you with it, but you talk to Mama D so you don't get yerself… tripped up. OK?"

"Yeah, sure, but what about—?"

"Like I said, you did good. But uh… you need to prepare yourself for… well, I don't think we're findin' those kids."

"What? Why not? We got the guy. I'm sure of it, Frank! I know—"

Frank pulled to the side of the street and looked at Del. "Da phone was out."

She blinked the information, slowly, to the back of her brain. "What? The phone?"

"Yep. The phone he said he got calls on, how he got his pickup and delivery orders? The special ones. That phone don't work. It's dead."

"Well… maybe it's just been turned off."

"It wasn't even plugged in. The wall connection is just loose wires hangin' out. No phone would work in that place."

Del looked around the car as if the answer had just slipped away into the shadows.

"But he said! He said he got calls! How can—?"

"If he's getting calls, they're in his head. That, or a ghost is callin' him."

Del deflated slightly. She looked at the scuffs on the toe of her boot.

"But listen here. Dis thing ain't over yet. We got a guy that can be held for twenty-four hours on suspicion, but maybe longer based on what's in da car. Dat's a lot more than what we had dis mornin'."

"I'm gonna go home and get a nap, shower and shave, then we'll meet up later. But, I thought maybe you'd like to celebrate your first successful manhunt." He pointed across the street to the Ice Cream Emporium. "I can pick you up later."

Del grabbed the rearview mirror and looked at herself. "Oh my god, where'd these circles come from?"

Frank was confused.

"Well, honey, it's just ice cream. I'll go in a get you—"

"No!" she pushed the mirror halfway back in place. "No, that's OK. I'll go in by myself."

"It's no trouble."

"Really. It's OK. You know, I think I would like to celebrate a bit. That's a good idea, actually."

Frank and his cigar suspected they were being conned, but didn't see the angle. "OK. You need a little money?"

"No, thanks." Del had stepped onto the sidewalk and was closing the door. "I'm an independent woman. I got it covered."

Frank wished he were a better detective during some of his conversations with Del.

"How 'bout I come back around—" He held his watch out as far as his arm would go.

"Don't worry about it. I can make it home from here. A long walk might do me good. There's some things I want to sort out anyway."

He eyed her closely, but knew she was more than capable of making it home. He yawned again and blinked through the smoke.

"OK, then. It's about one o'clock now. I'll run back by here around four, just in case. But if you're not here, I'm gonna assume you went straight home, so I'm gonna drive to Armand's, den—"

"Frank, I got it." She was in front of the car waiting to cross the street. "I'll be OK."

"Well, OK then. See you tonight."

He watched Del run across the street and skip onto the sidewalk.

CHAPTER 38

By the time Del's foot hit the sidewalk, she'd forgotten about Frank. She was taking a mental inventory of herself. She slapped her cheeks lightly and adjusted her headband. She checked her reflection in the window of the clothes shop, next to the Ice Cream Emporium. The window was dirty and had a glare from the sun, but from what she could tell everything looked fine.

What if he's not working?

She stood with her back to the wall. She didn't want to go in yet. She looked across the street and noticed Frank slowly pulling away.

Why is she standing there? he thought.

Why is he watching me? she thought back.

Frank started to stop.

"See ya!" Del waved and pretended to stretch her legs. She wasn't sure why she'd picked this activity.

Frank eyed her curiously as he crept his car into the street.

She's actin' kinda funny just for gettin' some damn ice cream.

She knelt and checked her shoelaces.

A horn blared at Frank and he dismissed them with a wave of his cigar. They needed to be patient. He took one final look, then drove away.

She stood up slowly and checked her clothes.

She wondered if she should peek first.

Don't be stupid. Just go in.

She took a deep breath, counted to three, then walked into the cool, sweet air.

A pair of brown eyes looked up from behind the counter. Johnathan shot her a quick smile and went back to scooping.

She wandered in and looked around. There were a few open tables. Thankfully, the group of teens weren't here, but if they came in, the snotty girls might see something unpleasant in their ice cream, she thought.

Del waited patiently for the grandmother in front of her to count out her final pennies. Meanwhile, the granddaughter eyed her up and down.

"What flavor did you get?" Del asked her.

"Strawberry," the girl said quietly.

"Mmm, that sounds—"

"Are you a witch?"

Del wondered if she heard her correctly. "What? I... uh..."

"You look like a witch."

"Girl, watch your mouth!" the grandmother scolded her. "Go sit down and hush up."

She snapped her purse shut and pulled two small napkins from the dispenser. "Sorry," she said, turning toward Del. "She—"

The woman stopped in mid-sentence. A look of surprise flashed over her face before she collected herself and politely tucked it away.

She pulled her purse close and turned quickly away.

She walked to the table and sat down, pushing the staring girl's face toward the street. The woman stole another look over her shoulder—which caused her to unconsciously lean away from Del—then inched her chair a bit closer to the window.

Del had no idea what that was about.

"Hey, how have you been?" Johnathan said with his back turned. He was quickly putting items back in place. "I was just getting ready to take a break, do you want to—"

He turned around.

His eyes told a different story than what they had promised when she walked in. A flicker of confusion ran through them.

The seconds began to tick.

Why doesn't he say something?

The silence seemed very long.

He doesn't recognize me.

He thought I was someone else when I walked in.

She saw his eyes searching. He inspected the details of her face.

"Uh, Del, right?"

She forced the best smile she could, but suddenly feared it would squeeze tears out instead.

"Yeah. Johnathan, right?"

"Yeah." He regained some composure. "Yeah, you were in the other day, right?"

"Mmm-hhmm." Hot blood crept up her cheeks. Then she added, "Yesterday or the day before, I don't really remember."

The lights seemed too bright suddenly. Why had she come in? This was a mistake. She felt like running out the door.

"Well, like I said, I'm going on break now. Do you want something?

I'll put it on my break meal."

Del's appetite for ice cream had disappeared within the last thirty seconds. She'd planned on sampling a few more flavors, but that didn't seem like a good idea right now. She couldn't even remember what she'd tried last time. "Strawberry, I guess," she said, borrowing from the little staring girl.

"OK, see if there's a table open outside. I'll be right out."

Del turned and walked to the door. The grandmother corrected the girl's staring face again.

A table was open to the right of the door as she exited. She took the far seat and waited. She chewed a nail and drummed a leathery rhythm onto the concrete. Skipping down the sidewalk towards her were two girls, their mothers trailing. The girls were drinking orange sodas, and Del suddenly felt thirsty. Her mouth was coated with something sticky, and her tongue felt too big for her mouth. She needed water. She thought about going back in, but Johnathan exited just then with two cones.

"I only have fifteen minutes, but it's good to see you again. I was hoping you'd come by."

Del tested the ice cream. Her stomach was unsettled. "Really? Why?"

He dug into his waffle cone with abandon.

No problem with his *stomach.*

Through a mouthful of cone, he mumbled, "I don't know, I thought you were cool. Not like the gossip girls that usually come in."

Well, that was something, she thought.

Del wanted to tell him that he had chocolate on his lip but was waiting to see if he'd lick it off or wipe it away.

"Sorry about earlier," he was saying.

She realized he was just a few shades lighter than his ice cream, but it was from his tan. He must work another job, outside, she thought. *He glows. He's his own shade of bronze.*

"Sometimes the lights in there play tricks. I guess I didn't realize you were older when you came in before. It was pretty busy that day and—"

What did he say?

He took another large bite. He was halfway down the cone already, still mumbling. Maybe she'd misheard him.

"But that's cool too. You probably know all the hot spots already."

Hot spots? Like bars?

Del stared into the street. How old did he think she was, anyway? How old did she look?

"...just graduated in May, but I'm almost eighteen. I started late because..."

I'm only eighteen! she wanted to say. What the hell was he thinking? And what's a few months anyway? Why would that—?

He thinks I'm a lot older.

She suddenly understood the problem.

Do I look that much older?

"...maybe... if you wanted..."

She halfway wished Frank would pull up. But that would only make the conversation more awkward. She looked down the street just in case.

"Whoa! Wicked scars. How'd you get those?" He was staring at the left side of her neck.

Turning to look down the street, Del had exposed the fresh scars that ran from behind her neck, out across her collar bone. Scars of her wonderful gift.

Her hand covered them instinctively.

"Did you get mauled by a bear or something?

Mauled?

This wasn't turning out anything like she'd expected. The stress of little sleep and extended trancing suddenly crashed over her, and all she wanted to do was go home and go to bed.

"No," she said, her voice hurting. "They're just scratches."

Water welled behind her eyes as ice cream dripped over her fingers and onto her lap. She couldn't look at him because of her stupid watery eyes and she couldn't wipe her eyes without exposing her scars or her messy hand.

Johnathan crushed his napkins into a tight ball and made a three-foot swish into the trash can.

"Hey, I didn't mean anything by it. I just thought there was an interesting story or—"

"I have to go," she said, standing up.

"Oh." He stood quickly, but didn't know what needed to come next.

She watched his feet shuffle beneath the black metal weave of the table. The awkward seconds stretched out.

Finally, he said, "OK. Yeah, I guess I need to get back to—"

"Thanks for the ice cream."

She sent half a smile at him, afraid anything more would knock the tears loose, then turned away.

She heard the grate of a chair leg against concrete and thought he may be coming after her. She didn't know if she wanted him to or not.

"Can I call you?" he said quickly. "Maybe we—"

Her stupid hand was a dripping mess. Her scars felt like they were glowing red on the back of her neck. She slid her left hand further back to cover them. Then the water behind her eyes finally broke loose. She couldn't even turn around to give him a number.

"Phone's out," she called over her shoulder. "I'll see you later."

She hurried away, watching her ice cream melt. It dripped onto her boots as she walked.

CHAPTER 39

Madame Broussard paced her showroom. She stopped and rearranged the items on the display table, again.

Where is he?

She circled the table twice more, then stopped.

This is ridiculous. Just go find him!

She *could* find him. It had been a very long time since she'd had to resort to that, but she could still do it.

And it wasn't even an issue of *if* she could do it, more of, *should* she do it?

She sat down and straightened her pearls. The day had started poorly and gone downhill from there. The disturbance this morning had her on edge. Whatever force had played tricks with her fresco demanded her attention. No one knew of her location, and for someone to suddenly locate her and start pulling at the fabric of the spell that concealed her, well, that would have to be dealt with swiftly.

The other issue, which at the moment was only an inconvenience, but could also become a major problem, was locating and training a new delivery person.

That wasn't easy.

It was hard to find exactly the right mentality.

Finally, she looked at the broken frame leaning against the wall—issue number three. It would take time to repair, but it would have to wait.

No one had looked for her for years. Why now?

The black perimeter was still in place around her hiding spot—and would likely never go away—so no one had to worry about her getting out. Likewise, the building had its own motivation to stay hidden—and survive—so she didn't have to worry about someone getting in.

Or did she?

She sat down in a large chair next to the display table and considered this last thought.

Some people got in—*the little ones.*

But she wanted them in.

They could be coaxed into just the right dream-state to slip through one of her shadow portals—which she kept closely guarded. But the secret to those portals was only known to her and the building that housed her—she had to delegate some duties, after all. Beyond that, nothing got through.

The few people she'd dealt with—that actually *saw* the inside of her showroom—had more cause to keep her secret than to expose her. So, she doubted it was them. And there was no one actively hunting her any longer—well, there was no one left to pay the bounties; the church had exhausted those funds a long time ago—so who did that leave?

Her fingers absently traced a finger bone of Alvie Foreshaw. After Mr. Scarmish's terrible behavior, what was left of him had been rolled onto a rug and lifted onto the showcase table. He was fragile, but the remains still had value. His clothes had burnt off or disintegrated. The skin had shrunk so tightly around the frail cage of bones it had nearly torn away in several places. Most of it was stuck to the bones the way detritus from a hurricane sticks to whatever remains standing. Paper thin shards, dried hard, pointing in the direction of the retreating wind. Only in Alvie's case, all skin-shards pointed inward—except at the base of his skull.

She inspected the finger bone she had been tapping on the table. Since the time of Alvie's unfortunate encounter, she hadn't truly inspected the remains. The whole mass of him seemed to have... shrunk. Even the bones were smaller. It was as if some great force had compressed him to two-thirds his original size.

What had Scarmish said? 'He's nothing but sinew and string'?

How apropos. It would take a lot of string to put Alvie back together again.

She filed the thought away and walked to the phone. She would try her contact one more time.

*

Block after block slid past Del and her running thoughts. She had already ditched the melting ice cream, licked her fingers clean and set her pace to a fast walk. She was vaguely aware of her location, but knew instinctively that she was heading towards the river. A landmark she could always navigate from.

She turned a corner and the sounds and smells of Jackson Square assaulted her. The square sat in front of the St. Louis Cathedral and stretched towards the Mississippi River. Covering a full city block in size, the square was sided by wide cobblestone streets that doubled as pedestrian walkways. The four sides surrounded a central park and a large bronze statue of a man on a horse. Large live oaks grew in the park and stretched their massive limbs above the streets, creating a kaleidoscope of skittering sun patches. There, under the shifting shade were dozens and dozens of painters displaying their creations; some good, some... interesting.

A deep courtyard extended from the majestic granite steps of the cathedral and transitioned to grass on one side of the park. Here, several groups of musicians had gathered and broken into impromptu renditions of blues, jazz or ragtime songs.

The food vendors were working overtime, supplying patrons with all manner of treats: fried catfish, hushpuppies, hotdogs, and powdered-sugar beignets served in small paper bags.

Two open benches sat on the side of the courtyard, one bathed in warm sunlight, the other sinking into deep shade. Del moved toward the first, but her scars flared in protest. She suddenly wished she'd worn a collared shirt, but doubted it would have mattered. The shadows invited her to the other bench.

She curled her knees tight against her chest and leaned back. She watched no one in particular, but felt as an outsider to everyone. It seemed that each person in the park had a part to play: some were there to make music, some to sell goods, while others brought laughter and squeals, and a few brought natural beauty, freely sharing it with anyone fortunate enough to look at them.

Del's hand slipped up to her neck and rested there. She had supplied the scars and shadows. In her own way, by making the edges darker, the other things looked brighter. Maybe that was her role.

After several minutes, the people around her blurred. The sounds faded to white noise. The scars of the day disappeared. She slipped into a trance and started to explore.

She saw herself sitting on the bench. This spot was as safe as any, she thought, and wouldn't require much balance work. It had just been a few days since she'd learned she could trance while standing. Maintaining her body's balance while floating around in a vision had been a major trick, but this would be easy. She would just go exploring.

She reversed the scenes of her journey to the park. She watched herself walking, seemingly at random, but in jerky backwards steps. The backwards motion was disturbing; like her life unwinding, or being *undone*. Normally, she picked a moment in time and watched it run forward to another point in time. But what if she tried to watch her life run back to the beginning? Could she do that?

On the park bench, her body shivered with the cold thought. Even if it could be done, it didn't seem like a good idea.

Her backwards steps were now heading towards the ice cream shop, where Johnathan stood on the sidewalk, watching her leave. She decided to skip over the next ten minutes. No sense reliving that.

Now she was in the car with Frank, driving backward, cigar smoke running against the wind to recollect at the tip of his cigar or stream into his mouth.

There was Spider's apartment; the telephone rang in the background. She replaced the hair on the pillow. Frank dropped the keys in the seat. Frank and the other officer were speaking on the back stoop. The telephone rang again. Frank searched the apartment. They walked backwards down the steps and looked into the trunk for the first time.

Del froze the scene in her head. Something picked at her mind for attention, then it dawned on her. She didn't remember the telephone ringing when they were there before.

What had Frank said about the phone?

She sped forward through the scenes. Frank had said, *"If he's getting calls, they're in his head. That, or a ghost is callin' him."*

She went back one more scene, but heard Frank's voice again.

"It wasn't even plugged in. The wall connection is just loose wires hangin' out. No phone would work in this place."

The phone rang again.

The phone's ringing! Why didn't we hear it when we were there? How could we have missed—?

Suddenly she understood. The phone is ringing *now!*

Her mind snapped forward to the present time. She didn't consider how she got there. It just happened. But she was back at Spider's apartment—in present time—and the phone was ringing!

She watched the empty apartment from outside the scene. No one had returned. And there was only one phone. It sat on a table next to the old couch. She looked closely and saw the phone line snake out the back of the base. It hung to the floor, then stretched toward the wall; there it ended. It wasn't even close to the frayed wires protruding from the baseboard. It was connected to nothing, but it rang anyway.

Del suddenly realized the person they were looking for was on the other end of the line.

CHAPTER 40

Snapping out of her trance, Del saw the day had grown late. The groups of musicians had changed; some were gone completely. The painters were packing up. The shadows had grown long.

How long had she been sitting here? Her mind told her she'd just sat down. However, her body ached in response as she stood up. A stiffness was in her joints, and one leg was asleep. Stinging nettles of pain ran up her leg when she shifted her weight. It made her limp awkwardly. She felt old and tired.

Maybe I do look old, she thought. A nap sounded good right now.

She limped through the thinning crowds, wiggling her foot and inspecting the paintings. The people were generally busy gathering their items, but some looked up when she approached, hoping to land a final sale. Their expressions were all the same. Each one, upon seeing Del, had a flash of surprise run across their face, their eyes widened, then they turned away.

Every response was the same.

What's wrong with these people?

It was as if a black aura suddenly hung around her that everyone could see but her. She wished she'd worn her old jean jacket suddenly. There was comfort in being covered with layers.

She left the square and quickened her pace. The sun was sinking, and Frank may be at Armand's house already. He'd want to hear what she had discovered about the telephone.

She soon forgot about the staring people from the park, but they would remember her. From time to time—even late into their own lives—they'd shake their heads and think back to this day. "*That poor girl,*" they'd say, "*I wonder what was wrong with her?*"

*

Frank's car was sitting in the driveway when she arrived back at the house. She smiled, anticipating a warm bath, a hearty dinner and lively banter. Washing away the stress of the day was just what she needed.

She bounded up the back steps and through the door.

"Hey, Frank," she said, "guess what I—"

Three solemn faces turned to greet her.

"What's wrong?" she said immediately. She closed the door quietly.

"Good God!" Mama Dede struggled up from her chair. "What happened to you?"

Del stared in confusion. "I walked back from—"

"And where you been? We got worried." Mama D grabbed Del's chin, turning her face from side to side.

"What?" Del pulled away. She felt all the eyes in the room study her. The *oddity* status had returned.

"Come here." Mama D led Del by the arm out of the kitchen and into the foyer. Positioning her in front of a mirror, she turned the girl toward her own reflection. "Girl, what are you doing?"

Del stared in disbelief at the image before her. It was her staring back, but she looked terrible. She blinked, trying to refocus the image, but it didn't change.

Over the last few hours, a thin film of age seemed to have crept over her.

The dark circles under her eyes had grown worse. She looked like she hadn't slept in days. Her normally glowing brown skin had an ashen-gray tint to it. Her eyes had a dull luster—as if cataracts were forming. But the most disturbing thing was the dried blood. Two small streams had formed, one from each nostril, and stopped at her top lip.

No wonder why everyone had stared at her. She'd walked home looking like someone dying of a terrible disease.

"Come on." The woman pulled her to the nearest bathroom and turned on the water. "Wash up. We got things to talk about."

Del tested the temperature and let the water fill her cupped hands. "I know what you're going to say." She washed the blood trails from her face. "I'll take it easy after we find the kids. But I just found another—"

"Jimmy had an accident." Mama Dedé dropped a towel in Del's hands, turned and left.

Del snapped the water off. She trailed the woman closely, drying her face. "What accident? Is he OK? When—?"

"Sit down." Mama D pointed to a chair.

Obediently, Del took her seat. She felt like she had just entered an interrogation room; Frank and Armand sitting as quiet witnesses to the proceedings.

The older woman stood with her back turned at a long row of cabinets. "Jimmy almost drowned today." She spoke with a methodical cadence, her hands busy with other tasks. "After you left, he spent a lot of time in the courtyard."

"But how did he—?"

A heavily ringed hand raised and stopped Del's inquiry. Having pulled several tin canisters from a cabinet, the woman began mixing herbs in a granite mortar and pestle. "It seems he was pretty upset about something that'd happened at breakfast."

Del tried to sink into the kitchen chair, but there was nowhere to go. Frank and Armand pretended to inspect their smoking paraphernalia.

"He said he was talkin' to the lady in the courtyard, but there was no one there." Mama D turned and carried a tea set to the table. "At least, not that we saw."

She nodded at Armand, then focused on Del. "Jimmy said he saw you in the water of the big fountain. That you were starin' up at him."

She placed a cup in front of Del and took the seat next to her. "He said he thought someone pushed him in, but wasn't sure. What he is sure of—at least he thinks he is—is that you grabbed him while he was in the water and tried to pull him down."

Del's mouth fell open as fresh tears appeared on her lids. She looked from one person to the next, but no words came to her. She blinked in disbelief, waiting for someone to defend her. Surely, they didn't believe this! Everyone knew that she'd never hurt Jimmy. Didn't they?

"If it hadn't been for Armand walkin' outside when he did…" The woman shook her head slowly.

Armand cleared his throat. "We were very fortunate today." He absently stroked his beard. "I'm happy to say that he is resting comfortably upstairs."

"I want to go see him." Del started to leave.

Mama Dedé motioned her down. "No. There's a few other things we need to talk about first."

Del's jaw clenched as the tears spilled over her lids. "You don't think—!"

"Psshh! Girl, what's wrong with you? I don't think you had any more to do with it than I think Frank's gonna grow wings and fly away!"

Frank frowned and looked at Armand for support.

"But I DO think that you in somethin' way over your head, so you need to listen now."

Del leaned back in her chair with arms crossed. She rocked rapidly, like an overwound spring drove her legs. She couldn't hide her flexing jaw and didn't care to try.

"You wanna' know why you look like death warmed over?" Mama D said.

Del felt a sharp sting, remembering Johnathan's surprise at the ice cream shop.

"'Cause you're either goin' too long, or you're goin' too deep. I don't know which, but I warned you about that already."

Her hand went up instinctively before Del could argue. With a pointed finger she said, "You wanna know why your nose is bleedin'? Too long, or too deep." Then the woman's voice quieted, and she leaned in. "But you wanna know why somethin' almost pulled Jimmy down today? Or why you been seein' *things* on his face?"

Del looked up in surprise.

"Yeah, I know about that too. Or why the shadows are gettin' deeper?"

A heavy silence fell over the room. Only an old, cantankerous clock could be heard ticking away the world's remaining time.

Del wiped her eyes and dropped her hands into her lap as the many eyes in the room inspected her transgressions. Maybe they were waiting for her horns to appear. She stared at the teacup with a dull focus. The cold shadows of the park scratched at her mind.

"You went too deep. And I think you made a crease."

CHAPTER 41

The black outline of Mr. Scarmish began to etch itself onto the glass mirror. Madame Broussard stood at the podium of her showroom, hoping the spell would hold. Small tracers of lightning-fire smoked and sparked as his face came into existence. He'd been *invited* again—everyone had to be invited—but the precautions were much stricter this time.

Instead of the full doorway and seating area that had been made available to him previously, this time he was restricted to nothing more than a large mirror. His feet would never touch the floor. His hands would not reach outside their designated area. His black spiked tongue would do no harm tonight. In fact, the precautions were so strict, he barely qualified as being *present*. It was more of a long-distance impression of him that was twisting into existence with its deadly fire.

As long as the spell holds, she thought. But it was too late to worry the small details.

The large silver mirror that contained him had rarely been used. It was a special device the woman had carried with her when she made the journey to these shores. The age of the devise was unknown. It was from the old country. Its original use had been lost to the ages, but its unique ability to facilitate communications over a long distance was a layer of protection she was happy to have right now.

The three-dimensional shadow-face had been forming for several minutes before the fire began on the surface of the mirror. It was as if he were far away in time and space, stretched spaghetti-thin, beyond reason, and was struggling to find his way back. Maybe if he never found his way back, that wouldn't be such a terrible thing, she thought. Although, it was good to have such powerful customers from time to time.

The sparks subsided and the shadow-face seemed to consider the barrier in front of it. The outline of the face glowed a dark orange amongst a swirling cloud that stretched backward into oblivion. The eyes were dark holes where small lightning storms flickered in the distance.

"Are they ready?" A hollow voice vibrated throughout the room. The surface of the mirror appeared to warp slightly with each syllable.

"Not quite," she said, touching her black pearl necklace. "We have a problem."

The face twisted. It looked like a Picasso. The eyes were in the wrong place. The head stretched in multiple directions, throbbing, processing her words. From far in the distance, long smoke-tendrils streamed toward the thin glass surface. Maybe the eyes were in the top of the head now. She couldn't tell.

The smoke-body crowded the mirror. Its weight gathered at the surface. The tension on the glass increased.

"Problem?" The air vibrated. "What problem do *we* have?"

The sound was inside her head now. Somewhere deep in her mind. Her pale skin tightened into tiny bumps.

Lightning-fire flickered and licked at the glass. It spread slowly across the surface—as if searching for a way out.

She kept her composure, but watched the structure of the mirror closely. "The supply chain has been compromised," she said.

"'Compromised'?" The mirror rattled against the brick wall.

"We always knew the supply chain was a risk," she said, "especially given my... well, under my current circumstances."

"'Current circumstances'?" The smoke roiled. The face had dissolved back into the toxic cloud, but the eyes remained. The many eyes of Mr. Scarmish looked in all directions. Lightning-vision flashed from across eons, smoky gray, burning red, then white hot. The glass surface distorted where one of the eyes pressed against it and a tiny spark popped from its surface—*into the room*—and fizzled away with a crazy snake-tendril of smoke. The eye looked deeply at her.

"You're a relic!" The voice shook the building. "That's *your* circumstance. And your value to me is nearly depleted!"

She gripped the edge of the wooden podium and red nails, hard as steel, gouged deeply into the cringing wood.

The coppery taste of blood from the inside of her own lip caused her pupils to dilate. She'd bitten herself in her anger. Her nostrils flared as her senses went into overdrive.

"We have a bigger issue than just a broken supply—"

"I need more root stock!" The deadly wind of Mr. Scarmish rushed at the mirror surface. Two more sparks popped free. "I'm close to finding—"

"I think a Spirit Hunter has found me."

"WHAT?" The twisting hurricane of energy slowed as the question echoed in the chamber. "It can't be." Lightning-eyes searched the room for the truth.

"It is." Then she added quietly, "I'm fairly certain, anyway."

"'Fairly certain'? 'Fairly certain'?! Well, are you, or aren't you?! Do I need to—"

"Mr. Scarmish! Don't presume to question me in my own home. Especially when you rely on the very sustenance *I* provide!"

"Graahhh! Foolish woman." A red cloud swirled behind the glass. "You provide nothing I can't find somewhere else."

She slammed her hand on the podium, cracking the heavy wood. "Remember that you *exist* because of me!"

"Exist? I'll show you what your world would be without my—"

"You'll do nothing that I don't allow!"

Here, she raised her clinched hands and began to chant. The steel-hard fingernails had already pierced her palms and the blood ran freely down her wrists. Suddenly, her fingers sprung open, spraying droplets of blood into the room, and the old walls drank what they could.

The Scarmish shadow froze and waited to be expelled from the viewing mirror. But she had something else in mind.

She stepped from around the podium, blood dripping from her fingertips. The chant filled the room and the room obeyed.

"BOY!" she yelled, holding out her right hand.

Something moved in the shadows.

"What? What did you say?" The voice came from the mirror. It was no longer in her head. Many eyes floated near the edge of the glass, looking, straining to see what was happening.

A wind started up and ruffled the pages of an open book. Candle flames cowered. The building awoke. And somewhere outside, the faded sign above the door that no one could see began to move.

"What are you doing?" Scarmish demanded.

Madame Broussard stood before the mirror, but stared far beyond it. Her rage blinded her to the present. She saw into her past, remembering a time of greatness, and longed for it again.

From out of the shadows, Willy, dirty, starving and hypnotized beyond fear, walked toward her.

It was a slow, shambling walk. He limped slightly on his right leg. His tears had long since been exhausted, and all he could do now was excrete a sour smell of fear. The last real memory he had was of wanting to save a little girl from a dark place. But he couldn't remember her name. A trickle of urine snuck out, but didn't even make it to his leg. He was nearly dried up. A quivering lip was the only outward sign he comprehended his fate.

The wind swirled, mixing the odors. Like so many times before, no droplet would be lost. The building had to be fed as well. The sign rocked.

"Wait! What are you doing?" The face in the mirror pleaded, but it sounded far away. A Scarmish-dream pestered her, but she was focused on only one thing.

Her nostrils flared again.

With one quick move, she snatched the boy up by the throat with one hand, twisting him toward the mirror, and sunk her teeth into the side of his neck.

"NOOO!!!!" Scarmish screamed. "Don't waste him!"

The boy's reflection contorted in pain as his eyes rolled back in his head. He appeared to be floating in mid-air. No sign of his suspension was reflected. His arms and legs did not flail, nor did they break off. He was thicker than Alvie and his consumer was more controlled—in some ways. But she still grunted with the same gluttonous, wet sound.

"I NEED HIIIMM!" The mirror rattled again. "What are you dooo-iiinnngggg?"

Madame Broussard released her bite and threw her head back.

"AAAHHHHhhhh!" she bellowed. "I feed… because I am…"

She stared at Scarmish with her own glowing eyes.

"ELEMENTAALLLLL!"

The sign rocked wildly outside, screaming at the night.

The smoke in the mirror flashed red and black as Scarmish screamed out in anger.

Everyone screamed.

Except Willy.

CHAPTER 42

F rank looked at Armand with the question of what to do next. It was his house after all, and these women were a part of it. Besides, he didn't like the sound of Del having made a *crease*. Whatever that was.

Armand stood up, trying to capture a fleeting thought. There was something here that would help lighten the mood. He searched for the thought with his nimble fingers, randomly dancing the air. He muttered to himself as he walked. "Let's see... chair, counter, sink, dishes... no, not dishes, counter, cabinet. Yes, of course!" He spun around. "Would anyone like a cookie?"

Mama Dedé, Frank and Del all looked at him with varying degrees of question on their faces. The elder woman questioned the timing; Del, the appropriateness; Frank wondered what flavor.

Armand took down an old cookie jar from the cabinet and said, "Almond windmill," then turned toward the foyer. "They go quite well with an apple brandy I've been wanting to open." He disappeared through the door trailing smoke.

"Well, in dat case." Frank was up and heading towards the door.

Mama Dedé huffed. "We ain't had supper yet!"

"Come, come," called Armand from the staircase. "A change of location is in order. And perhaps Del would like to take one to Jimmy."

Del sprung up like a jack-in-the-box. "Good idea!" She bolted through the door and passed Frank before he reached the stairs.

"Damn!" the woman muttered. "Apple brandy fools!" She gathered the tea tray, then went to the cabinet and added a small bottle. "Besides, everyone knows amaretto goes better anyway."

As Frank settled into his usual chair in the second-floor library, Del returned from Jimmy's room.

"He was sleeping, so I left the cookie on the nightstand."

"That's good." Mama D handed her a cup of tea. "This'll perk you up." Del took it and sat on the loveseat by the rail.

Armand stood behind his worktable, inspecting stacks of papers. Smoke curled above his head and seemed to dance merrily off his wild hair. With his beard and moustache, Del suddenly thought Armand would make a good Santa Claus. Actually, Frank and Armand together, squished into one body would be perfect. She looked at Frank and saw that the brandy had already warmed his cheeks.

Yep. Perfect.

Why the thought had come to her, she didn't know. She'd never thought of it before—and hadn't thought fondly of Christmas for many years. Would they all still be together in this house for the holidays? Had Jimmy ever known a real Christmas before?

Presents! How would she afford presents?

Old anxieties tried to surface, but she pushed them back down. She'd think about that later. She still needed a job, but right now she just wanted to enjoy the evening. The last several days had been a rollercoaster. She sipped her tea.

"Mmmm," Frank munched a cookie that he'd dipped into his brandy. He then looked at his cigar, dipped the end into the same glass and put it in his mouth. Savoring and puffing, he inspected the combined flavors.

"MMMM!" He was quite pleased with the combination.

"Frank," Mama Dedé said, "try to keep it to a low moan." She'd joined him, taking the chair facing the fireplace. "Me and my amaretto would like a quiet evening in front of the fire."

She turned towards Armand. "That's a nice fire you built Armand. I like a nice fire."

Frank snuck a dip of his cigar into her glass of amaretto and inspected the new flavor combination.

Armand caught the quick movement of the amaretto thief; his eyebrows betrayed his surprise.

"Frank, why can't you build a nice fire like—?"

She caught the look on Armand's face and spun on Frank. "What-he-do?" She inspected herself quickly as if expecting to find an errant stain. "What'd you do?"

Frank settled back into his chair and puffed. Instead of drooping like a dog-ear, his cigar stood proud like a peacock. His grin was wide.

The elder woman picked up her glass and eyed him suspiciously. "I'm watchin' you." She sipped the liqueur, then blinked in surprise. Something wet and slimy hung from her lip.

She sputtered and spit. "Ooo... Blech! What is that?" She pulled a stringy mass off her lip and held it in the air. A small strand of tobacco from the cut end of Frank's cigar had peeled away and stuck to the rim of her glass.

"You stuck that nasty thing in my amaretto? What's wrong with you?"

Frank smiled on. With a poor French accent, he said, "Ze flavor profile iz ex-qui-zet! Mon sherry!" Then he winked.

"Psshh!" She waved him off. "Damn..." She picked at the rim of her glass looking for remnants. "...that was the last of my amaretto..."

Del's teacup clanked loudly as her head nodded forward. "Oh!" she said, sitting up and rubbing her eyes. "Woo. I thought you said this would perk me up?" She yawned and shook her head. "It's not working very well."

Mama Dedé set her glass down and pointed at Frank, "I just put a spell on it. If you touch it again your thing will fall off."

She didn't wait for a response. Hefting herself out of the chair, she left Frank to ponder his own demise and walked to Del. "It *will* perk you up honey, but I didn't say when." She took the empty cup from Del's hand and set it on the worktable.

The girl yawned again and rubbed her watering eyes. "What did you put in that?" The yawns lined up in her throat. She could feel them waiting to emerge.

"Just something to help you sleep." The woman's large hands pulled at Del's smaller ones. "You got to let your mind rest. Which means shuttin' down the outside signals as well." She pulled Del up and whispered in her ear. "They can't find you if they can't feel your pull."

"Wha...?" Del blinked in confusion.

"Now, let's get you into bed. I know it's early, but you need it. I put a few more things around in your room. It'll keep out the... visitors. The ones that already know you're here."

Frank and Armand exchanged concerned looks.

Del mumbled something to each as she navigated her way

through the room, followed closely by her mentor.

When the women were out of range, Frank joined Armand at the table.

"What was dat about *visitors*?" Frank asked.

Armand cleaned his pipe and considered the question. "I can only theorize, but I suspect our young Del—whether she wishes it or not— has a certain attraction to... to whatever lurks on the *other side*."

"Ho-ly hell."

Armand looked up. "Precisely."

A chill ran down the back of Frank's neck. He thought about the events of the day, and how much Del had helped him. After dropping Del at the ice cream shop, he'd returned home and napped. Arriving at Armand's house a few hours later, he'd learned of Jimmy's accident and updated the adults on the progress of their search.

He hadn't shared all the days' details. Not that he was hiding anything really, but he simply didn't know how to explain the event that occurred when Del was trancing, or if it was even related. But he suspected it was.

"Why did she look so... sick?" Armand asked. "What do you think is the cause? It appears to be something other than mere exhaustion."

"I'll tell you what the cause is," Mama Dedé said as she reentered the room.

Armand topped off his and Frank's brandy and poured one for her.

She stood at the table and sipped. After a long sigh she said, "It's her Well of Life. She's using it too fast."

A newly struck match flamed near Armand's pipe, lighting his eyes. "Well of Life? You mean, she looked... haggard, because she was tired? Burning the candle at both ends?"

"No, Frenchy. That's not what I mean." The woman walked to her chair and sat. The men followed. Armand stoked the fire as Frank set the brandy on the small fireplace table.

"Trancin' is hard on a person. I've said that before. It's also dangerous. And I've said why. I taught her to drink the tea before trancing. She thought it was so she could get *into* the trance, but it was really so she could get *out*. Anyone who can trance should drink it. Anyone of us could go too deep by accident."

Armand raised his hand slightly. "When you say, 'too deep,' what does that mean exactly? How does one go... *too deep*?"

Firelight inspected the question on the woman's face, brightening it briefly, then fled off to fight with the shadows in the corner of the room.

"Like I've said before, when you trance, you watch the scene, but from *outside* it. You have to be careful because sometimes you can move too close and pass right *into* the scene, like going through a door. When you do, you've passed into the *other side*. At least—"

"Wait! Pardon me, but this is quite fascinating. Are you saying that you pass into the realm of the dead?"

She considered the words he used. "Don't know for sure. But you've passed *out* of the realm of the living. And that's where the problem starts. As far as I know, there's not just *this side* and *the other side*. It's more like layers. How far *away* from *this side* you go, the more damage you do to yourself and the harder it is to get back."

Frank whistled his concern and sipped. A new cigar was plucked from his shirt pocket.

Armand quietly inspected the concept of *this side* or *that*. His pipe smoked as his fingers drummed against one another. She waited patiently.

After several finger raises, half thoughts, head scratches and eye squints, Armand formed his question. "*The further you go, the more damage is done*. So, the deeper Del trances—somehow going past, or into, a scene—she's inflicting damage on herself and risking her ability to return. But if the damage is not due to exhaustion, and presumably you can't physically touch anything, what is there to incur damage from? How does that even happen?"

"Evaporation."

Both men shook their heads in sync.

"I'm sorry, what?" Armand asked. "Did you say—?"

"That's what I said. Evaporation."

"But... how...?"

"Think of a glass of water. You leave it out too long and what happens? The water just disappears."

"Yes, but that can be explained."

"On *this side*, we're a glass of water; a *well* in most cases. A Well of Life. On the other side, the well is empty. Dried up. The deeper you go, the drier it is. When you cross over and come back, it breaks you down a little. It tears at you, your... essence, your soul. Your Well of Life can repair that. It can patch the small tears. But the well isn't endless. No one's is. And when you're on the other side, besides the small rips, it's dry. At least, I've heard it's the driest place you can ever imagine. And it pulls life-water from you like the air pulls water from a glass."

"Oh my!" Armand exclaimed. "Then every time young Del ventures forth... Frank, when she was looking for your culprit..."

Frank supplicated his hands. He didn't realize the danger either.

Armand ran a hand through his wild hair. "We must do something. We have to tell her of the danger."

"Tchh! Welcome to the program, Frenchy. Why do you think I've been harpin' on her? Just so I get the *mean parent* label and you and Frank—"

Her fist clenched as the words slipped out, but they wouldn't come back. She knew she wasn't Del's parent, nor ever would be. But someone had to look after her.

Both men sat quiet. Armand inspected his pipe. Frank brushed his shirt. They both knew they were far outside their areas of expertise.

CHAPTER 43

As Willy's Well of Life dripped away, the building fed. Tiny, imperceptible ripples ran across the floor. Willy was delicious.

Madame Broussard had fed enough for now, but wanted more. In her anger, she'd started something that would now be hard to control. During her isolation she'd learned to be controlled. It was needed to pass the long years. But now, feeding so soon—and so passionately—she knew that her future had just taken a dramatic turn. Where it would lead, she couldn't comprehend.

Mr. Scarmish stared hungrily from his void; he would not feed tonight, nor any night soon. And he was deep. It was very dry where Mr. Scarmish was.

The woman picked Willy up and sat his crumpled remains on the display table. He fell over. His head—still attached—rested in the bone-lap of Alvie-the-boy-made-of-string. They looked like two friends, exhausted after a long day of games.

Madame Broussard returned to her position behind the podium

and gathered herself. She tucked strands of hair behind her ears. She straightened her pearls. She wiped the blood from her mouth and inspecting it on her fingers, shaking her head in disgust. *What a waste.*

Placing her hands on the podium, she resumed the discussion of business.

"Now, what just occurred here was completely unacceptable. We are now—" She corrected herself, "*I* am now down to one full rootstock. And she will *not* be wasted. She will be saved, perhaps even groomed."

"But what of him?" The smoke swirled as lightning-eyes leered at Willy. "There is still life there. I can feel it. He still breathes!"

Without breaking her gaze with the mirror, she said, "You know very well, that one is now mine. He's been marked, admittedly by accident, but nonetheless, he's now bound completely to me. And, considering the circumstances which we still need to discuss, I have other plans for him. For them both."

Several of the fire-eyes disappeared and the face changed shape again. A faint flash of lightning backlit the deep void of Scarmish's world. But he was still listening.

"The most pressing matter is the Spirit Hunter. I haven't identified who it is, but there's no other explanation for what I felt. They were… aggressively exploring the past. I felt they would see past the veil that hides me. And I should not have to state it, but *both* our worlds are at risk if that happens. This type of power cannot be left to lurk about.

"However, there was something else. It was a clumsy sort of probe. They were nearly on top of me, but didn't realize it. Or… didn't have the patience to look closely enough. It felt rushed. It felt like… inexperience to me.

"I fear the break in the supply chain is due to this person, so they're already looking for something. They may not know *what* they're looking for yet... besides... the children perhaps."

Understanding painted her face with surprise, then caused her to shake her head in disbelief.

How silly of me.

"What?" the mirror asked.

"Times are changing, Mr. Scarmish. We now have someone who cares about the orphans of the world. That's who's looking. AND, they're a Spirit Hunter."

"Yes..." the mirror hissed. "I have felt something myself. I was busy with other matters and ignored my instincts... but I will heed what you say."

The cloud-face swirled blue and thoughtful. It was satisfied with the conclusion.

"I can find the Hunter," Scarmish said. "If he's as powerful as you say, he'll leave a trace."

She nodded agreement. Scarmish would be best for this job.

He continued. "And if he's as inexperienced as you think, he may have already left a crease."

She saw the plan of action spread out before her. "I'll work at reestablishing the supply chain. It may not be completely broken— perhaps only delayed. In the meantime—"

The face shimmered with excitement.

"Yes... I'll find the Spirit Hunter."

CHAPTER 44

When Jimmy finally awoke and made it down to the breakfast table, Del was just finishing his Mickey Mouse pancakes. She'd been up for hours—having slept the deepest sleep—and heard him stirring upstairs. Her timing was perfect.

She'd bounced around the kitchen all morning, helping Armand with odd chores. 'Radiant Del,' he'd said, when she had first appeared. She wasn't sure she felt radiant—happy at least—but couldn't deny the spring in her step. She smiled cautiously as Jimmy approached.

"Hey, sleepyhead. Pancakes are ready."

Jimmy stopped in the door of the kitchen and eyed Del. He leaned protectively against the heavy wood trim.

Del retreated to the far side of the table and sat down, giving him space to approach.

"Jimmy," she said softly, "I heard about your accident yesterday. I'm really sorry I wasn't here to help you."

He rubbed his eyes and blinked. He remembered that a lot of

things happened yesterday—he'd taken several naps for one thing—but wasn't sure what Del was referring to. Taking his seat, he looked at Mickey with his strawberry-eyes and bacon-mouth. A slight smile moved his lips.

"You know you can see all kinds of things in water, right? And that I'd never ever do anything to hurt you. You know that too, right?"

Jimmy shrugged. "Yeah, I guess."

Del sighed a quiet relief.

"Hey, guess what?" Jimmy said.

"What?"

"I found a cookie ona my night tand."

"You did?"

"Den guess what?"

"What?"

"I ate it!" Jimmy cracked a wide smile. "Ike 'dis, cunch, cunch, cunch!" His fingers gripped into claws.

Del said a silent *thank you* to the heavens and hid her tears with a napkin and a generous laugh.

"You know what I think, Jimmy Wawoo?"

"Wha?" Part of Mickey's ear stuck out of Jimmy's mouth.

"I think today is a good day for playin'. Who wants to go watch the trains come in?"

Jimmy thumbed his chest. "Dis guy!"

*

Frank arrived at the station at nine a.m. sharp. The report on Spider was that he hadn't slept the night before. The night guard's report stated: *Agitated and Talkative.*

He was that and then some, Frank thought, when the guards led Spider into the interrogation cell. Watching him through the one-way glass, Frank immediately saw the signs of nicotine withdrawal. The wiry man constantly flicked at an invisible lighter with his right hand. And he was talking too. A lot. As he gestured and spoke, sometimes the invisible lighter would switch hands, but he'd flick it habitually just the same.

"Morning, Frank." The captain entered with two cups of coffee in white Styrofoam cups and handed one to him.

"Mornin', cap'n. We didn't by chance get a confession, did we?" Frank nodded his thanks for the coffee.

"Sure, we did. Spider's got a thing! All night long, from what I hear."

Frank shook his head in dismay. "Yeah, I was afraid ah dat."

"That was until he started talkin' to himself. I think that kept him occupied the rest of the time."

"Gggmm…" Frank muttered. "I thought we'd get somethin'. Didja happen to find anything else? You know, in da trunk?"

"We found a bit of hair, some gum wrappers, stuff like that. But nothin' we can use. It's still not enough to hold him past his twenty-four hours."

"Damn…"

"Why you think he's the guy?" The captain watched Frank closely. "Pilla and blanket in the trunk is suspicious, I'll admit, but not unheard of."

Frank thought back to how adamant Del had been. She was certain they had been on the right track. He hoped he'd been right in following her again.

"Just a hunch."

"Yeah, that's what they all say."

"A magician doesn't reveal his tricks."

The captain grunted. "It'll be more than a trick if we find those kids alive. Be a damn miracle."

"Yeah, I know." Frank slugged down the coffee with a grimace. "Haddie make da coffee?"

"Yeah, how'd you know?"

Frank showed a covey of coffee grounds stuck to the bottom of the cup, then dropped it in the waste basket.

"Mind if I have a minute with him?"

"Better do it while you can. He's only got another four hours or so, then I have to release him. You want me to lock him down first?"

"Nope. I wrestled a bigger shit than him this mornin'." He hitched up his khaki pants and smoothed his shirt. "But, can I bum a smoke from you first?"

"A smoke?" The captain grabbed the pack from his pants pocket and knocked two free. "You finally give up the stink turds?" He handed over two unfiltered Marlboros.

At the same time, Frank pulled a fresh stogey from a leather, three-cigar carrying case attached to his belt and bit the tip off. "Nope," he said with a grin and spit the tip in the trashcan. He stashed the smokes in his shirt pocket.

Frank lit the cigar in the hall before entering the interrogation room. Spider spun around when he heard the door open. A thick cloud of smoke greeted him.

"Mornin' Spider," Frank said as he took the seat closest to the door. A gray metal table, bolted to the floor, sat between the two men on the left side of the room. The right wall held the one-way observation mirror. Spider flicked his invisible lighter as he watched Frank work his cigar.

After several seconds Spider focused on the man's face. Then his twitchy fingers pointed. "Hey, I kn-know you. You, you're the guy who ran into m—"

"Wrong." Frank blew another thick cloud towards the twitchy man. "I'm the guy who caught you, Spider. Or, should I say, Willis Lewis Morris?"

Spider walked in a tight circle at the back of the room and consulted his shaky hands. He stopped behind his chair and looked down at the ripped seat.

"S-say, y-you wouldn't happen to have—"

"A smoke?" Frank said cheerily. "Just so happens…" He pulled the Marlboros from his pocket and sat them on the table in front of him.

Spider sat in his chair with wide eyes. Although his right shoulder leaned against the beige wall of the room, he was at full attention.

"But… I need some information first."

Spider squirmed and rubbed his head, but his eyes never left the cigarettes. Small beads of sweat broke across his brow. Finally, with a rubbery neck, he looked at Frank. "What?"

"You know *what*. It's da same damn *what* I asked you yesterday. Where're da kids?"

Wiry legs began scissoring together beneath the table. Spider's head was on a loose swivel, and loped from side to side. "Man, I told you. I don't know nothin' about no kids."

Frank snatched up the smokes. They headed for his pocket again.

"Wait!" Spider said.

Flick. Flick. Flick.

"Just… just wait. I, I, I'm tellin' you the truth." He scratched at the tabletop with nicotine-stained fingers. "Now, just wait."

"What da hell am I waitin' for?" Frank leaned forward on his thick arms. "For you to have an epiphany?"

Spider's head was hurting, and his feat drummed the floor. There was a far-off sound picking at his mind.

"I... I... don't know about any..."

He suddenly felt that he was missing an appointment.

"...ohhhh... ...uuhhmmm..." The sounds snuck out of his throat as he tried to remember his steps.

He had steps for this sort of thing. A man of his profession needed to be organized and prepared for just such an occasion. He was sure he'd read them somewhere before. He kept notes. He just couldn't remember the exact order.

Should he ask for a lawyer first, or the smokes first?

(But the sound is coming.)

If he asked for a lawyer first, they'd think he was guilty of something. But if he asked for the smokes, he'd have to tell them something—even though there was only one other person in the room with him, that person was still *Them*—and *They* could be tricky.

The far-off sound got louder. Spider turned in his chair and looked behind him. *Where's that sound coming from?*

"Spider?"

Flick. Flick. Flick.

"Wait. J-just... wait."

Spider leaned forward in his chair and listened to the table. No. The sound wasn't coming from there.

"Where're da kids?" Frank asked quietly.

Spider looked at Frank, then at the dark mirror on the wall. He leaned towards it slightly.

No. The sound wasn't there either.

(But the sound is coming.)

He nodded. Yes. He was sure the sound was coming.

"The deliveries. Where do they go?

Flick. Flick. Flick.

Spider's eyes were wide and searching. The sound was close.

He turned to his left and looked behind him again, but this time at the wall he'd been leaning against. No wonder he didn't see it. It had been directly behind him the entire time.

He stood up and took two steps towards the back of the room.

"Spider?"

A steady right hand rose in the air as Willis Morris looked over his right shoulder at Frank. "Just wait, please," he said. "Spider has a thing."

Willis Morris turned back around, and Spider reached out with his left hand and picked up an invisible telephone receiver. The sound in his head stopped.

"Hello?" he said quietly.

CHAPTER 45

Madame Broussard put the finishing touches on her project, stood up and wiped her hands clean. She'd been working feverishly over the display table all day.

With Scarmish gone, off looking for the Spirit Hunter, this little project kept her mind occupied. She didn't know how long Scarmish would be gone. She wasn't sure how deep he'd explored before, or how much he could remember when he came back. But that wasn't her concern.

What she was addressing *now* was her concern. With the supply-chain compromised, and her picture frame broken, she was blind to the world and needed an alternative.

The circumstances that caused her to become imprisoned in this place were painful reminders of what she'd once had, so she had pushed them deep into her mind long ago. However, the damage to the picture frame was recent. It stung her with a feeling of vulnerability that she hadn't felt in... well, she couldn't actually remember when.

She thought she could fix the frame, but its magic was old. It would take a lot of energy to repair it, and she had more pressing matters now. Alvie was a better choice.

She looked at the Boy Made of String—for that's literally what he was now—and wondered if she could make the transference work. It was a tricky spell, and although she'd had a long time to study it, she wasn't naturally gifted with binding. Hers was a different power.

She was decent with trancing, but that always left a trail, and despite her careful efforts to remain hidden, that trail could still lead something to her. That's why she didn't trance. And that's why she'd spent so much time putting Alvie back together again.

Yes, Alvie, the boy who was nothing but skin and bones, string and sinew, had just received an extra bit from his donor-friend, Willy: just enough sinew to hold him together. His shrunken bones were still strong enough, but with the loss of nearly all his muscle tissue, the joints just fell apart. And without sturdy joints, he couldn't stand. And if he couldn't stand, he couldn't do what she needed.

Willy, on the other hand, still had all his parts—and was still breathing, she was happy to see. Faint, but breathing. She felt he'd finally stabilized, having begun his transformation, but was not far enough along to technically make him off limits to feeding. She liked Willy. His curly hair and fat cheeks gave him a loveable look. And he made adorable squeaking sounds occasionally—faint, but adorable. But that's not how she knew he was alive. No. She could *feel* his life force, for it now flowed through her.

With the supply-chain broken, she couldn't be wasteful. Thankfully, Willy was a plump, healthy boy. He could last a long time if she kept the building away from him. The little girl on the other hand, was an enigma. So small and precious she was, but with a rich, thick rootstock. She would be saved for something special.

After the unfortunate discussion with Mr. Scarmish—and her anger-fueled feeding frenzy—she'd placed Willy on the table next to Alvie. Both boys were turned away from the viewing wall—the one Scarmish had been so graciously invited through two nights past—and faced inward toward the podium.

She propped the boys up on the table, wedging hand-forged pieces of iron behind both. The iron pieces were also very old—as her things were—and looked as if they were metal frames to a chair back. They were made from rough iron bars: one that formed an upside-down 'V' that supported the back, then another bar that formed crude arms. Each boy's arms were draped over the iron bars which supported their weight. Their heads tilted toward one another as if they'd fallen asleep after an exciting adventure.

She walked to a large bookshelf, but didn't peruse the dusty old volumes as eccentric researchers would. She knew the book she was looking for, and it wasn't on display. Pulling a key from her pocket, she slid aside a small wood panel and exposed a keyhole. She inserted the key. It turned without a sound. Another wood panel dropped quietly down and exposed a hidden drawer. She pulled the drawer out and despite its infrequent use, it made no sound either. But the building knew it was open. She carefully removed the book and a thin, stained veil from the secret drawer. She took both items to the podium and set them there.

The veil unfurled with a dusty flourish as a slight breeze stirred ancient particles from it. The strands seemed to barely hold together, and if it weren't for the magic that had passed through them over the years, she thought they would have surely let loose of one another like little Alvie-bones. But Alvie no longer had that problem.

She draped the veil over the heads and faces of the two boys, then absently straightened her pearls. Everything had to be just right for the spell to work. A steel-hard fingernail sunk into Willy's wrist and came back with a precious drop of blood clinging to the tip.

Returning to the podium where the black book lay waiting, her elegant fingers slid over the binding until they found a scarlet-red book ribbon that marked a special passage. She breathed deeply and swallowed, then opened the grimoire to the thirteenth passage.

Across the high ceiling, nervous candlelight danced. Little patches of light jostled for position—nothing wanted to miss the spectacle—but like summer days and shooting stars, their life was short and most faded to black before the miracle happened, only to be replaced by another anxious flicker.

The pages of the grimoire that held the Thirteenth Passage appeared to be blank, but she knew the power was there. She could feel it. The book was waking up.

She smoothed the two pages back with her hands, then ran the blood-soaked fingernail down the length of each one. The book twitched once with the influx of life and the spell began.

Ancient, scrawling script suddenly appeared on the pages of the Thirteenth Passage. Crimson-red and gold, the words of the spell wrote themselves, and waited. The next part was hers.

The woman read the words slowly and clearly as the candle-light voyeurs clung to their fleeting existence on the ceiling. The swirling air slowed. The candles burned slower. The sign outside began to swing.

By the time she'd finished speaking the words, the pages had already begun to swell. She watched in fascination as the blood of Willy—just the single drop—had multiplied. It was inside the pages of the book now, and was nearly ready. The blood was infused with shadow-life giving properties that had to be transferred to Alvie. But not a drop could be wasted.

She picked up the book with both hands and noticed for the first time two small holes, one on each side of the inside binding, that were nearly perfect imprints of her own bite. At least one of her ancestors had performed this ritual before. She didn't have time to wonder who—the pages were swollen almost beyond capacity. She had to perform her part quickly.

Bringing the bottom of the book toward her mouth, like a child drinking the last remnants of milk from a bowl, she lowered her mouth to the pages, opened it wide, and let her teeth find their place in the meat of the grimoire. She felt the scarlet-red book ribbon slip past her tongue and the process began. Instantly, the blood began to flow. The engorged pages released their life-giving fluids in large spurts, which surprised her. The book shivered under her bite. It was an unholy union. The blood flowed into her mouth faster than she could store it and several times she had to tilt the book one or the other to keep the precious fluid from spilling away. It was almost too much. The book had produced more than she'd expected, and she was afraid she would spill it. She gulped the liquid without feeding on it— it still had to be transferred. If she could just digest it. It was meant for something else. The coppery-tasting fluid flowed into the back of her throat, expanding it, filling every crevasse it could find. It covered the top of her mouth, thick and metallic. She felt it fill her nasal cavity. She gagged. It flowed beneath her eye sockets. Her eyes swelled tight and began to water. It pushed deeply into her throat. She convulsed. She drank. She held her breath. It was nearly over.

Finally, the taste of the book turned dry and papery and she knew it was over. She dropped the book and lunged toward the bones of

Alvie before she spilt it. All she had to do was get to one bone.

Her head came down over an exposed thigh bone and her teeth sunk deeply into it. The transferred blood gushed from her throat in large splashes, flowing over and into the bones. At this point she didn't care where it went, as long as it was out of her. But the blood knew where to go. It wanted to be alive. And it flowed to that which could live.

When the last of the blood was expelled, she staggered backwards, gasping for air. She fell into a large chair near the display table and watched. The book, having fallen back onto the podium, remained open to the Thirteenth Passage and was enshrouded by a red mist. Her rings swirled green and yellow eyes, one on each hand, that looked out to watch the transference. Strange wisps of light shot up from the book and hovered in the air. The cloud floated over the two boys and settled onto their veiled heads. Tiny sparks flashed along the frail material, sensing the imbalance of life. Then, a faint but steady flow of light pulsed towards Alvie. The imbalance was being altered.

Madame Broussard could only sit and marvel. The awful taste still lingered in her mouth, but she dared not move. The process was working.

After a long time, the light began to fade from the veil. The tiny sparks slowed and dimmed, and the red haze around the book began to fall back into it.

A final crack of static arced across Willy and Alvie, lighting the room. The force sent the veil flying high into the air. A faint burnt smell wafting after it. The veil fluttered its annoyance and floated toward the grimoire, falling gently over the book.

The woman held her breath and waited. What was next? The spell was complete, as far as she knew. When would the transference be—?

Her question had just been answered. She sat with wide eyes and marveled.

Alvie's foot had just moved.

CHAPTER 46

Frank sat in his car beneath a shade tree and twisted the radio dial. He was looking for a ball game. He wanted some common-ground background noise playing. That tended to put people at ease.

Spider walked out of the NOPD district #1 at two o'clock in the afternoon. His twitchy fingers discarded the butt of a cigarette he'd inhaled during his short walk down the hall. He fumbled for another—the last in the pack. He hit the sidewalk in front of the parking lot, turned left and walked at a steady pace. He didn't see Frank slide up behind him.

"Hey there, Spider," Frank said, as he inched the car forward.

Spider convulsed in surprise and sent his cigarette tumbling through the air. He reached to catch it, but it escaped down a drain opening in the curb.

"Man! What's wrong with y—?" He stopped when he recognized Frank. "Y-you stay away from me. I got nothin' to say."

"Hop in, Spider." Frank patted the car door. "I'll give ya a ride."

"N-no thanks. I think... I think I'll just walk."

Twitchy spider-fingers searched pockets for another smoke, but came up empty. Squinty eyes shot glances at Frank, then searched for all manner of escape routes down the sidewalks.

Frank crept the car forward, but was about to run out of parking lot. He knew Spider would have to decide quickly as to which way to walk. And following him at this pace down the streets would be problematic.

"Spider! You have a phone call." Frank stopped the car and held up his own invisible receiver. "Yeah," Frank said into his hand, "he's right here."

Spider stared at Frank. His eyes twitched from the man's face to his raised hand and back. He didn't hear the phone ring.

Flick. Flick. Flick.

"Who... who are you talkin' to?" His hands were deep in his pants pockets, searching. Now they were out, rubbing lint into tiny balls. The energy from his hands traveled up his arms and slid down into his legs. His feet were nervous now. Maybe he wasn't the only one who had *things to do*. Maybe he wasn't as special as he'd thought. If this old guy got calls as well... Maybe he was higher up in rank. Yeah, that could be it. A network. You had to have a hierarchy of command. Maybe this guy was testing him. Maybe this guy could promote him.

Frank watched the Wheels of Spider spin. They were slow, but they moved along methodically. The twitchy man was trying to reconcile something in his head. He wanted to understand, perhaps even to believe. Something about a simple raised hand cradling an invisible phone had the man transfixed. Frank suddenly realized he'd found a way in.

"That's right, Spider. I get calls too. But you're not getting this one." Frank hung up the phone with a slap on his dash.

"BAH!" Spider made to grab the phone through the open window of the car. "That might be important!"

Frank blocked the reaching hand with his thick arm and seized Spider by the wrist. "It was important, but you missed it." Transferring the twitchy hand to his right, he pulled Spider closer, controlling his upper body by the front of his shirt. "Now listen to me, Spider. I've been watchin' you for a while, and you're gettin' sloppy."

The watery eyes of Spider searched Frank's face for pity, but found none. "I— I— I ain't been sloppy!"

"How da hell did you end up here den, if you ain't been sloppy?"

Flick. Flick. Flick.

"L— listen… I— I— I need to get home in case…"

Frank released him and let the car creep forward. "You'll go home and wait!"

Spider now paced the car with a staggering walk. He held tight to the car door.

"Wait? Wait for what? I need to know if—"

"You'll go home and wait for me. I'm takin' your calls now."

Spider's eyes were wide. "Whaatt?"

"That's right. All calls go through me now. You're too sloppy. Go home and wait for me to call."

With that, Frank pushed his hand away and pulled onto the street. He darted into traffic without hesitation.

He didn't like the fact that he'd played the man's emotions so hard— something was clearly wrong with him. But he needed more time, and thought he'd just bought some. Plus, he needed to explore this new opening. He needed to get to Del immediately.

Spider stood on the sidewalk flicking his fingers. He badly needed a smoke.

CHAPTER 47

Del and Jimmy took the long way back from the train station. She thought he'd like an ice cream.

Several times that day she'd caught a glimpse of herself in a mirror and felt that her old glow was back. She knew it was. What a difference a good night's sleep had done her.

Despite the trick Mama Dedé had played on her to get her to sleep, she wasn't mad. Del knew she only wanted to help, and it had. Her youthful glow was back, her eyes were bright, and her scars had seemed to fade some. The sickly gray hue had left her skin, which looked warm against the bright yellow t-shirt she wore.

Jimmy chattered on about what flavor he would try as she pushed the door open. The sweet cool air wafted over her and she smiled. This was now one of her favorite smells.

A girl looked up from behind the counter. She smacked her chewing gum as she spoke. "Can I help you?"

Del looked through the door that led to the storage room. "Hi. Uh, is Johnathan here?"

The girl eyed Del with something close to suspicion. "No. He's off today. Why?"

Del felt the vibe the girl was sending her. And it wasn't friendly.

"Hon, hon," the girl said, motioning at Jimmy. "Don't lick the glass. Jeesh."

Jimmy, pressing his face to the glass to get a closer look at the flavors, had let his tongue slip out. The cold glass felt good.

"Sorry," Del said, pulling Jimmy back from the glass.

"Hey, I recognize you," the girl said. "You were in here a few days ago."

Del recognized the girl behind the counter as one of the teenagers that hassled her the first day she came in.

"Well, don't worry about Johnathan. He's taken." She smacked her gum. "In fact, I'll tell him you dropped by when I see him tonight." She cocked her hips to one side and blew a bubble at Del.

A flash of red went through Del's mind and reflected out through her eyes. The girl, attempting to stare her down, glimpsed the flash and turned her head slightly. Looking directly at the pretty girl in the yellow t-shirt had suddenly become uncomfortable.

Del placed their order and the girl quickly filled it. After paying, she simply said, "Tell Johnathan I said hi," turned and headed toward the door.

"Freak!" the girl yelled as the door swung closed behind her.

Licking his ice cream, Jimmy said, "Why'd she say fweak?"

She stopped to stare back at her through the window. Her heartbeat pounding in her ears. They were standing beside the very table she and Johnathan had sat at yesterday.

"I don't know, she's just—"

Del's focus moved from the girl inside the shop, to the picture of the girl taped to the inside of the window. The flyer stated:

Missing: Clara Boynell

6 years old. Brown hair. Brown eyes

Last seen at St. Augustine Orphanage.

Call NOPD District #1 with information.

The missing kids!

Everything she'd done the last few days suddenly flooded back into her mind.

Frank. And Spider. Oh my gosh, what am I doing?

Here she was, taking a leisurely stroll, looking for a boy who she didn't even know, and the kids were still missing.

The hair!

She franticly felt into the pocket of her jeans and found the hair. She'd meant to use it yesterday when she got home, but after the meeting with Johnathan, then the trancing session in the park, she'd forgotten.

Whatever Mama Dedé had put in the tea did more than just cause her to fall asleep. She'd been walking around in a daydream until just now.

"Come on, Jimmy. We have to get home."

"OK, but—"

"Please. Let's just walk a little faster. I forgot to do something."

Jimmy licked his ice cream as he tried to keep up with Del.

A large black cloud crept silently overhead. It was the forward scout, casting a cold shadow over the ground and down the street. The shadow trailed behind Del and Jimmy at its own pace. It would overtake them sometime later. The storm was just beginning to form.

Somewhere in the dark, Clara was sleeping.

CHAPTER 48

A lvie The Boy Made of String sat up on the display table. His skeleton legs dangled down and clacked against each other. They swung like mistimed pendulums, slowly winding down.

The top half of him kept a wobbly balance as it swayed from side to side. His arms hung down onto the tabletop where bone-fingers made a dry scratching sound against the wood.

The remnants of tattered skin fragments that wrapped around his bones gave him the appearance of motion even though he was sitting still. Like Hermes—the messenger of the gods, who had winged feet— Alvie was to be a messenger now. Although his tiny skin-wings jutted about wildly, as if an invisible tumult blew him in all directions.

Madame Broussard watched with fascination. Willy lay beneath the table and blew a snot bubble from one nostril. One eye leaked fluid onto the floor. The wood planks were thankful.

Alvie leaned forward and propelled himself from the table. The woman thought he would crash into a hundred pieces, but his bone-hands flexed just in time to cushion his fall. He landed like a staggering animal, on all fours, and sent a shower of dust and skin particles floating in the air. His head snapped down at a sharp angle, then sprung back up. She feared he surely would have broken some of the borrowed sinew, but it held. After several seconds, he stood up on his own two feet and began to walk.

It was a stumbling, leaning walk. His head—just the skull and jawbone really—seemed to be too heavy for the little neck bones—especially after they had been severed. The head flopped from one side to the other, always pulling him this way or that. He staggered about the room like a drunkard. His body careened to the right as his head looked left, then vice versa. Through an errant turn, the weight of his skull fell backwards and hung awkwardly between his shoulder blades. This caused his bone-body to tilt back also, and he backpedaled into the wall. His head bounced forward and this sent him running after his center of gravity, with short, stubby steps; his arms hanging loosely behind him. The whole time, his bones knocked together with a sickening *CLACKITY-CLICK-CLACKITY* sound that echoed off the high ceiling.

In due time, Alvie The Boy Made of String found his stride. It wasn't perfect, but it would allow him to do what she needed. He was a Creature of the Night, now. That's what the Thirteenth Passage had created. That, and her ability to transfer blood.

She shivered at the thought of the taste. Hopefully she'd not have to perform that again.

Because of Alvie's new status, he could travel the Shadow Roads. He could pass beyond these walls and return. She only had to pick a shadow that had never been used before—this way nothing else would know it—point him to it, and she could safely send him where she needed. With her picture frame broken, she needed a view to the outside world. He would be her eyes. It didn't matter that he no longer had any. Whatever he saw, or heard, whatever he *absorbed*, he could bring back. She had another perfectly good set of eyes to be used for viewing. They were beneath the table right now.

She decided to use the shadow she kept inside the large cabinet—the one that had held her picture frame. That seemed like the appropriate relationship for this task. Her picture frame had been her view onto the world, and she'd kept it safe in that cabinet. She'd never considered what to do with the shadow in there.

As if by divine intervention, she felt a chill settle over the building. Her skin prickled at the cooling of the air.

A storm was coming.

She could feel the electricity far away, but it was coming. The timing couldn't have been better. The shadow roads would be many in just a matter of hours. They would be deep and wide and spread out like a network of veins. Many Creatures of the Night would be traveling the roads soon. And Alvie would go about virtually unnoticed.

In just a few hours, Alvie would slip into the shadows. By the very nature of his making, he would seek out power. He was drawn to it as if it were infused into his bones.

He was like a bloodhound now. He would first follow the telepathic trail she'd been sending for so long to Spider the Dragon King. She didn't understand the significance of the name, but that was the image her contact portrayed. Alvie would look for this person and report back. She'd received garbled messages from him just this morning, but knew that he was at least still alive. Once she knew the status, she could plan what to do next. But she needed information. After that, Alvie would be free to roam where he wanted. She knew he would naturally follow the strongest shadow-paths. He couldn't make many decisions on his own yet. And once he was on the larger paths, she assumed it would lead him to a powerful source. If Scarmish was right, and the Spirit Hunter had made a crease without realizing it, it would be easy for Alvie to follow. In fact, it would be like him floating down the current of a swollen river, only in reverse. All things would flow to the source if the crease was deep enough.

Then she would know who the Spirit Hunter was. Perhaps even before Scarmish got there.

CHAPTER 49

Somewhere, in a strange place of beginnings and endings, walked a thing known as Scarmish.

The shimmering entity had been a man once, in a past time. But he only resembled the form now by the faintest of faint memories. His shape came from the *idea* of something he'd been before; the idea of what he knew to be on the side of the living.

The life-forces on that side were food that drew him back occasionally. That was the only reason he went back, but it helped him to remember. Out here, in The Desert of Dust, it was hard to remember. But there were reasons he came here. There were dark things here that he wanted to find, secrets that he needed to learn.

He walked the desert with slow, dragging steps. That was the only way to traverse the desert, all his other power was used just to keep himself intact.

He had tranced here years ago, finding it accidently—*slipping* into it. He'd barely survived that first incident. Through some odd circumstance he'd found his way back out, but could not heed the warnings of his logical mind to stay away. The draw to the place was too powerful, and it tore at his mind. He came back whenever he could, but he'd only been able to explore a small part of it. It was infinitely large and growing deeper all the time. The dust grains always fell.

The desert was a hurricane-inferno that stretched on and on. The tempest winds of eternal destruction blew forever and buffeted him from all directions. The fine grains of dust sandblasted his being, sanding him down and polishing him to a deep, translucent color. He was a thousand shades of black and his surface melted and reformed constantly in this place.

He felt his mind expand when he was here—dangerously large. Whether it reached out on its own, or something pulled at it he couldn't tell, but it wanted to stretch. It wanted to *see* and *be seen*, consume knowledge and be consumed. If he wasn't careful, his existence could simply end here.

The desert was a barren place, static-gray and stripped of color. There was nothing to be seen but the always swirling dust, but he knew that something else was here.

As a bat senses its cave, he too could sense this world. Invisible static lightning punched through the forever-clouds, illuminating strange horizons in his mind. He needed and feared the lightning. It was his only light source in the infinite gray, but sometimes... if he looked just right... he saw things in the distance. He sensed they were gigantic, lumbering things, a thousand years away, enormous beyond comprehension, but he knew they were there. And they moved ever in his direction. No matter where he was in the desert, the things on the horizon always moved towards him.

No longer able to remember how he found the desert, he simply let himself *fall* towards it when he was trancing and ready to come back.

He'd formed his own crease here—a pathway in his mind—he'd come so many times. There was power in this place, real power. He felt that it all began and ended here. He wanted to learn it. He dreamed of controlling it.

The finest dust fell from the sky. Constantly. It fell from the black space high above where any cloud could form. It just came from *above*. Whatever it was, there was an endless supply of it. As long as he'd been coming here, as long as he'd explored, as far as he'd walked, the dust always fell. And when it did, it would eventually be caught up by the furnace-winds and turned into a cutting agent. If you stayed too long, eventually, everything was cut down by the winds—even memory itself.

His progress was slow because the dust was deep; he sank up to his ankles with every step. Despite having arrived here from the power of his mind, physical walking was the only way to move about. It was exhausting work, which made his stay even more dangerous. He still needed the strength to get back off the desert floor, and trancing his self away was tricky. Yet he came here anyway.

He trudged along and thought about the stupid woman who'd wasted his rootstock. Her name had already been blown away from his mind, but it didn't matter. She was just a means to an end. He suspected she would still be imprisoned in her little cage a hundred years from now if he stayed away that long. Something had happened… something… that he knew about long ago, to cause her to become trapped. But what did he care? Humans and the first-generation aberrations that haunted them were no longer his concern. When he'd discovered the *layers*, that was his first glimpse into how the universe worked; how the power worked. Unsure how many layers there were, he'd searched for decades and had been able to go no further than this place. How many layers he'd traveled was a mystery. Over time, they all blurred together.

The hurricane-furnace-winds changed direction, whipping sideways at him, and burnt the left side of his being. The front right side of him cooled by a fraction of a degree and solidified. His face was deep glass, pure and translucent. Any semblance of human features had melted away—or sunk inward. He had no need for eyes in this place, so made no effort to manifest them. The *memory* of an eye was infused in his being. He could call it from his marrow when needed.

The heavy dust clouds hid much in this world, but through some ability cast upon him by the stars, he was able to find things in the dust. He'd found the beginning of a few creases before. They were stubborn things to find, nearly invisible and thread thin. But he could see them on occasion. The ends—or beginnings really—of the creases formed tiny dust-devils in this strange place. Some force caused them to begin here, and upon a chance following, he'd discovered what they were.

They were attracted to him, he thought. It was as if he were a magnet for them. If one was close, he could feel its energy. And if he'd saved enough of his own energy, he could stand still and let the winds blow it towards him. Eventually, he could see the shrieking dust-form. The twisting tunnel of energy—like the tiniest thread—always led up and away from the desert. It soared away into the black void of space, growing ever wider.

Eventually it would lead you to the one who created it.

CHAPTER 50

The bones of Alvie passed into the cabinet shadow and were gone. Without noise or fanfare, one moment they were there, the next they were not. Madame Broussard had to blink twice and convince herself that he *had* actually been there just a second earlier.

The storm outside was still forming and the shadow roads weren't all in place yet, but Alvie's maiden voyage was only to be a short one. She felt Spider the Dragon King was close by, and the sun was low enough to cast long shadows in many places. Her new messenger could manage. Besides, he had to learn the ropes somehow. And based on how quickly he disappeared into the shadow of her cabinet, she wasn't concerned about someone seeing him. Oh, they may catch a glimpse. But as soon as they did, the next second he would be gone. Then they'd convince themselves it was all in their imagination. She'd relied on this one human flaw for a long time.

She stood up and looked at her fresco. It had finally come back into focus after the prying eyes of the Spirit Hunter had distorted it. How long had that been? Just yesterday? It seemed longer than that.

So many things had happened since then.

She thought about calling out to Spider again, but barely had the energy. The process of using the Thirteenth Passage had drained her. She shivered slightly at the memory. Instead, she gazed absently at her fresco. The shadows crept slowly around the streets as the black sun made to sneak beneath the horizon. Then she noticed something.

Had she never seen this before? Had it always been there, and her memory had finally started to slip? She didn't think so, on either account.

Watching with fascination, she saw that one shadow moved faster than the others. Independently. They'd never done that before. The whole world of shadows could be seen on her fresco, but as a large, living mass. The mass was stronger or weaker in areas, depending on the rates of births and deaths and many other things. Sometimes the shadow mass would shift, blown by an invisible tide-wind to collect heavy on some shores and light on others. But she never saw individual shadows moving against the flow. Why would it suddenly—?

Alvie?

Is that what she was seeing? Her very own creation moving amongst the shadows?

It must be. But why?

She poured herself some wine and sat down. Even from here she could see the shadow move. It was as if her eyes were drawn to it and couldn't look away. It *was* Alvie.

For some reason...

Willy!

She stood up and walked back to the wall. Her mind told her this anomaly was connected to Willy somehow, but the full explanation was still forming.

The tiny, moving shadow had the slightest glow to it, which caused it to stand out from the others. On the inner wall of her building, it looked like a physical thing, like a flaking section of plaster that was being pushed away from the wall.

But on the fresco drawing, it had its own presence. It floated on a faint illumination and slid easily in any direction. And she now understood it was because of Willy.

In her anger with Scarmish, she'd snatched Willy up and given him a near-fatal bite. It was completely out of character for her, but it had happened nonetheless. She'd been able to retard the process that was trying to transform Willy's body—which came from her own deadly bite—but then she'd made another mistake. When preparing for the Thirteenth Passage, she only had Willy to use—he was still alive after all. It was his blood that she'd transferred to the grimoire with the scratch of her nail. His blood that was *already transforming* into an unnatural being. Then, after the spell changed the blood *even more* and was transferred to Alvie's bones…

The wine glass shattered as it hit the floor.

It was unclear to her what she had created from these unfortunate events. In the history of mankind, she wasn't sure this had ever been done. She could see Alvie traverse the shadow-roads because he had a bit of her power in him. It was faint… at least, it *had* been faint, before the grimoire transformed it. But she could see him in the shadows of the fresco as if he were of her own flesh and blood.

Her heart leapt into her throat.

This meant the other things that had hunted her for years could see him! To the hunting shadows, Alvie would look just like her.

And he was heading back to her hiding place now!

CHAPTER 51

Mama Dedé sat down with a gush of air and wiped her brow. She'd been trancing all day, and was exhausted.

"Well?" Armand said, looking up from an old manuscript. He walked around his worktable and joined her at the fireplace.

"Well what?"

"Are we haunted?" Armand tweaked his moustache gently.

"Frenchy, you about the strangest man I ever met!" She waved him off. "I get paid to make these things go away and here you want to invite 'em to supper."

Despite her exhaustion, she popped up from her chair and headed toward the railing.

"Oh, now," Armand began, "please don't misunderstand me. I don't wish for anyone to be harmed in any way. But…"

He stood up and returned to the table with the open manuscripts.

"But, if something were here…" He patted the books. "In this very house. And if we were able to communicate with it…" His fingers slid delicately over the pages as he dreamed. "What might we be able to learn? What secrets of the past could we see?"

"I can do that now!"

"Huh! I know!" He grabbed at his wild hair. "And how fascinating that must be."

She turned towards him, shaking her head. Her elbows jutted out from her hips. "Why is it that men always want to go peekin' into the corners? Shinin' a light in every damn crevasse lookin' for the boogey man?"

The look on Armand's face clearly said, *My dear woman, because it's there!*

Mama Dedé heaved a sigh and walked to the table. Her voice became low and somber. "Do you still have the gris I made for you?"

"But of course! I would never—"

"And you remember how little it helped then?"

"Well..." Armand grabbed his pipe and began cleaning it. "Those were quite extraordinary circumstances. Surely, you don't think that—"

The tilt of her head stopped him. "How do you know what I think?" Her lips were a tight line across her face.

"I... I just thought..."

"I know what you thought, but here's what you don't know." She looked around for snooping ears. "Yes, we have visitors here, in this house. They're here right now."

"Right... now?" His eyes glanced sideways as if to catch one sneaking.

"Not so much in the day, but yes. I can feel them. And I've seen a few."

"Really?" His eyes were wide with excitement.

"Frenchy, don't make me knock you." She shook her head again. "I saw some that were after Del and Jimmy the other night. You know, the night she spilled the soup."

He nodded, remembering.

"I didn't know what was goin' on at the time, but I knew somethin' was up."

A tentative finger rose. "What do they look like?"

She expected the question. "Don't know, really. They keep to the shadows. Can't tell how many there are either, but…" Her lips puckered as she debated saying the words. "It's more than I've ever seen in one place. Short of a cemetery."

Gray, furrowed brows showed his first real sign of concern. Armand's fingers tapped the end of his empty pipe. It jutted from a clenched jaw. He turned and looked at his books, then turned quickly back. "What do you think they want with…" His finger went around in a circle. "Why are they here? So suddenly."

"You been callin' 'em up?"

He shook the confusion from his face. "What? No, of course not."

"Didn't think so. But someone has. Whether they're trying to or not, someone's calling out to them."

Armand rubbed his hands and stared absently past the woman. Finally, he said, "Jimmy's accident… in the fountain. Do you think our visitors had anything to do with that?"

"Haven't looked into it yet, but I'd guess yes."

"And will they get more aggressive? These advances?"

"They normally don't just go away on their own. They're here for something. I'd think they plan to stick around."

More hand rubbing. "And you can't just… shoo them away?"

"Shoo 'em away?" Her hands went back to her hips. "Psshh! They ain't puppies!" She turned and headed for the stairs. "Your damn questions are makin' me hungry."

*

"Mmm-mm!" Frank said, walking into the kitchen. "What's cookin'?" He tried to see what was in the pot, then added, "Good lookin'!"

Mama Dedé rolled her eyes as she stirred the pot of spicy potato soup. "Oh, were you thinking about staying for dinner? I'm not sure I made enough."

Frank stretched and rubbed his large stomach. "Don't worry, I eat like a bird anyway. Say, where's Del-bell?"

Before Mama D could respond, Del called from the second-floor library. "Up here Frank! Come quick, I've been waiting. You wouldn't believe—"

A hot spoon came into Frank's view. One end dripped potato soup; the other end was gripped tightly by a ringed fist. "Listen here. She just got rested up. Don't go sending her on no—"

He clamped his mouth over the spoon in an impromptu taste test. "Mmm... grdd." She pulled the spoon back in disgust.

A deep sigh of resignation sunk his shoulders. He considered his words and lowered his voice. "I really need her help. Our guy got released today."

"What?" She dropped the spoon in the sink. "Why's that?"

"Not enough damn evidence. But I think he's our guy. And Del found him." He pointed his cigar toward the stairs. "Problem is, he's nutty as a fruitcake."

"Why you say that?"

"Come up and I'll tell you." He headed towards the foyer.

"But I'm—"

"Just let it simmer," he said. "Besides, it needs more pepper."

A heavy lid clanked behind him. "Oh no it doesn't!"

He chuckled as he headed for the steps.

"Frank!" Del called from the railing. "Did we get him? What happened today? I've been wondering when you were coming. I thought about calling, but then thought you might be busy or not home yet and I didn't want to bug you but I remembered something and—"

"Whoa! Whoa!" Frank pleaded. He puffed up the stairs, his cigar glowing red with every other step. "Jus' gimme a minute."

Frank topped the stairs and saw a radiant Del smiling at him from the sofa.

What a difference a good night sleep makes, he thought. This was the beautiful young woman he was used to seeing.

Armand was stooped over a chess table at the opposite end of the room. He was showing Jimmy how the chess pieces moved.

The large stained-glass windows twinkled with light as the streetlamps came on from below. The sun had disappeared behind an unexpected thunderhead that had formed in the west. A storm was on its way.

"Well?" Del froze in anticipation, another flurry of words threatening to explode from her at any moment.

Frank inspected the growing assortment of liquor bottles that had collected at the end of the table. He poured two fingers' worth and sampled it.

Frank rocked the liquor in the glass. "They let Spider out today."

"What?" Del joined Frank at the worktable. "Why?"

He explained that the police could only hold Spider for so long without more evidence. The pillow and blanket just hadn't been enough.

"I can't believe that!" Del paced the room. Her arms crossed tightly. "Why can't they... Did you question him? You can make him talk, can't you?"

"As it turns out, I did question him."

"And?"

"And... he's been talkin' to Casper."

"Wha...? Who?" Del asked.

Armand looked up from his chess lesson.

"He's hearin' stuff, honey." Frank twirled his finger in the air. "I think his coocoo got clocked. He's talkin' to weeba-jeebas or somethin'."

Del looked at Armand for translation.

"Mon ami? W*eeba... jeebas?*"

"Yeah." Frank was matter of fact. "Weeba... you know," Frank whistled the tune to *The Twilight Zone*. "Dat sumbitch is nuts. He's hearin' voices, talkin' to Martians, I don't know. He's even gettin' imaginary phone calls and—"

"OH MY GOD!" Del pointed at Frank.

Frank jumped, sloshing his drink out of his glass.

"The phone call! That's it, I—"

"Hold on now," Frank said, raising a hand. "That's what I was gettin' at." He glanced at Mama Dedé, who had just joined them. A look of caution was etched onto her face. He turned back to Del. "I uh, well... I thought... maybe... ah hell! If he's expectin' a call, what can it hurt for you to ring him up? You know." Frank wiggled his fingers again.

"Frank!" Mama Dedé said sternly. "What did I just—?"

Frank pleaded, "He already thinks he's gettin' calls, so—"

"He is!" Del blurted.

Frank's fingers stopped in mid-air. Mama Dedé cast her look of concern to Del. The room fell silent as all eyes turned to the young woman.

Mama Dedé said, "We're all ears now."

Del looked at the small shadow her foot made as she tipped the toe of her boot from one side to the other. Her mouth twisted slightly as she debated what to say. Finally, the words tumbled out.

"He's getting phone calls, not just imagining them in his head. They're actually happening. I heard one."

Mama D's tone softened. "What do you mean?"

Del told them about stopping in Jackson Square the day before, sitting on the park bench and retracing the days' events in a trance.

"His phone was ringing, Frank. The one that was unplugged. I heard it. I meant to tell you but," she looked at Mama D, "my magic sleeping potion made it kind of hard to remember some things."

Mama Dedé fanned her heating neck. "Well, I just thought you needed some rest. Besides, it wasn't magic, just a bit of—"

"OK, so, what does this mean?" Frank looked around the room.

"Wait a minute," Del said, turning to Frank. "How did you know about the phone calls?"

"It seems our Spider is a bit complicated. Sometimes he's a normal guy pleadin' his innocence, but when he starts talkin' about himself in third person..." He shrugged.

"Really?" Armand said.

"Yep, then add da invisible phone call and we got us a very unreliable perp."

"What do you mean by *the invisible phone call*?" Del asked.

"He got one right in da damn cell when I was questionin' him. Walked right over to da wall, picked up a receiver that no one else could see and said, 'hello.'"

"I can call him!"

Mama D. protested. "Wait a minute."

"No," Del said. "I can call him. At least, I think I can. It's *my* gift, right? You were trying to teach me anyway. What good does it do for me to have this stupid thing if I can't use it?"

Mama Dedé looked at Armand for support. At least *he* knew what she was concerned about. "I want you to be safe," she said. "Besides, you don't know," and her voice rose as she stared at Armand, "what else might be out there."

Armand pulled at his moustache. He believed that Del had the power to pull this off, but knew that Mama Dedé was only being protective. And admittedly, he didn't know the scope of the problem— or the threat—so he felt he wasn't the best mediator for the situation.

"Frenchy…"

He puffed at his pipe, but it had gone out. "I believe…," he began slowly, "that some caution should be observed… when undertaking an important decision… where all the facts may not be understood… by all parties involved."

Del's mouth twisted as she stared at Armand.

Mama Dedé glared.

Frank's cigar drooped. "You runnin' for office or somethin'?"

"Alright," Del said, turning to Mama D. "What aren't you telling me?"

CHAPTER 52

Madame Broussard watched with horror as her creation—
Alvie, the Boy Made of String—moved across the fresco.
His presence, represented by a strangely illuminated
black spot, moved through the shadow roads on his way home. She
silently prayed that he not bring home any *pets*.

In a blink of an eye, his shadow disappeared from the fresco and
she heard a loud commotion in the cabinet. Alvie had traveled the
shadow road and instantly arrived back home. He was suddenly
ejected out of the cabinet and onto the floor. She stood motionless,
waiting.

The Alvie-bones lay sprawled like a bundle of branches. They were
still connected to one another, but the makeshift tendons had allowed
them to flail in all directions. When he'd tumbled out, he was thrown
face first onto the floor and now lay in a twisted pile of bones. His
skull was wedged at the corner of the floor and wall; his right forearm
was stuck above his head and jutted up as if he intended to climb the
wall; his left leg had fallen forward at a disturbing angle and lay over

his left shoulder blade as if it wanted to walk up the wall. And all the time, the jutting remnants of skin pointed in all directions.

She looked back at the fresco and her secret place on it. Her eyes moved back and forth from the map to the shadow-cabinet. After several long seconds, she breathed a sigh of relief. There was no new activity on the wall. Had something been following Alvie, she thought she would have seen the result by now. Her existence remained secret.

With a twitch and a rattle, Alvie began to move. First, the right foot turned, and the toes began to move. They curled as if trying to grasp the air. They were looking for solid footing. Thankfully, many of the smaller tendons had survived the ferocious feeding from Mr. Scarmish. Stitching together the tiny toe bones just so he could keep his balance would have been a monumental task.

Next, the fingers of his right hand began to scratch at the wall. Tiny bits of plaster floated down from his effort and settled onto the remaining skin that clung to his skull.

He was trying to get up.

His left foot—just moments ago laying against the wall—convulsed and flew backwards, pulling his shin bone in the same direction. In fits and starts, his bones were reorienting. The left foot, now pointing away from his head, clawed against the floor and pulled his femur away from his shoulder blade. When both legs were extended behind him, his right hand dug into the wall and he started to get up. First, he knelt, then he leaned back on his knees. His skull was jammed back so that he stared at the ceiling and his left arm—which had torn loose from the violent windmill action of the first assault—dangled, unresponsively. Those tendons had not held.

The compressed skeleton of Alvie finally stood up, and with a dead

CLACKITY-CLICK-CLACKITY, the bones began to walk about the room.

She watched with pride as the little creature stumbled and bumped its way through the world. She almost righted the skull, but stopped just as it flung itself forward. Now it was staring at the floor. He seemed to be looking for something.

She walked around behind her podium as the Alvie-bones stumbled toward the viewing wall. This was where he'd met his fate just a few days earlier. He bumped along the brick, and dried pieces of skin broke off and fell to the floor. There they were quickly absorbed.

Alvie, suddenly orienting on his target, tripped or flung himself forward and disappeared beneath the display table.

Madame Broussard peered beneath the table, expecting to see a pile of unusable bones—the magic having exhausted itself—but was surprised again. She looked just in time to see the Alvie-mouth open abnormally wide, and with two new sharp teeth, clamp down on Willy's foot and begin to feed.

With the slightest whimper, Willy announced that he felt his brother's violation. For weren't they made of the same blood now? Alvie suckled only briefly, then fell silent. His energy spent. In response, Willy twitched twice, and his left eye flew open. Although Willy was laying on his right side, facing away from the woman, she knew his left eye had opened, for spreading across the floor, emanating from the eye, was a dim light. It shone out like a feeble ray from a dying flashlight, but it was strong enough to be seen.

She knelt on the floor, tucking her legs beneath her, and watched with wonderment. Shining out of Willy's eye was a scene. The very scene that Alvie had absorbed when he first traveled outside her hidden building. Alvie's exploration of the shadow roads and the living world outside had been recorded and transferred to Willy. It was replaying across the floor.

For the first time in many years, she saw the outside world as it really existed.

CHAPTER 53

S carmish trudged on. The hell-wind bit, shifted, and bit again. His energy was nearly exhausted. His last impromptu meal had served him well, and he had other means of sustaining himself, but he feared he'd have to leave before finding the crease.

His mind felt a surge of lightning as it scorched the barren desert. He tried to look away, but something would not allow him, and he saw the monstrosities again. The gargantuan, lumbering things beyond his own existence were still moving towards him. Forever they moved in his direction.

He was now up to his knees in dust. He'd traveled nearly as far as he could go. He couldn't quite remember why he'd come back, but knew his time was short. He was looking for something. A source of power. Or an answer.

Without warning, his mind sensed a vibration. One moment all he knew was the hell-wind, the next moment, a distinctive warble. A signal, in the distance. He was close to something now.

He teetered on nonexistence. He may have stayed too long this time, but whatever he'd been looking for must have been important. It must have something to do with the power. A hint as to where the power came from or where it went.

A crease! Yes, he was looking for the source of a crease. That was the sound he felt. It was near, and it felt terribly deadly. Surely created by someone very powerful.

He stayed himself against the wind and called the thread to him. It would be hard to see. Somehow, he knew that what he sought was hard to find. He would have to open his mind to it; more open than ever before.

Opening his mind to this strange place was like turning on a lighthouse light in a storm. It shone like a beacon. When he did, he immediately felt the twisting thread move his direction. But he felt other things move his direction as well.

The lumbering things from the horizon, seeking out his very existence, were closer now. He felt them closing in. As if in a strange dream, he'd thought they were a thousand years away, but now gauged the distance to be closer, to be mere hundreds.

But the thread was close too.

He pulled at the fiber with everything that was left of him. It moved closer, but at its own stubborn pace. The twisting filament of power that led to a crease that led to a person, skittered across the desert like a butterfly on a summer breeze. It jumped in fast, crooked arcs. How it moved was a mystery, but it was a deliberate thing. It skittered past him, only to reappear on another side.

The lumbering things were only days away now.

He wavered with exhaustion. He was nearly depleted. The thread of power skittered and danced just outside his reach. It mocked him. His mind was open, shining like a beacon to pull the thing in and it mocked him, making his presence known.

An insane, monstrous thing plodded just beyond his mind, only hours away now. He couldn't turn around and face his tormentor, for surely, he would be undone with the first glance. His mind began to unravel. Soon he would become dust and bury his own ankles.

The thread struck his hand with an electric shock. Out of the dark, the thread had found him. He grasped at it and felt its power flow into him. It was enormous! It was a thread unlike any he'd felt before.

Suddenly a smell came rushing up behind him. Something was there. He'd lingered too long. The lumbering insanity from the far reaches of this place had found him and now towered behind him, blocking out all else.

He grasped at the twisting thread of power, enduring the shock of the electricity and was ripped from the Desert of Dust just as oblivion overtook the place. The monster from the horizon had arrived a second too late. Its anger bellowed out in long, low waves that shook the desert like an earthquake. The remnants of Scarmish were pulled away from annihilation and fell through time and space; they drifted along the current of a source of unwieldy power.

CHAPTER 54

D el sat on her favorite couch with her feet curled beneath her as Mama Dedé explained what she'd seen lurking in the corners of the house.

"Where'd they come from?" Del asked quietly.

"Not sure, honey," the woman said. "I've been trying to figure that out the last few days."

"Ho-ly hell," Frank said. "You mean to tell me we got another hellish spirit on da loose?"

"Frank!" Mama D glared at him.

Armand interrupted. "I think what she is saying, is that we have again found ourselves… well…"

"It's because of me, isn't it?" Del said quietly. "I think there's something wrong with me."

Frank interjected. "Now Del-bell, dat's not what I'm sayin'—"

"That's OK. I've known for a while. Or at least, I've kinda felt it. Something's happening."

Mama Dedé stood up. "Honey, you're just goin' through the same thing we all do." She glared at Frank as she walked to the worktable. "Us women, that is." She poured herself a small glass of brandy. "You got all kind of things happening right now. Your body's changing. Your mind's changing. These two lunkheads don't know anything about that. You have to give yourself some time to grow into who you'll become. You can't rush it."

Del wanted to sink into the couch. She hated the attention. The scratches on her neck itched as the heat of embarrassment rose through her.

"As I was trying to say," Armand continued, "it's quite possible that these poor souls have lingered in this old house for many years. The previous owner was quite fascinating. Did I ever tell you the sto—?"

"Yes!" Frank and Mama Dedé said in unison.

"Oh. Well, of course." Armand puffed at his pipe. "I must have. Anyway, there are so many memories in this house… and in these books." He spread his arms. "It's a wonder that I haven't realized we have visitors before now."

Frank cleared his throat. "Look, all this is swell. Maybe you two can ask da spirits over for tea and crumpets, but I still have a perp that's walked, and kids dat are missin.'"

Armand and Mama Dedé exchanged hurt glances.

I'll do it, Frank. Del thought this to herself and Frank jumped as the thought entered his mind.

He looked at Del in surprise. Mama Dedé and Armand were protesting somewhere in a far-off conversation, but he was focused on the voice inside his head. His thick eyebrows wrinkled in question.

Del wasn't sure if what she'd just done qualified as a trance or not. It had happened so quickly it was over before she knew it. The other instances: at the ice cream shop with the snotty girls, and with Ronnie-

mister-indoor-sunglasses, she'd consciously thought about trancing—
projecting really. This time it was just a reaction. She shrugged at Frank
as if to say, *I don't know. It just happens.*

"I'm going to help," Del said. All conversation ended when she did.
"Mama D, if you could… you know, kind of, *back me up*, I'd appreciate
it."

Somewhere in Frank's mind he imagined Del had just winked at
him.

Be careful, he thought back, but wasn't sure if the message got to
her.

"But I don't want the tea," Del added.

The older woman protested. "We've talked about this—"

"No tea. Just your help." Del looked calmly at her mentor. "It should
be easy, right? It's just the projection of a phone call."

"Well…"

"It's no different than the image of the butterfly I sent to Jimmy the
first day you taught me."

Mama Dedé stabbed the air in front of her. "Of course, it is! You're
gonna try to talk to some man who's already got someone talkin' to
him. Who do you think that other person is?"

"I don't know," Del said. "But with your help, I should be safe,
right?" She turned her attention to Frank. "What do I need to say?
Who does he think is calling him?"

Frank grumbled. "I wish I knew. But let's just see if you can ring
him up. If he takes da bait… hell, I don't know. Just ask him to come
back for a pickup."

"Come back where?"

"Don't know. But *he* should know. We gotta hope he does, anyway."
Realizing a prime opportunity for collaboration, Frank redirected

the conversation. "Mama D, do you think it's possible to pick up our perp—once Del rings him up—and take over da trackin'?"

"Of course it is," Mama Dedé said.

Del shot a question at Frank's mind. *What are you doing?*

Frank kept his gaze fixed on the elder woman, but spoke broadly. "Now, just go with me on this." Del pulled back. "You're right to be concerned. I am. If Spider ain't crazy, he's at least lookin' for it. Dere's no tellin' what she may run into, if she can even send him a call. And *if* he," Frank made air quotes, "*picks up*, who knows what da hell's gonna happen. I'd feel a lot better if you were to take over the *followin' part*, if we can even get him on da move. Dis way, we can keep her out of it, if it gets messy."

Del understood what Frank had just done, but sent a glare into his mind anyway. She wasn't a little kid, after all.

"Get!" Frank waved his hand at an invisible gnat.

Mama D stared at Frank, but his eyes never wavered. She could feel a sales job when it was being laid on, but there was some truth—a lot, actually—to what he'd said. "OK, Frank. I'll buy it. I think you're right. It'd be safer all around."

She looked at Del, who returned a restrained smile. They appeared to be in tentative agreement.

"Settled," Frank said, and headed for the worktable. Armand was already there, refreshing his drink. He poured three-fingers for Frank this time, then clinked his glass quietly.

Well done was the message.

CHAPTER 55

Jimmy sat on the back porch and looked for rain drops. The adults were talking about Del again, and he was tired of playing with the chess pieces. He rocked slowly as the dark clouds gathered overhead.

The stone maiden that stood over the fountain beckoned to Jimmy, but he was ignoring her. Since his accident, he'd been told not to play around the water. He couldn't quite remember what happened or why he shouldn't play there, just that it was dangerous. But there were lots of dangerous things in Armand's house.

The rail along the second-floor library was dangerous. He'd dreamt that some little boy had jumped off that rail and squished his head on the floor below. He'd even watched him do it a few times.

Armand had some really sharp knives in the kitchen—they were dangerous. They were sad that they hardly ever got used. Sometimes they rattled in the drawers when Jimmy walked by. They wanted out.

Even all the candles near Armand's books were dangerous. The flames wanted to jump off the candlesticks all the time. Jimmy heard them say so. If someone could just knock them over—they weren't heavy after all, even a baby could do that—they would be happy and wouldn't have to live in one place the rest of their lives. Wouldn't that be nice?

The stone maiden whispered to Jimmy again, but the wind blew her words away. A white, shadowy arm moved in the darkness. She beckoned him close. She needed him to hear her words.

He looked away and saw something else move in the garden. The shadows were moving more than usual. It didn't feel windy on the porch, but it must be in the yard to cause all this movement. Goosebumps ran up his arms. He felt it was time to go in.

*

"Well dat was a damn bust," Frank said as he poked at the fire. Sparks shot up angrily in agreement.

"I'm sorry," Del said. "I thought I could do it."

"You did," said Mama Dedé. "You can't help it if he was passed out drunk."

"I should have expected it," Frank said. "I gave him a pretty good scare today. Hell, probably my fault he's like dat anyway."

"So, what do we do now?" Del asked. She picked at the last few oyster crackers on her plate and nibbled them.

"I know where to look," Mama Dedé said. "I'll pick him up in the morning and see what I can find out. When his head straightens out, you can call him again."

"If you do," Frank added, "tell him to return at nine a.m. I'll be watching his apartment and trail him from there."

Del looked around. "Where's Jimmy?"

No one had seen him for quite a while.

She jumped up in alarm and looked over the rail. "Jimmy? Are you down there?"

No sound could be heard.

"Jimmy?" Del descended the stairs. Her quick stomps echoing from the ceiling.

She heard a drawer close as she entered the kitchen. Jimmy turned around and looked at her with glazed eyes.

"There you ar—what were you doing?"

The boy stared at her with blank eyes. His hands fidgeted behind his back.

"Jimmy, are you alright?" Del stepped forward, only to see Jimmy step back. He stopped when he bumped against the counter.

"What are you holding?"

He seemed to be in a dream. His gaze went past her to a faraway place. He fidgeted.

Slowly, realization came back to him and he focused on Del's face. "Hi, Deh."

"What's wrong? What were you doing?"

"Talkin'."

Del glanced around the room. "Talkin' to who? I don't see anyone."

"To da mouse."

"The mouse?"

Jimmy walked toward her. "Yeah, he tuck in da dwawer. I was gonna 'et him out."

"A mouse was stuck in the drawer? How do you know?"

"He toad me. But you scawed him away."

"Oh, I'm sorry that I scared him. Are you sure it was a mouse?"

Jimmy's empty hands dropped to his side as he brushed past Del. "I'm tiad. I'm gonna bed."

"OK, sleepyhead. What? No hug?"

"No. I'm yust tiad."

Del watched Jimmy ascend the stairs up to his room. She made a mental note to check on this scene later. He seemed out of sorts tonight.

She walked to the counter and pulled open several drawers. If there was a mouse, she'd tell Armand. She didn't want to have to deal with it. But she doubted there was.

"Good night," Armand's voice floated down the stairs. "Don't let the bedbugs bite."

Rummaging through the drawers, Del only saw an odd assortment of utensils: old, tarnished silverware, miscellaneous knives, and some things she had no idea what they were used for. The other drawers held similar items, but no mice.

Leaning against the sink, she thought about all that had happened in the last few days. Even today had been long. No wonder Jimmy was tired. She rubbed her forehead and listened to the banter float down the stairs. The night owls seemed to be winding up for another late one. She knew each one had their own opinion on what she should do and how much she should be involved. She appreciated each person for who they were—even if Mama D could be kind of over-protective. But she wanted to be free of all the mothering. She wondered when she ever would be. She wondered how all of this would end.

The wind had been listening to her thoughts, and knew the answer. It knocked a branch against the side of the house and foretold a dire warning: it would not end tonight, for there was a long night to come.

But no one heard.

Behind her, a dark shadow had also been listening, and had an opinion. It slid out from the drainpipe and crept a black path across the white sink basin. Silent as death it slid up the cold porcelain toward the warm girl. To the shadow, she was like the life-giving sun.

With her hands wedged into her jean pockets, Del kicked her hips and launched herself off the sink edge just as the shadow reached the top. The shadow lingered on the lip as its sun departed, then slipped back toward the drain. There were many pipes in this house.

Her hand slipped further into her pocket and like a static shock, she felt it. The fingers of her right hand came out holding a fragile item. The lock of hair she'd found in Spider's trunk was still in her pocket.

Damn it! It had slipped her mind again. Why hadn't she used it before now? This was probably her best chance at finding at least one of the kids, and it had been within her grasp for over a day now.

Tucking it away gently, she headed for the stairs. It was lucky the other three were just catching their second wind. She guessed they'd stay occupied late into the evening, and Mama Dedé wouldn't bother her.

Mustering the biggest yawn she could, she primed herself for a quick diversion. By the time she reached the top of the stairs, her eyes were red and watery, and another yawn was following it.

"You guys have fun," she said, waving at them absently. "I'm bushed. The days are catching up to me."

"Wear your gris," was the only warning Mama Dedé gave before Del passed out of sight down the hall.

No one noticed the shadows gathering in the high corners as Del disappeared into the dark.

CHAPTER 56

The liquor bottles sat warm and inviting on the end of the worktable. Long planned, the firelight leapt from their flames and danced across the etched glass. Like a bee with only one chance to sting, each flash of light danced its glory, then died quietly, another flash always ready to take its place.

The dance was lithe and seductive. It was meant to attract. The bottles glowed with a subtle yet unnatural brilliance tonight. Many pairs of eyes looked longingly over the warm, inviting bottles. Every pair of eyes knew the effect of the bottles, but only three mouths would drink from them. It was a good plan.

The shadows had watched the three elders for a long time. It took a long time because it was hard for the shadows to communicate; each driven by its own need; each trapped in its own time and place. Some, perhaps arriving late to the party, were not sure why they were here. But at least *here* was somewhere. At least *here* was a direction toward the living. So, they agreed it was a good plan.

The promise of the bottle would work. The liquid inside the bottles was soothing; it must be. The three elders loved the bottles. The firelight danced *on* the bottles and the three elders danced *with* the bottles.

The liquor inside was dark and hid the shadows. It was a very good plan.

Frank pulled the stopper from the bottle of brandy. It looked magical as the firelight danced off the cut glass. It seemed to sparkle more tonight than he remembered. This would be a good way to start the evening.

The aroma—like a genie from a bottle—snaked out and soothed him. It promised a warm, loving night. A night of not thinking about his wife and missing her. He could let his guard down here. Why not? He was among friends.

Mama Dedé watched as the dark red liquid splashed into her glass. It ran down the inside, silk over crystal, soft warmth over hard edges. It reminded her of a night, long ago. A night with a lover, dark and feverish. She let some of those thoughts warm her. Why shouldn't she? She was among friends here.

Armand felt the sting pass his lips and coat the inside of his mouth. He let the feeling consume him and fill his mind. Specially hidden memories were uncovered and brought back to life. Dark secrets remembered. Why not feel happy about them? He was among friends here.

The three elders sighed, each lost in their own memories, and they smiled at their secrets. They glowed slightly in the firelight, errant flashes dancing exotic across their faces.

This was a good plan.

"Tell us a story," Frank said. He pointed at Armand with his glass. "Oui?"

"Yeah, da kids are in bed. Surely you ain't run out of—"

"No, no," Armand said quickly. "Mon ami, do you think I would not have a—well, they're not *stories* really... I, I prefer to think of each one as its own theory. A theory attempting to describe one of the many mysteries of the universe."

"Yeah, OK." Frank walked to the fire and poked at it. He settled into his usual chair and turned it towards Armand.

Armand was carefully twisting his moustache. Each turn seemed to increase the sparkle in his eyes. By the time he was done his eyes were nearly a different color.

"Let's see..." He began a slow walk behind the table. Mama Dedé joined Frank at the fireplace. She brought the brandy with her.

Armand's safe-cracker fingers danced on the air as they opened the folds of his mind. Enormous stacks of research lived there—leaning precariously amongst the gray folds—and threatened to tumble out. At the same time, his swinging hand toppled a stack of folders and the written notes within went skidding across the table.

"Oh, my," he said. "What a jumbled mess."

Without even having to perform his word association ritual, the obvious choice of a story came to him.

"Of course!" He pointed at them with a wide grin. "Have you ever the story of the Tangled Spirit?"

Mama Dedé had heard the term recently, but couldn't recall where. Armand saw the question on her face.

Frank had filed it away better. "Say, didn't that come up when we were talkin' about Spider da other night?"

"Very good, mon ami," Armand said. "You would make a good detective someday." He began what the others thought of as his *lecture walk*. A leisurely but purposeful stride moved him around the room.

"Yes, young Del did mention it, just two nights ago. It was very much in passing, but we were focused on other things." He pulled a long draw from his pipe. "As we should have been!" The mouthpiece pointed at them. "But it stuck with me, and I was able to do some research. It's quite the fascinating story."

"You don't say?" Mama Dedé was getting impatient.

"Yes, quite fascinating." Armand was in his element, and missed the slight. "It took a lot of digging. There is little information on the... legend."

Frank cleared his throat. "Well, what is it?"

"Not what, but who. You see, it seems the St. Augustine Orphanage—the very one that Del called home for so long—has had a problem keeping track of the unfortunate for many years. After much research and a bit of luck, I discovered many cases of children that were simply labeled as *runaway* or *missing*."

"So?" Frank said. "Lotsa kids run away every day."

"Yes, I agree. And I doubt the record keeping was much better at the other orphanages. But the number missing from St. Augustine's seemed quite extraordinary. Where did they go? How did they get out? Why so many from one place?

"I wondered if there was some pattern to the disappearances. Were the children ever found? Did they return?

"I considered the possibility of them simply slipping out and never returning. But it's hard for children to disappear on their own; even harder when they are eight years old; and most difficult yet, when they are twins."

"Twins?" Mama Dedé said.

"Yes. Twins. In 1845 two twin girls were found huddled in an alley. They were sent to the St. Augustine orphanage. I have seen the registration documents. There was even a small article written about them in a newspaper. I have a clipping of it somewhere. It describes the girls as mutes—perhaps from shock, who knows—but with no knowledge of their names or family. They simply appeared one day."

"If they couldn't talk," Frank began, "how'd they know they were twins? They must have been identical. Did they look identical?"

Armand threw his hands up. "Mon ami, please. I have no way of knowing. But perhaps it was because the head mother kept daily notes *about* the twins." His smile promised intrigue.

"Anyway, the strange thing was not the girls themselves, but the events that surrounded them. The daily logs indicated that the girls seemed to communicate with one another by silent gestures, or as one entry recorded: *an innate understanding.* Several transfers to other orphanages were initiated, but they were never completed. Doesn't that seem odd?"

He sent the question to Frank, but continued.

"Additionally, it was reported that several of the younger children came down with—and I quote, *acute cases of malnutrition.* A type of wasting disease. But the whole orphanage didn't suffer, only the youngest, who presumably would have been housed in the same room."

He pointed at Mama Dedé for confirmation, but continued.

"And on top of all that, after the girls disappeared, the malnourishment malaise affecting the others simply disappeared." He wiped his hands once for emphasis.

"Well…," Frank said, scratching his head. "Da trail of clues is kinda… loose"

"Oh, but it's not," Armand countered.

"It ain't?"

"No, it… ain't!" Armand exclaimed with a point of his finger. "It's precisely at this time that the Tangled Spirit comes into the rich mythos of our city."

Armand poured himself another drink and savored the rich aroma. "I say, the brandy seems especially delicious tonight. It's going down quite easily."

Raising his glass, Frank said, "I concur with your conclusion, counselor." He'd been sipping his slower than normal this evening. He had some indigestion flaring up.

Mama Dedé waved her glass as well and said, "Be a dear and bring your handsome moustache over here and pour me a little more. This is yuummmy. I'm having some cozy feelings with this batch."

Armand wiggled his eyebrows at them as he approached. He danced a soft-shoe across the floor.

Mama Dedé hummed a tune into the glass she held against her cheek.

Armand poured, then danced his way back to his speaking position.

"So… where was I?" His hand waved lazily in the air, trying to orient his thoughts. "The twins… the twins, the sick children, the… brandy… yes of course! The Tangled Spirit."

Frank nodded his understanding, but blinked his eyes at a wavering Armand. He suddenly looked unsteady.

Firelight leapt from bottle to bottle, casting a final, hypnotic dance.

"Within a year of the twins' dish-appearance," His words suddenly came out mushy. "Oh, my." He patted his numbing lips and sipped again. "We find the firsht reference known… the firsht… to a haunting known as the *Tangled Spirit*. And do you know where the hauntings began?"

His finger jabbed the air triumphantly, which pulled him off balance again.

"Preshisely! In orphanages."

"You don't say?" Frank was intrigued, but also concerned at the sudden change in his friend. "In orphanages?"

Armand nodded as he strolled the room. "Yesh, I'm 'fraid so."

"So, if we're talkin' about ghosts of da girls, why they tangled up?"

Armand, facing the stained-glass windows, stopped and shrugged. His wobble was more pronounced, like a top losing momentum. Frank willed him to be still, lest he take a nasty fall.

"Hee, hee, heee..." Mama Dedé mumbled into the glass that was still pressed against her cheek. Her eyes were closed, and she was whispering. "That was a funny story, Samuel. Tell me another one."

Frank looked at his companions, then at his glass of brandy. It sparkled invitingly at him, although he had barely touched it.

He set the glass on the table and grabbed the other from Mama Dedé's hand. "All right you two, I think this is a wrap." He suddenly felt a driving need to be clear of this room.

The firelight protested and danced frantic across the room. It exposed itself, naked and inviting. A sinuous fire-dance spread across the floor.

Armand spun around to protest, but the shadow beneath his feet was waiting. The tassels of the rug were bunched together, catching Armand's foot and sending him sideways. In slow-motion he stumbled toward the railing.

Frank made two quick steps, then lunged on the third to intercept him before he tumbled over the rail. With a quick jerk of Armand's arm, Frank redirected his momentum to the floor by the edge of the couch. Armand went down hard, teetered on his butt, then righted himself as his legs rocked him upright. His glass rolled across the floor and the dark shadow within it escaped into the floorboards.

"Whoa der, hoss!" Frank exclaimed. "You alright?"

Armand shook his head and looked around.

Frank said, "Say, did you break out a new brandy or somethin'?"

"Mon ami." Armand floated his hand in the air, looking for assistance.

"Yeah, that's what I thought." He pulled Armand to his feet and steadied him. "You make it down da stairs alright?"

Armand nodded and moved gingerly around the couch and grasped the rail.

Frank helped Mama Dedé up and pointed her down the hall. "You too, huh?"

"Nigh-night, Frank," she said. Her arms stretched out as she bumped her way down the hall.

"I'll lock up on my way out. Y'all feel better in da mornin."

Outside, Frank welcomed the cold air. His head immediately began to clear. The upstairs library with the rich furnishings and warm fireplace had coerced them to stay up many long nights, but it was on overdrive tonight, he thought.

Starting his car, he glanced back at the house and saw the second-story lights click off one by one. He pulled out of Armand's courtyard and made a right turn. With the top down, he clearly heard the old gate motor groan to life and begin to shut the heavy iron gate. He didn't remember Armand shutting it before, at least not since the gang started living here. It was easier for everyone to come and go that way. But, better to be safe with the condition he and Mama Dedé were in. They were unlikely to hear anything tonight.

Yes, safer that way, Frank thought as he drove away. Nothing could get past the tall wrought-iron fence and stone columns that surrounded the house. And the heavy iron gate was sure to lock them in tight.

CHAPTER 57

When Del had closed the door behind her, she'd stripped off her clothes and threw on the first nightgown she could find. Several long white gowns had been left in the chest of drawers, and they seemed to be a favorite of Mama D's, so they were always on top. She lit a few candles and turned off the lights. The room seemed darker than usual, but she assumed that was because of the clouds rolling in. Even the streetlamps were having trouble shining light through her window.

She sat on her bed and bunched the pillows up behind her back. The banter from the library was in full swing. This was perfect, she thought. Frank and Armand would keep Mama D occupied most of the night. This would give her a chance to locate who the hair belonged to.

She'd only used a personal item once before—the night when they all fought the Gris-gris man. But everyone had freely given their hair, even Frank. She remembered the warning from Mama Dedé: that if the person didn't give willingly, it could make the magic go bad. But

Del wasn't even sure if what she could do was considered magic. She didn't feel magical. And until just a few months ago, she didn't believe in this stuff anyway.

What harm could it do to try and locate someone with the hair? It's not like she was going to try and control them.

She wrapped the piece of hair around the inside of her little finger and closed her eyes. Slipping into her trance had become so easy, she almost didn't feel the transition anymore. Her mind quickly jumped backwards to Jackson Square, to the ice cream shop, to Frank's car, then to Spider's. Like landmarks on a long journey, those scenes stuck out to her. There was no need to look at every detail going on around her just to get there.

The shadows in the house found this fortunate.

Watching her day-old self take the hair from Spider's trunk, she knew what to do next. She would track the nervous man through his daily routines *before* she and Frank caught him. She wanted to see what else he'd done that day. It would be much slower, because she hadn't watched this particular movie-reel before, and she'd have to look for clues, but she had all night.

She slipped out of the trance just quick enough to pull the covers up to her chin. The ventilation seemed to be on the fritz again, and the room was getting colder. She wanted to be able to concentrate. Without another look, she snuggled back into the pillows and let her mind drift away.

*

Jimmy had been watching the train move around his room for several minutes before he heard Del's door close. They had the two rooms down the hall past the fireplace. Mama Dedé had a room on the other side of the library, but the hallways ran past both sides of the big bookshelves and connected at the back of the house with another hall that ran between them. This way, people could go way past the library, circle behind it, and come out on the other side.

The colored train was an image cast from the shade of his night light that sat on a side table. The night light was really a small lamp with a cylindrical shade on it. The heat of the light bulb made the shade spin slowly around, which made the image of the train move around the room. He imagined he was driving the train, and hoped he'd dream about it tonight.

The train looked fun and a little scary at the same time. Fire and smoke billowed backwards from its smokestack as it flew down the tracks. A large iron grill stuck out from the locomotive to clear any cows, tumble weeds or bad guys that may have wandered onto the tracks. Even the steel wheels seemed to be turning fast.

He'd also been watching the shadows move along the walls as the train went around. He'd had the train light for a while now, but didn't remember it making such funny shadow shapes on the wall.

They looked fun and a little scary as well.

CHAPTER 58

Madame Broussard watched in amazement as her new liaison clambered around her showroom. For that was how she now thought of Alvie. He was more than just a means to transmit a message. He was becoming more than just a vessel to absorb the life outside her window and bring it back to her. The little boy made of string with the compressed bones and tattered skin was almost that: a little boy.

She had given life to him after all, hadn't she? Her usage of the Thirteenth Passage had been her sacrifice. Who knew what long term affects may come from that? He even had a half-brother. The two of them were forever linked, albeit in an unusual way.

The woman marveled as Alvie stumbled around the room, his bones *CLACKITY-CLICK-CLACKING* as he bumped along of his own will. That was one of the things that amazed her. The first time she'd sent him out, he was under her suggestion. She knew he would follow the psychic signal she'd been sending to Spider. The signal was his guidewire. All he had to do was propel himself and he would end up in the right place, eventually. But now, now he was exploring the room on his own.

Granted, he *was* clumsy, but she could overlook that. After all, Scarmish had sucked out all his muscle and organs. But to see her little creation move around on his own was an experience she hadn't anticipated. It was much different than letting a transformation happen, such as the one Willy was going through. That was different.

But the thing that amazed her the most, and that linked the two boys in the most unusual way, was that whatever Alvie *saw* with his empty eye sockets, Willy *showed* with his working eyes. After the first transference of sight had occurred where Willy replayed what Alvie had seen, it was as if a mental channel had been created between the two of them. Whatever Alvie saw *now*, as he stumbled around the room, was projected out of Willy's eyes as it happened.

When she realized this, she picked Willy from the floor and propped him up in a chair, facing the wall. By another odd happenstance, the fresco characters on the wall *consciously moved* outside the two circles of light that Willy's eyes cast upon the wall. It was as if the fresco was making way for this new form of viewing. Within the two circles shone the stumbling, leaning view of what Alvie was seeing.

After several minutes, she knew he was ready. She walked to the dark chifforobe and opened the cabinet door. Alvie's crusted head immediately turned and looked behind him. Echoes from the cracking neck bones bounced off the walls and fled into the darkness.

He felt the pull of the shadow road. It beckoned to him.

Walking backwards, dead eye sockets looking deep into the shadows, Alvie took several steps, fell into the waiting shadow and disappeared.

Madame Broussard closed the cabinet door and took her seat

next to Willy. She didn't know where Alvie would end up, but quietly hoped her intuition was correct. Alvie was a creature of the night, neither living or dead (in his unique state), and would follow a path that all night creatures did.

Granted, most of the night creatures had their own desires and could go where they wanted—resisting the natural flow of the shadow roads. But some were lazy—or new to being dead—and could only go where the power was the strongest. She hoped this was the case for Alvie.

If so, it didn't matter which thread of power he started with. The most powerful always created the bigger crease. Like water, other things naturally flowed to it. Alvie would stumble his way along the shadow roads until he was caught up in a current he couldn't resist. This current would twist and turn, but eventually (and usually) would end at a great source of power.

The tricky thing about shadow roads and creases was they weren't attached directly to the person who created them, more to the location. Madame Broussard knew this. They weren't like phone lines that only went to one phone. They were more like worn paths in an old carpet. You could see that many people had traveled through the front door and into the main room (an obvious crease of traffic), but after that, the worn path faded off in many directions. A crease did the same thing because the person who created it was not always in the same place when they tranced, but if you could just find your way to the right house, you could find the person with the power, regardless of which room they were in.

Not only was there a chance Alvie could end up at the house of the Spirit Hunter, but Madame Broussard would be able to find them simply by feeling the pull of their power. She only hoped Scarmish hadn't already found them.

CHAPTER 59

In her trance, Del followed Spider's car. He mostly ran errands and stopped at a lot of bars. Whatever his job was, it seemed pretty easy. He was on the road a lot.

The other thing she noticed was that he talked to himself a lot. Sometimes he talked to the radio, as if responding to what was just said. Other times—like while walking—he had conversations as if someone was standing next to him. It was difficult to tell if the conversations were instructions or not.

She quickly skimmed the day scenes and several of the evenings where he'd stayed in. Finally, she got to a night where he was leaving. It was pretty late to be taking a drive, she thought.

As soon as he pulled into the alley behind St. Augustine's, she knew he was the guy.

Unknowingly, Del clenched her toes and fingers in anger. Her mind was far away, but the knowledge of what Spider was about to do had a physical effect on her body.

In her room, the shadow that had crept between the sheets pulled back slightly at the unexpected movement. It thought Del had fallen asleep sitting up. It had watched her for so many nights, it knew she fell asleep in different positions. It had watched the Positions of Del for a long time. It was drawn to the subtleness of the lines; they stirred something in its past.

Del watched the scene before her carefully. Spider parked; he got out of the car and walked away. The image lost focus again.

Her leg flinched.

It was the same thing as before! Why couldn't she focus?

The scene jumped ahead, but it was still the same night. And he was driving away with someone! She was sure of it.

Del felt another presence in the car with Spider—perhaps two. And there was something familiar about it. She felt like she knew who was in the car with him.

Who is it? she screamed in her mind. She searched the scene from all angles, but saw no one else. She kicked her leg out in frustration, catching the shadow by surprise. It was caught by her heel. It had waited a long time to feel her touch, and Del had finally come to it!

Not wanting to break the spell, the shadow lay still, warm and gentle. From experience, it knew that the living typically had an adverse reaction to its touch, so it had to go slow. It had to let the warm skin adjust slowly to its presence. Ever so gently, it slid itself around her ankle and inspected the pores and fine hairs there. The tiny hairs reacted with revulsion, but it wasn't enough to send alarm signals. It would be patient.

Many other shadows—previously frightened away by the gris the old woman had cast—looked on wantonly from the corners of the high ceiling. They would brave the gris for a touch of Del.

*

Jimmy's train loomed large on the walls of his room. It had grown considerably over the last several minutes. He lay huddled with his covers drawn up to his chin. The train went around and around the room. The smokestack billowed smoke and fire. He thought he heard it growl.

He almost got up and turned it off, but he'd have to walk across the dark floor, and it looked like it was moving also. He tried to be brave like a lion, but was pretty sure lions didn't have to face things like this.

The lightbulb pulsed brightly. Something was wrong with it. It was too bright. Jimmy thought it might catch on fire. The light pulsed, the heat surged, and the painted shade spun faster and faster. The growling train sped around his room in a mad attempt to fly off its tracks. It was going so fast, sometimes it looked like it was going backwards.

He whimpered and tried calling out to Del, but his voice was lost in the blanket he'd pulled tightly around his face.

Forward and back, forward and back. The light shining from the smokestack searched his room. It flashed and pulsed, again and again. He couldn't stop looking at it. Something was in the train. Something was driving it into his mind. He could feel the bright light probing his eyes, sliding around his eyeballs into the back of his head. He tried to shut his eyes but couldn't. He didn't want it in his head, but it was in there now.

Forward and back, forward and back. The mad train went so fast it had settled into a slow, rocking rhythm. Like a magician swinging a gold watch, his open eyes grew heavy. The train was in his mind now, a surprisingly vast mind. And Jimmy felt himself fall under its spell.

*

Alvie traveled the night road for an unknowable amount of time. The Boy Made of String, now with his own instincts, let the road take him where it would. His hollow eye sockets saw the dark void of space and time, and let the ancient forces jettison him along. He felt a great pull on his being. He was heading towards a powerful source.

Suddenly, he was flung off the night road and floated somewhere in a group of shadows. He was still mostly shadow himself, so nothing noticed his arrival.

Madame Broussard watched with anticipation as Willy's eyes cast the scene of Alvie's arrival onto the wall.

Alvie had arrived at a grand house that stood three stories tall. Across from the house, the Lafayette Cemetery #1 sat, cold and silent.

Was that a coincidence, she wondered? How interesting that the house of a powerful Spirit Hunter—if that's where he was—would be right next to one of the oldest cemeteries in the city. Perhaps it was not coincidence, however. A person with that type of power could have many uses for a cemetery right next door.

Alvie's dead eyes captured the image of the stone crypts that lay in close rows. The shadow he rode had settled onto the branch of a large tree that had originated in the yard of the grand house, but had stretched all the way over the road and touched the cemetery wall. It was this branch that he now walked.

With careful steps, Alvie picked his way along the outstretched wooden arm, toward the house. The limb was so massive, it could have supported a whole army of Alvies and not felt the strain.

The roots of the giant tree must run deep, Broussard thought. Deep beneath the yard, twisting around the foundation, above and below the road, always reaching toward the dead.

A faint *CLICKETY-CLACK-CLACK* emanated from Alvie's bones and floated away on the wind. The sound could have easily been from two branches—quarrelsome old spouses—settling into their nightly slumber, so the sounds caused no alarm.

Then, as his boney foot stepped onto a substantial shadow, Alvie was transported once again. In an instant, Madame Broussard's view changed from the exterior of the house, to a dark view inside a bedroom.

A heavy-set woman was sleeping in a large bed, snoring lightly.

CHAPTER 60

Del watched her own scene in frustration. She wanted to know who was in the car with Spider. She fought with the scene and it fought back. Something was distorting it. Spider drove slowly through the dark streets. Something in his trunk made a noise. It was a voice! Del was sure of it. But she watched in horror as Spider reached out and turned the radio up. He didn't want to hear what was in the trunk.

After several long minutes, Del watched as the car slowed halfway down a block. The area looked familiar. Spider crept the car forward as if not sure where to stop or turn, then suddenly, he made a right into an alley and completely disappeared.

Del almost came out of her trance, she was so surprised. She couldn't believe what she was seeing—or not seeing. One minute the car was there, then it wasn't. She waited to see if the scene would correct itself or not.

It didn't.

After several minutes, his car reappeared. Like magic out of thin air, his car suddenly came out of the alley, made another right turn and went down the road.

What just happened?

Del hovered in her trance, trying to think what to do. She moved away from the scene in her mind, giving her a bird's eye view, and immediately knew where she was. She and Frank had been on this very same block just two days ago. This is where she felt the strange presence.

This has to be where the kids are! But why didn't we find it when we were there? Why did—?

Where's Spider?

She fast-forwarded through the scenes and found Spider still in the car. He was heading home. And he was alone. Somehow, she knew.

She turned her attention back to the dark city block. Something was there she couldn't see, and discovering it was the key to finding the kids. She was certain of that.

With all her concentration, she focused on the center of the block. She willed herself to see it. Somewhere, far away, her leg was beginning to tingle. It must have fallen asleep. But she was too close to stop now. It would just have to tingle. With a final push, she felt herself rush toward the space in the scene where something should exist. She meant to pierce the veil that was hiding it.

Like a lightning flash, white light exploded around her and she tore through the fabric of the present. She'd slipped again, landing in an old building. There were people here.

And the screams were horrifying.

*

As the spirit of the train pulled at Jimmy's mind, he felt the annoying gnats return. This time they were trying to fly into his ears.

"Bah! Pllttt! Geh away!" Jimmy pulled the covers tight around his head to keep the bugs out.

The things were flying, like tiny spirits of light, out of the train's smokestack and swarming around his head. Some of them flew at his eyes, only to trick him into uncovering his ears so others could fly in. Then when he stuck his fingers in his ears, they flew at his eyes again. But he couldn't close his eyes. The forward and back motion of the train had stuck them open, and his eyes were filling up with mean bugs. And he hated mean tricks.

"Aahhh, tupid bugs!" He swatted his ears and eyes as fast as he could. His cheeks were stinging. His eyes were blurry with tears. "Geh away! Geh away!" He cried and rocked in his bed.

Other shadow things began to crawl from beneath the rug.

*

Mama Dedé slept a deep sleep. Deeper than ever before. Her heart rate slowed to an abnormal pace. It was tired also. It worked hard pumping blood around her large frame, and something tonight had made it sleepy as well. The brandy had been delicious and had coaxed her entire body to simply go to sleep.

*

In his downstairs bedroom, Armand had been quiet for a long time, then let out a loud, ragged snore. He liked sleeping down here because it was cooler. Also, because he couldn't hear anything through the thick floors and high ceilings. He never heard a thing from his housemates.

He gasped for air in his sleep, then fell quiet again. He had fallen asleep with the covers over his face, which he'd never done before. He'd barely made it into bed before he fell into a deep sleep. He hadn't even had time to wonder if Frank would try to close the outside gate.

*

Alvie traversed the shadows of the grand house, but was somehow aware of a disturbance that was building behind the walls; the air pressure was changing. He could feel it getting tighter as if the old walls were stuffed with too many things. There were simply too many shadows trying to get in.

Madame Broussard leaned forward and stared at the fresco. The entire landscape of the city had shifted and reoriented itself with Alvie in the middle of her line of sight. Next to her, Willy's eyes burned brightly as the scenes from the house were transmitted from Alvie, back to Willy. She was seeing what Alvie was seeing, but at the same time, seeing what was happening around the house. The fresco made sure of that. And the combination was unlike anything she'd seen before.

The ring of shadows that surrounded the Spirit Hunter's house was enormous, maybe just as large as what surrounded her own hiding place. Granted, they did live next to a cemetery, but she doubted that could account for all the activity. Something was happening. Whether because of Alvie's presence or some cosmic coincidence, she had tapped into this house just as something big was about to happen.

Shining out through Willy's eyes were the details of a home that slumbered under the false presumption of privacy.

A large woman slept soundly in a bed. It was hard to tell, but Madame Broussard thought she might recognize the woman. She felt a kinship to her.

As Alvie slid down the shadow of the wall, a commotion from the first floor pulling him down. There in another bedroom lay a sleeping man. Although she thought he wouldn't be a sleeping man for long. It sounded as if he were suffocating. And the night things that crawled over his chest weren't helping his breathing.

She glanced at the fresco; the black ring around the house had grown even larger. She almost feared for the people inside, for surely if they were this powerful to pull so many spirits to them, they deserved a chance to defend themselves. Broussard was well aware of the shadows that kept a constant vigil around her. Some had honor, others... they were there simply to feed.

She willed Alvie to get a better look at the man. She wasn't sure he would respond to her suggestion, but she hadn't seen the inside of another home in so long, she couldn't help herself. Just as she thought the covers over the man's face would slip down, she heard someone yell out: "GEH AWAY 'TUPID BUGS!" And Alvie's view of the sleeping man was ripped away. It was as if he had stepped onto a conveyor belt that instantly swept him aside. He'd hit a crease. Or perhaps, one was nearby and had just pulled him to it.

Willy's eyes projected a view of the world that she didn't understand. Shining upon the fresco, flashing with frantic color, was the picture of a train running around and around a bedroom. But Alvie wasn't looking at it from a hidden shadow in the corner. He was seeing it as if sitting on something. And he was slapping himself in the face. Somehow, Alvie was seeing a train fly around the room while he was slapping at his eyes. And his hands had skin.

CHAPTER 61

Del, having just slipped, cringed at the sound of the screams. High-pitched and frantic, they were a mix of human and non-human sounds. Although they were muffled from the thick floor she was standing on, she could hear the pain.

She'd landed in the attic of an old building that was stuffed with crates and cobwebs. It appeared to not have been used for many years.

She knew she had slipped again, and felt it was an older version of New Orleans. It felt familiar.

"What was that?" Mumbled words floated up through the floorboards.

Chants and screams continued. A metallic screech dug at her nerves. Whatever was happening below must be terrible, and she feared what she would find.

Still unsure what her limitations were in this past reality, Del took a step, listening, then another. She didn't want to give herself away.

She heard another mumbled protest from below, but couldn't make out the words. The thought to project herself in different clothes had not occurred to her (and would not, this long night), so she ventured forth, testing the old floorboards with her bare feet as her nightgown swished in the dark.

Concentrating, she imagined the wooden planks like the surface of a lake. If they were water, she could look beneath. She felt the boards dissolve, which allowed her body sink beneath them. Then she saw the room below.

A chaotic scene played out before her.

The room was large and sparsely furnished. A few chairs sat in the far corners. A bookcase adorned one wall. A single doorway in a second wall led to the interior of the building. And the other two were bare brick.

In the center of the room, a large circle, four feet across, was drawn upon the floor. It was surrounded by strange markings and symbols. Two smaller circles were drawn at its base, with similar patterns. Where the circles intercepted, in that rounded rectangular shape, a white light shot up from the floor.

Sitting inside the large circle was a person; a man, she guessed, but it was hard to tell. The air around him was distorted and feverish. It sucked at him, pulling ribbons of matter from his head and body. He was changing.

Inside the smaller circles were two girls. Raggedy clothes and tangled hair whipped about them from an unseen wind. Ribbons of light and color danced around them, flying in all directions. They were changing as well. But they were disappearing.

The man was chanting. The girls were screaming.

Outside, a metal sign was screeching.

*

Jimmy slapped his face and screamed. The bugs had gotten in his head. He could feel them. Something was inside him. Something bad.

He clawed at his scalp to get the bug outs. He felt the hair tear away. Hot bee stings. They were all over him now.

"DEH! HEP ME! AAAAAAHHHH! DEH!"

Jimmy scrambled off his bed and flung open the door. He had to get Del.

But his bones wanted something else.

Jimmy didn't understand why his body made a left instead of a right. Del's room was to the right, down the hall, but his body went the other way.

Not under complete control, Jimmy shambled down the hall and out into the library. He lurched and cantered, sometimes leaning sideways, sometimes shooting forward in two or three quick steps. He screamed and slapped his face, which was now red and starting to swell. Tears and snot ran down it as he spun around, looking all directions.

"GAAAHHH! DA BUGS! I GOT DA BUGS!"

He tried to run away from the bugs. He remembered one time when Del told him about the bees, and that if he ever got stung, he needed to run away from that spot. He tried to run now, but the bugs were following him. They were inside him and following him because they knew where he was trying to go. The bugs were moving his arms and legs.

"I GOT..."

He stumbled over the rug and sprawled onto the floor. Rolling upright, he slapped at his stupid feet for not working.

"Da tings...

"Ahh, daa, daa, daa."

Now his stupid tongue wasn't working. He stood up and wobbled toward the worktable. It looked familiar and scary. It sent a chill running through him.

His mind wanted to hide away from the table. He remembered one from a long time ago. Something bad had happened on it and he didn't want to remember.

He'd been scared and alone in the dark before the bad thing had happened. When he was scared, he liked to sing. Sometimes it made the bad things go away.

His tongue, thick and sticky, tried to sing the song.

"I got... no tings..."

He looked around wildly. The bugs were singing and moving his tongue.

"To hoad me down..."

His tongue remembered the words.

"I got no tings, to hoad me down..."

He stumbled away from the table and down the dark hallway, singing the song of a boy made of string.

CHAPTER 62

el saw the ritual underway, but didn't understand it. Ribbons of light arced off the girls and man, swirling about their bodies. A dark mist encircled them, distorting their images. Faces twisted and arms dissolved, only to reappear seconds later. The man continued to chant. The girls continued to scream.

Whether by some outside force, or her own terror, Del was frozen into inaction. In her trance, she was hovering in the upper corner of the room. She looked down in horror, not knowing what to do.

A movement from one side of the room caught her attention. There in the shadows stood a woman, elegant and tall. She wore a black dress and absently fingered a black pearl necklace. She was watching the ceremony with curiosity.

Why had she slipped into this building? Del wondered. And where *was* this building anyway? She was looking for Clara and the two boys. She thought the hair would have led her to where they were hidden. Instead, she'd ended up here.

An arc of light was thrown off the girls and floated toward the ceiling.

Torn away from its energy source, it began to fade immediately. The dying glow of light passed through the space that Del's mind occupied and voices sang there like a lost memory. It was a child's rhyme.

We are pretty, we are twins,
We hid and fooled them all again.
Quiet-quiet, not a sound,
Forever-ever, won't be found.

It was a rhyme game the girls used to sing to each other in their heads. It was their way of 'hiding' from people, because no one could hear them.

The man was chanting loudly now, almost yelling, to be heard above the roar of the wind and the screeching metal. Something snaked out of the man, hovering in the air, then slithered toward the girls. Something black. It made Del think of a tree root that had come to life.

Then she saw two more root-shadows, fine and wispy, come out of the girls. Their ends quivered in the air, like tiny worms emerging from the ground. The roots of the girls were tentative, surprised at their exposure. The black root of the man was not. It sought the other roots and it found them.

His root shot out in two quick strikes, snake-like, and caught the smaller ones. They twisted in agony, but would not get free. The girls' eyes flew open as they convulsed in pain. That's when they locked eyes with Del.

She felt their stares and knew they could see her. Through the swirling mist Del recognized the tormented faces. It was the girls she'd seen in old New Orleans. Only she hadn't realized at the time they looked the same. As the mist spun and the girls screamed, Del realized she was witnessing some macabre ritual being cast on a set of twins. Tangled together, the roots of the girls were becoming part of the man's. When they did, a noticeable change in the arcing light could be seen. Instead of flying off in all directions, the arcs—like needles aligning to true North—now pointed to the man. Whatever energy the girls had was now feeding him.

Scarlet and Misthal were the girls names. Del knew this.

HELP US! The girls screamed in Del's mind. She was rocked by the blast of energy, and nearly slipped out of the scene.

HELP US! PLEEAASSE!

Del panicked. She wanted to help, but didn't know what to do. Her head pounded for attention. Nausea startled her. She felt her stomach flip, whether from here or from her body that was sitting safely in Armand's house, she didn't know, but she felt ill. Her head pounded and her ankle hurt for some reason.

STOP IT! she screamed. She remembered seeing the bugs on Jimmy that night in the parlor. She'd blown them away somehow, but it didn't work this time. She focused on the top of the man's head and tried to fly through him, but was stuck. The energy pulsing off the three was greater than she could muster.

"What was that?" the tall woman said. She was no longer watching the ritual. She was looking at the ceiling.

The chanting man raised his arms and spoke the final words of the incantation.

...help us... The girls whimpered one last time.

The fading words of the twins dissolved in the mist. With a final flash of light, their bodies collapsed into a dark pool of tar and the man fell backwards, nearly disappearing. The spell was complete.

He lay still, tendrils of smoke and energy fluttering off his shadow body. What had been two girls in two separate circles was now a black mass that lay on the floor. A thing forever tied to the man. They would feed his existence until they were used up.

Del screamed for the girls. She didn't care if the monsters of this world heard her or not. Her eyes spilled feverish tears and she heard her cracking voice from far away. She had no power to help anyone here.

The tall woman looked at the ceiling again. Something was there. Although the hell-wind had stopped when the girls dissolved, something was moving the cobwebs in the corner. And nothing had ever gotten into her building that she didn't let in.

Del felt the woman's gaze. Maybe it was looking *through* her, or *past* her, but it knew she was there. She knew the woman was seeing something. Del could feel the eyes penetrating the thin veil of reality that hid her.

The shadow-man on the floor moved and pulled the woman's attention away.

"Where am I?" he asked weakly.

"Where you ended… and began," the woman said.

"Remade?"

"Yes."

He sat up and his head moved as if to look around. The features of his face were still struggling to form, so she couldn't tell if he was actually looking at anything. His fingertips brushed the edge of the drawn circle and a slight spark nipped at them. He looked at the fingers as if discovering them for the first time.

"You remade me…"

"No. You paid for rootstock and privacy. That is what I provided."

"Remade…" He trembled. "I've been remade."

He stood up and Del saw that his shadow-body—although not completely reformed—cast its own mishappen shadow along the floor, into the pool of tar. Then it began to move.

In a revulsion that she could barely comprehend, Del watched as the black pool—now connected to the man—tried to move away from him. It rolled and twisted to escape. Beneath the black surface something swelled. The bubble became larger and larger. It looked like a small head.

Yes, beneath the black surface was first one head, then two, trying to reform. The pool stretched, as shadow arms pushed it up. The shape of a child formed, then another. The essence of the twins was still there. They now existed in an elemental form, but they were there. And they were trying to crawl away from the man they now fed.

"Now that you are remade, what will you be known as?" the woman asked.

The shadow-man, now solidifying to a constant color, looked at the floor and the pool of energy that lay at his feet, feeding him.

One by one, shadow-hands motioned to the two small circles. "Scarlet and Misthal. They now feed me."

The frantic shapes of the girls—with surfaces nothing more than primordial tar—crawled across the floor, stretching an unholy bond that would never break.

"I am now Scar-mish. And I have been remade!"

Feverish and dizzy, Del screamed at the horror one last time and let herself fall backwards out of the scene. The trance had drained her. Her head pounded for attention and she tasted blood in the back of her throat. She'd gone looking for Clara and the boys, only to find something worse. The girls from old New Orleans, the strange building, the shadow-man and the elegant woman, she felt all these things were related to the missing kids. It was all too overwhelming, too much to consider in her exhausted state. She needed sleep. She needed Mama Dedé's help.

She let the cosmic winds blow her back towards Armand's house. It was strange how easy it had become. As if on a rail, her mind slid along with little conscious effort.

She felt her bedroom rushing towards her, but instead of comfort, a twinge of panic filled her. It didn't feel right. Something was wrong.

As her mind and body rejoined, she was assaulted with pain and dread. A hot fire shot up her leg, causing her to cry out. A palpable feeling of death floated on the air. For a moment, she thought someone was in the room with her. Adrenaline surged through her stomach, turning it sour.

"Get off! she screamed at the shadows. Slapping away whatever had bitten her leg, wave after wave of nausea flooded her.

Then she heard the sounds in the hallway.

CHAPTER 63

J immy was growling.

It was a sound she'd never heard him make before. Guttural and raw, it was a screaming growl and it came from a deep terror. Its power ebbed and flowed.

"GGAAHHHH! I got no tiiNNGGSS! IGOTNO TINGS. Ggghhhrrr… TOP TINGING!! ..mmmhhh.. top ting…iiinnnggg…"

She could hear him stumbling through the hall, bumping into doors.

Jumping out of bed, her tingling foot hit the floor and sent her sprawling.

"OWW!"

Pain flashed through her eyes as she grabbed her ankle.

"DEH!" Jimmy cried from the hall. He stumbled toward the door. His voice was dark and raw. Like a pneumatic lung, the words labored forth. "hhrrggg… hhrrggg…. ggrrhhhhepppp mmmeeee…"

Now it didn't sound like Jimmy at all.

As she rolled upright, Jimmy made it to the door. For a brief second, she wondered if she'd locked it earlier, then the handle turned.

Jimmy fell against the door and it slammed open. There in the doorway, backlit by an errant light, was the face of true torment. An overwhelming smell of urine and sweat assaulted her as the air rushed in. His eyes were wide with fear and surprise. His face was red and swollen and she knew he'd been crying. He'd busted his lip on something and the blood dripped down his chin. He shook uncontrollably and his arms flailed at his head.

"Ggrrhhhhepppp mmmeeee…"

He took one step forward and that's when she saw it. Something was on him. Or coming out of him.

She scrambled backwards over the bed, despite her screaming leg. Like a double vision, she saw Jimmy and something else at the same time.

She screamed.

As the screams emptied her lungs, her mind struggled to comprehend what she was seeing.

His bones are coming out! Oh my God, his bones are coming out!

The thought, as crazy as it was, jumped into her mind.

She was now standing on a desk chair that sat along the far wall. She didn't know what had happened, but she couldn't get far enough away from him. A faint shimmer swirled around his body as he flailed his head and face. Sometimes she thought she saw bones, sometimes not. Sometimes it was his tormented face, other times… she thought his skull was separating from his body.

She slapped herself, hoping she'd wake up. But it was real.

She flashed into a trance, high above the room. She only had a second or two, as her weakened body could barely support itself now. But that's all she needed.

In that instant, she saw the thing that inhabited Jimmy, that possessed him.

"GET OUT!" she screamed at the spirit, and snapped back into her own body as it nearly lost balance.

A flicker of surprise crossed Jimmy's face when she screamed. He flailed his arms in response and stumbled toward the end of the bed.

"GET OUT! GET OUT!" she screamed again, but didn't feel the same power as that night in the parlor. She was exhausted and could barely stand. She didn't risk another flash-trance to see if the thing was gone. She didn't need to. Now she could hear the bones. A faint *clackity-click-clack* floated on the air and the thing inside Jimmy saw her. Dead, socket eyes looked out from Jimmy's face and his lips curled into a sneer. She saw two long teeth on either side of his mouth.

"Ggrrhhhhepppp mmmeeee…" he pleaded as the teeth punctured his bottom lip.

Jimmy, controlled by The Boy Made of String, had made it to the end of the bed and suddenly lunged at Del. It was clumsy, but caught her by surprise. She leaped in the air, barely avoiding his grasp. Landing on the soft mattress, it sagged, nearly spilling her backwards. Throwing herself forward, she bounced off the bed and onto the floor. Jimmy was crawling up the bed right where she'd been. She lunged forward, hitting the open door, then slammed it shut as she ran into the hall.

She had to get Mama D.

*

Madame Broussard stared at the dark images that shone out of Willy's eyes. Alvie, and the body he'd been pulled into, was facing the closed bedroom door, trying to pull it open. But that was of no interest to her.

She'd watched the entire episode unfold. She now sat in utter shock at the magnitude of the coincidence. She recognized the Spirit Hunter's face.

One day, long ago, she'd provided rootstock to a new customer. Little did she know who that customer would become. She remembered a strange thing that had happened during the ceremony. She had a good memory and recalled it as if it were yesterday.

The ghost face in the corner of the room. The one that moved the cobwebs. It was this girl's face she'd seen that day; just a hint of it. Like a vision from a dream, the face came back to her and she knew she'd seen it before.

She'd been linked to the Spirit Hunter all these years and hadn't known it.

The implications were maddening.

CHAPTER 64

Del ran into Mama Dedé's room and locked the door behind her.

"Mama D! Wake up!" she whispered as loudly as she dared. "Wake up, quick." She shook her shoulder lightly.

Jimmy was stumbling down the hall.

"hhggg… I GOT no tings, I got no tings… hee-hee…" His voice moved past the door and down the hall.

She shook the woman harder. "Mama D, wake up, please!" Del recoiled at the woman's temperature. She felt cold despite the blankets that covered her.

"Mama D?"

She was breathing, but slowly. And she wouldn't wake up, no matter how hard she shook her.

Del sat on the floor as her mind grappled with the situation. She grimaced at her burning leg; it wasn't just asleep. Everything had happened so quickly she hadn't had a chance to look at it. In the dim light of the room, she could see a dark red shadow around her right ankle. Touching it, she realized the shadow was inflamed skin, and it was leaking tiny droplets of blood and pus. It felt like a thousand tiny pinpricks had stuck her during her trance.

Creeping forward, she listened at the door. She had to get to Armand's room next, but realized she hadn't heard Jimmy for a few minutes. The house was quiet tonight. In fact, it was too quiet. She didn't even hear the normal creaks and groans.

She reached for the doorknob, then pulled back, shaking her head. What was she thinking? There was no reason to go into the hallway blind.

She sat back, yawning. Just thinking about another trance made her tired. But she'd search for Jimmy this way first.

Her vision flipped and she saw herself sitting on the floor. The shadows of the room pulled back slightly from direct observation, but she ignored their movement. Nothing obvious was wrong with Mama D from this view. She wanted to look back, earlier in the night to see what may have happened, but felt her time was short. Too many things were happening, so she looked wider.

There in the library, beneath the worktable, sat Jimmy. She didn't need to see his dazed eyes and panting breath to know he was still under the control of something; she could see the *something* quite well.

The ghost of a boy—the ghost of his skeleton really—hovered in and around Jimmy. Fading in and out of Jimmy, she couldn't tell if the thing wanted to be in him or was stuck there somehow. Why he'd stopped singing or crying out, she couldn't tell. He looked exhausted—like her. Only his was worse; he looked like he was in shock.

She quickly scanned Armand's room. He was sleeping quietly as well. Too quietly. The covers were over his face, but she didn't see him move. Unconsciously, she held her breath, counting the seconds between his breaths. Her lungs began to call out as the time ticked on.

He wasn't moving! Why wasn't he moving? She called out in her trance, hoping she could wake him. Nothing.

She tried to peer into his dreams, but his mind was blank. Or something was blocking her. Quickly looking back at Mama Dedé, she saw the same blankness. No dreams. No scenes. It was as if their minds were gone.

Did he breathe?

She focused back on Armand. Did she hear something?

Breathe! Please!

A ragged snore broke the silence, but it was weak.

The blankets were suffocating him!

A sick feeling sat like a weight on her stomach. Something was in the house! The spirits that Mama D had warned her about were attacking them.

Del's vision snapped to high above the house. The view was dark shadows and rain. A storm had started, and the view of the house was blurry from the rain cascading over it. But one thing was unmistakable: the ring of shadows that encircled the home was not from the rainstorm.

She had to get to Armand now!

Out of her trance, she found herself standing at the door, pulling the skeleton key from the lock. She slipped outside and locked it as quietly as she could. Mama D's room was on the other side of the library, across from hers, but all the rooms were connected by a long back hall. She needed to draw Jimmy down one side and escape out the other to get downstairs. She didn't want to risk getting grabbed by whatever was in him.

"Deh?"

She spun right and saw Jimmy standing in the hallway entrance. He'd heard the lock turn.

"I GOT NO TINGS! HA HA HA!" He ran towards her with his arms out.

She screamed and bolted the other way.

"DEH! COME BACK! I GOT NOT TINGS! I GOT NO TINGS!" Two voices echoed out at her: a terrified boy and a hellish boy, but they were sounding more and more like one.

She ran to the back of the house, made a right, down the back hall, then a second right, and could see the fireplace chairs in the library. She sprinted towards them and caught the glimpse of Jimmy's hand just as it reached out. He'd gone the other way when she ran and had cut behind Armand's worktable. She jumped, but the hand caught her foot and she tumbled into Frank's chair, the closest to the stairs. She sprawled onto the floor as her nightgown twisted and bunched around her waist. The combined boys leered and crawled towards her as she tried to cover herself. Sometimes he reached for her and sometimes it was a skeleton hand, but they crawled closer. She kicked her feet and rolled toward the stairs. In one quick move she was up and descending the stairs two by two. She was only a few seconds ahead.

A long hall that ran beneath the library led back to Armand's room. She twisted the doorknob, fully expecting it to open, and jammed her shoulder into the door when it didn't. She heard the key she'd been carrying bounce once against the wall and fall silent. It lay somewhere in the dark.

She felt frantically for it as she listened to Jimmy stumble down the stairs. He usually took them slower, but whatever was driving him was in a hurry. Her hands flew over the carpet. With a quick swipe, she sent the key sailing off the carpet runner and bouncing against the floorboard.

"Deh?"

She held her breath. The echoes were tricky sometimes, and it was darker on the first floor. Feeling around quietly, she flash-tranced and saw a vision of Jimmy tiptoeing from the base of the stairs. He took careful steps. He was stalking her.

She felt the cold metal of the key and grabbed it. A faint scraping sound escaped the floor and echoed through the silent air. Then a sickening sound returned.

CLACKETY-CLICK-CLACK echoed off the paneled walls and the sound of running skeleton feet came at her.

She jammed the key into the lock and twisted it back and forth as she slammed against the door. She missed the faint click of the lock tumblers and fell into the room as the door gave way. A scrawny hand, partially covered in flesh, snagged her gown as she did, and a long strand ripped away. Falling onto her back, she looked up and saw a slobbering mouth and possessed eyes searching for her in the dark. She kicked the door shut with both feet, and the pain from her injured leg overwhelmed her. She felt like she was going to black out.

Just then, she saw the doorknob turn and realized the key was still in the lock.

"HELLLPPPPP!" she screamed over and over.

No one in the house heard her. Although several things did.

CHAPTER 65

Madame Broussard paced the room as the scene went dark. The bedroom door in front of Alvie had just slammed shut.

The wild events of the evening were not what she expected at all. Why Alvie had attached himself to this other body, this boy with the speech problem, she couldn't tell. And this girl? If she was the Spirit Hunter, why hadn't he attached to her first? And if she were so powerful, why hadn't she put Alvie down by now?

Fingering her pearls for inspiration, she turned back to the scene playing out on the wall. Willy's eyes were still projecting.

A deformed hand has fumbling with the doorknob. Half bone and half flesh, she couldn't tell if Alvie was regenerating skin, or if the host body was pushing him out. But there was something else going on here that she was missing.

She watched the hand struggle at the knob, then saw a surprise. How careless! She just caught a glimpse of it, but it was there. The key was still in the lock!

Had it not been for the malformed hand and the clumsiness of both boys, she would be seeing inside the room right now. They were able to get the door to open occasionally, but it was always pushed shut from the other side.

What she wouldn't give to trance again and see on the other side. Just once. The Spirit Hunter *was* a lovely girl. Even more lovely in her flight of terror. A damsel in distress, fleeing her tormentors through an old house. And in her nightgown no less! How exciting!

*

Del's legs trembled as she stretched her toes out and pushed against the door. It kept trying to come open. When she'd tumbled into the room, she'd landed between the door and a small loveseat that faced Armand's bed. She'd had just enough time to slam the door shut with her feet before she saw the doorknob turn. Fighting to stay conscious, she reached her arms over her head and found the legs of the loveseat. It was just close enough that if she stretched her toes out, the weight of the couch could help her keep the door shut. But her arms were trembling just as much as her legs. She couldn't keep it closed for long.

Although she tried to fight it, the tears flowed as deep sobs wracked her body. She was exhausted and freezing. Armand's room was too cold. And it wasn't because of the heating system.

It was because of her.

Mama Dedé and Armand were sick because the spirits had followed her. Jimmy was possessed because of her; simply because she was here.

She was here and the kids weren't. She couldn't find them. She'd been too busy visiting the ice cream shop, and why? Because of a stupid crush that only existed in her mind. Because of the stupid thought of playing detective when she didn't know what the hell she was doing.

She should have sensed what was going on in the house, but hadn't.

Somewhere deep in her mind a faint sound echoed. It was a warning sound, she thought, but didn't understand it. It seemed far away. Drips of water. In her panic, her mind was spinning, and she imagined the sound of dripping water. She pushed it away.

More thoughts flooded in. Del remembered when they'd all come to Armand's house. Even though it was Sister Eulalie that caught Mama Dedé's house on fire, ultimately it was because of Del. The Gris-gris man had been looking for her, and she'd been in the house, trapped in a trance. The only friends she had almost died getting her out. Jimmy had been lost then too, because of her. He'd snuck out of the orphanage hoping to see her, and would have been sucked into the void if it hadn't been for Jo; a friend who had died because of her. A friend who had saved her from being pulled into the blackness. A blackness of her own making.

This would keep happening. She was sure of it now. This gift of hers—this curse—hadn't saved anyone yet. Not the lost kids. Not the poor twins. No one. It wasn't any good to her if she couldn't save the people she loved. She could have protected everyone if she'd just paid more attention. She could have protected them by not even being here.

As the wind mocked her pity, she heard the sound again: rain drops, or drips of water somewhere in her head. They sounded louder. She listened.

A plan began to form in her mind. Slowly, a series of images emerged, one after another.

She wondered where they came from. She felt too tired to have thought of them on her own, but they emerged nonetheless. They were awful thoughts. Terrible. Dark thoughts that surfaced from a deep, black pool. Only a monster would think such things. But maybe that's why they'd come to her. Her curse had caused her black mind to think of these terrible things. The monster was inside her, trying to get out. The monster was her.

Tears of anger now replaced those of fear. She hated what she was thinking, but was consumed by it. A fever burned in her mind, fueling the terrible thoughts. If this was to be her fate, if she were to die in this place as a monster, then she would do monstrous things to save the little family she had. That was the least she could do.

And if she really were a Spirit Hunter, then tonight, the spirits would know her.

CHAPTER 66

"Deh!" Jimmy whirled on his wobbly legs, then started down the hall after her. He hadn't seen her come out, but there she was, standing at the end of the hallway. "I got no tings! Hee-hee-hee-hee."

Jimmy-Alvie ran after Del as she slipped out of sight. They reached the foyer just as she turned down another hallway. They followed.

In Armand's room, Del scrambled off the floor, ripped the covers from Armand's head and slapped him hard in the face. He let out a startled gasp and breathed a deep breath of air, but remained asleep.

She only had seconds, but flashed high above the room and saw the loathsome spirits that crowded it. They were sucking tiny strands of energy from the air, but she knew ultimately the strands were coming from Armand. She could hear the drops evaporating from his well.

"Whed she go?" Jimmy said in the dark foyer. He heard something from the bedroom, and thought Del was playing a game with him, but then caught a glimpse of her run down the other hall. He followed again.

Quietly, she snuck out of Armand's room, locked the door behind her and tiptoed toward the front of the house. She was panting and her nose had begun to bleed. It was difficult maintaining her balance while sending the false visions to Jimmy. She hoped she could maintain it long enough.

"Hee-hee… I got no tings, I got no tings…" His voice bounced off the old wood, giving false locations.

She limped to the front of the hall. She had to get somewhere safe, but there was something to do first. She kept sending false visions to Jimmy, which right now had him looking for her in the back hall.

She made it to the parlor, where just a few nights ago she'd seen the things crawling over Jimmy's face. It was cold in here as well, and the shadows were deep. She hoped this wasn't a mistake.

The parlor normally stood open, but could be shut from the rest of the house by large pocket doors that slid into the walls. She assumed there was a lock on those doors, but wasn't sure.

She heard Jimmy's frustration as his voice floated up from the back of the house. His voice grew dark again. "hhhgggg… Tupid Deh! Whed you go? Cunch, cunch, cunch!" His teeth clicked together.

The doors slid out with a loud groan. Somewhere in a dark hall Jimmy stopped to listen.

There was a keyhole in one door, but this was a different kind of lock. Since the sliding doors had to meet in the middle, the lock had to reach from one door into the other through a small metal slot. It didn't look very sturdy. It hadn't been designed to hold monsters in.

Guilt made her cringe. She couldn't think of Jimmy that way. It wasn't his fault what was happening to him.

Like a whisper, she heard faint sounds.

Clack. Click. Clack.

"hee-hee. Hhggg..."

Click...

Click...

He was still stalking her.

Tiptoeing to the foyer, she crouched behind a side table and held her breath. If he saw her here, she could only go out the front door, but thought she wouldn't survive it. The wind howled its invitation and the shadows formed a dense, dark ring. Waiting.

She forced her mind to focus, and sent her image out to Jimmy again. In it, she was smiling and inviting him into the parlor to play. This was a deadly game indeed.

Jimmy spied the image and ran towards it. The Del-image slipped inside the parlor and waited. Jimmy came to the sliding doors and stopped. The Alvie part of him was anxious to go inside, but what was left of Jimmy's mind thought something was wrong. He didn't know this room had magic doors. They went right inside the walls. He didn't remember that before. Besides, he had a bad feeling about this room. There'd been a lot of bad bugs in here before, and this is where Del had hit him. Well, one of the places. And he didn't like that either. He began to whine.

Del saw the hesitation and fear in him. She felt sick to her stomach for doing this, but knew of no other way. The Del-image called to Jimmy with all the friendliness she could muster, but it was weak. She felt the ominous spirits in the parlor. They seemed to have anticipated her plan. And they'd gathered early.

Jimmy pushed on the pocket doors to see how they worked. They slid apart and banged against their wooden stops deep inside the wall. They were as far apart as possible now. Happy with his understanding, he stepped inside to play with Del.

She ran on tiptoes to the parlor door and began pulling them shut. The extra motion, and exhaustion, caused the Del-image in the room to fade away. Jimmy was confused.

Hearing the doors close, he turned and saw Del, now behind him. She was shutting him in!

"Deh!" he cried and ran towards the doors.

As the large wood doors banged shut, they bounced slightly apart, and a small hand came between them. She couldn't shut the doors on his hand, but had to get them closed. With Jimmy trapped inside, she could tend to the next part of her plan. She just needed him to let go for a second. Without thinking, she sent the image of a monstrous face through the door and Jimmy screamed. Throwing his hands up, he stumbled backwards and tripped, landing hard on the floor. She pulled the doors together and said a quick prayer that the key would work here as well.

It did. With a scrape and a click, a metal finger came out of one metal hole and locked into another. Jimmy was trapped.

And screaming in terror.

CHAPTER 67

Del covered her ears and ran up the steps. She blocked out the terrible sounds, but couldn't resist a quick flash-look into the room. There in the center of the floor lay Jimmy. The ghost skeleton was half in, half out, unsure if it wanted to stay in its host. The shadows were thick in all corners of the room, and several stretched out across the floor.

She shut the scene from her mind as Jimmy screamed about the bugs.

Slamming open Mama Dedé's door, she knew the woman was near death. The room was ice cold and thick with shadows. She could barely see despite having flicked on the light switch.

She jumped onto the woman's bed, shoved her head and shoulders up and squeezed between her and the headboard. Her skin was cold, and pulled warmth from Del's own body as soon as they touched. Del pulled the covers beneath the woman's chin, wrapped her arms around her and closed her eyes.

She was far away in an instant.

*

Spider woke up in a panic. He was late.

His pounding head reminded him how much he'd drunk when he got home from jail yesterday. He rolled to his side and squinted at the clock. It was ten minutes after three. It was dark outside. It was still last night. Sort of.

His heart slammed in his chest and wouldn't slow down. Something was wrong. He thought he'd heard something.

He swung his legs off the bed and listened. Had he been dreaming?

Blood rushed through his ears. It sounded like he was listening to a seashell. Maybe it had just been—

There it was again.

His phone was ringing.

He must be late for a thing!

He stumbled out of the bedroom and down the hall, hoping his heart wouldn't explode along the way. What a time to be getting a call! It must be important. Like a top-heavy boat, he bobbed back and forth as he made his way into the living room. He fell into the chair and grabbed the receiver. He held it in the air for a split second, then put it to his ear.

"Hello," he said quietly.

He sat listening without saying a word. He'd feared this call ever since getting home. He was afraid he'd have to explain what happened and plead his case, but there was no time for that now. There was no need for questions. The directions were clear.

Yes. Spider had a thing.

*

Del's arms clung to Mama Dedé as she imagined her own Well of Life. It was deep and silent. She was young and strong and her well was deep. She could use it. She had to.

Her mind was far away, searching for her well, but she didn't know how to find it. In her trance, there were no scenes. She wasn't focused on a person or a *normal* place. There was just blackness. She'd heard the drips of water once before, when she'd first learned to trance. She had to get back to it.

She let her mind *sink*. That was all she could think to do. If wells were deep, you must have to go deep to find them. They were deep and cold, like this room. The cold made her want to sleep. Her exhaustion made her want to sleep. Everything in here wanted her to sleep. As her mind fell backward, a strange sensation enveloped her. This didn't feel like a normal trance. This felt like floating in a warm, black dream. Her mind sunk quickly.

She felt the fear of the situation begin to fade. Her heart stopped pounding. Her leg stopped hurting. She felt calm in her falling. She was invisible and floated on an infinite thread of energy.

A strange thought came to her. The people in Armand's house were like all other people. They all died, eventually. It would be painless for them once it happened. Why did she worry so much about them? If they died tonight, wouldn't their suffering end? Wouldn't they be happier? Jimmy wouldn't fall down anymore. Armand could chase an infinite number of theories. And Mama Dedé could talk to Marie all she wanted.

If her friends died, they could all float like this. Each on their own thread of energy, floating away forever in this deep, cold place.

The stress flowed from her shoulders and her fingers relaxed their grip on the old woman. She wanted to slip into the cold warmth of the darkness. She wanted to follow this thread.

Here in the void, that's where the real power was. She felt it call to her. It washed her fear away. She felt she could live forever here.

She shook her head hard. What was she thinking? What kind of place was this?

It was a dangerous one. She knew that now. The power was intoxicating, and it pulled powerful things to it.

She forced herself to think about Jimmy's frightened face. She willed herself to feel Mama Dedé's cold arms. Those were the reasons she was doing this.

Then, like a tiny drip from an old faucet, she heard it, somewhere far away. She forced herself to fall faster. She'd never been this deep before. Not on purpose. It was cold and silent here. The only sounds were the water drops, dripping backwards out of the well. Further and faster she fell. Space and time raced away like a fleeting dream. Then, she suddenly stopped.

She was somewhere near water. She could smell it. The cool, sweet aroma of a forest pool in summer. Dark. Calm.

Only something was wrong.

The single backwards drip she'd heard before wasn't here. At her well, it was backwards raining.

CHAPTER 68

Flick. Flick. Flick.

Spider lit a cigarette as he drove the Plymouth down the street. This was a special thing he had to do tonight, and he couldn't mess it up. He felt lucky to have this new chance. Yesterday he thought he was out on his ass due to his getting arrested, but knew he had a chance to fix it. His good standing would be restored. He'd be the golden boy again. He'd be Spider the Dragon King again. This was much different than anything he'd been asked to do before.

Usually, he just drove somewhere, then somewhere else. He didn't have to *do* the thing. But this time he did.

Spider turned down the street and gawked at the house. It was huge. And it looked haunted. Maybe it was the pouring rain and the sheets of water causing a dark mist to float up around it, but it looked creepy as hell. And it didn't help that it was right next to a cemetery.

Spider hated cemeteries. That made this task even harder. Instead of driving down a dark alley and checking for lights, he had to park next to a cemetery and wait. And he'd just arrived.

He pulled a small bottle of bourbon from his glove box and took a swig. It helped calm his nerves. It also took the edge off from the pounding rain. The clouds had opened on his drive over. All he could hear was large raindrops pounding the roof, and all he saw was an old creepy house and cemetery. He shivered and took another drink.

He squinted through the windshield, waiting for his signal, hoping he wouldn't screw up.

*

Del's spirit opened as if taking a deep breath, and she felt the water of life fill her. A renewed lifeforce pulsed inside her, filling her core. She drank from the well and felt alive like never before.

Faraway, the pains in her physical body subsided. Her inflamed leg began to heal. Her skin radiated life-giving heat that a cold body absorbed. The shadows recoiled like mold from a blistering sun.

She felt her true power for the first time.

Wave after wave radiated from Del. Mama Dedé stirred in Del's arms and let out a slight sigh. Her ringed fingers clasped at the blankets and pulled them tighter.

Del sent her focus to Armand.

There, looking down upon the bearded man, she saw regular breathing. His eyes fluttered as if breaking the final hold of a bad dream. He twitched and groaned, finally rolling to one side. The shadows in his room pulled back, waiting.

Del went to Jimmy. He was writhing on the floor.

She sent all the energy she could to him. She flooded his mind with butterflies and trains. She called to him.

His body twisted and he suddenly stood up. He cantered around the room like a drunkard. Two minds pulled the strings of Jimmy, and they wanted different things.

The parlor shadows fell back, nervous of the new energy that flowed into the room. The energy was rich and full of life. They wanted to feed from it, but were nervous. It was too rich. It may be more than they could take. It may be a trick. But they could be patient like the other things that gathered outside the house. They had been waiting a long time already.

"Deh? Hep me..." Jimmy said weakly.

She sent wave after wave of happy images to him. She wanted him to know that she hadn't left him after all. She was here to save him. If only she had enough time.

CHAPTER 69

Spider sipped his bottle and watched as a pair of headlights careened down the street.

Damn drunks, he thought.

He hoped the idiot wouldn't crash into him. That would really screw up his night. But instead of sailing past him, the car screeched to a halt outside the house he was watching.

The hairs on his neck stood up.

The car, a red convertible, had almost run into the iron gate of this house. It was like the guy expected the gate to be open or some—

"What the hell?" Spider said quietly. He squinted through the rain-blurred windshield, watching a large man exit his car. He rubbed his eyes and looked again, then slipped low in his seat.

"It's that d-damn, cop," he said to himself.

What the hell is he doing here?

"I-I don't know, but I d-don't like it."

Frank was out of his car, frantically pushing the call button of the old intercom speaker attached to the stone pillar.

Peering just over the top of the door, Spider sipped again. The first drink had warmed him; the second had calmed his nerves; now he was feeding his anger.

Crazy old fuck. I oughta—

"You're not gonna do anything, so just shut up," he said to himself.

Oh yeah?

He didn't waste the breath to respond.

Spider watched as Frank hustled up the sidewalk, inspecting the tall iron fence. He pulled on the bars, seemingly at random.

What's he—?

"He's looking for a way in."

No shit. He's looking for a way in.

"He's looking for another gate."

Now his job was really tricky. He was supposed to come here and wait for someone to call him, then he'd sneak in and find some boy.

I guess he has the package.

But how the hell could he do that with a cop snooping around?

Flick. Flick. Flick.

Three quick flashes lit the inside of the car.

Things in the dark noticed.

*

Madame Broussard shielded her eyes as image after image flashed against her wall. They beamed like spotlights from Willy's eyes. Butterflies, trains, the moon, a blue frog, all created from the mind of the Spirit Hunter.

She didn't believe the images were actually being seen by the boy's eyes. Just in his mind. Afterall, who had the power to manifest actual images? But that would imply that Alvie was somehow *seeing* what was in the boy's mind as opposed to seeing simply from his eyes. And that was equally perplexing.

She paced the room. This had gone on long enough, she thought. She'd found the Spirit Hunter—an incredible talent—and knew where she lived. Now all she wanted was to call Alvie back in one piece. There were plans to be made. She couldn't be hasty.

Short of trancing, Madame Broussard wasn't sure how to bring him back. She'd already called to him—pulled at his being—but to no avail. It was as if another great source of power was keeping him locked to the stumbling boy.

Maybe she *could* risk a trance, just this once.

*

Del flashed from one room to the next in quick succession. She knew her arms still clung tightly to Mama Dedé—she felt the cold body absorb her warmth—but her mind was a jumble. It was in so many places at once, it didn't register the blood that ran from both her nostrils. And she'd forgotten about the backwards rain—*her Well of Life emptying at a terrifying pace.*

She could maintain enough presence in each room to keep the shadows at bay, but some seemed to be anticipating her rhythm. The shadows in Armand's room had retreated to one closet and beneath the bed, but were constantly trying to slide up between the blankets. The parlor-shadows were worse. They were now moving in a slow, circular pattern, like a whirlpool, around Jimmy, waiting for an opening. She knew they were waiting.

And then there was still the shadow-ring outside.

Outside!

What was happening there?

She flashed a look outside and saw one shadow—in the thousands that were there—move by the fence. She recognized it immediately.

FRANK! she screamed.

Outside, Frank jumped and pulled the pistol from his shoulder holster. He'd heard something. He spun around, looking in all directions.

Frank! Help!

"Del?" Frank shielded his eyes from the driving rain. "Del! Where are you? Open the gate!"

Help! Please…

He looked up at the towering house, hoping to see her in a window, but instead saw a nightmare. Crawling up the walls and over the roof were shadows not made by the storm. At least, not by any storm that he knew of.

Frank ran to his car, started it and threw it in reverse.

*

Spider sat up when the cop got in his car. He guessed that the rain had driven him off, but would have sworn that he'd just been talking to someone.

Maybe he got a call.

Spider felt a tinge of jealousy.

"Yeah, maybe he did."

He said that he was gettin' the calls now, and that I wouldn't get any.

"Cause you fucked up."

I didn't—!

He stopped in mid-thought. He'd been watching the cop pull away in the rain, but now…

Holy shit, he's going to ram the gate!

Spider watched in amazement as the crazy old cop steered his car straight for the iron gate. With a deafening crunch, chrome and candy apple red steel met rust-covered iron. The right headlight shattered on impact and the glass tinkled to the sidewalk. The iron gate stood.

Squalling tires announced his retreat, then the car shot at the gate again, spinning on the wet pavement. This time the right front tire hit the curb and knocked the car off track. The front end bounced high—losing momentum—and hit the gate on a downward angle. The gate groaned but held.

Spider thought he could see a bit of steam coming up from the engine compartment. The long sleek hood had a crease near the front, but the car was tough. This time, the driver backed away slowly, straight across the road from the gate. He was taking a different approach.

Gingerly, he backed the car up onto the curb and as close to the cemetery wall as possible. Spider imagined that the man was trying to be gentle with the tires, a strange alternative to its treatment the last few minutes, but then he realized why. He was looking for more traction.

The car rocked as the man revved the motor. Spider thought briefly of 'Big Daddy' Ed Roth and one of his hotrod caricatures, waiting for the green light of an insane monster race. Then the car let loose.

The traction from the concrete sidewalk was exactly what the car needed. It shot across the street in an instant. Hitting the low grade of the drive entrance and bouncing up with a shower of sparks, the three-thousand-pound car sent all its force into the iron gate. A bolt of lightning and crash of thunder punctuated the collision and lit the calamity. Spider watched in slow motion as the bottom of the iron gate kicked backwards and the whole thing flew up in a slow, lazy somersault. It made three-quarters of a turn before its weight slammed it down onto the hood of the car, shattering the windshield. The car honked once and sat still, steaming.

Expecting to see neighborhood lights flip on, Spider made to turn on the ignition and make his exit. But he stopped and waited. Nothing stirred in this place—except the shadows. He remembered then that he was sitting on an empty street, between a mansion that took its own city block, and a cemetery. That and the crack of lightning meant no one heard the commotion.

Then to add to his surprise, the door of the car swung open and the crazy cop stepped out, wobbly but walking. He made his way to the house.

CHAPTER 70

In Del's mind, everything was screaming. The boy she'd spent so many years protecting in that awful orphanage was screaming. The thing that inhabited him—whether trying to get out or burrow deeper—was screaming. Even the shadows, the dark unnatural things that moved against the grain, that crept towards her, that watched her, that felt and tasted her, those things screamed in their dead-tongue language. And Del heard them all.

Her mind was in splinters. It was everywhere and nowhere. It blurred through the house, keeping the spirits at bay. But her energy was running low.

Jimmy slammed into objects and bounced from wall to wall. She had to get him to slow down somehow so he didn't hurt himself. She needed just a bit more time in order to let Frank get inside.

If she could actually see the spirit inside him, she thought she could bring him to rest somehow, but it was elusive.

Mama Dedé stirred beneath her arms and shivered. She moaned slightly, which Del thought was a good sign.

Taking advantage of the slight improvement, Del focused more energy on Jimmy. She'd seen enough of the tormenting spirit inside him to know what to look for. If she could track the thing, maybe she could figure out how to get rid of it. She tranced hard and deep. The night's scenes began to peel away.

Like dying thoughts, the scenes flashed through her mind. One by one, she relived the night's horrors to find the beginning. The number of spirits that she now detected in the scenes was terrifying. They'd been here all along, and she never saw them. Now they were all she could see.

There it was! The scene had just passed her. One moment Jimmy was swatting at bugs, the next moment he wasn't.

She'd found it.

The skeleton boy—for that's what he looked like—came through the wall from Armand's room. He'd been watching Armand, then Jimmy screamed out about the bugs, then he was in Jimmy.

Before Armand? He'd watched Mama Dedé.

Before her? The scenes led outside to shadows and a large tree. He'd walked across the street on a branch.

Before that?

Del saw the path the skeleton boy had traveled. What exactly she was seeing, she didn't know. But she could see it. And she knew it had led the thing to her house.

She inspected the scene, trying to determine what was wrong with it. It looked like there was a slight indentation in the air. An odd gust of wind twirling the mist. Or a heat shimmer. Yes, it was more like a heat shimmer, but it in the shape of a small tunnel that twisted away into the night.

And they were everywhere!

Now that she knew what to look for, she saw them everywhere. They twisted and flowed in all directions: away into the night; up through the clouds; down through the ground. This new mystery fascinated her, and she pulled at her Well of Life without thinking. She needed the energy to comprehend, to look deeper. The backwards rain flowed like a torrent into her mind.

A brave shadow that had crept down the wall reached out and nibbled at Del's earlobe. The pain she absorbed. The interruption enraged her. In a flash, her head turned and an animal sound escaped her throat as her teeth snapped at the shadow. "HHHRRRAHHK!" The spirit disappeared with a flash of light and the other creeping things retreated.

Her eyes wide and staring, she snapped back to the air tunnel that had brought the skeleton boy. It twisted and doubled back, but she followed. She saw the remnants of other shadows that had traveled here. She felt a part of the path was newly formed—the part closest to Armand's house. But other parts were very old. It was a road for the dead, and the dead traveled upon it.

There were many branches and openings that joined the air tunnel she was following. This road for the dead had many exits. She imagined this might be what arteries and veins looked like in her own body; small tunnels branching in all directions, combining, and splitting apart. Only these tunnels carried nothing for the living. She followed the image of the skeleton boy backwards through twists and turns. Several times she thought she'd lost the trail, but would then catch a good glimpse of the living skeleton. She felt she was getting close its origin.

Suddenly a void opened in front of her. The tunnel she was following had ended at what seemed to be a giant distortion in the air. She'd call it a bubble if it hadn't been so large; an *air cavern* maybe? Several other tunnels ended (or began) here, but not abruptly. The ends of the tunnels seemed to dissolve and become the outer membrane of the cavern itself. Almost like an imaginary forcefield she'd seen in a recent sci-fi movie. The membrane of the cavern shimmered with light and images of things that had traveled here in the past. Del felt like this place had been here a long time, and that many things had come.

Then a set of eyes were there, staring at her from the end of the tunnel. They weren't dead or evil eyes; they were wide and inviting. They froze, neither retreating nor advancing, only watching, curious. They were elegant eyes that Del had seen somewhere before. They were attached to a regal face. Below the face hung a strand of black pearls.

Del and Madame Broussard had finally met.

The woman's face retreated backwards out of the tunnel and into a large room. Del followed.

As Del reached the end of the tunnel—which was somehow the starting point for the skeleton boy—she saw the woman smooth her black dress and fold her hands in front of her. The woman showed no sign of fear, only an amused curiosity toward her visitor. Del knew this woman.

Through the end of the tunnel Del could see into the same room that she'd peered into earlier tonight. Only then, she hadn't seen it as it existed today. Earlier in the night, when she'd slipped during her first trance, she had been focusing on the scene where Spider disappeared. It had happened at this building. Only in her trance, she'd slipped past the current time of the building and into some dark history of the same place. In that history she'd seen the same woman observing a strange ritual with a man and twin girls. Somehow the girls had seen

Del. Tonight, *a hundred years ago*, the girls had pleaded with Del for help. Now, in the present, Del was the one seeking the help.

The woman smiled at Del. Curious as to what she was thinking; watching the emotions run across her face. They were getting acquainted.

Del searched the past scenes of the brick room. There was dark history here; ghost upon ghost; horror upon horror.

She couldn't see everything and wasn't sure why, but assumed it was the same reason she and Frank couldn't see the building that day in the car. It was well hidden. But she saw enough. Del was beginning to understand.

The woman saw the understanding break over the girl's face. This young Spirit Hunter, she thought, so beautiful and wild, yet so careless with her trancing, was beginning to understand the ways of the world. It was a mysterious world, the one Madame Broussard inhabited, beautiful and dangerous. Given the impressive feats she had already witnessed tonight, she thought Del could play an important role in it. Granted, it would be a dangerous liaison—someone like her teaming up with a Spirit Hunter—but the events of the last few days had rekindled an old desire in the woman. Besides, a girl had to have some fun.

(We meet at last.)

Del heard the woman speak in her mind, but said nothing. The vision was fighting her, and she was struggling to focus.

(You won't see much here. You're not able.)

The woman seemed confident, but Del ignored her. In her trance, the seconds ebbed and flowed, stretched into long minutes, then snapped back. Already, she couldn't tell how long she'd been here, but it was long enough to know that others were present.

The woman spoke in her mind. Something about existential power and its seduction. But Del was exploring elsewhere.

She saw the room and it felt her presence. It tried to hide its history, but Del the Spirit Hunter laid it bare, layer after layer. She saw the brick walls and strange iron hooks; the long display table with the skeleton of a six-legged monstrosity; the old voodoo doll with a metal pin running through it (these last two items felt strangely familiar); then she saw the boy.

She instantly she knew it was one of the missing boys. He was still alive, but his condition was wrong. He was being eaten, or consumed, by some dark force that lived here. Time sped up. Scenes flew past her. Her attention was pulled from the chair, where the boy slumped, to under the table (he had lain there not long ago), to his encounter with Alvie, he was bitten, he was on display, hidden stairs, dark rooms, creeping, a picked lock. Clara!

The little girl was here! And she was alive!

Del reeled with the impact of finding the girl. Through the strangest coincidence, while fighting for her own life and trapped in an upstairs bedroom, she'd let her mind roam free and somehow found the missing girl.

She had to get her out. But how?

(Release Alvie.)

Del snapped back to the woman. *What did she say?*

Madame Broussard saw the question ripple across Del's face.

(Release Alvie.)

Del heard but didn't respond.

(He's of no use to you.)

What did she mean, release him? She wasn't—

She thinks I'm holding him somehow. Why would she think—?

Wait!

Alvie?

The skeleton boy. That used to be Alvie. In her frantic exploration of the room, she'd caught a glimpse of a ceremony with a book of blood. That's how the bones came back to life.

Willy—what was left of him—was slumped in a chair over by the wall. He was watching something.

And Clara. She was still alive as well, but Del didn't know how to get to her. She felt sick imagining the same terror that happened to the twins happening to Clara. She wondered if—

What is that? Her attention broke off to a strange movement.

Del went back to Willy. What was he watching?

That looks familiar.

She looked closer at the scene on the wall.

That looks like... Frank.

Panic blacked her mind as she realized what she was seeing. Projected out of Willy's eyes were scenes from her own house. She was seeing Frank wobble unsteadily up the garden path. His car was crashed into the gate. Jimmy (and Alvie) were watching him from the parlor window. Then she heard the boys laugh.

"Hee-hee. Cunch, cunch, cunch."

CHAPTER 71

Spider jumped. He'd just heard something. He looked around the car, wondering if he'd dozed off. The windows were fogged with moisture and he could no longer see outside.

He'd just watched the cop ram the gate. He couldn't have fallen asleep that fast.

Had he missed his signal? He didn't think so.

He looked around the car, wondering where the sound came from. Maybe a branch fell on his car?

An unpleasant, squirmy feeling settled in his stomach. He needed to pee.

Then the phone rang again.

Spider sat up in his seat, staring with wide eyes. His heart suddenly pounding in his chest. He didn't remember having a phone in his car. He'd never received a call here before. But there it was right on the dashboard. And it was ringing.

Shaky fingers reached out and touched the receiver.

He picked it up.

"Hello?"

Thirty seconds later the Plymouth sped away from the curb and down the street. He'd missed an appointment!

Frantically wiping at the fogged over window, his twitchy fingers left nicotine stains where he wiped the glass. With the defroster on high, he squinted through a low clearing of windshield near the dashboard.

"Stupid! Stupid! Stupid!" His hand slapped the dash.

How could you have missed the first stop?!

"I didn't! Those weren't the instructions!"

You did! That's what the phone said.

"I swear! I remembered it right!"

"You didn't remember shit, because you're Spider the Fuckup King!"

Don't say that. I'm not! I remembered right. I—

"—remembered right. I—"

Spider flailed at the windshield and the lights that reflected there. The streetlights and raindrops made halos dance across the glass. To Spider it looked like a hundred cars driving at him, trying to block his progress.

"Get out of the way! Get out of the way!"

The Plymouth careened and skidded down an empty street, under the cover of a dark rain.

Frantic and squirmy, Spider wove his way through the ghost traffic. He no longer had to pee. The smell of urine and sweat filled the car, but he didn't notice. He just needed to make this correction and get back. He'd almost fucked up again, but he could make it right.

He'd do this thing if it was the last thing he ever did.

*

Outside, on the back porch of Armand's house, Frank heard the dimmed screech of car tires. The sound barely registered with him, and he thought about it no more. What he did think about, for a long time, was the doorknob.

For the strangest reason, he was transfixed by the doorknob on Armand's back door.

He'd turned this knob hundreds of times in the past. There was nothing special about it.

He knew the door was locked. He remembered locking it earlier that night.

He knew how the door jamb would break when he kicked it. He'd done that to dozens of doors in the past and they all broke the same way.

All these things he knew, but he looked at the doorknob anyway. Whether he was experiencing a new symptom of old age—some type of delayed decision making—or his mind was running so fast it just seemed like he'd been standing here a long time, he couldn't tell.

But he was very aware that he *was* standing here. And he had the oddest feeling that it just *wasn't* time to open the door yet.

CHAPTER 72

Clara woke to the sounds of a soft voice. It was coming through the wall again, not from beneath the door. She thought her angel was back, but it must be a different one—taller—that's why the voice was coming from near the ceiling.

Maybe she was dreaming of her angel. Or maybe she was just dead. She didn't know the difference.

A faint light began to glow in the corner of the room, and a shape appeared. First, it was a swirling cloud, then it was the outline of something. A white dress billowed high in the corner as the outline of a person appeared. It was her angel!

Pushing her hair back from her eyes, Clara sat up to talk to her angel. She was anxious to get out of this place and to see Pickle. Maybe she could even see Mommy again. She rubbed her eyes and stared.

Something was wrong with her angel.

It didn't look like she expected. She couldn't see the wings, but it *was* floating in the air, so it must have them. Maybe they were invisible wings.

But where was the angel's face? And the halo?

Then the angel came into full view and little Clara screamed.

Her angel was bleeding.

*

Madame Broussard felt a ripple in the air and turned away from the image of the Spirit Hunter. She glanced at the wall inspecting the chaos playing out of Willy's eyes, then turned her attention to the building. She thought she'd heard something, but was more concerned by the prickle that ran across her skin. Something wasn't right.

She walked quietly around the main floor. She knew every creak and sigh of the old wood, but there was something new here.

Had she just heard the patter of feet? A cry in the night? Perhaps the little one had stirred. The little one? What was happening below?

Just as the thought entered her mind, she caught a glimpse of a shape moving in the dark. A small shape in the back room, near the stairs.

Who was that? Was the girl out of her room?

She hastened through the back room and down the stairs. Had the girl gotten out? How was that possible?

She hurried through the lower level and to the last room. Unlocking the door, she threw it open and stood in dumb surprise. The bed was empty! Somehow the little girl had gotten out of her room!

Just then a loud thump echoed through the ceiling as if a large weight had fallen onto the floor above. She hurried back up the stairs and found Willy flailing on the floor. Somehow, he'd toppled over in his chair and was staring toward the attic.

Madame Broussard went to pick him up, then heard him whisper. Once again, she was to be surprised, because typically no one this far into their transformation had anything to say. She leaned in close.

"…girl…" he whispered, staring past her at the ceiling.

Girl?

She looked at the ceiling. Faint images projecting from Willy's eyes were cast there. The ceiling was too high for the images to be clear, but the concept of movement caused her mind to latch onto an idea. Willy was telling her the girl had made it up to the top floor!

Madame Broussard ran for the next flight of stairs. This was getting out of hand.

*

Spider arrived at his destination in a panic, despite having made the trip in record time. In reality, the two locations weren't far apart, and there was no traffic at this time of night. But in his mind, it was the power of Spider the Dragon King, soaring through a dark storm, that got him here.

He pulled into the hidden alley that led to the building no one remembered and went into a dream. He knew how to get there, but could never remember where it was when he left. Granted, he didn't try terribly hard to figure it out—that wasn't his style. He simply took the message, didn't fuck up, didn't ask questions, then did the next thing. And that's what he was doing now.

In his waking dream-state, he parked the car, opened the trunk and walked away. There was only one alley in his dream, so it wasn't hard deciding where to go. He simply left the car behind him and walked away. As soon as he'd walk away, the alley became a long street with foggy lights off to each side. It would lead him somewhere—it always did. Fortunately, every time he came here it looked the same— less to remember.

The street was old cobblestone—but there was a lot of that in the city—and it felt both familiar and not at the same time. He never thought about taking a side path, or turning around. He just walked. He'd get to his destination eventually.

This place was always foggy, sort of like after a hard rain. No one else ever walked here—at least no one he could see, and certainly no one he wanted to meet. He felt as if something was just beyond the fog walls, but as long as he stayed on his path—and didn't turn around—he'd be fine. He wouldn't dare venture off the path. He knew that would be bad, without being told.

He couldn't remember how long the walk was. But his spider-instincts told him it was never too long or too short. And just as he thought this, he saw his car up ahead. He'd recognize the silhouette of the grill and the distinctive headlights anywhere.

He didn't know how he knew this, but it was now time to leave. He climbed in, started it up and drove out of the fog, exiting his dream.

Back on the street, the old fear of being late settled over him and he pushed down the accelerator. A sour, sweaty smell stung his eyes.

The car tilted as he slid around a curve. That's when he heard it.

Noisy packages.

He turned up the radio and squinted through the glass. He had one more stop to make. He still had a thing.

CHAPTER 73

Fearing he'd missed his signal, Spider snuck up the back steps of Armand's house and listened at the open door. He'd just arrived, and had left his car parked in the same spot, next to the cemetery. The engine still pinged from the heat of his frantic race back.

He stared into the dark void of the kitchen and wondered what to do. Someone had kicked the door in. Wooden splinters from the door jamb were laying on the kitchen floor. The red car was still smashed into the gate, so he assumed the crazy cop was still here. He must have kicked open the door. For as big as he was, the guy was pretty nimble, Spider thought. And he had a light step. There was no telling where he was.

He slipped past the open door without moving it. He didn't want to risk a squeaky hinge. Spider was cautious. He'd do this last thing and set his world straight.

A sliver of light shot across the floor of the kitchen. Someone had just turned on a light in another room. Spider stood against the wall in the shadows. The shadows were dark here. He could hide forever in this house.

He knew he was outside of his initial instructions, but thought this was the right course of action. He felt it. He felt good that he was taking charge, making his own decisions. He was exactly where he should be at this moment. Something important was going to happen tonight—in just a few minutes perhaps—and he was going to be part of it. Someone had called him here and was guiding his footsteps. He trusted the voice in his head.

In the dark, Spider smiled for the last time.

*

Del snapped back to her trance of the house. The road of the dead that had led her to Madame Broussard's dissolved like a whisper. Her last image of that horrible place was the woman frantically searching the upstairs. She was chasing ghosts.

Gray static clouded Del's trancing scenes. Her mind wavered. Her energy was nearly spent.

But there was still one she had to save.

She flashed to Jimmy and found him in the hall. Frank was now in the parlor—having spent quite a long time waiting on the porch—with his back to the door. Spider was here also! He was in the kitchen. And the shadows were waiting.

A floorboard squeaked as Jimmy crept from the dark, and Frank spun on him. His gun drawn.

"Hee-hee," he whispered, "I got no tings."

"What?" Frank recognized the boy, but knew something was wrong. His shape was... fluid. "Jimmy? What's wro—?"

"HHGGRRRR! I GOT NO TINGS!" Jimmy ran at him.

"NO!" Del screamed in Frank's mind as she saw his finger move to the trigger. "The kitchen!"

Frank kicked a chair into Jimmy's path, which sent him toppling over.

"Ow! I— hhggrrr!"

"Del, where are you?" Frank yelled.

"The kitchen, quick!"

Frank ran from the parlor. As soon as he entered the foyer, Spider stepped from the kitchen door with his arms open.

"Come here, buddy," Spider said in a strange voice.

"What da hell?" Frank pointed his pistol, but his hand shook. In all his years of being a cop and detective, his hand had never shaken. But he'd never seen this before.

"Frank, move!"

The voice of Del was in his head, but seemed to be coming out of Spider's mouth at the same time. That was because Spider and Del were standing in front of him. Frank thought he was seeing the ghost of Del. The shock was too much for him and his chest suddenly tightened, causing him to grimace slightly. He thought she was dead.

The image that floated in front of Spider was loosely attached to him, and moved a split second after he did. It was like a bad 3D movie, where the filming was out of sync. As Spider walked forward, so did the image of Del. Only the contrasting images froze Frank in his place.

Spider's face was blank with surprise. Del's face streamed blood from her nose.

Spider's shirt stuck to him from rain and sweat. Del's nightgown clung to her from blood.

Spider's steps left footprints of water. Del's steps left a single trail— the right foot—and it was of blood.

Frank's chest seized again as tears filled his eyes. "Del-bell... honey..."

"Frank move," she pleaded. Her voice was weak.

A part of Frank's mind obeyed as the rest went blank. Like a man who'd lost everything, he was barely responsive. He took two slow steps to the side, just as Jimmy ran past him.

"Come here, buddy," Spider-Del said, now on their knees. They welcomed the boys with open arms. "I've been looking for you."

Jimmy screamed in horror at the sight of Del; Alvie screamed in delight. The energy was strong. It drew the Alvie-bones to it. And they ran.

A flash of light erupted as Spider-Del and Jimmy-Alvie collided. A sharp crack of electricity echoed the halls, announcing a new union. Del's spirit fell back from Spider, just as the Alvie-bones left Jimmy. They'd found a new home.

Frank stumbled to a chair and watched in disbelief as bodies and spirits separated and recombined.

Jimmy bounced off Spider and rolled to the side. Spider fell backwards, clawing at his chest. Something was in him! He screamed and kicked as he flailed on the floor. Something was burrowing inside him!

He felt squirmy!

"Frank," Del's voice was weak in his head. "Get Jimmy. I'm upstairs."

Frank stood up and checked his balance. His blood pressure made his head swim, and speckles danced before his eyes. He pulled Jimmy up by the arm and headed for the stairs. The boy was catatonic but walking. His hands and arms trembled with fear.

Looking up at the long staircase, Frank wondered if he could make it to the top. Del had sounded weak, but there was still a crazy guy in the house.

"Go find Del," he said to Jimmy. Frank turned to find Spider.

Supporting himself with furniture, Frank stumbled through the foyer. His chest sent warning shots down his left arm, but he marched on.

"Get out! Get out! Get OUUTTT!" High-pitched screams cut the air as Spider beat his head and clawed his chest.

The Alvie-bones, still feeding on the Del-energy left inside Spider, tried to work the new body, but the body fought back. The wiry spider-muscles were stronger than the boy's. But once the bones had time to settle, it would be a wonderful new body. Spider crashed through the kitchen and out the back door. Both he and his bones wanted to get away from this place.

"Come 'ere you sum'bitch!"

Frank grimaced as another pain shot across his chest and he stumbled sideways. His legs were trying to give out.

He followed the trail of destruction through the kitchen. He didn't know why Spider was at the house, but that was far too close to Del. If this was to be Frank's final act, it would be ensuring Spider wasn't around after he was gone. He was determined not to let Spider get away.

Sprawled on the courtyard stones, Spider kicked and tore at his flesh. Something had tangled his feet on the way down the steps, and he'd hit the stones with the top half of his body. His face was scraped, and his mouth bled; his torso—now missing a shirt—had deep scratches where he'd clawed himself.

Frank made his way onto the back porch and steadied himself against the rail. He watched Spider as he flailed on the ground.

Spider had gone mad from the unholy invasion. Babbling and screaming, he was a man of many voices—some were dead voices, but not all. Not yet.

Then a horrifying sight came to Frank. The shadows of the courtyard crept out of their dark places and stretched toward Spider. His torment was not over.

Frank raised his pistol.

Spider convulsed over onto his stomach, and with a surprise spring of his arms and legs, leapt sideways behind a large stone planter. Frank adjusted, firing where his body should land, and exploded the corner of the planter. Suddenly, Spider was up sprinting toward the gate.

Frank tracked ahead of the fleeing man. He had to run past his car, which was still wedged under the iron gate, to get out. But Frank knew where the gas tank was on the car. All he needed was one good shot.

His chest seized again, and he bit his lip. Then he saw the light.

CHAPTER 74

Whether it was blood-vessels popping in his brain, or his mind shutting down, Frank saw lights where none should be.

In the center of the courtyard, illuminated from within, the stone maiden began to move. Its granite eyes saw the dead things, for they were of the same world. It knew the shadows that had invaded the house, and loathed them. It felt the power that radiated from a second-floor room and feared it. Most of all, it despised the abomination that was running towards it. Some things should never be joined.

Like splintering ice echoing from the heart of a glacier, ancient sounds of grinding rock cracked through the air as the maiden began to move.

A long white arm reached out and snatched the running man as he passed near the fountain base. A surprised squawk escaped his lips as he was suddenly lifted eight feet in the air. Staring skyward, and for the briefest moment, he felt like he was flying. Spider the Dragon

King flying away on a magic wind. Lightning flashed high overhead, marking the occasion.

Then he was falling toward water.

He hit the dark pool and gasped, breathing the water deep. His lungs screamed. His arms flailed. Shock overwhelmed him. Images flashed through his mind, *flick-flick-flick*. This wasn't supposed to happen. He still had a thing!

The stone maiden, having stood in judgement over the courtyard for a hundred and fifty years, cast its eyes upon Spider. It saw no redemption. The stone eyes closed in an act of mourning.

Spider's body convulsed as he tried to save himself. His wide eyes stared at an infinitely deep pool of water. Images of his life swam there. His life surfaced, scene by scene, then faded away. There was nothing beyond today. Then he saw the dead things swim up from the deep. They were hungry.

A lightning bolt of pain shot through his back and he gasped a second time. A large stone arm pummeled him under the water. Again and again it swung, first breaking his ribs, then his left arm, just below the shoulder. Spider screamed in pain as he gulped his last lung full of water. The air fled from him in frantic bubbles as his eyes clouded over. With two feeble kicks of his legs, he fell still. The last vision to register in his brain was a mouth full of teeth swimming up at him.

The Alvie-bones exited the dying body. A skeleton hand reached out of the water and clutched at the capstones. It churned the water as it pulled itself up. It needed a shadow road to get home, but not the one at the bottom of the pool. It clambered to the top of the stone circle and the maiden pummeled it again. Fragments of bone and stone flew into the air. One creature breaking itself to destroy the other. This was what the maiden had been after the entire time.

The skeleton boy crashed to the stone courtyard as its windmill arm came off, bouncing high in the air. The sinew couldn't hold against the brutal attack. The arm bone landed on the capstone and teetered into the water.

The skeleton began to crawl away until the stone maiden crushed the skinny spine with a mighty blow. The whole thing collapsed as a skeleton mouth turned and gnashed at the air over its broken shoulder. The right arm scraped against the ground as the stick fingers clawed toward a shadow.

Another stone hand swung high in the air, preparing the final blow. The maiden's intent was to turn these unholy bones into dust and let the storm winds take them. As the hand swung its final arc, the skeleton fingers reached out and touched a shadow that had ventured forward. Even the dead took sides.

The bones of Alvie, The Boy Made of String, disappeared into the shadow just as the stone hand hit the courtyard. The last few strands of sinew kept the dead legs, crushed spine and other broken pieces connected to the outstretched fingers, and they all disappeared with a wink.

The stone maiden cared not what happened to the human body or other bones that had been in its pool. They were no longer there. The black things had pulled them down. Creaking with the ancient sounds of time, the maiden looked out over its courtyard and settled itself back into place. It observed the fleeing shadows and knew the inhabitants of the house were safe for a while.

As Frank collapsed, he thought he saw a circle of light, like a shockwave, radiate out from the maiden and race across the courtyard. He did see the clouds part and glimpsed the faintest hint of dawn.

He thought of Del as his eyes closed, and wished he could see her again.

The long night was nearly over.

CHAPTER 75

S everal hours later, Del heard Mama Dedé call to her. She thought she had slipped off to sleep and the elder woman was starting to wake up, but in fact, it was the other way around.

Del twitched defensively, trying to pull herself from the deep sleep she'd fallen into, but the woman soothed her mind and she went under again.

*

Del dreamed of blood and shadows and saw herself lost in a dark place. The vision spun around her like a whirlwind. She remembered a void and heard a great, sucking wind. Somewhere a man chanted, calling to her. A girl screamed and disappeared. Del slipped from dream to nightmare and was lost to all.

*

Up and down her mind swam. She dreamed of water, silent and deep. She wanted to bathe in a deep pool and absorb the water there. She felt dry and brittle. She dreamed of a hot wind baking her skin, little pieces flaking off and blowing away like autumn leaves.

She dreamed of high-pitched screams that exploded brittle bones. Dust and fragments swirled in the air and recollected as deformed stick figures. They danced about, mocking her, singing a song fragment that scratched her mind. Then the figures scuttered away with a dreadful, click-clacking sound. Hours later, she coughed up warm liquid.

*

It was dark when Del opened her eyes. She flinched and tried to get up, but her body was unresponsive. Her head pounded and her leg throbbed a warning to stay still. Her bones ached from deep scars that had settled at her core. Her tongue found a loose tooth.

She recognized voices that floated down the hall. They were hushed and somber. She tried to trance out to see who it was, but a sharp pain flashed behind her left eye and a wave of nausea crashed over her.

Her mouth was pasted together with dry saliva. It glued her tongue to the roof of her mouth and stuck the insides of her cheeks to her teeth. She needed water, but was too weak to call out. Her mind fell backwards into sleep once again.

*

Still dark. Her stomach was empty, but no longer hurt. She no longer shivered uncontrollably. She'd just drank something warm. It washed away the taste of blood.

She smelled incense and pipe tobacco. They were familiar smells, but they weren't complete.

More hushed tones and somber words. Someone was missing. Someone was here.

Something was wrong.

CHAPTER 76

Madame Broussard stalked her showroom. Her lips, set in a tight line across her face, squeezed out all hint of color. She was enraged.

The empty eye sockets of Alvie followed her from the tabletop. The skeleton body couldn't sit up, it was too badly broken. It looked longingly at her when she passed by, hoping to soon have its strings fixed so it could move again. But it would have to wait.

The actions that had taken place over the last twenty-four hours were still unbelievable to her. She'd wracked her brain trying to understand the sequence of events, but the entire picture eluded her. Not only had the Spirit Hunter found her, and managed to destroy her creation, but the little girl was gone as well.

It was a complete and utter violation of her world, her sanctuary. It cut at her core and would not go unpunished.

The night the Spirit Hunter visited, she'd wondered why a more overt attack hadn't been made. Or at least, some attempt at rescue. Now she understood.

The girl had seemed hardly able to trance when she appeared from the shadow road, confused and barely able to focus. Honestly, Madame Broussard had expected more from her. But she'd played her part well: the poor bleeding orphan, not understanding what she was seeing. And the whole time Madame Broussard was lecturing her about existential powers, she was not only trancing through the building, she'd found Clara, tricked her into hiding beneath the bed, then sent the distracting sounds around the building, facilitating the wild goose chase.

Madame Broussard remembered being surprised when she saw Clara's empty bed. Had she only looked beneath it where the drooping cover hid her...

How deceitful!

Then the fortunately timed fall from Willy sent her hurrying up the stairs, then to the attic, only to leave the bedroom door unlocked.

Very clever, actually.

Of course, the *coup de grâce* was when the girl had managed to call Spider and send him back to the building for a pickup. How she knew the building would handle the transference of the rootstock was still a mystery—perhaps even dumb luck—but choosing to manipulate Spider the way she did—seemingly at the last minute—said something about the girl's character. There was a dark side to her. The decisions she'd had to make could not have come easily. Unless...

Madame Broussard fingered her pearls. Some people had black streaks—buried deep. Sometimes they never emerged, the catalyst never presenting itself. But others... their black streaks flowed just below the surface, waiting to bubble up and burst free. And those people—Madame Broussard had met some—those people just needed a tiny push. Sometimes just a prick of the mind and the black streak would emerge. And in many cases, those people who were right on the edge gravitated to situations that would eventually tip them over. Like a moth to a flame, they couldn't resist.

Coming back to the present situation, Madame Broussard wondered what to do about the rootstock now that the little girl was gone.

That was the first problem.

The second issue was what she saw on her fresco.

Looking at the caricature of life that played out on her wall, she stared at the ring around the Spirit Hunter's house. Just twenty-four hours ago it had been as black as the ring around her own building. Now, it not only wasn't there, it had been replaced. Whether a trick of the light or her own imagination, she couldn't say—perhaps it was a trick left over by that deceitful girl—but it looked like a ring of light had begun to form around the house.

It was a harsh color compared to the black ring that still encircled her own building, but its implications were clear: some spirits were sympathetic to the Spirit Hunter. And those spirits were beginning to mass. It seemed getting at the Spirit Hunter would not be easy now.

And it also seemed as if her own dark night would never end.

CHAPTER 77

But Del's finally did.

She had slept all day Sunday, through the evening, and into Monday morning. When she awoke, she sat up on the side of the bed. Disoriented and sluggish, she felt like she was coming out of a long sickness. Her head was light, and her legs shook a bit, but at least she had the energy to sit up. It would be a long time before she felt normal.

She listened to the house. Its familiar squeaks and groans comforted her, but there was a sadness in the air. The emptiness was palpable. And someone was crying quietly in the library.

Standing up and reaching for her housecoat, she caught a glimpse of herself in the mirror. Her eyes were sunken with dark circles. There was hardly any shine to them. Raw skin covered her top lip, just beneath her nose. She remembered tasting blood. Her skin had a grayish tint, and the scars on both sides of her neck stood out with a sickly white pall. Her right leg twinged when she put pressure on it. She didn't want to see what the scars looked like beneath the bandages. She looked away from the image, slipped on her robe and opened the door.

Shuffling down the hall, she felt sick with apprehension. Mama Dedé rocked in Frank's chair. Del sat down in Armand's and stared at the woman, awaiting the news.

Without looking up, Mama Dedé said, "Frank had a heart attack."

Tears sprang to Del's eyes. "And?"

"It was mild. The old bastard was lucky." She smiled through a pinched face as a new stream of tears wet old tracks. "But it could have been worse."

"Oh, thank God!" A smile cracked Del's face, but came out as a grimace. "Ow…" She massaged her neck gently. She imagined deep scars running from the back of her nose, down her throat and into her stomach. "Where is he? Can we go see him?"

"Armand's picking him up today. Frank's complaining about the bed. Says he can't sleep without his pilla. And that if the nurses don't stop poking him, he'll have a real heart attack."

Del chuckled at the thought of Frank grousing at the nurses. Images tried to flicker to life in her mind, but it was too weak to entertain them.

"Where's Jimmy?" Del asked cautiously.

"With Armand. He's been asking about Frank ever since he found him on the back porch."

"Found him?"

"Mmm-hmm. If it hadn't been for Jimmy finding Frank, then waking up Armand, well… I just don't know."

"Jimmy found Frank?"

"Yeah. And that's not all he found."

"Clara!" Del said as images flooded back to her. "Oh my gosh! Did someone—?"

"She's safe. Jimmy found her in the trunk of Spider's car. She's at the hospital as well."

Tears spilled down Del's cheeks as she slapped her hand to her mouth. *Thank you, thank you,* she thought to whatever invisible force may be listening. "Is she going to be OK?" The words were muffled through her fingers.

"They think so."

Del let her head fall back as she wiped her eyes. A wave of relief washed over her, but was replaced by a bubbling spring of guilt. It welled up inside her as she thought of the little girl, laying terrified inside the trunk. She tried remembering that night, wanted to see that Clara hadn't been completely traumatized, but it wouldn't come to her. Not yet.

After a long minute of searching the ceiling, other questions emerged. Del looked at Mama Dedé. "Jimmy found her?"

Mama D nodded.

"How did he know to even look for her?"

Mama D shrugged.

"And then he got Armand?"

"Yeah, why?"

Del thought hard. How did Jimmy get into his room? Hadn't she left Armand locked in? Had Frank picked the lock first? She didn't think so. And how was Jimmy even able to function after the night's events?

Elbows to knees, Del squeezed her head, trying to focus her brain to make sense of this. She wished she could remember more details, but regardless, thought Mama Dedé would be more forthcoming with information.

"What's wrong?" Mama Dedé asked. Her hands sat in her lap.

Del curled her legs beneath her and leaned into the chair. She wasn't sure if she was ready to unravel the visions she'd had over the last twenty-four hours. She wasn't even sure if they'd stopped. Everything had run together into one long nightmare. "I'm not sure… what's been a dream, and…"

"Had me some funny dreams as well."

"But, Jimmy's OK?"

"Seems to be. Oh, he may be a bit rattled about the break-in. Been hanging around Armand a lot, but he'll get over it."

Del's face went blank. "The break-in? What do you mean?"

"Don't worry now, Armand's got the door fixed back. It'll take a while to get the gate fixed, but we'll be safe."

"I don't understand, safe from what?" Then Del added, "That a gate could stop, anyway."

"Well, Spider of course. He's the one that broke in. Most likely coming after you to get back at Frank."

"Spider? But he's—"

"Don't worry now, you'll be safe. The police found his car parked outside. They haven't found him yet, but they're on the lookout. Thank God Frank was driving the neighborhood and saw him."

"Driving the neighborhood?"

Del sat in stunned silence. The story didn't make sense. She searched her mind for an answer as to why her mentor didn't have a clearer picture of what had happened.

Del questioned her again. "And you're *sure* Jimmy is OK?"

"Yeah. Why wouldn't he be? Not sure what woke him up the other night, but Frank's lucky he did. Unusual though. That boy normally sleeps like a log."

Del nodded. "Yeah… Unusual."

Something was wrong. She needed to speak to Frank.

*

Del sat in the kitchen, watching tea drip from her spoon into her cup. She'd spent most of the afternoon here watching the courtyard for Armand. Her energy was low, but returning. The aches in her body were still present, but the simple act of staring out the window put her mind at ease—somewhat. Each time she tried to run through the scenarios of what had occurred that night, and during the day she lost to sleep, her mind crawled to a stop. Sluggish and tired, the images were hidden like old dreams. She barely had enough energy to make the tea and take a cup to Mama Dedé, who'd stayed in her room all day. Trancing was completely out of the question.

Armand had already cleaned up the broken items in the house. Most things had just been toppled over, but an expensive looking vase from the parlor was gone and the door jamb from the back porch into the kitchen was broken. She thought that was from Frank. But why did Mama D think Spider had done it?

As Armand pulled into the courtyard, she stepped onto the back porch. Frank was with him.

Jimmy stepped out of the car and waved. "Hi, Deh! You seepyhead!"

Another weight floated from her chest. She couldn't believe there was no sign of trauma.

"Hi, Jimmy!" She waved as she limped down the steps. "How's Frank?"

"Mmm… he petty good, I guess. I saved him."

"Ha! You did? And Clara too! You must have been pretty brave to do that."

"Yeah… petty bwave, I guess."

Jimmy walked past Del and up the steps.

"Hey, wait! Don't I get a hug or something?"

Jimmy hugged her quickly, patting her shoulder as if to comfort her. It was a strange gesture.

"Hey, what's the rush?"

"I go hep Mama D now," Jimmy said.

"Oh. OK."

She watched him walk through the kitchen bobbing his head, humming under his breath.

She turned and saw that both men were still in the car, waiting for her. She hobbled over to Frank's side and stuck her head through the window.

"Del-bell." Frank hugged her weakly with his right arm. "How are you, honey?"

"Me? How are you? Oh my gosh, I've been so worried. I sat in there all day wondering how you were, and I thought about calling the hospital, but knew that Armand was coming to get you out, but I didn't know when and I didn't want to call and keep you there any longer, but I was wondering and I was hoping—"

"Ha! Whoa, honey. You like to put me back in if I try to listen as fast as you're talkin'. Hop in. Mr. Moustache going to run me home."

Del jumped into the backseat before Frank got his arm settled back inside. She pushed a duffle bag with Frank's clothes out of the way and scooted behind Armand.

"So, what'd the doctor say? Are you going to be alright?"

Frank struggled around to look at her. "Oh, it wasn't much of nothin.'"

"Mon ami!" Armand said sharply as he backed the car out of the courtyard. "That was not what—"

Frank raised his hand. "A bit worse than bad indigestion, but I'll be alright."

Armand's eyes widened. "Indigestion?"

"Eh!" Frank cut him off and pointed at his chest. "You're givin' me indigestion right now, so let me tell it."

Armand huffed and his moustache flattened into a straight line. He took off down the road with a jerk and drove in silence.

Frank turned back to Del. "Da question of da day is, how are *you* feeling?"

She sighed and sat back in the seat. "Tired… and confused. I'm trying to put the pieces together, but it's hard. Some things just don't make sense."

"What do you remember?" Frank asked.

CHAPTER 78

By the time they got Frank settled into his house, the story had become clearer, but several pieces were still missing.

Del knew that the missing kids had been transported by Spider and kept hidden in a building they still couldn't find. How the kids got out of the orphanages was still a mystery. The only place Spider had gone inside, as far as Del knew, was Armand's house.

Armand told of the shadows that Mama Dedé had warned him about, and suspected they had something to do with their near demise, the night they all drank the brandy. Although he'd never heard a story of a spirit spiking a bottle of liquor, he vowed to research it thoroughly.

Frank told of hearing Del scream for help in a dream, but silently doubted it was a dream at all. He'd been compelled to drive to Armand's house early that morning. Upon arriving at the closed gate, he was sure Del was calling for him then. He apologized for destroying Armand's gate. Under the circumstances, Armand assured him it was alright.

Del knew that Alvie was gone and that Willy was beyond saving. Both men commented on what a fortunate turn of events it had been that Spider was transporting Clara right before he made his final stop at Armand's. Del had a different impression of what happened but remained silent, since the details were foggy. Besides, Jimmy being the hero of the night was a pleasant thought. She also felt that Willy deserved a supporting actor award, for his role in The Great Deception of Madame Broussard, but thought the topic too complicated to explain.

When Armand questioned her as to the kidnapping mastermind—Spider obviously wasn't the brains of the operation—she could only explain it as, 'a malevolent force,' which piqued his interest even more, but she said no more.

The source of Armand's sore jaw came to light when Del retold her frantic run through the house, avoiding Jimmy, so she could remove the covers from his face. He thanked her profusely for the valiant act of saving his life. Frank asked her to reenact the part where she smacked Armand, because he wasn't clear on what happened.

Armand interrupted. "But what was wrong with young master Jimmy? Why was he chasing you?"

Del looked at Frank, who at that moment decided to inspect the ceiling. "Maybe… it was one of the spirits?" she said.

Armand stroked his beard and considered the answer. There were simply too many questions to explore in one evening.

The interaction between Spider-Del and Jimmy-Alvie was avoided. Frank cleverly talked around Armand's probing questions when it came to Frank and Spider meeting in his parlor.

"But," Armand said, "why was he even there? And how did Del know to call out to you? Was this after he broke in? If so, how did you get here so quickly?"

Sitting on Frank's couch with her feet curled beneath her, Del rubbed her head as she looked at the floor. A headache was starting behind her left eye again. She didn't know how much she wanted to say. "I'm not really sure about the timeline. When I couldn't wake Mama D, and knew something was wrong with Jimmy, I got scared. I just called out for help, trying to wake somebody up... I don't know... maybe he heard me."

Frank watched Del closely and understood the unspoken signals. She was struggling with a decision she'd made—a decision regarding Spider. In fact, he thought she was struggling with many decisions she'd made that night, most of which had probably saved their lives. *But at what cost?* he wondered. What terrible trade-off had she made?

"Well," Frank broke in, "I don't see what da timeline really matters for. I knew that sum'bitch was involved somehow." He reached for his cigar box, but grimaced as his weak left arm fell short of its mark. "Well, hell..." he mumbled and left the box alone.

"Do you want something else to drink?" Del asked. "I'll make you something."

"No, honey, that's OK." Frank rubbed his arm. "Anyway, like I was sayin', I don't think we're gonna see dat sum'bitch anymore." He slipped a look at Del. "Ya think?"

Now it was Armand's turn to watch the unspoken messages. He felt that Del was holding back. But as anxious as he was to understand these fascinating powers, he wouldn't press her to talk about something she didn't want to. But he knew there was more.

"Well, I don't think so?" She looked at Frank for help, because she truly didn't remember this part. "Did you see where he ran off to? I haven't been able to look yet... my head, you know."

"Hell, all I saw was flashin' lights right before I went down. I imagined I was seein' all kinds of things, but... well, I don't know what da hell I saw."

"Did you see him run past your car?" Armand asked. "Despite the blockage, that would make the easiest escape."

An image of his beloved red car flashed in Frank's mind, the heavy iron gate laying casually in the shattered windshield.

"Can't say I did."

Armand nodded. "Then did you see him run past the fountain at least?"

Frank felt an uneasiness creep into his chest. "No."

"I see. Well, after you mend, we should inspect the fountain. It has some interesting marks about it, and I'd like your professional opinion on what put them there."

"Intrestin' marks?"

"Yes, very interesting. After I returned from the hospital that morning, I discovered that the extent of the melee went well beyond the house proper."

"It did?"

Stroking his beard again, Armand's eyes sparkled. "Yes, it did." He pulled his pipe and tobacco pouch from an inside vest pocket. He began cleaning it, then pulled back in dismay. "Oh, my! I am sorry, mon ami."

"No, no. Go right ahead. It was smellin' a bit stale in here anyway. I'll just sniff a little from over here."

Armand smiled and winked. "Thank you. Now, what was I saying? Let's see..."

"The interesting marks?" Del asked.

"Yes, of course!" His finger shot in the air. "The interesting marks around the fountain."

Del snuggled into the couch and pulled an afghan over her shoulders. She wished they were in Armand's library with Mama Dedé. A tinge of guilt passed through her for feeling better, when she wasn't sure how Mama D was doing. She decided she'd stop Armand if the story ran too long, so they could get back to her.

"As I was saying, when I returned from the hospital that morning, I quickly surveyed the house. Which of course was when I discovered tiny Clara sleeping on the couch in the parlor. Young master Jimmy had tucked her up tight!"

Frank interrupted. "But wait, before dat. What woke you?"

Armand considered his pipe, the flaming match highlighting his curiosity. "I thought I told you. That was Jimmy as well."

Del broke in. "Yeah, what about that? How did Jimmy get in your room? I'm sure I locked the door after... well, after I tried to wake you."

"And how'd you wake him again?" Frank asked with a grin.

Del smirked at him.

"That's interesting," Armand said. "I remember a bit of a dream where I got hit, but in the dream, it was that hellish doll from... you know." He shivered and nodded over his shoulder. "Then it was a jumble of images, then... I recall Jimmy standing at my bedside yelling for me to wake up."

"He was in your room?"

Staring into the distance, Armand tried to remember. "He must have been. I saw him standing over me, telling me to wake up. Then... my head was very heavy, you see, and... by the time I sat up, he was gone. He must have run back to Frank, because by the time I got there, he was already there."

"You went straight to Frank?" Del asked.

"Yes, of course."

"How did you know where he was?"

"I don't know. I suppose Jimmy told me."

"When?"

Armand shook his head. "I... I'm actually not sure."

"Was your door locked?"

Armand searched the depths of his memory. His widening eyes told the tale. He thought the door *had* still been locked. Finally, he said, "That old lock is cantankerous. It is unreliable at best, but..." His head nodded as the implication settled over him.

"But what about da courtyard?" Frank prompted.

Slowly, Armand came back to that part of the story. "Yes... yes, the courtyard. When I found you—and saw the gate—I thought you'd driven here looking for help, or... I didn't know what had happened, but recognized the signs of your... pain. Upon returning from the hospital, I discovered the extent of the... events, and went exploring. I found Clara, then I found Jimmy. He'd taken tea to Mama Dedé in her room. She was..."

He turned to Del. "Why were you in her room? Had you—? Oh! I remember now. She was tending your bloody nose."

Del's eyebrows raised. "I don't remember much at that point, but, yeah... something like that." An image of the cold woman and a deep well surfaced, but she didn't feel it necessary to explain the details of what had actually happened.

Armand contemplated the smoke from his pipe. "I was still sluggish then. I called the authorities, but simply wandered the house. Something was different about it. Something was off. When they arrived, I explained that you were already at the hospital and that the missing girl had been found. When they asked how she had come to be asleep on the couch, Jimmy explained that he'd rescued her from the trunk of the wretched car. The officer said he would follow up with you and—"

"Yeah, I already gave him my statement," Frank said. "They knew I was workin' da case."

Armand nodded. "Yes, of course. I think I mentioned it as well. After they left, I checked on everyone, then at some point made it into the courtyard."

"Hallelujah, we made it!" Frank said.

Armand chuckled. "Yes, mon ami, we have finally arrived at the interesting part of the story. But it is a part that is difficult for even me to believe.

"You see, the day of Jimmy's accident," Armand said, "I had been speaking to Mama Dedé about some things." He remembered it had been about Del and the dark circles below her eyes, but didn't mention it. Looking at her now, he wasn't sure if the circles were better or worse. But this spirit business was taking a toll on her, that he could tell.

"We spoke at length, then I went downstairs for something. I thought I heard water dripping in the sink, but upon reaching the kitchen, knew the sound was coming from outside.

"I remember the clouds were strange that day. They'd cast an eerie gloom over the courtyard, and as I stepped onto the back porch, that's when I saw it."

"Saw what?" Del hugged her knees to her chin.

"I've felt a thread of guilt, ever since that day, about the notion that I saved Jimmy's life. Oh, I was there to push the water from his lungs, but… I wasn't the one to *pull* him from the water."

Frank and Del exchanged questioning looks.

"What I saw that day," Armand continued, "is hard to explain. The clouds, you see. They had cast a strange glow over the courtyard. But as I stood on the back porch searching for the sound of the water. I thought I saw the maiden pull Jimmy from the pool."

"Da maiden?" Frank said.

"The stone maiden?" Del's eyes were wide.

"Ho-ly, hell," Frank whispered.

"Perhaps," Armand replied with a nod.

An image came to Frank: a searing white light, rippling across the courtyard as he'd clutched his chest. He would remain silent on this topic for now.

"One moment, I thought I'd seen the maiden pull young Jimmy from the water. The next, I was pushing water from his lungs as he lay silent on the wall. I don't even remember crossing the courtyard."

Armand tapped cold ashes from his pipe into an ashtray. Frank and Del waited.

"I didn't think to inspect the pool at the time. When Jimmy began to cough, I only thought to get him to Mama Dedé. She met us in the kitchen, having somehow been aware of our distress.

"After that, the stone maiden was forgotten. Until yesterday. When, upon arriving home and inspecting the grounds, I found new evidence of disturbance on the maiden and around the outside of the pool."

"Disturbance?" Del asked.

"Yes. The stone courtyard is old, and with no large trees in the middle of it, has no reason to heave or settle. The slabs are over two inches thick and weigh a great deal. I had to straighten one by the carriage house once. Dreadfully heavy things. But there is now a stone slab that has a fresh break in it. And surrounding stones that are freshly chipped. Quite extraordinary if you ask me.

"In addition to that, the maiden herself seems to have incurred some... accelerated aging."

"Aging?" Frank asked. "How so?"

"She is pure granite. Quite a lovely creature. And despite the unkept nature of the gardens when my," here he looked at Del, "family arrived, I had spent many days and evenings walking the garden, admiring. Over the years I've inspected every fold of her gown and crease of her arms.

"Yesterday, I noticed several new hairline cracks about her. It seems that a great pressure has begun to work against her."

The three sat silently absorbing the implications. They had no words to describe their thoughts.

CHAPTER 79

On the drive home, Del's mind swam with questions. After updating each other with as many details as they could remember—and felt comfortable sharing—they told Frank they'd check on him in the morning. He dismissed the need for such babysitting, but when Armand reminded him that his car was undriveable, and that a condition for his early release was that a nurse would be over first thing in the morning, Frank grumbled and agreed. Del still wasn't sure it was a good idea leaving him alone.

"Armand, I've been meaning to ask you something."

"Yes, I have questions for you as well."

Del watched the late afternoon slide by through the car window. "What does Mama D remember of the last few days? With all the sleeping I did, I'm not clear on what she knows and…"

Armand considered the question. "I don't have the wonderful ability to see into someone's thoughts, so it's difficult—"

"Why did you tell her it was a break-in?"

"Ah, young Del, so perceptive. But perhaps I should ask you: is there a reason to not believe it was a break-in?"

Nervous energy rushed through Del's legs and her boots tapped a rapid distress signal on the floorboard of Armand's car. *WARNING! PROCEED WITH CAUTION. WARNING!*

Finally, her answer came. "I guess not... for now."

Armand nodded. "Yes of course. Therefore, a break-in is a perfectly reasonable theory. For now."

He clamped his teeth around his pipe, then removed it, pointing the mouth-end to an important idea in the air.

"I assure you my intention was never to mislead her. And given the hectic circumstances, I did, initially, consider the possibility of a break-in. But as the day unfolded, and I began to understand... I knew the truth would come out eventually. Although," he looked at her knowingly, "it appears it will come in pieces."

Del wasn't surprised that Armand had his suspicions about what she'd told them. "Yeah, you're probably right."

"Yes, as I thought. The prudent path, I would say. Very wise. One cannot be too careful with delicate matters such as these. The line between what one knows and what one *believes* they know is thin. It's not to be toyed with or manipulated. Sometimes it's the only thing that separates a person from sanity and... insanity."

"What are you saying?" Del turned towards him.

"Over the many years, I have learned a few things. And one of the most important is this: the human psyche is as fragile as it is resilient. It can withstand the horrors of humanity seemingly unscathed, then one day the slightest offence can shatter it like a discarded teacup. You never know what will tip the scale. And it's impossible to guess. We all experienced unnatural events this past weekend. They came at us from different directions, but they came at us nonetheless. I believe it will take time before we see the scar-tissue of these events surface. They will manifest differently in each of us. Only then will we understand how deep are the wounds."

Del's heartbeat quickened, but she didn't know why. The answer to her question was close. But Armand wanted her to arrive at it on her own.

"What was Mama D doing when you found her that morning?"

"As I said, she was tending to you."

"To my bloody nose?"

"Yes. That's what she said."

"She described it that way?"

"Yes."

"Did she say anything else?"

"Only that she awoke to find you had crawled in bed with her. She thought perhaps you had bumped your nose in the middle of the night. You were quite... well, the amount of blood was... disturbing."

Something like anger bubbled in Del's mind, but she didn't understand why it was there.

"A bloody nose? She thought I had a bloody nose?"

Armand sighed as he pulled the car into the courtyard. He stopped just inside the broken gate. His car was used as a makeshift blockade until the gate got repaired. He let the car idle.

"She hasn't said much since the morning I found her. In fact, she tends to only answer 'yes' or 'no' to basic questions. Anything more and she... wanders away, as if to look for the answer."

"'To look for the answer'?" Del was livid now. "What do you mean? It takes her two seconds to look for the answer, all she has to do is—"

Armand raise his pipe. "Not anymore," he said.

"What do you mean?"

"Her ability to find the answer she seeks seems to have… degraded a bit."

"Degraded? But she's going to be alright, isn't she? Isn't she? Maybe she needs to see a doctor. We should—"

"To which doctor should we take her? And what would I say are her symptoms?"

Del looked wildly around the car, searching for the answer. She could no longer keep track of which pieces of story she'd told to which person, and the words tumbled out. "But she has to be OK! When I saw she wouldn't wake up I went to her. I tranced and took her to my well. She was cold, but now she's not. I warmed her up. She's not cold anymore, so she has to be better!"

A grave feeling settled over Armand. The researcher in him knew they were on a dangerous path. Warning lights flashed in his mind. They were at a dangerous line of realization; he was close to understanding what truly afflicted Mama Dedé. He needed to step across that line, but felt with all his heart he had to leave Del on the other side. He felt a scale in his mind tip precariously. It was the scale of Del's psyche, and it had just received an unexpected blow.

"What are you saying?" Del's voice cracked. "Why does she still think it was a break-in?"

"I believe that is the easiest for her to understand."

"What do you mean, 'understand'?" Del was outside the car yelling through the open door. "She has the power! She can just look for herself and see what happened!"

With great pain, Armand said the words he'd been avoiding all day. "Perhaps she has forgotten how to look."

CHAPTER 80

The next several days were slow torture. Del spent her time between Frank's house and Armand's. She and Jimmy took to riding the bus back and forth. They'd spend time at Frank's helping clean around the house—which wasn't much work—cooking some meals and keeping him company. At least there they had someone to talk to.

Returning home was a grim reminder of how things used to be. Mama Dedé spent most of her time in her room or sitting in one of the chairs by the fireplace. Del would hear her crying on occasion, but she always said she was fine, just fine, when Del asked if she needed anything. Armand was busy with contractors making repairs to the gate, the stone columns and the back door. He also gave Frank updates on the repairs being done to his own car.

As Del healed physically, so did her mind. She remembered more, she understood more, and she accepted more. The decisions she had made would be part of her the rest of her life, she knew this. The cuts from those decisions would heal in time, but they would all leave their mark. Those decisions wrote the story of Del. She was a book of a thousand blank pages, and the scribe had set his quill deeply. Her story would be long, and she would bear every scar.

A new one would be made very soon.

CHAPTER 81

Madame Broussard let her hands run over the strange curios on the display table. After her initial anger of being betrayed, she'd become oddly melancholy. Willy was winding down. He would soon fail, and she needed to decide what to do. Alvie was still a pile of bones. The tedious process of stitching him back together didn't interest her now. Instead of tending to her business, she'd spent hours watching the fresco. Watching for a change in either the black ring that encircled her, or the glittering ring that encircled the Spirit Hunter. Neither changed. Therefore, her circumstance remained fixed. She was still trapped, and the lovely girl was even more protected. How the girl had managed it, she didn't know. Normally, this type of challenge excited her; now, it made the days agonizingly long.

Her finger caught on something sharp, and the faintest sound floated up from the table. She'd never heard the sound before, and almost played it off to a wandering mind, but hers did not wander. Her mind did not imagine things that weren't there. She'd missed something about the object on the table.

Inspecting her finger, she saw the small drop of blood clinging to it. Inspecting her table of items, the same red color showed brightly from the tip of a needle. A hat pin really. It had been shoved through the shoulder of a nondescript voodoo doll, and protruded from between its legs. She'd forgotten all about the object, and now couldn't remember when she'd received it or where it came from. She associated it with the strange little skeleton of the six-legged animal that sat near it. But neither had ever made a sound before.

Lowering her finger to the end of the long needle, she positioned it against her skin, then looked at the doll. Slowly she pushed and felt the needle slide into her finger. As the red bead eyes of the doll began to glow, she heard the sound again. A very faint, *ngyihng...* escaped its red bead mouth.

She looked from the doll to the bones of the six-legged creature, then over to the fading Willy. A lovely idea took shape in her mind.

Outside, a sign that couldn't be seen began to swing in anticipation.

CHAPTER 82

Del picked up her jacket as the grandfather clock struck. It was four o'clock in the morning. She'd barely slept, and had been waiting for this hour. She was nervous and excited at the same time.

Night after night she'd sat with Mama Dedé, but nothing seemed to help. The woman who had mentored and cared for Del seemed to be affected by a lethargy that drained her spirit. Del thought of the shadows that had haunted them. Every time night fell, she wondered if a spirit was lurking in the corner, sucking the life from Mama Dedé. She feared trancing out to see; she didn't want to pull anything else to the house. She didn't want to even think about her *gift*. It had caused enough damage already.

Over and over, she thought about the warning that Mama D had given Armand about the shadow-spirits. Del understood now why the woman hadn't told her. Mama D must have been afraid that if she told Del, it would only make Del think more about them, which would pull more in.

Without trying, Del had become the most dangerous monster of all, one that couldn't control itself, and pulled death and destruction to it. No one would ever be safe around her.

She slipped on her motorcycle jacket. The veve that Mama Dedé had drawn on the back was still there. She figured she'd need all the protection she could get. She threw her backpack over her shoulder; it carried a few changes of clothes, two gris bags—one with money in it—and her colored headbands. Four written notes, each in a separate envelope, were held in her other hand. She slipped through the bedroom door and quietly closed it behind her.

She breathed deeply as she walked through the library. The smell of old books and pipe tobacco was something she would surely miss. She glanced at the large paintings in the foyer. She remembered the first day she'd stepped into this house: how much she loved the old wood, how cozy it felt, how much she wanted to live in a place like this. She was glad she'd gotten to experience it.

She dropped the envelopes on the table, then turned back and arranged them in better order. She changed the order once or twice, then decided to put each at the individual's breakfast spot. Frank's letter was left at her own spot.

The letters all said the same thing, only in different ways that each person would understand. Armand's had been the easiest to write. Sometimes he was the most perceptive, she thought, and didn't let her age interfere with his advice. He was like the eccentric uncle that didn't mind the nieces and nephews sneaking out at night, because that was part of the learning experience—even if they got in trouble. But she didn't want people to think she was sneaking out or running away, especially Armand. She simply told him that she was off to continue her ten-thousand-hour journey.

Frank's letter was difficult to write because he was still healing. Even though he was already walking the neighborhood, she wanted him to take it easy. She said that she'd be 'checking in on him' from time to time, to make sure he went easy on the cigars. She didn't want him to worry about her—although she knew he would. And, he shouldn't worry about any Ronnie-mister-indoor-sunglasses getting the better of her. She knew what to look out for now.

Jimmy's letter described how proud she was of him that he'd found Clara and kept her safe. It was a brave thing to do, helping someone else, even if it was scary for him. She knew there had been some bad things happen around the house lately, but she wanted him to be brave like a lion. She had to take a train ride for a while, but would come back some day and tell him the adventure. She was pretty sure that all the scary things would go away when she left.

Mama Dedé's letter was the shortest. She had lost something, and Del had gone to find it. But, in the meantime, she should wear the gris bag that Del had left for her.

She wanted each person to understand that she'd made this decision for very personal—and adult—reasons. She was her own woman.

It was nearly four-fifteen, the perfect time. She'd picked this time because it was the closest to when the buses would start running, without risking an early morning encounter with someone in the house. She held open the kitchen door and looked back. The room was blurry from tears. But she had it memorized. She closed the door quietly and walked quickly down the steps. A minute later she was walking along the sidewalk, heading for the bus station. She'd yet to decide where to go, but knew for everyone in the house, they'd be safer with her gone.

A tingle of energy quickened her pace. The wind of freedom and adventure propelled her forward. This was the beginning of a long journey, and wherever it took her, it would be of her own making.

She looked back at the lovely house and thought she saw a shadow slink down the outside wall. It could have been a trick of the light, but thought it better to be safe.

"Come on," she said quietly. "I'm going this way."

CHAPTER 83

In the fading night, dark clouds roiled as a black tattered wind took shape. The air parted, not wanting to touch the black thing, and flew off in all directions. The ethereal shape was not of the normal elements. It came from a deeper place, and was changed because of it.

Within the roiling cloud, a hint of red whispered as if a single ray of light had lost its way. Twisting and twisted, the light struggled into existence.

The red light pulsed, a feeble first breath, sucking at the energy that flowed here. The tattered wind had come so far, had delved so deep, it had nearly been destroyed. But it had persisted. Some deep desire existed in the tattered element. For once, a long time ago, it had not been tattered.

The black cloud with the red spot that roiled in the air began to think. It had traveled so far—much further than expected—it had nearly forgotten how it began. It had followed the shadow road for so long, so long the journey had been, the concept of time had left it. But it began to remember:

Furnace winds. Lightning. Cutting dust. Annihilation.

A thread of energy.

A tiny thread that pulled it from the place of annihilation. It had been searching for the thread. It had been something more than just tattered black wind. Once, it had had form and substance. Once, it had had a name.

An eye formed and looked out onto the mortal world. It was at the end of its journey now. It had survived! It had found the thread of power, and through the harsh winds of the universe, followed it. Twisting and twisting, the thread wound through millennia. It was an old thing, the thread. It had an old beginning. But the end had just been reached.

The thing once known as Scarmish looked out of the red eye and surveyed its world. It had once been searching for a great source of power. A Spirit Hunter.

It had finally found the end of the crease the Spirit Hunter had made. A well-worn path that wound through the fabric of humanity ended above a house near a cemetery.

It had found the place where the powerful rested.

As the remnants of Scarmish peered through the clouds, past the brick walls, its attention was drawn to the sleeping inhabitants; one by one it inspected them.

Traces of power, like ribbons of lightning, floated off the crease, surrounding the house, hampering the inspection. Surely a trick of the Spirit Hunter, for the threads of energy had called many protective spirits to it. They surrounded the house in a solid ring that Scarmish could not penetrate; not yet.

Determined to find a way to the Spirit Hunter, the Scarmish-thing descended through the clouds and decided to wait. Across the street from the grand house lay row upon row of crypts; the Lafayette Cemetery #1 would sustain him until his strength returned.

A cold wind blew down the dead alleys of the cemetery, and the remnants of Scarmish settled into the shadows of a tall crypt. Here it would feed and watch the house for an opening. Here it would contemplate its next move, for it had just—at this very moment—glimpsed the powerful one through the wall. As the dead things moved away from the tattered shadow, its red eye peered through the walls and into a dark bedroom. There, its cold gaze fell upon a sleeping boy.

And his mind was endless.

A NOTE FROM THE AUTHOR

Thank you for reading *Scars of Redemption*!

I was excited to revisit Del and the gang. Their wellbeing is important to me and I'm anxious to see how they handle this new twist in their lives. I must admit, I thought the story would end differently, but was happy with the outcome. I hope you were too.

If you enjoyed this book, please think about leaving a review at your favorite retailer. Reviews help the book get discovered by others who may also enjoy it.

ACKNOWLEDGEMENTS

Thanks again to my wonderful wife Mary for the long hours reading and discussing this story. You were right, the first ending was bad. Del, Clara and I appreciate you pointing that out.

Also, many thanks to the close family and friends who read this story in its imperfect state. Please keep the feedback honest.

MORE BOOKS BY D.S. QUINTON

If you're looking for another read, maybe explore where the supernatural power came from. Remember, Armand had a theory about this, based on the diary of a very unfortunate boy.

That theory is FREE to download and read…

The Phoenix Stone – A Dark Beginning

Would you die to expose the secret of mankind's origin? Otto just might…

Desperate to journal his grandfather's discovery before his capture, young Otto hides in a secret Egyptian chamber avoiding nomads and flesh-eating beetles to chronicle an amazing story—How we began. Will the story be lost? Will the nomads find him? Or…does the unthinkable happen?

This short story is the dark beginning of all things.

Get *The Phoenix Stone* FREE at www.dsquinton.com/my-books

And as the dark beginning splinters into infinite shards of kaleidoscope dreams, one story tumbles headlong into the future of human evolution, A.I. and government conspiracies with the genre-blending novel...

Devel Django - The Evolution Series Book 1

A near-future thriller that whispers at the fundamental question of humankind—Where did we come from?—and gropes at the undefined space between science and religion.

It is a unique tapestry woven with coarse threads of horror, hybrid metal synapses, and detailed with a fine, ancient brush from a long-lost palate of knowledge.

Get *Devel Django* at www.mybook.to/DevelDjango

Finally, for anyone that grew up on *The Twilight Zone* or *Night Gallery*, check out *Circus Sideshow*. You may find something you like.

Circus Sideshow - A Supernatural Oddity

Act One:

A pompous actor. A small-town sheriff. A dark secret in a place called Devil's Backbone.

When an arrogant second-rate actor runs afoul of a small-town sheriff, he learns his place in the world. Through a series of strange encounters, the actor is introduced to the people of Devil's Backbone and their unique contribution to the world.

Act Two:

A quaint town. An honest man. An ancient horror in disguise.

The small town of Devil's Backbone experiences its first brush will true evil. The Making of Polly Three-Tongues is a warning tale to the human predators that walk among us. Don't come to our town.

Get *Circus Sideshow* at www.dsquinton.com/my-books

A TASTE OF THE FUTURE

I very much hope you enjoyed *Scars of Redemption*.

If you did and would like more in the same vein, here's a sneak peak at the third book in the *Spirit Hunter* series...

CHAPTER 1

Del walked alone and felt the eyes upon her. She always felt the eyes.

In the light of day, the eyes of people she didn't know glanced at her, inspected her, leered. Sometimes they saw her beautiful face, sometimes her scars. At times they were repulsed, other times they lusted. But they always looked.

At night the eyes were different. Night eyes always came from shadows and dark places, regardless of the light. These eyes were dangerous.

Night eyes were hungry.

Having just finished her shift at *The Hidden Note* jazz club, she walked home via the best lighted street she could take. The lights meant safety for most people, but to her, it just made the shadows darker. And she knew what slept in the shadows.

Her ears still rang from the loud music at the bar. Despite the place being advertised as a jazz club, tonight—being a slow Tuesday—they'd had a young band of four guys whose only real talent was turning the volume knob up too far. *Louie, Louie* by The Kingsmen, was played over and over at the screaming request of a few drunk groupies, and Del couldn't get the song to stop playing. Her head pounded from the thumping bass and she smelled like smoke, but she'd made almost fifteen dollars in tips. That wasn't bad considering she had to pay for the tray of beers she'd dropped.

As the fresh air cleared her head, she thought of her eccentric family and wondered what they were doing. When she'd left, almost a month ago, she was full of nervous excitement, but hadn't realize how much she'd miss each one. Each night she fought the urge to trance-out and check on them. She wanted to see their faces but didn't want to draw anything else to the house, which was why she left in the first place. This was the only way to protect them, she reminded herself. She'd keep them safe this way until she could learn what had happened to Mama Dedé. Then her mentor could help her set the house—and spirits—back in order.

Del rubbed her eyes and yawned. The shadows slid past her as she walked. She hadn't realized her shifts would be so late when she took this job—her first *real* job. Happy to have found work so quickly, she accepted it without knowing exactly what was involved. She knew she'd be taking customer's orders but didn't realize that *customer service* meant different things to people. Some people were pleasant enough, but others had their own idea of what *service* she needed to provide.

She wasn't sure if she'd be any good at this job but was determined to stick it out. For now, she only worked the slow nights; the girls with more experience worked the busier nights. They probably made a lot more in tips, she thought, because they knew how to move through the crowd and handle the drunks. Del didn't know that. She also thought they made more money because of the way they dressed. But Del didn't have any clothes like that either, so she'd have to make do.

Walking the dark streets hadn't bothered her when she used to sneak out of the orphanage. How much her life had changed since then—for good and bad. Those nights sneaking out of the orphanage and walking the alleys had seemed like magic to her. It was a hint of the freedom that was to come, without the worry of what could happen. Now, after a crash course in what life could really throw at you, she was more mindful of things. But she still felt a swell of pride knowing she'd found the job on her own, so she'd work the hours she had to, even if it meant walking home late.

Turning her focus back to the street, she felt a new set of eyes following her—three pairs in fact. They were from the three men who had just finished peeing in the alley across the street.

Here, away from Armand's house and her family, she wasn't afraid to trance. So what if she created a *crease* in a place where she wouldn't stay long? And her light trancing—*flashing*, was how she thought of it when it was done quickly—had become so second nature to her, she didn't think it did much harm. Flashing didn't produce deep insights, but it was useful to tell if someone was ready for another drink. It was sort of like reaching out and mentally touching them.

Del flashed to the three men across the street. Not only had they noticed her, but they had noted that she was alone. She felt this in their pulse somehow. They had decided to follow her.

Usually—from her limited experience—the guys would cat-call her, whistle, and shout, but not pursue her if she showed no interest. These men were different.

The three men following her now had said nothing when they

turned in her direction. In fact, she felt they were trying to be very quiet.

She still had several blocks to go, but those were the darkest. She'd just left the lighted area where the clubs and their neon signs competed for patrons and had transitioned to an ill-lit residential area. The type that always surrounds seedy bar areas. Here, the live oaks stretched their gnarled limbs out over the street casting long shadows and hiding alley entrances.

Del felt for the wrench she kept tucked inside her leather jacket. Why she'd picked it up that day from the street, she didn't know. Laying there, discarded, covered in grease, the wrench had slipped past the view of its previous owner. Just a bit of the untarnished chrome had glinted at her, catching her attention. Taking it home and cleaning it, she found it felt good in her hand. It had weight, but not too much. It fit awkwardly in a large pocket inside her jacket.

She took the wrench out and held it in her right hand. She didn't brandish it like a weapon, but she didn't hide it either. It glinted a dim warning that was lost down the dark alleys.

Running footsteps! While Del was fishing for the wrench, the men—having made silent signals to each other—split across the street and quickened their pace. By the time she heard them, they were nearly on her. She broke and ran. Quiet curses and pounding feet chased her. Even in pursuit they were careful to stay quiet.

Sprinting into the street, she opened a slight gap, but the men stayed close behind. She heard muffled commands—a pursuit strategy—but couldn't risk trancing, not even a flash, to learn their plan. If she lost her balance the pursuit would be over quickly.

They ran like young hunters.

Up ahead, her street was coming to an end. It ran into a cross street and ended there. She had to decide left or right. She moved right, then made a quick left. Her apartment was to the right. She didn't want to lead them that direction. Staggered breath echoed in the night air: both hers and the men, but she ran on. Someone gave orders behind her and one man broke off through an alley to her left. They seemed to know this part of town better than she did and were anticipating her retreat.

Dim shadows obscured the uneven cobblestone of the streets, and she nearly fell twice as she fled. Old streetlamps, tall and stoic, observed the chase without emotion. They'd seen this playout before.

She was gasping for air now and felt panic tighten her throat. The long shift in a room full of smoke hadn't helped her. She was tired and slowing down. In a few minutes she'd have to stand and fight.

Following the dark street around a slow curve to the left, she saw the third man running up the street at her. He'd cut through a short alley or backyard, knowing the winding street would turn this way. With nowhere else to go she turned right, down the first alley she found and suddenly realized her mistake. This alley was a dead end.

She was trapped.

CHAPTER 2

The old woman felt a commotion coming and came out of the shadows to peer down the street. At her age the nights were long, and she no longer slept, but still, she didn't much care for commotion. She preferred the night because of the solitude, but now someone was about to disturb it.

Her clouded eyes scanned the twisted silhouettes, and she took inventory. She knew every tree, every odd angle from a streetlamp that had begun to lean over. She even knew where the trashcans typically sat and how they looked through each season. She'd been here a long time and was observant, so she *should* be able to recognize these things. And yes, the things were in their usual places. But something new was coming.

Of course, there were always transient images—people and things just passing through—but she recognized them for what they were. She'd seen so many over the years, she no longer worried about cataloging them and let them pass from her memory. But she felt a permanence growing in the air now and thought to be ready.

She licked a crooked finger and swiped the air in front of her, like flicking off a light switch. By doing so, she marked a spot in the air where the moon sat bloated in the sky. To her eyes the swipe in the air shimmered with moonlight and began to glow around the edges. She knew the moon was typically silent on matters of the human race, but occasionally it had an opinion. She studied it for a moment, then nodded slightly. Tonight, the moon was in a place for mischief, so mischief was afoot.

Looking to the right, she peered down the empty street. The mischief would come from that direction, she thought. The air was different down there and changing quickly. She adjusted her stance slightly as an old moonbeam tried to peak around the edge of a tree and see her. Tricky moonbeams, she thought. They were always playing silly games. Just like children they were. Children or old lovers actually, full of mischief.

She watched as a girl ran into the middle of the street. She'd made a left at the dead-end. Had she made a right, the mischief would have gone away, and the woman would have gone back into the shadows. But now she was interested because the girl was bringing the mischief right past her.

As the girl approached, the woman licked her finger again and held it aloft. With a quick swipe, she marked right where the girl passed and studied this. She rubbed a whiskered chin and looked back at the moon for confirmation. Its opinion hadn't changed.

The woman saw that the girl was followed by two men. Then she saw a third man coming from the other direction. Someone was in trouble.

The old woman steadied herself against a rickety fence; the gentle wind testing to see which it could topple first. Across the street was an opening that looked like an alley but ran up against the back of an old structure: *Claudine's Chicken Shack*. Claudine had abandoned it years ago, but the neighbors said that sometimes it still smelled of grease in the hot summer. This neighborhood—just off the river, smelled like a lot of things. The cobblestone streets were bad to soak up everything and not let it wash away. Over the years, the smells of cooking grease, engine grease, mop water, urine and the sweet rotting smell of magnolia fruit had built itself up, layer upon layer, into a rich *street stew* aroma that was unmistakable. Some even said the dead could recognize their own street by its unique smell.

As the girl turned down the alley towards the back of the chicken shack, the woman shook her head and moved a little closer to the street. She couldn't help now. The three men had just arrived behind her and were blocking the alley. Another smell would be added to the streets soon.

The woman wondered… If she'd been younger could she have helped? *Would* she have helped? Before she could answer herself, the screaming began, and she forgot the question. The moon was right again.

The trees and buildings seemed to lean together slightly, muffling the screams from the alley. Neighborhoods in the Crescent City were private places and liked to keep their secrets.

She'd heard plenty of screams before, but not like this. This wasn't just fear or pain. This was true terror. For the first time in many years, the old woman was hearing a scream of terror. And she was curious.

Something unexpected was happening in the alley across the street…

ABOUT THE AUTHOR

D.S. Quinton was born in the Midwest USA and attended the schools of daydreaming, foosball, and mixology. His is an avid student of the unknown and grew up on Greek mythology, the Twilight Zone and Night Gallery.

He is the author of the Spirit Hunter supernatural thriller series and the Circus Sideshow supernatural oddity series, along with a few other interesting tales.

Although his guitar slide is rusty, the piano keys are warm, and despite the lure of many untraveled paths, his feet are generally moving forward.

You can find him at dsquinton.com, some social media platforms, or on his deck solving the world's problems with his wife and a good bottle of wine.

Made in the USA
Monee, IL
27 November 2021

83153501R00259